THANK YOU

YOU

for the

SHOES

RAFFAELA MARIE RIZZO

THANK YOU

for the

SHOES

the story of an extraordinary ordinary man

Giro di Mondo

THANK YOU FOR THE SHOES
Copyright © 2015 by Raffaela Marie Rizzo

This book is based on the life story of a real man, true locales and historical events, brought to life by the author's creativity and imagination.

Published by Giro di Mondo Publishing, a subsidiary of The Ottima Group, LLC
Fernandina Beach, Florida

Printed in the United States of America.

Cover and interior by Roseanna White Designs
Cover images from www.Shutterstock.com

FIRST EDITION (Hardcover print)
ISBNs: 978-0-9966687-0-5 (Hardcover)
         978-0-9966687-1-2 (Paperback)
         978-0-9966687-2-9 (Digital)

Library of Congress Control Number: 2015952218

It has taken me decades to articulate this understanding
and to write this song of praise.
For
My father and My mother

FOREWORD

Everyone living in the United States of America with an Italian last name or an ancestor with Italian roots often experiences a kind of knowing bias that conjures up the word "Mafia."

The truth is that for the few who fell to the seductive lure of the mob made famous by the books of Mario Puzo, millions of other Italian immigrants embraced the new world with a fire in their belly to do good for themselves and provide a future for their families. Through hard, honest work and with God ever present as their guiding star, they persevered. Most came with their heads full of dreams fueled by one of the most deceptive and effective public relations campaign ever launched. Instead, they arrived at our nation's shores to face unimaginable hardships. Their leap of faith in leaving their homeland to sail into the unknown was akin to any one of us leaving earth in a rocket ship for Mars without any space or flight training, no special equipment or clothing and the controls on the vehicle as foreign as hieroglyphics to the average second grader.

While the word Italy conjures up visions of the magnificent art and architecture of the Renaissance or the ancient grandeur of Rome, the peninsula in the shape of a woman's high-heeled boot, did not become a nation until the 1860s. It is a land of texture and color based on the cultural history hammered to a fine patina through the numerous invasions, political divides and regionalism. Curiously, the largest wave of emigration to the USA started in 1870, after Italy became a unified country, and most especially from the South. The Southerners mostly came because they were starving, or *morte di fame.*

As they were processed through immigration, clerks labeled them, "Italian" and they immediately became the fodder that helped build our country and in doing so became part of the fabric we call America. Among the millions who came, was a 13-year-old, fatherless, man-boy, baptized Michelangelo Rizzo from a little mountain town in Calabria.

This is a story of big hopes, setbacks and small triumphs. A story of love and legacy, a story, that will resonate with anyone who is a first- or second-generation immigrant from Europe and other parts of the world, and for the millions of people in the United States who have made tracing their roots a passion.

Dear reader, what follows are my thoughts and interpretations from conversations with my father and mother, as well as stories recounted to me by sisters, brothers, other relatives, friends and *paisani* in Italy, Australia and America. I have blended those numerous conversations and interviews with my own research and investigation, experiences, observations and imagination.

I offer this work in a spirit of love and remembrance.

- Raffaela Marie Rizzo,
September 12, 2015, Amelia Island, Florida

PART ONE

Chine lassa a via vecchia e pia chilla nova sa chillu chi lassa ma un sa chillu chi trova
~ old Platanese proverb

He who leaves the old road for the new, knows what he leaves but not what he finds

CHAPTER ONE

The moon was still visible and the sun but a suggestion, slowly clawing its way over the mountain crest, as Michelangelo trod slowly down the rock-strewn mountainside. He followed a path well worn by the ancient Greeks who had settled the southern Italian town called Platania centuries before. Heading toward Nicastro, the market city center in the valley below, he was intimately familiar with the dirt and rubble road from Platania, having traveled it more than twice weekly in his short thirteen years of life. With it etched in his mind, he could find his way down the treacherous path in the dark.

As he made his way, he mentally noted the tremendous significance of this trek. It would be the last time he scaled the trail to the base of Monte Reventino, he thought. He did not intend to return, ever. Once down the mountain, he would eventually head to the Commune di Nicastro where he would catch a train later in the day to the port of Vibo Valente. A small vessel would take him to Naples where he would board the *Duca D'Ostia* ocean vessel that would take him across the Atlantic ocean to the port of New York—America.

But first, he needed to detour to the outskirts of the Commune di Sambiase, to an area in the valley known as *La Chianta*. Alternatively called *La Pianta*, depending on which dialect you spoke, it was where his mother's brother—his *zio*, or uncle—Luigi Folino and his enormous family, lived. Michelangelo's mother, Rosa, was one of six children. Of all his many relatives on his mother's side, he most especially wanted to see Zio Luigi's children.

Though he loved all his Folino cousins, he felt drawn the most to these four children—Angelina, Petronella, and twin brothers Antonio and Michele. He had always felt more related to these four than all his other maternal cousins. He wasn't sure why, maybe because they were all close in proximity of age, or maybe because they all had radiant blue eyes and infectious smiles. The two Folino sisters especially had nurturing warmth that belied their steel-strong character. Their twin brothers were just male versions of their sisters. He enjoyed being with them and always felt welcome there.

He thought back to the night just ended only a few hours ago when he had bid his mother a last goodbye. It had been a gut-wrenching affair. Trekking along he became lost in his thoughts and began to relive not only the scene from last night, but also scenes from the past nine years.

"U shachu che non ti vido ciu, cum tu patre," she had wailed in the distinct *Petronese montagnaro*, Platania's mountain people's dialect. "I know I will never see you again, Michele. Just like your father." He realized that his mother had always known that this youngest of her children would follow in his father's path and perhaps even

his father's date with destiny.

She had lost so much—an infant son first, and then his brother Carlo, who had been sickly since birth; his death at nineteen was still a blow to Rosa. She had lost her daughter Rosanna, and her husband Antonio, both dead. Michele's sister Angela had left when she was twenty; she married her Italo-Argentine husband and followed him to his adopted country in South America. Now with Michele's departure, only Rosa's adopted daughter, Marianna, would remain.

He was sure his mother had never doubted this time would come for him. In fact, she had told him that she knew he would leave her almost since the day the terrible news arrived telling her Michele's father had died in America. "I knew from early on that when you were older, you would want to find some shred of him, something that would help you know him. You are so much like him," she had sobbed.

Each year on November 2, the entire community, in fact, all of Calabria went to pay respects to their lost loved ones at the cemetery. The first Day of the Dead, All Souls Day, he could remember was just after he had turned five years old. That day the gray sky threatened rain, though the 4.3 degrees Celsius temperature was about average for this time of year. His mother had prepared for worse with a black shawl covering her head and shoulders and her wool stockings ready for the possibility of damp and cold. She had said aloud many times that the clothes she had bought with the money Antonio had sent were proving useful. As she muttered often, she did not know when, if ever, she could replace the wool stockings so vital in the mountain winters.

With Michele in tow as she approached the Nicastro cemetery, it appeared that the entire valley was flocking to the site with flowers and small tokens made with last spring's palms. It was an annual pilgrimage.

He remembered asking her, "*MaMa, dov'è PaPa?*" MaMa, where is my father buried? Why can't we bring flowers to his grave? Where did he go?"

"Stop. You are stabbing me in the heart," was her response.

But Michele remembered pushing forward, his inquisitiveness not being quelled.

"Are you doing this just to give me pain?" she had asked without expecting an answer.

"MaMa, I don't understand. If PaPa died, shouldn't he be here in the cemetery so we put flowers and light candles?"

She shushed him again as she purposefully strode directly to the grave of her parents. He remembered wondering why it seemed everyone was staring at them. Everyone knew who she was. Antonio Rizzo's widow, the one whose husband died before he could return from America. A few who knew her well stopped and inquired about her situation as well as her children. Making remarks about how fast Michelangelo, whom many called "Michele," her nickname for him, seemed to have grown. They spoke as if he wasn't even there.

A few more paces and another stop. "How is your boy Carlo?" asked someone else. Then, spying Michele, who was trying to disappear behind his mother's dress, a nosy woman asked, "Who do you have here? Is that Antonio's last son?" Michele recalled his mother's lamenting responses to all the questions.

"I would have left Michele with Marianna, you know, my adopted daughter, but my son Carlo is so sickly. It's a lot for her to handle and Carlo's disposition is none too pleasant either. Poor thing, she is grieving, too," Rosa said.

"Michele is a good boy, but he asks a million questions. He's curious about everything. Between Marianna and me, we have to keep our eyes on him every minute. Thanks to God, he is sturdy for such a small boy. He never complains about our long journey from our mountain abode to the valley and back up again," she boasted to the inquiring woman.

As she passed others, she shared with them that her parents were buried in Nicastro. It was well known that people from the valley of Nicastro felt superior to the mountains. To have a family member buried at the Nicastro cemetery was almost like saying you were well off. Otherwise, the local cemetery in Platania would have been just a short walk for her.

After they left the cemetery and had nearly scaled the mountain and just as their modest home came into view, Michele remembered announcing, "Someday I'm going to find my father's grave and bring flowers."

He looked up at his mother as a loud wail came out of her mouth; her face had turned pale.

CHAPTER TWO

Rosa had been a lovely woman with milky white skin and blue eyes. A testament to the numerous invaders in the Calabrian region over the centuries. The oldest of six children, she had helped her mother care for the large family as well as work the fields that were bits of land scattered across the valley. After her marriage, she had lost several children as well as her husband.

A few years after she became a widow, her oldest son, Carlo, had died, and she had become even more attached to Michele, the only remaining son of her marriage to Antonio. "I see your father every time I look at you," she had told him often as he grew. He recalled how she had clung tightly to him during those first five years after she was widowed. Though he often tried, he could not remember his father. Though Antonio Rizzo had died when Michele was nearly four years old, he had been gone from home since Michele was about a year and a half old, still a babe sucking milk at his mother's breast. There was no possible memory he could conjure up of him. All that he knew of him had been shared by others; early on, by his mother, her brother, his Zio Luigi, and a few townspeople. Marianna, his adopted older sister, remembered Antonio vividly; he had constantly pressed her for information.

For the first few years after his mother was widowed, Marianna and Michele's sister Angela had been a great comfort to Rosa. Rosa had reminded Michele almost daily that he had a sweet spirit, just as his father had. Now, despite all that had passed, Michele knew that his mother prayed every morning and evening for his well-being.

The most difficult part for Michele was not only that he had never known his father, but that he had no paternal grandparents. In fact, he had never known anyone from his father's family—siblings, aunts, uncles and cousins all dead either before he was born or shortly thereafter. Though Rizzo was not an unusual name, Michele was well aware that he was the last living male in his family lineage to carry on the Rizzo name.

From the time, he could ask questions, he was enflamed with a desire to know more about his father. It seemed as if he was on a never-ending search as a toddler, then a boy. His questions had been incessant. He always hoped to understand something about the man whose blood ran through his veins. Through persistence, he had by the time he was ten years old pieced together the struggles and decisions that had made his father leave his family for America. He recalled how he had often questioned his mother. When he did, she had shared the bare facts with him of where his father went, and about his life in America; however, if he pressed for more than that, she became defensive. He couldn't remember exactly when he became aware that perhaps she felt a sense of guilt. It was after all she who had insisted Antonio take a second trip to America, leaving the little boy fatherless.

In the last few years, his times alone with his mother were rare, since she had remarried when he was nine. He recalled that it was about that time when he told her that he felt certain the answers to all his questions had to be in America where his father had died.

CHAPTER THREE

Antonio Rizzo, son of Carlo Rizzo and Rosangela Gallo, was born April 19, 1850, in Platania (often-called Petrania in the local dialect) in the province of Catanzaro in the region of Italy known as Calabria. Calabria, a melting pot of Mediterranean and non-Mediterranean cultures, is a place distinctly different from the Rome, Florence or Venice that most tourists visit or read about. Each state within Calabria (Cosenza, Catanzaro and Reggio Calabria—a fourth state, Vibo Valente, was created in the 1990s) is as different as the countries of France, Spain, Italy and Russia.

The Calabrian region is essentially dominated by the Appennino Calabro mountains, surrounded by an 800-kilometer coastline formed by the Mediterranean, Ionian and Adriatic seas, which creates the bottom of the country's shape of a woman's high-heeled boot. Calabria stretches from the toe to the heel up through the instep and ends just before the ankle of the boot, abutting the region of Campania. The state of Catanzaro, with its capital city of the same name, is the area from the instep to the arch of the boot. With a breathtaking coastal landscape, Calabria is much more mountainous than flatland, defined by its majestic pine and birch forests, lakes and rivers.

Its natural beauty and the historic sentinels are witness to the fragments of cultures and customs of all the various conquerors mirrored in the faces, mannerisms and dialects of the Calabrian people. Greeks, Iberians, Romans, Saracens, Byzantines, Normans, Jews, Aragons, Swabians, Spanish, Moors and Bourbons are some of the invaders whose imprints were left behind in genes and influence.

For Calabrians, Garibaldi's unified Italy, so desired and anticipated, instead created misery and famine. After unification, highway robberies flourished in the region. While ordinary people begged for a plate of change and political stability, the serving for Calabria was instead comprised of radicalism and socialism, inadequate replacements for feudalism.

To be Calabrese could mean being a blend of the best of many cultures, or, as Michele preferred to believe, it meant you are from a race of supreme survivors, people who adapted, grew and conquered their circumstances if not other people—a proud heritage. Sometimes Michele felt that the blood that ran in his veins was perhaps a fine blend of both. He was not unaware that the rest of the boot-shaped peninsula raged that the government needed to deal with the "problem of the south and of Calabria."

When Antonio Rizzo left Platania, he was part of an almost thirty-year migration to the New World to relieve the hunger, misery and the indignities of the times. During this period in southern Italy, many children were born, but few survived past their teens. If they did, often they left to find a future in the Americas or in North Africa, where many helped build the Suez Canal that opened in 1869 after nearly ten years of construction.

Michele's father and mother had married in 1881 when his father, Antonio, was nearly thirty-one years old. Rosa was twenty-four. Together they had had six children. Yet now, it was up to him, Michele, the youngest and the only living male child of their marriage, to carry on the family name.

Michelangelo, who was affectionately called *Michele, Miche* or *Micchuzzo* by the townspeople, was very proud of his name. In fact, the main church in Platania was San Michele Arcangelo, named after his patron saint as well as that of the town. Michael the archangel, revered in Catholic tradition as the protector of the Church, was part of the lore Michele heard often. He knew how the saint was called an archangel because he was placed over all the angels, as prince of the seraphim. The itinerate priest who said mass at the tenth century church located in Piazza Vittorio Veneto in Platania's main square, had said that San Michele Arcangelo was also a special patron of sick people and mariners.

Michele had often pondered the statuary in the church, which clearly depicted the saint's emblems and his powers—a banner, a sword, a dragon and scales. He had called upon the angel frequently from when he was very little. After a long hiatus in his prayers to his namesake, Michele now implored San Michele Arcangelo to protect and defend him on his journey.

Driven by curiosity and despite his mother's meager responses, Michele had relentlessly badgered his mother's siblings, cousins, neighbors and others until he managed to glean the circumstances that compelled his father to leave home again for America shortly after he was born.

It was 1898, when Michele was twenty months old. His oldest sister Angela had reached an age where she would soon need a dowry. Antonio and Rosa were facing the realities of the times and circumstances. Their daughter Rosangela, born three years after

Angela, had already died. Their oldest son, Carlo, suffered an arrested development from a congenital heart disease. He was now seven years old, and it was clear to Rosa and Antonio that Carlo would not live into adulthood. Their son Francesco, born two years after Carlo, had lived only two weeks.

Moreover, they had an adopted daughter, Marianna. Marianna's birth mother had died giving her life, just one day before Angela was born. Rosa had been overflowing with milk from Angela's birth. The couple's mutual compassion for the motherless baby caused the Rizzos to take the child so Rosa could serve as her wet nurse. After Marianna's father remarried, the new wife was disinterested in the child. So Rosa and Antonio adopted the little girl and raised her as their own. Not uncommon in places of high infant mortality, a *figlia di latte*, or milk daughter, was a cherished member of many families.

Marianna was a humble girl completely devoid of even a trace of arrogance or guile. She had been a great help to Rosa with Carlo and the helplessness he suffered from his disease. And when the new baby Michele was born, she acted like a little mother to him.

Then, when both Angela and Marianna were fourteen years old, Antonio set off for what was his second trip to America in four short years.

On the first trip in 1894, Antonio had found some work through the help of Rosa's brother, Luigi, who had gone to America two years before him and had settled in Bridgeport, Connecticut. Luigi had helped him find work immediately as a day labor. Though back-breaking, it had earned Antonio some decent money. Back at home, raising the highly prized silkworms to supply the cottage silk industries that peppered the mountains during that period, Rosa had helped supplement the family's earnings.

On his first trip, Antonio had sent a steady stream of money home to his wife, by living in a rooming house with other men doing similar work in the area. The American dollars had afforded them more than just the ability to buy needed food and supplies. It had put them in a unique position compared with much of the Southern Italy peasant class.

Antonio was lonely without his family. And, though there was his brother-in-law Luigi and other *paisani* from their area of Calabria, they were all boarding at different houses. Immigrants had to take whatever there was, wherever there was a bed. They were frugal to the point of being parsimonious because their goal was to save all they could.

As misfortune would deal a short deck, Antonio's first trip to America was truncated. He arrived during the aftermath of a bank panic and financial depression that had evaporated many jobs. While he did find some work fairly quickly, it was not steady work. Where his plan had been to stay for two years, he and Luigi returned to Italy after only a year and a half, despite the urging of many *paisani* who said, "Ride it out, America won't stay down for long." He missed his family. Antonio came home, saying. "I don't need to be greedy. I've earned enough for my family to live more comfortably."

After his return from that first trip in late December of 1895, they used his savings to acquire a small plot of land on which to plant some vegetables and to build a rustic house. Those who lived within the city, in the buildings near the square, would have described the Rizzo abode as little more than a hut. Nevertheless, the loose stone structure Antonio had built for his family was one of the better ones in their area among the rural mountain dwellers. Antonio and his wife coaxed out a variety of vegetables, including potatoes, during the spring, summer and fall seasons. Winters were harsh on the mountain, yielding virtually nothing. During the producing months, they took the small harvest of whatever was in season to sell at the *mercato,* the marketplace in the valley. The largest town in the area, Nicastro, had many well-heeled residents and professionals who would pay some *ducati* that could buy the necessities that the Rizzos didn't grow themselves. Though Calabria now used the lira established in 1861, Antonio and his family all referenced the monetary unit of Venice, *ducati di oro* of Florence, or *scudi di Marche.* Those older currencies held sway in world trade and many of the southerners were skeptical of the unification as well as the monetary system.

With the birth of the baby, Michelangelo, or Michele, in September of 1896, and the looming needs of a marriage-aged daughter in post-republic southern Italy, Rosa implored Antonio, saying he had no choice but to go back to the well, known as America.

Rosa later would share with her son that his father lamented making a second voyage to America. Antonio had told her he remembered all too vividly the stench of the long trip in steerage class with no windows and people being sick everywhere on that first trip across the Atlantic. He expressed to his wife that he had missed his family enormously while away. Unlike many other men, he found no solace in drinking and loose women. So many of the men that he had seen on his first trip avoided returning home at all costs. Sending money home to their families in Italy, they justified their loose morals by telling themselves that they were making huge sacrifices for their families. Sadly, Antonio realized that many of them had no intention of ever returning to Italy. When he had come home that last time, he had vowed never to go back to America without his wife and children.

CHAPTER FOUR

By 1898, it was evident that instead of improving, the economic and political situation in southern Italy appeared to be headed into a downward spiral. A disturbing lawlessness prevailed and famine was even more widespread than before Garibaldi's unification. At the same time, there was more and more talk in Nicastro that America was on the move again. With a new president, there was sure to be more work, and the railroad bankruptcies of the 1893-1894 were giving way to more building and construction. America needed good workers again.

Feeling the weight of his obligations toward his family and Rosa's persistent harping on the case for Angela's dowry since even before the baby Michele was born, Antonio was softening.

Moreover, now there also was the need to help Marianna, who already had a boyfriend.

But at forty-eight, Antonio said he didn't feel young enough to withstand the rigors of the strength-sapping voyage, and the harsh work and living conditions. It had been bone-breaking work on roads and construction projects in the cold and heat, with squalid living conditions in rooming houses, with as many as four men to one bed.

He had always prized his own personal cleanliness, a trait he had imparted to his children. He knew that upon his return to America there would be no such luxury as personal space or cleanliness. Though they had little in Platania, Antonio felt they had a space of their own, sunshine and fresh air and family nearby. Sadly, though, he could not see a future there for his children.

America, Antonio had confided to Rosa, was not the land of milk and honey that so many would have you believe. Although Rosa knew her husband to be a truthful, honest man, she, like so many of the townspeople, did not quite believe the stories of hard work, unscrupulous bosses and difficult conditions. She felt that perhaps he had embellished a little to gain sympathy. How could it be that bad in America when many others had sent letters raving about the riches there?

According to Antonio, those who had no intention of returning were the worst. They sent illustrious depictions of the money that could be made without effort. Indeed, many had made some sizable fortunes, albeit less than honestly. They spoke of wonders never seen in the land of the *Mezzogiorno*, the traditional term for the southern regions of Italy. They spoke of the big houses that *i'mericani* owned. And they raved about how someday they would buy a big house and then their families could come, too. They promised their wives would live like queens. In the meantime, they claimed to live modestly saving every dime so that their families could reap the riches of America. Instead, Antonio observed that many didn't save a cent. After sending some of their earnings to their families, each week they drank away more than they sent back to Italy. And what they didn't drink away they spent on evenings at the local brothels.

Antonio was ashamed of the behavior of some of his countrymen, *paisani*. To be fair, he also knew many that were like him—homesick and completely committed to working, saving and getting back to their families. However, it seemed that those who were less than good, God-fearing sons of the *Mezzogiorno* seemed to have more money and were more favored by the bosses. Antonio didn't quite understand the patronage system.

No, Antonio did not have the stomach for returning, Michele's mother had said. She had often boasted that she finally came up with the ultimate lure. Finally, when their "milk daughter," Marianna, was about to be married in the early spring of 1898, though only fourteen, Rosa managed to sway Antonio. Marianna was betrothed to a strong young mountain man. Eight years her senior, at twenty-two, Augustino was a hard worker with a rough but kind demeanor. Marianna's birth family had promised a little something toward the customary linens and marriage garments, but little else. Antonio was pleased with the upcoming nuptials.

While no one would have described her as beautiful, Marianna was by no means ugly. She had even features, a pert little nose and high cheekbones. She was scrawny and strong. A sturdy worker with a big heart. While there was almost no dowry, the young man prized the young woman who often worked alongside him to remove stones from the fields. He jokingly had bragged that she was more agile than a mountain goat.

Marianna was a simple person. Thoughts flew from her head to her lips in an instant. She was completely open, but most of all she was a very loving and generous spirit. The couple was to be married just before Marianna's young husband would accompany Antonio on this second trip to America in 1898. The plan was that they would stay three years—May 1898 to May 1901.

When they returned they would have earned enough money for them to recoup what they paid for the passage, while keeping some money coming back to the family in Italy, and to buy some additional land. They would be able to build a sturdy house for Marianna, and

Antonio's earnings would keep the baby Michele and emaciated Carlo well fed.

Best of all for Rosa was that she could build a proper dowry for Angela so she could marry well. *La bella figura*, ensuring that a good face was presented to the community, was central to Rosa's view of the world. She herself was from the valley of Nicastro. Her marriage and move to the mountain was considered a step down not only in the eyes of others, but in her own eyes. Yet her brother Luigi had often reminded her that Antonio had been worth it. He was loyal, faithful, trustworthy and handsome.

Rosa had told Antonio, with conviction, that their son-in-law would be doing the same for himself and Marianna. Taking him to America on this voyage could help assure that their adopted daughter, who had been such a godsend to them, would have a stab at a much better life with the earnings her husband would send back.

Michele thought of all this and much more as he trudged down the mountainside, leaving to go abroad himself. He reflected that to his mother and father this all must have sounded like a good plan at the time.

CHAPTER FIVE

Atlantic Ocean—1898

Antonio Rizzo left Platania with his son-in-law, Augustino Caruso, to embark on the ship the Britannia from the port of Naples on May 17. The passage of twenty-one days to New York, though long, was not as horrible as Antonio remembered from his first trip across the Atlantic. Perhaps it was the better ship. Built in Glasgow, Scotland, the 3,069-gross-ton, twenty-year-old, three-masted ship with a single funnel was 350 feet long and 38 feet wide. With compound engines and a single screw, it carried along its 654 passengers, almost all third-class, at a service speed of 11 knots. There were a handful of first-class passengers, but the small vessel basically scurried from Kalamata, Greece, to Messina, then Naples to New York, profiting from the mass travels to the new world under the British flag for the Anchor Line.

Antonio had warned young Augustino of the rough seas and admonished him about not drinking wine, as it would enhance his seasickness. Though certainly not flavorful, the food too seemed a little better to him than the first voyage, though perhaps he was now not surprised at what the English called food. He was just happy to get some.

The time passed more quickly perhaps because the seas were a little calmer this time of year than on his previous voyage. And, though it was a crowded and smelly trip, Antonio walked up on deck frequently taking in the fresh, salty air.

At night, he often played *scuppa* and *briscola*, the card games endemic to southern Italy, and he sang songs with his fellow *paisani*. Perhaps it was the time of year, spring as opposed to winter, or the championship of his son-in-law, or that he had braced himself for the horror of his first trip, but despite the cramped quarters, the lack of privacy, the heat below deck, Antonio found himself thinking this crossing tolerable. This time, there were more families and less single men. And, where there were women, things were just a little cleaner.

This crowd of fellow steerage passengers seemed more jovial than on his first trip. There was almost always someone singing and sometimes even dancing. People were sick, but not to the degree of his first crossing. He himself had learned what to avoid and his stomach was faring much better. Regretting the difficulty he had caused Rosa over making this second trip, he began to focus not on the work he would have to do ahead, but on the trip home and bringing money for a good dowry and a better life for his family and that of his adopted daughter. He began to fantasize about bringing Rosa and the children to America.

Though Augustino had been seasick for nearly a week, Antonio's newfound optimism infected his son-in-law and they both disembarked with smiles on their faces that spread from their first sighting of the Statue of Liberty and didn't even get defeated as they endured the dreaded Ellis Island processing. Soon they were safely at the home of a trusted *paisano*, Antonio Negri, a rented row-house in Bridgeport, Connecticut. Negri, as he was called by friends, had been widowed with four children. After a short time, he had married a widow with two of her own. The family of eight took in two boarders to make ends meet and somehow made the tiny space accommodate ten people.

Antonio's letter to Negri several months before their departure had said he would need a bed for two. His response had been, not to worry; we'll find you a place to board. Only when they arrived did Antonio learn that he and his son-in-law could stay with the Negri family. The wife would cook, wash and clean for the whole brood; what was two more, said Negri with a confidence that was not matched by his new wife of only a year. The Negris had only been at 588 Pembroke Street for a short time.

Negri had now been in America for nearly five years. When Antonio had been here the first time, he and his brother-in-law, Luigi Folino, and Negri had all worked for the railroad as day laborers. Negri, though, had stayed and had gotten a better position with steady work.

Angela Negri prepared a delicious meal for all of them. The aromas of Calabrian food were comforting. As they feasted on full plates of pasta and an oval-shaped meatball made from veal and pork, Negri bragged about his wife's talents. They talked for several hours about the townspeople, family back home, and conditions, specifically in Platania, and Calabria in general. Then Negri showed Antonio and Augustino the sleeping accommodations.

"*Dormiti qui,*" he said. They were to sleep in an area of the small house that Negri called the *porcchia.* Antonio figured out that it wasn't Calabrese, but an Italianization of the American word for *portico anteriore.* Extremely tired, the two men fell asleep instantly despite the fact that they were sharing a small sofa bed on the miniscule enclosed porch.

"*Io viau a fatigare sta sirra,*" Negri said over coffee in the morning, explaining that he was going to be working a night shift so he could take Antonio and Augustino to find work.

Despite the tight sleeping accommodations, they had awakened, rested, to the blinding light of a sun-filled day with an azure sky, nary a cloud overhead, and zero humidity. The weather and beauty of the day invigorated Antonio. Young Augustino couldn't contain himself. *"Sono in America,"* he effused. The air was dry and the homes and yards all sported colorful flowers and greenery in their front yards. As they walked, Antonio explained to Augustino that spring here in Connecticut was similar to Platania. His previous trip to Bridgeport had lasted long enough for him to experience the entire change of seasons.

Maybe it was the exhaustion from the transatlantic voyage, but after the three-mile walk, Antonio felt winded when the three arrived at a shack where a sinister-looking man smoking a cigar sat at a small table. The man barked what sounded like greetings and Antonio was impressed at Negri's seemingly excellent English, as his friend seemed to express himself with such facility. Of course, he reminded himself, he could not judge Negri's English language skills, with none of his own. After a lengthy exchange of which Antonio and Augustino didn't understand a word, Negri finally said, *"Abbiamo fatto l'affare. Incominciatti lavoro domain."*

Antonio was pleased that the deal had been struck, and the two recent arrivals would report to work tomorrow. He did not want to waste any time to start earning money and sending some back home.

Back at the house, Negri told them that they would be digging trenches for a new railroad line. There would be some blasting to clear rock so prevalent in the area. Negri chuckled. "This Connecticut is full of hard rock. But nobody digs ditches better than we Calabrese do! And we know about rocks from our hometown, *Petrania,* which means rock-strewn. Well, at least that's what its over-name means," he joked, as he knew full well, that the town's actual name, Platania, came from a tree, the platen, that grows profusely there, and not the rock-strewn nickname, though indeed the mountain and the town had no shortage of stones.

The next day, the two newcomers reported for work. It was backbreaking labor. Augustino came home at the end of the day with welts and blisters, a splitting headache and his back screaming with pain. Though not unaccustomed to backbreaking work, the two men's muscles had been in disuse for nearly three weeks.

Antonio felt bad for his son-in-law. Despite his own muscles aching, he helped get Augustino into the tin tub and soak with some salts. He told Augustino his muscles would adjust quickly and it would all get much easier. "*Tu si, giovanne; fra pocchi giorni ti sembra un giocca di bambini.*" You are young. This will seem like child's play before long.

CHAPTER SIX

Bridgeport, Connecticut—1899

The days progressed with working, eating, sleeping and letters to the family in Italy dictated to a *scrivano*. The beautiful spring weather gave way to the summer solstice turning things hot and humid. And the noonday heat was intense. Augustino remarked to his father-in-law one morning, "I thought Americans were so smart, but unlike in Italy where we work very early and get out of the sun and rest from one o'clock until four in the afternoon, and then start up again for a few hours, here they work right through with only a short thirty-minute break. Don't they know that this intense sun is not healthy?"

While Antonio empathized with his son-in-law, he did not want to indulge him and said, "America is growing. They have no time for long rests. You make sure you drink lots of water on the breaks. That's all I can tell you. And do not go suggesting that Americans are not smart. They are smarter than our country that even after unification can't create jobs for us peasants who are willing to work. Remember how many times you have gone to bed hungry before you dare criticize the way they do things here."

Though he hadn't spoken in a loud voice, his tone had been nevertheless excoriating and Augustino was cowed by his father-in-law's admonitions. He would keep his thoughts to himself in the future, he decided. Though each morning they woke up soaking in sweat and returned broken, burned and exhausted each day from the hard labor, they both said to Negri how grateful they were that he was able to find work for them so quickly.

In August during the height of the heat wave, Antonio and Negri sat outside in late evening after everyone had gone to bed. Negri smoked a shriveled, short, skinny cigar that the *i'mericani* called "guinea stinkers." Lulled by the heaviness of the air and the screaming pitch of the cicada, Antonio explored some new territory with his friend.

"Che ti pensi c' aggia fare per portare tutta mia famgilia ca? Io sacchio che Rosa vo venire al'America."

Negri explained the process he went through to get his first wife and children here. He also described a hair-raising scene that happened to his second wife. When she arrived at Ellis Island, one of the children was sick. Apparently, she had nearly died of fright that they would turn the child back. They stayed in quarantine for a while. But finally the child's chest congestion cleared and they entered. "It's a good thing," he said, "because I'd be here with my motherless children going crazy."

Eventually, Antonio brought up his boy Carlo. Based on what Negri had said, it was clear that Carlo would never be accepted into the country with his congenital heart condition; his withered body and arrested development would be apparent immediately. And that was only if he could survive the ocean journey itself.

Dejected, Antonio talked with his friend until into the wee hours. He and Negri discussed when Antonio planned to repatriate to Italy.

"If you stay until you reach your goal of staying three years in the spring of 1901, you will go back to Platania with a sizable sum of money," Negri predicted. "You would be able to build a *palazzino* in the center of town, perhaps. With the American money you'll be saving, you and your wife and children could live like barons."

His jocularity evaporating suddenly, Negri said, "My poor first wife died so young. And my second wife's husband the same. The work, not enough decent food, our homeland failed us. Now we live in our adopted country, think of every way we can save a few pennies. Angela works night and day to cook, clean and manage the children and the boarders. She also takes in sewing and ironing. It's no different here, the work is difficult. But I have hopes for my children. In time, they will live better than we are living.

"Tell me more about the situation back home. I was sure that Garibaldi would bring about important changes for the better," pried Negri. "I even sent money from here to the cause for unification. From what I heard, the fighting was ruthless, but he pulled it off. Garibaldi is magnificent!"

"In Italia le cosi vanno molto male. Chi sono molto vagabondi e niente future per I nostri ragazzi," said Antonio quietly.

Negri was shocked to hear Antonio's description of the lawlessness and the marauders who roamed the countryside.

"People are starving everywhere around us. If it wasn't for the money that comes from those of us who are fortunate to have family in America or make a trip or two ourselves, we would all be dead from hunger," Antonio added.

"But why?" asked Negri incredulously. "I thought things were better because of unification. Garibaldi is a great man to achieve what other men of high title could not do."

"We all thought that. My family is a little better off now but not because of Garibaldi, but because of my first trip here, and that is now long gone," he confided in his friend.

"We all had high hopes for the unification. There were several from Petrania who joined Garibaldi in the fight, all brave men. But sadly, unification has brought more troubles to the *Mezzogiorno* than ever before," Antonio said with a palpable melancholy.

Antonio had no great desire to leave Petrania permanently, but there was no future for the young people.

"Carlo is one matter, but Rosa and I are happy that at least the new baby, Michele seems strong and healthy," he said.

"I can't shake the terrible foreboding that Petrania will not be able to sustain our baby Michele as he grows, though. At some point, he will do what so many have done. He'll grow up and leave us for other places. Unless we can all move here, I believe we are destined to spend our old age alone with no children around us."

"Cheer up," Negri joked. "Stay focused, Antonio, on the money you will bring back that can change your life and those of your children. *La moneta combia tutto,* he declared with a raised wine glass to the notion that money changes everything.

"What an interesting thought," mused Antonio, suddenly feeling a bit better. He vowed to tackle his labors joyfully, although this past week they had been blasting rock and he didn't fare well with each blast. He felt as if his whole being was sucked out of him each time. Nevertheless, he decided he would make his friend's words, "money changes everything," a mantra of sorts. Along with his daily prayers, he felt he needed something to keep him going. Normally an optimistic person, these recent years had been a downer for him. He didn't know why, but he felt an impending sense of doom. Whenever it overtook him, he worked to shake it off quickly with a prayer to St. Antonio, his patron saint.

In his next letter to Rosa that he dictated to the scribe, he expressed his optimism that with the American money, the baby would grow up respected as a son from moneyed people. Their daughter, Angela, would marry a fine young man and while nothing would change Carlo's condition, they could provide him with a more comfortable home and more care from the doctor.

CHAPTER SEVEN

Bridgeport, Connecticut—1900

Antonio and Negri didn't get to see much of each other over the next three months, because Negri had been working the night shift the entire time. They saw each other briefly in the mornings. Like ships passing in the night, they tossed a joke or two and some pleasantries, but not much else.

Then, one morning as Antonio and Augustino were basking in the solitude of the quiet, drinking their coffee on the front stoop before heading for the blasting site, out of nowhere appeared two men. Antonio thought it odd that visitors would come when it was barely light out. He had a sudden flash of the marauders that often attacked the families in Southern Italy, snatching young girls and boys right before their mother's eyes.

The household was still quiet as Antonio and Augustino often prepared the coffee themselves and left before six a.m., just as Angela was waking the children and starting her day. With her husband working the night shift, she had a short space of time before he came in around eight a.m. to get the noisy chores completed so he could rest after the children were off to school.

One of the men addressed the pair on the stoop in Calabrese.

"Tu se u fratti di Negri?" he asked. No, not his brother, Negri's friend and boarder Antonio answered, and then quickly asked, "Has something happened? Where is Negri?" he suddenly felt pained.

"Mi dispiace." I'm sorry to have to bring bad news, but we must talk with his wife." Before Antonio could go inside to knock on the door upstairs where the Negri family slept, Angela appeared dressed for the day with some mending in her hands. She stopped when she spotted the two men behind Antonio.

"What's happened?" she cried.

"Your husband collapsed at work."

"Where have they brought him? I must go to him."

"He's gone," said the other man in almost a whisper. "There was nothing to be done."

Stunned, Angela screamed. The children came running. In an instant, the stillness was replaced by chaos. Antonio had no words. He heard the men tell him that his friend Negri had not suffered. He felt at a loss as to what to do next. He and Augustino had to report to work or the bosses would let them go. He suddenly realized that he really knew nothing about his friend Negri's affairs and financial situation. He asked Angela if there was someone he could fetch for her. She was limp in a chair, ashen, with all the children around her. Their saucer-sized eyes were incredulous. Antonio was struck by the notion that these children were not strangers to death. They had suffered devastating loss once before.

As if out of nowhere, a neighbor woman appeared and seemed to take charge of Angela and the children. She begged Antonio to find out where Negri's body had been taken. The two men already had walked almost to the end of Pembroke, and Antonio ran after them. Shouting to Augustino to head to their work site and to tell the boss that he would be along soon, Antonio accompanied the men to the undertaker so he could confirm the identity of the body. After the painful identification, Antonio asked some questions about what would take place, and proceeded to arrange a small funeral for his friend, as his widow was in no condition to handle anything.

When he finally arrived at his worksite, Antonio was winded. Forcing himself forward, he went to talk to the railroad boss about any provisions for Negri's family. He was relieved to learn that unlike himself, Negri was not a day laborer, but a real employee. That meant, he was told, there was a railroad insurance that his family was entitled to that would help pay for funeral expenses.

The next afternoon at the visitation, Antonio was pleased there were a lot of the *paisani,* or fellow *Petranese,* and some distant relatives that had showed up. Dying was serious business among the *paisani.* Everyone respected the dead. Antonio had only met a few of them during his relatively short time in Bridgeport. Judging by the size of the crowd, Antonio surmised that his friend had known just about everyone in town.

At the funeral mass on the following day, the property owner of Negri's house approached Antonio and asked if he wanted to rent the apartment. Antonio explained that he would not be remaining in America permanently, to which the proprietor said, "I'm sorry then, I'm going to have to evict the widow and the children. Everyone will have to be gone by the end of the week. I have to rent the place."

After the funeral, Antonio and Augustino went back to collect their belongings and asked what they could do for Angela and the children. Apparently, a distant relative was taking them in temporarily. The general consensus was that she would go back to Calabria where her parents, though elderly, might help her.

Disconsolate from the events of the past few days, Antonio and Augustino trudged to a rooming house on a nearby street that someone had told them about after the funeral. The price was slightly higher, but it was certainly far less than if they had to rent an apartment. This way, the men could continue to make efficient use of their hard-earned dollars. Antonio couldn't fathom how Negri had paid for the house. Though he had boasted a few times to Antonio about having saved a lot of money, when he asked some of Negri's coworkers how Angela might access some of his savings, they didn't sound at all encouraging. He was told that if Angela wanted to remain in America long enough to probate his estate, it could take perhaps a year or more, and even then, there might be nothing for her to inherit. She would have to let it go. She knew less than her husband's co-workers about his money, if indeed he had any at all.

It was all so bewildering, Antonio thought. America, the land of milk and honey, was so fragile. He knew Angela was not looking to profit from her husband's premature death, but how would she manage? She didn't even have passage to return to Calabria, she had said.

At once, Antonio wanted to get away from Bridgeport, Connecticut. The sooner the better. An inexplicable fear overtook him. He was sure the place was cursed. The next day, Antonio and Augustino went back to work with black armbands on their sleeves, out of respect for the loss of their dear friend. Antonio's heart felt as black as the cloth encircling his right bicep. He was as depressed at the death of his friend as he was when he buried the last of his own relatives in Italy. While he considered that his wife's family overflowed with siblings, and all of their children and grandchildren, it deepened his melancholy thinking about how he had no parents, siblings, aunts, uncles, nieces or nephews remaining on this earth. His wife and children were an ocean away. Despite Augustino's companionship, Antonio felt an enormous sense of abandonment; it was as if he had been an orphan.

He scolded himself. "I'm a grown man with children. Orphans are children with no parents." Yet for all the pep talks he gave himself, he could not shake the feeling of a boat adrift without an anchor. He felt helpless against the tide. He recognized that these feelings were an anomaly; he was normally an optimistic person.

Despite the depressed feelings, he didn't lose sight of why he was here in America. He summoned his reserves, from where he did not know, and resolved that he would see it through. However, with Negri gone, Antonio was no longer tempted to stretch the trip out into May of 1901 as they had originally planned. That night, he and Augustino discussed what they could expect to earn in wages and even though they now had a higher expenses for room and board, they lived simply. Together, they determined that if the finished out the year working in America, they would still have done well.

"If we work till then, we will have earned good money. We can leave in November or December; it's only six months before we planned. We'll be home for the start of the new year!" Antonio said for Augustino's benefit, but he didn't feel the optimism that his words were imparting. "There is no work here in the dead of winter anyway; it's all frozen. You well remember last January through March, when we were sweepers earning almost nothing," he said, sounding like the voice of experience and knowledge. Deep down, Antonio felt lost.

Augustino had moaned that if they waited until the spring to return, it would be three years since they had left. To the young man, it seemed an interminable amount of time to be away from his wife, Marianna. He missed her so much. In fact, the young man spoke of nothing else. He often said he would get her pregnant the first night he returned.

"I know you miss her, as I miss my Rosa and the children, though it seems like forever, but in the scheme of life, it's not much," said

Antonio in a small, quiet voice. Yet he had been more than happy to give into curtailing the stay in response to his son-in-law's wishes. The letters continued back and forth across the ocean to their wives lamenting their separation and how hard life was without them in America. As Antonio always included some money in each letter, Rosa back in Platania felt the sacrifices were worth it.

As time passed, she wrote, "Our son Carlo grows weaker each day. On a happier note, our son Michele is now quite a little man, talking and helping us with small chores. At three years old," she reported, "he's smart enough that we can leave him to tend to his sick brother while Marianna and I go into town or to gather the silkworms. Michele fetches things for Carlo, who doesn't have the strength to walk across the room. Carlo is so weak; he spends each day stretched out on the little divan."

In America, the two day workers went from the railroad projects to work on a new dam of the Bridgeport Hydraulic Company near Beaver Brook, in the upper part of an area called, Stratford. The bosses had said that this job would shut down at Christmas time and work would not resume until late March. Armed with that knowledge, Antonio and his son-in-law set their return passage to return to Italy for December 24. While he would have liked to be home for Christmas, Antonio found the cost of passage lower on that date; it would allow the two men to work till the last possible day.

Then, on December 17, a week before their planned departure, the Antonio and Augustino were working at digging away at an embankment while blasting was going on at another area of the construction. The blasting explosions had become routine and no one really worried about them except for Antonio. He hated them. His work group had just stopped for a water break. He stood with a ladle in hand and watched as the crew where his son-in-law worked became fodder for the cave-in that occurred before his eyes.

As Antonio watched in horror, he saw the upper part of the bank suddenly collapse above them and about 30 men buried alive. Dumbstruck, he realized his son-in-law along with some of the men he knew, had just perished before him. In the chaos that followed, no one noticed Antonio as he gripped his chest and slumped to the ground. Seeing what had happened, all the men he was with rushed to the cave-in site and started digging to extract the men. The site was overrun with people and horses who brought Doctors Lewis, Ivers and Adams of Bridgeport to the victims' aid. When finally Antonio's co-workers spotted him on the ground, they assumed he had been overcome with grief. They carried him back to his rooming house, but never fetched a doctor until the second day, when they recognized Antonio was barely moving. When the Dr. Ivers arrived, he announced after examining him, "This man has suffered a massive heart infarction."

The massive coronary had debilitated Antonio tremendously. In his weakened state, Antonio asked that his co-workers contact his family. Unfortunately, even before a telegraph could be dispatched, Antonio died.

CHAPTER EIGHT

Platania–October 1900

The telegram delivery boy, always a harbinger of bad news, was universally perceived as an ill omen. In Calabria where the main channel of communication was word of mouth, everyone dreaded the telegram delivery boy coming their way. When Rosa saw the young man on the bicycle approach her door, she screamed. Then the boy read the telegram to her. With the news fully absorbed, she keened with rage and fury. "Not only have I lost my devoted husband, but what am I to do with a little boy, a ten-year-old son with heart trouble who can't help work the fields let alone take care of himself, and a daughter getting closer every day to the age of marriage," she wailed.

"This is every Southern Italian mother's nightmare—no dowry with which to make a good match for my daughter." In a singsong lamentation, she cried her fears that Angela would be forever a burden to her family, not to mention the shame of an unwed daughter who was not in a convent.

And, of course, there was Marianna. Heartbroken. A widow at

eighteen. "What are we to do?" Rosa screamed as she tore at her face. Her guilt at having practically forced her husband to go on this trip would follow her to her grave. "It's my fault. I should never have insisted they go. I have committed a grave sin," she declared to the world.

Little Michelangelo had developed a strong bond, a solid kinship with his "milk sister," Marianna, from the day he was born. Marianna was not yet married then and though only a teenager, she had tended Rosa with the birth. Even after marriage, having no children of her own yet, and later an absent husband, it was easy for her to lavish the little boy with all her love and attention. His own mother, too, had paid considerable attention to the baby from the time he was born. His hazel-colored eyes and full lips made her often declare that he was her little cherub, the apple of her eye.

Though not quite four years old, he understood the seriousness of what he was hearing from his mother now—her anguished cries, then joined by Marianna as the news reached her that her Augustino would not be returning. Over the next several months, Antonio's premature death rendered Rosa more and more despondent. She paid little or no attention to *Michuzzo*, her pet name for him. Now, even more than working and tending children, there were greater issues at hand. Whatever money Antonio was saving was gone. No one knew what happened to either Augustino or Antonio's stash of earnings.

Marianna had been less demonstrative. She went around hugging Michuzzo, doing chores by rote, weeping quietly. Her pain was different, she realized, than her mother's. Rosa for her part screamed words that didn't register, "You are a young woman with no children. You'll soon marry another good man."

The distance, the lack of education and knowledge about America made it impossible to lay claim to anything. Rosa went to the priest to see if he would write an official letter, but the priest though accommodating was not encouraging. "Rosa," he said gently, "America is a wild place. If he didn't send it to you, then it's gone. No sense building up false hopes. Whatever there was is gone. It is God's will."

Dejected, she trod home, hugged her children, keened, ranted and cried some more. Rosa knew that in a place where lawlessness reigned, a woman alone with two daughters, a baby and a sickly son had much to be concerned about. Her situation was precarious in Calabria with no money or man.

To cope with her grief she made herself imagine at first that Antonio was coming home in six months. But as time passed, the lack of letters and money drove home the harsh truth. She would no longer have the warmth and stability of her fine husband. One afternoon after having gone to the *mercato* in Nicastro, she detoured on her way back to Platania to pay her uncles and cousins a visit in Sambiase. They offered her something to eat. She felt guilty accepting it, but after refusing it three times, on the fourth offering she ate.

Tears slid down her face. She barely had anything to feed her children, she confided. Her uncle and cousins all advised her that finding and marrying some good widower was her only salvation. She protested that she could do it alone. No one could replace Antonio, she declared. She wanted no other husband.

A few months later, when winter raged its frigid fury, she realized that she and the children were all getting weaker and weaker. Her family's words rang in her head and it finally dawned on her that they were right. A widower who needed her help could be her family's savior. She needed to find someone who had lost his wife. She needed to have others convince him that Rosa would be a suitable wife for him for the sake of all of them. It would be a marriage of convenience. Unlike the love and burning attraction she had experienced with Antonio, this union would just help them stay alive.

Was there such a man who would have her? She wasn't young, the bloom had left the rose, she thought. She examined herself in the small hand mirror she had received as a wedding gift what seemed eons ago. Her face was unlined, though she was closer to forty than thirty. And, her bosom was still ample. Yes, she was indeed saddled with children and problems; nevertheless, she went to call on a woman in town known for bringing the 'mbasciata. A matchmaker. She would help.

———————————⸼⸽⸾⸻⸻———————————

In summer of 1904, as she approached her fourth year as a widow, and the state of the Rizzo family had deteriorated, Rosa married Domenico Scalizi, a widower with several children. Her youngest son, Michele, was nearly eight years old. A virtual little man always helping his mother and serving his sickly brother Carlo, Michele had not been asked his opinion about his soon-to-be stepfather. Yet he had overheard his mother talking to his older sisters and to the town matchmaker, and from what he had heard it sounded like his mother was not too thrilled with the match herself. He had overheard her say, "It's the best I can do; otherwise, we will all be lost."

Six months into the marriage of convenience, Michele came to realize that the man his mother had married was providing a roof over their heads and some food for their bellies, but he was also inflicting plenty of pain and suffering.

CHAPTER NINE

He had been living alone for almost a year now. Michele had left his mother and stepfather's home after he gotten into a fight with the man trying to keep him from striking his mother again. It had been a terrible scene. But when his stepfather struck Michele as well, his mother had not defended him. She merely tried to hush him so as not to provoke further disputes. Michele had not been able to stomach the abuse that his stepfather had dished out regularly, not only to him, but to his mother as well.

Realizing that his mother had resigned herself to a situation that he wanted no part of, he left. At age ten, he moved back into the old Rizzo home that they had abandoned when Rosa had married. It was what his father had secured with the earnings from his first trip to America. He lived there alone in the crude structure. Though it was typical of the Mercuri area of Platania where the peasants lived; fashioned from loose stones, which were plentiful in the mountains, it served to keep the elements at bay with clay, hay and an eclectic collection of nature's throwaways shoved in between the crevices.

Summers were epic in Platania. The tangy mountain air spiked with pines and crystal-fresh springs, kept the temperature much cooler than the valley of Nicastro, where the residents fled to the beaches to escape the intense heat of August. The mountain springs ensured good drinking water year-round for the *Platanese*, but for those in the rural areas, it was a long walk to get it. At least we are not as bad off as much of Nicastro where lack of water is a way of life during the arid summer months, thought Michele often to soften the daily demand for fetching water for cooking and personal needs.

On the mountain, the drinking water was clean. However, water to bathe, cook and wash was difficult to secure during the months of January, February and March when the temperatures hovered around .7 degrees Celsius. Those who resided in the Platania town center had sturdier structures that kept out the winds and cold and kept in the warmth from *caminetti* and *scaldapiedi*, the fireplaces and foot-warmers that were popular with the well-heeled townies.

However, in the more remote rural areas where Michele's family lived, there was little to fend off the bitter cold and ice. While picturesque three seasons of the year, Platania, in winter, cloaked itself in an aura of mourning, as food and forage were difficult to find. Michele's house, like most in his area, turned into a meat locker, with the only chilled game being himself.

This frosty February Tuesday was no different than most. Michele had gone on his usual expedition to gather *frasche,* forest branches, sticks and kindling for a fire, as well as to look for small game, birds or dig up some roots that he might sell or to help contribute to the simple meal that his sister Marianna would cook. His feet, bare most of the year, were wrapped in old rags, which did little to stave off the numbness. He had set out at first light since the winter days were short. This morning, he had awakened with a stiff neck. His arms and neck hurt. He had not undressed because it was so cold, but his body felt itchy and he noticed he had what looked like a rash on his abdomen. He just felt generally unwell and sluggish. Yet he pushed on.

As on many a winter's day, he was working his way to Marianna's house to arrive there close to the noon hour so he could help her. Marianna had married again, well before his mother had, within two years of losing her first husband. Michele had been Marianna's comfort when she first was widowed and she had his undivided attention. She had smothered Michele with hugs and kisses, but her unbridled affection stopped when she married Francesco Fruscino. Fruscino was a good man. A sturdy peasant, he was simple, amiable and hardworking. Two years older than Marianna, he was handsome of face, but best of all he had a good heart and he adored his wife. While Marianna no longer lavished Michele with hugs and kisses, it was clear she still loved him very much. Most mornings, Marianna and Francesco would spend their time either working their small parcel of land on the hillside or walking the approximately five kilometers into Nicastro to sell their meager produce, which was almost nonexistent this time of year. During the warm months, Michele would often join Marianna going to the *mercato,* thus leaving Francesco behind to work the fields. The pair would make the return trek at the height of the mid-afternoon sun after the market closed at one o'clock. In the summer, Platania was always much cooler than Nicastro even on the worst day. Somehow, the thought of the decline in heat and humidity made the uphill trek home easier to deal with.

Now, in the dead of winter, Marianna and Francesco were grateful for the bundle of branches and small food bits Michele brought. On most winter days, Michele helped make the fire for cooking while Francesco tended the goat. The three would eat together. But today when Michele arrived, Marianna took one look at him and saw a scary sight. Instead of the big smile he always sported for her,

Michele crumbled to his knees, pale and shaking.

Marianna and Francesco's home was like those of many peasants in the Mercuri—one sparsely furnished room. Year around, all the cooking happened outside, though the rustic table with benches was indoors. As she stretched Michele out on the bed, she was shocked to find that his body appeared to be burning up with fever. By the time Francesco arrived less than five minutes later, Michele was delirious and talking nonsense.

Francesco did not need to be told. He knew how many had succumbed to the awful sickness of the previous year—cholera, they had called it; several of his family members were among those who did not survive it. He turned on his heel and immediately ran the distance to the doctor's house in the center of town a good thirty minutes away. When he returned with the doctor, Michele's body was not only afire, but his brain was too.

The small, neat little man immediately went to Michele's side and started feeling his neck, under his armpits and his abdomen, all the while pressing Marianna for information.

"Da quando e` cosi?" How long has he been like this? His grave look and his probing questions told Marianna and Francesco that time was of the essence.

"Before he became delirious, Michele said he had awakened ill when it was still dark out and that he had been sick to his stomach, and his head and neck hurt terribly," she explained. Too shy to look at the doctor because of her extreme consciousness of the class difference, she went on to share, "Michele said he felt itchy like with a rash. Yesterday he looked and seemed fine. Please help him to be all right."

The doctor had no trouble understanding her mountain dialect with the words clipped at both ends.

"We do not know if we have gotten it early enough, but we may have since he appeared well yesterday," he told her. "It's good that he made his way here because the Lord only knows when someone would have found him."

Marianna was very embarrassed by the doctor's presence in her modest home. She knew he tended the fine families of the town as well as the rural population, but those who lived in the *compagna* mostly saw the doctor when they went into town to his office. She offered him coffee, then immediately realized that what she had was probably not what the doctor was accustomed to drinking. Their coffee was made from boiled dandelions.

To her relief, the doctor said, "Thank you so much for your graciousness, but I had just had my coffee when Francesco arrived."

In short order, he announced in what Marianna thought was the most learned voice she had ever heard besides Monsignor at San Michele Arcangelo on Sundays, *"Meningita meningococcal."* The doctor spoke in his mountain dialect refined by his years away at medical school in Catanzaro and now used only to put the rural people at ease. *"C'e pocco che pottiamo fare,"* he said with a grave look on his face while shaking his head. "There is little we can do."

He reached with his small, uncalloused hands into a leather medical bag. Emerging with an eight-inch hypodermic needle with metal grippers in his right hand, he gingerly fingered a clear vial filled with fluid with his left. He plunged the needle into the vial after he had removed the protective metal case. Knowing what was coming, Marianna turned her head, to avoid watching as the doctor jabbed the needle into Michele's thigh and pressed slowly on the plunger until all the contents vanished. Michele flinched and moaned.

The doctor told Marianna the shot would help him if they had indeed gotten it in time. He explained the meningitis disease came from Africa but could occur anywhere and, like the cholera of the year before, it was now sweeping through the area in epidemic proportions. He said the next forty-eight hours were critical. He gave Marianna instructions on what to do; stay with him, place wet compresses on his forehead and try to get him small sips of some clear broth.

The doctor showed her how to wet rags to cool Michele's body, but he offered little hope that Michele would survive. Determined that he would not die, Marianna kept vigil throughout the night, continually wetting the rags and bathing Michele's body. When it grew colder, she kept the chilling breezes off him by wrapping him in a woolen blanket. In his delirium, he raved of things that did not make sense. Trembling with fear, she sent her husband to alert Rosa. While she waited, she rocked back and forth citing a litany of requests to the Lord to save her brother.

Hearing the news, Rosa started gathering some of her precious stock of medical herbs, but then fell to her knees and began keening a litany of pleadings to God when her husband forbade her to go to her son. She knew he would either strike her or leave her if she disobeyed him. She had been on the receiving end of his quick hands often, which was why her son no longer lived with them. Every day she regretted the marriage. She was filled with self-loathing as she squirreled the herbs into Francesco's pockets and told him that she would pray to God to spare her son.

"Dio, non ti lo piare anche, Michele, comu patri e u fratto." Not him too, like his father and his brothers, she cried. Her heart, though hardened as the stones scattered along the mountainside, bled for her youngest son, who never had known what she felt was a happy moment. She cried for herself, her dead husband and her dead children as well as the one who was now at death's door. How could all this tragedy be heaped upon her? What she had done to deserve this pain, she wondered. Her rosary in hands, she prayed it aloud.

The next morning more than forty-five hours after the fever's onset, Rosa's and Marianna's prayers were answered. Marianna saw a slight stirring. When she checked, she found Michele was cooler to the touch, though his lips were crusted and parched. She placed a moist rag to his mouth and went off shouting for her husband to come and sit with him, while she went for fresh water at the public fountain at least a ten-minute walk each way. She took the jug sitting in the corner and after wrapping a handkerchief into a cruller shape and placing it on the crown of her head; she set the jug upon it and went with a sure-footed flurry to fetch the water.

She yelled to her adopted mother as she passed her dwelling. Since Domenico had already left the house, Rosa scurried to Marianna's place to get a peek at her son. Once there, she moved slowly toward him, touched his forehead, then fled quickly lest her husband return and suspect she had been to see him. Michele's eyes opened at her touch, and he thought it a dream when she said, *"O pregatto a dio e mia rispoto; grazie di Dio, tu va bene."*

Once back at her house, Marianna struggled to make a fire, so she could prepare a hot broth for Michele. Putting some grasses and herbs in the water, she was within an hour getting him to take microscopic sips. She spent each day for a week coaxing a little broth into him and praying for full recovery. Slowly regaining some strength, Michele began to realize that not only was he wobbly on his feet, but his eyesight had somehow been impaired. He was so elated to be alive that he did not complain, yet he struggled to see things clearly at any distance more than a few feet away.

Later that week, the doctor looked in on him. When he said something about his vision, the doctor told him it was often a result of the fever, that and a weakened heart. But he felt certain that Michele would be okay because he had been a strong and healthy boy before the attack of the debilitating disease.

As the weeks went by and life returned to some normalcy, Michele moved back to his own house as the temperatures grew warmer and the days longer. A month later, Michele found himself at Marianna's door. Looking in, he felt his heart swell with love for this simple woman, his adopted sister. Others felt she was somewhat slow or behind in her mental development, but her heart was huge. She was full of love for everyone, especially for him, often referring to him as *tessoro mio*, my treasure. That morning he realized that without her loving attention, he would have died. For that and for her many, many kindnesses, he would be forever grateful.

CHAPTER TEN

A s the mountain began its annual ritual of cloaking itself in flowers of every hue and umpteen shades of green, Michele began to realize that although his bout with meningitis had impaired his eyesight, he was now even more sharply focused on his dream.

Early in 1907, Nicastro was abuzz with the usual men who wore their best jackets and talked politics and expressed their opinions of world leaders, their decisions and its impact on everyone.

Every market day since he was very little, Michele had listened to even the tiniest morsel of news concerning not only the local items, but also those beyond Italy. He most especially paid attention to anything with connection to the United States of America, mostly referred to as *'merica* by the locals. Recently, he heard it discussed that America was continuing to grow bigger. The current president, Theodore Roosevelt, was a robust and courageous man who was bent on expanding the nation.

Just this morning Michele overheard a man whom he saw most mornings in the square holding forth. This man was always well dressed and spoke in educated Italian. Each day, he sat on same bench in Piazza D'Arme reading the daily newspaper. He invariably was joined by a group of similar-looking men within thirty minutes after he arrived. The other men referred to him as *Professore* Julio.

"I read in the paper that America has just gotten larger. Why, they just added another state called Oklahoma," the man declared.

Michele inched closer to hear the conversation better without appearing to be eavesdropping.

"They do great things in America," effused one of the man's cohorts. "In fact, a few years ago, two brothers flew like birds in something they built called an *aeroplano*."

Through these bits and pieces, Michele learned that America was seeking strong workers because they wanted roads and trains to drive across the vast continent. In the opinions of these local men of politics in Nicastro, it would not be long before the United States annexed the entire continent. Then they would need more Calabrese to build roads, lay train track and dig ditches. They gave a hearty laugh at this discussion because they said no one could dig ditches better than the *montagnaro Calabrese*—the hillbilly Calabrian.

They spoke of how rich everyone was in America. They all had shoes and several changes of clothes. *"Abbigliamento non si vede mai qui."* Suits and outfits that you would never see here, with extra clothes, some for Sunday and others for every day. *"Buttano via più cibo di quanto abbiamo mangiato qui in una settimana."* This morsel about how in America they threw away more food that anyone here had to eat for a week caught Michele's attention. He found it hard to imagine that anyone would throw away food. His belly always unsated, he struggled to understand that kind of wealth.

Michele absorbed these crumbs of information. Later, he would find someone to chat with at the *mercato* and ask questions he did not dare ask the *politica*. He was most interested in the rules about getting into the country. He sought every morsel he could find out from people he thought were knowledgeable and would not steer him wrong, because often he had heard that some people after paying passage and suffering the long trip had been turned back upon arrival.

This particular morning he wrapped up the sale of his small basket of produce he had brought down from the mountain and he slipped away before the stores and offices closed at one o'clock for the afternoon.

It was ten minutes to one when he walked into the *agenzia turistica*, three blocks off the market square.

Hearing the door, the man at the desk stood to greet him without looking up. Once at the counter, he took one look at boy and thought to himself, "steerage." He was a bit puzzled at the audacity of this young man coming into his office; usually people of his class sent someone older and more learned to handle voyage matters for them. As he glanced at the clock, he knew it would be but a few minutes until he told the boy it was closing time, for nothing interfered with the midday meal and the *riposso* of the office worker. However, business was business so he decided to invest a few minutes with the boy and not brush him off just yet.

"*Che cosa, vuoi,*" the agent asked curtly.

Michele answered modestly, "*Buon giorno. Per favore mi dice quanto costa un biglietto di seconda classa?*"

The agent appeared shocked. He had never had a peasant, and especially one from the mountains, come to inquire about fare above steerage class. Could this youngster with no shoes really have that kind of money to spare?

Michele had learned through much inquiry that if you went at least second class there was less chance of being turned back. Because he felt sure his eyesight would be an impediment and he might even be found to have a bad heart, he feared that while probably vastly cheaper in price, steerage would almost surely result in his being turned back.

The man told him the price of the ticket and assumed that would be the end of the conversation. Instead, Michele immediately thanked him and then asked a barrage of additional questions.

"How much ahead of the ship's sailing do I need to buy the ticket? From where does it depart? How do I get to Naples? Is there a time of year when the ticket costs less? What documents do I need?" Lastly, Michele broached the immigration questions with the agent.

The stunned agency worker made a mental decision that this boy really had something of a different streak in him. So he decided to help him all he could. The agent's abrupt manner dissipated and he proceeded to explain patiently to Michele all he needed to know.

In a careful instructive tone he said, "Ocean liner fare is generally less expensive November through May, Then it goes up dramatically. You will need to take a train to Vibo Valente; there you can board a small vessel to Naples. In Naples, you will go through a presentation of your documents and then board your ocean vessel to America."

The agent also explained, "To be admitted you must have some money with you. Not too much, but you need to carry at least the equivalent of twenty-five American dollars. You will have to declare that money upon your arrival. Those that are without money or too poor are suspect and may not be admitted. You will need an address of a relative or friend, someone you have to claim you will be visiting. This is very important. If you don't have it, you can't go in," he said emphatically

As if writing the words down in his head, Michele hung on every word that agent said.

"How is your health? You look strong, but do you have any infirmities I can't see?" Without pausing for an answer, the agent continued. "With the steerage fare, after you arrive in New York harbor, you will be transferred to another smaller ship and transported to a processing center called Ellis Island. All the people going through Ellis Island undergo a health examination. If you are found infirm, ill or they think you are crazy, they will send you back."

Michele took it all in, committing every word to memory. Then he asked one more question, "Does everyone have to undergo a health examination?"

The man eyed him looking for signs of infirmity; seeing none, he was a bit puzzled, yet he decided there had to be a reason. Perhaps he was asking for someone else. "No. It is mandatory for only those traveling in steerage class. Higher classes of fare only go to Ellis Island if, when they ask some general questions, you are found to be a criminal, act crazy, seem sick, don't have someone in America who is expecting you, don't have the funds I told you about, or are limping. Otherwise, you will be admitted without difficulty. Of course, if you are an American citizen you are not sent to Ellis Island."

"Did your father ever go to America?" the agent asked.

"Yes. He did."

"Well, ask him if he became a citizen; perhaps you can claim USA citizenship under him. We have some locals whose parents went to America in the old days, worked in the coal mines. They were either born there and then their parents brought them home here as babies, or their father became a citizen prior to their birth; even if born here in Italy, the children have rights to American citizenship."

Michele remained quiet for a moment, then answered, "No. My father died there too quickly after arrival to have become a citizen. I was just a baby when he went."

Observing the pained face, the agent was sorry he had brought up the subject. So he added brightly, "In America, they want strong young men like you."

As if to confirm his statement, he handed Michele a colorful brochure with a picture of a huge ocean liner on the cover, knowing that those of this boy's socio-economic class could not read or write.

Nevertheless, Michele took the brochure and for a few moments stared at it intently as if it would tell him something, he did not know.

Expressing his gratitude to the agent, he said, "*Io ritorno.*" I will be back. He left that office in May of 1907 more adamant than ever that he would make this happen before long.

Throughout the next couple of years, he looked for every possible way to earn a little more money. He stayed tuned in on all that was going on around him and every bit of news available. Occasionally, he would hear of some of the rest of the world's troubles and even some kinks in the health of the United States. Only a short time before, he had learned that there had been a war between the Russians and the Japanese and that in a place in America called San Francisco there was an earthquake that had killed about 3,000 people.

Despite the bad news stories about America, he had wanted to get away from the hunger, cold and the ever-present gloom of death in Calabria. The news of the natural disasters had frightened Michele perhaps more than most of what else he had heard because not long ago, there had been an earthquake in Southern Italy; the subsequent tsunami had destroyed the city of Messina in Sicily, as well as across the straits to Reggio Calabria. In the end, he had heard there were more than 60,000 people dead in Messina alone, many homeless and displaced and scattered throughout Italy and even to the Americas. Yet if America was bad, why would the homeless go there? he asked himself often.

He had felt the shocks in Platania where they were only some eighty-six miles from the epicenter. But being in the mountains,

Platania was spared the forty-foot waves. The news had traveled worldwide, and the King of Italy had even gone to the center of the devastation.

Since his bout of meningitis, Michele had concentrated on earning enough money to buy passage to America. He listened closely to the men who read the newspapers and discussed them in the town square both in Platania and in Nicastro. He hired himself out as a laborer to the landowners of the region, often walking sixteen kilometers in a day, sleeping by a roadside just to be there for the harvest or planting job that day.

While other young men his age already had started finding their way to the cantina to buy wine, he never did. He had no use for waste or for creature comforts. All that could wait until he went to America. He knew America was hard. He had no illusions about it. He knew it had killed his father and Marianna's first husband. Yet his soul amplified with a sense of certainty. Deep in his gut, he knew as surely as there was a God that it was his destiny.

In America, he would find his father's grave and pay his father honor by placing flowers at his gravesite. He felt compelled to make a solid connection with the man he imagined his father to have been. Every one of his relatives who had known his father had said Michele looked, sounded and acted like him. He often felt absolutely no connection to his father, yet at the same time felt he was his father incarnate. It was a strange feeling.

The cruel man who was his stepfather, had been a friend of the family and had known Antonio, Michele's father. Michele often thought that was why he seemed to resent him so much. Scalizi, Michele felt sure, could never measure up to Antonio. Michele promised himself he would right a terrible wrong that had been meted out when his mother married this poor excuse for a human being.

Somehow, Michel knew with certainty that he would find what he was seeking in America. He lived for nothing else.

As God planned it and time would teach him, Michele was both right and wrong.

CHAPTER ELEVEN

Platania—October 1909

When the rooster crowed, he jumped up from jumbled dreams. He poured some water from the terra cotta jug he had filled yesterday into a small basin. The icy water served his washing needs and sharpened his senses, scattering completely any grogginess. He pulled on his pants and shirt and grabbed his things, a small bundle containing one change of pants, shirt and underwear. Before starting down the mountain, he had one very important thing to do. All else was ready.

As he walked, he could hardly believe the time had come. He had paid for the passage. He had the documents he needed. He was mentally ready to leave everything and everyone he knew behind him. Yet he knew he would miss his sister Marianna very much. He would also miss his cousins, *'ianchi,* or "the Whites," as they were known by their over name. They bore the surname Folino, his mother's birth name, but no one referred to them other than "the Whites" most probably because they all had fair skin compared to most of the *Meridionale.* He would stop to visit them once he descended the mountain and before heading to the train station in Nicastro.

So much anticipation welled within him. He also began to feel a sudden nostalgia for Marianna and he had not even left yet. Her house was his last stop in Platania before he hiked down to Sambiase and on to Nicastro to catch the train.

Though still dark out, she had been waiting for him. *"A Miche,"* she said in her distinctive mountain dialect. She was a tall scrawny woman, almost his height, with not an ounce of fat on her. A virtual mountain goat, he had thought hundreds of times as he had watched her trek easily up the mountain carrying produce and other goods bought at the *mercato* in Nicastro. Her body was a result of that and the equal number of treks down the mountain loaded with a basket on her head or shoulder filled with items to sell at the open air market. In his mind's eye, he always pictured her with the *vozza*, an earthen jug, containing water, on her head. He stared at the hardness of her calloused hands that had so tenderly cared for him.

She grabbed his shoulders and made him look right into her face as she continued in a tone that sounded like she was chastising him, but instead was her way of expressing deep affection. *"Sta atttento; non ti mettiare cu chelli maliandrini. E quando ti fai ricco, mi venatrovare."* Be careful. Stay out of the way of those who are involved in the bad life. When you get rich, come and visit me again, she had ordered. Her scowl was replaced with a huge smile as she hugged him, and then her eyes lit up and welled with liquid love that flowed freely from them in giant drops.

He smiled at her simplicity and her loving aura. He had been her baby for his entire life, more so than his own natural mother. He thought of how destiny had brought him and Marianna together. She, needing a mother and father, and he needing the same.

Marianna's husband also hovered around Michele. In a limited

Petranese, he expressed that he would miss him, especially when they worked together. He begged that Michele not forget them, especially his sister.

Michele was elated that his sister had found a love to replace her lost husband. It was apparent to him that together, Marianna and Francesco would someday have children and make a wonderful family. Though she loved Francesco, she still spoke of her first love on occasion to Michele. She would often say, *"Prego che dio si l'abbriacchiato allu petto sua."* I pray God has embraced him in his bosom.

Michele broke from his thoughts and said, *"È tempo che mi ne vado."* It's time for me to go.

They hugged again without words. As they separated, Michele watched as Marianna bent down and then took off her shoes. The work boots had been a present from Francesco to her when they married. No one in the rural area had shoes. It was clear to Michele that the two had discussed what happened next. She said, *"Miche, non voglio che arrivi ala America squazzo come tutti l'altri montagnari. Va culle scarpe mia e ti fai un riccune subbito."* She seemed to think that if he didn't arrive barefoot as so many other mountain people did, he would get rich quickly in America.

Michele was stunned. He had been barefoot all of his life. In winter, he had wrapped his feet, like many of the Petranese peasants, with whatever they could find—bark, large fig leaves and rags bound with raffia. The remainder of the year, they developed hardtack soles on the stones and brambles as they went barefoot.

Gathering his emotions, Michele insisted he couldn't possibly accept this gift. "This is too much. You've already done so much for me. You packed some bread, *supressate* and cheeses that I know you were saving for the Christmas dinner next month," he protested, pointing to the bundle wrapped in a *tovagliolo*—a cloth napkin, tied securely in a knot. He knew the food would sustain him through his arduous journey until he reached Naples to board his ship to America. He had been told his passage included meals for the transatlantic crossing.

Marianna ignored his protests about the shoes and insisted that he put them on. Reluctantly, he acquiesced, all the while thinking, these shoes are over the top. The realization struck him that he had not given much thought to luxuries like shoes, but they would be needed because he wasn't traveling in steerage class. Without them, he would stand out if he didn't have shoes in the upper-class area.

He wondered how Marianna and Francesco knew that he had purchased the higher-class ticket. He had kept his own counsel on all the matters concerning his plans. Suddenly, he was seized with an overwhelming sense of gratitude that his adopted sister, whom all regarded as simple, had been smarter and a much better judge of what was needed than he had.

With threatening tears, he laced up the leather boots and found them even a bit big. As he stood, Marianna said, "You will grow into them." His sister and brother-in-law beamed at him. Over his protests, they shooed him along so he would not miss his train.

He tried to say a proper goodbye, but his voice failed him. He choked up and hoped that Marianna could see the love and gratitude in his eyes. He hugged Francesco. Then he took the shoes off and said, "I don't want them to get dirty before the trip." He would not wear them until it was time to board the ship. Not only did he not want to get the shoes soiled or worn, but also he wanted to feel every rock and sharp bramble all the way down the mountain for one last time.

With his shoes tied together and slung over his shoulder, the tears that had made a tiny appearance in front of Marianna and Francesco turned into a waterfall as he began his descent to the valley. Blinded by the torrent on his face in the dark before the dawn, he thought he heard someone behind him. He suddenly was concerned. There had been reports of robbers and murderers in this area. If someone had let slip that he was going to America, they would assume correctly that he had a little money on him. His heart began to race and his legs picked up the pace. His bag, lighter than many of the bundles he had hauled into the mercato on so many Wednesdays, didn't slow him down. He quickened his step and then took an unusual turn, not his normal path down the mountain, though it was more difficult.

After a few minutes on his alternate route, he began to relax. He had lost the sound of someone following. Then as he caught a glimpse of the lights of Nicastro, he suddenly became aware that whoever or whatever was following was behind him again. He prayed. "Dear God, I am so close, please don't let me beaten and robbed before I can go to find my father's grave."

CHAPTER TWELVE

The Port of New York—November 1909

This truly must be hell, Michele thought as he tried to stand and his legs buckled. His head felt like there were rocks rolling around inside an empty box. He had never seen so much food as he had that first day on the ship. He had made the short voyage from Vibo Valente to Naples on the small vessel without trouble. After one night in Naples, he had boarded the Duca d'Aosta the next morning of November 10, 1909, a beautiful sunny day. He remained on deck and watched the colorful Bay of Naples get smaller and smaller. He basked in the gentle breeze on his cheeks and in the azure sky and the snappy air. He had never felt more alive and full of hope.

He noticed everything that day, especially the way people behaved and their clothing and footwear. When they had embarked, he watched, as many of those going to below the waterline were barefoot, while no one in the second-class cabin deck had naked feet. His throat had closed up as he remembered his sister's kindness. He had been so grateful especially because he understood her sacrifice. Shoes were truly a luxury for the *montagnaro*.

Now, as he looked at his fellow second-class passengers, he felt Marianna would never know how truly important the work shoes covering his feet had proven to be. His clothes, though the best he had could scrounge, smacked of hunger and the mountains just like his hard, lean body. He had no coat, only a second-hand jacket with sleeves that were too short and shoulders that could have fit another person inside with him. On deck, he eyed an American family arrayed in charcoal-colored woolen coats with fur collars. He thought the coats were crafted perhaps by tailors in Rome or Milan. He promised himself that someday he would own a suit made from Italian wool and tailored to fit his body.

The Duca D'Aosta was a marvel to him. The 7,804 gross-ton-ship was 475 feet long with a 53.3-foot beam, two funnels, two masts, twin screw and sailed at a speedy 16 knots. The ship had accommodations for eighty, first-class passengers, sixteen in second class, and 1,740 in third class. Built in Palermo, with engines by a Sestri Ponente firm, she had been launched a little over a year ago by *Navigazione Generale Italiana.*

Michele was one of nearly 2,000 traveling on her maiden voyage that started on the ninth day of November when she sailed from Genoa for Naples and on to New York. He learned quickly that the ship served three meals a day and there was something to eat almost any time he felt hungry. Moreover, it was not just a bowlful—there were amazing choices and quantities enough to feed his entire *Mercuri* hamlet back on the mountain of Platania for several days. He had never seen so much food. There were heaping plates of meats, poultry, fish, vegetables and many different types of breads. The wine was liberally poured just for the asking.

There were little pastries and sweets that appeared to be crafted purely for show; surely, no one would bite into those works of art, he thought. That afternoon and evening, he had stuffed himself until he couldn't breathe. He had tried to be discreet. He didn't want those seated nearby to think he was crude. But little by little, he was feeling that he couldn't fit any more. Then he had gone to the tiny cabin shared with three strangers from Naples and had fallen asleep thinking America could only be better than the ship.

At about three a.m., he awoke. His stomach lurched and all that he had eaten was suddenly all over him. His cabin mates had urged him to go on deck and get some air, and he dragged himself up there and lay out on a deck chair. At about six-thirty, aromas of food preparation reached his nostrils and the smell of food made him ill again.

He spent the rest of that day in bed. The seasickness not only affected his stomach, but he could not hold his head upright. The sickness enveloped and totally incapacitated him. He became a bit delirious. His cabin mate told him he needed to go to the ship's infirmary. But Michele refused. He took small sips of water, as it was the only thing he could stomach. He was confined to bed for most of the remainder of the trip.

Lying in his cabin, he knew there was so much around him that he had never had, food, company, entertainment, and he was too ill to partake of any of it. Surely, he would feel better soon, he thought.

To the contrary, the seas only got rougher as the voyage progressed. Then his cabin mates became ill also. They all languished in the tiny space.

Michele began to think this was penance for his sins. He prayed for forgiveness. He confessed to God that he knew he was stubborn. He thought back to all the times he had been obstinate and vowed to try to do better.

The agent had told him the ticket would be cheaper this time of year. He now understood why. He also began to think that he might die before he arrived in America. All the warnings about steerage class and that he might be turned back because of his eyes and heart throbbed in his mind. He knew that when he arrived, although his class fare would not automatically cause him to undergo the processing at Ellis Island, he could still be turned back if they thought he was too sick. He was grateful for one thing. If he was sick in second class, those completely below the water line must be nearly dead, he thought.

Now, eighteen days later as the announcement that the ship was close to arriving, he summoned some small reserve of strength to pull himself on deck. Though his legs wobbled and his head spun, with sheer determination, he dragged himself up and then leaned on the small basin to wash his face and rinse out his mouth. He smoothed his hair with his hands and grabbed his small cloth handbag and dragged himself on deck. He felt as if he had been just released from prison. The air was biting cold, but the sky was clear. He watched with tears in his eyes as the ship came in sight of the famous Statue of Liberty.

The ship's whistle blew hard just as it had when they sailed from Naples. It seemed to announce to America that he was here. He had done it. He thanked God for the strength to have survived the voyage. He had crossed the Atlantic to a new world.

He tried to ask those around him where he needed to go, but many looked at him and moved on. "*Sie solo raggazzo?*" asked a smartly dressed, middle-aged man. When Michele answered that he was indeed alone, the man quickly responded in a low voice saying, "*Stati con me; io ti metto sotto il mio alle.*" Stick with me; I'll take you under my wing. Michele recognized the dialect as Sicilian. Through his foggy brain, he remembered the admonitions administered by his cousins of lessons learned from their father's forays to America. Instead of following him, Michele turned and moved into the crowd to lose the man.

His legs seemed made of rubber. The dizziness and nausea he had experienced for many days on board ship had left him totally depleted. People around him were speaking rapidly. Most of it he did not understand. Now and again, he would pick up a word or two and recognize it as Calabrese. He was shoved into a line; he saw that those around him were much better dressed, carrying real valises, instead of his cloth bag. As confusing as the activities swirling around him were, his research soon paid off. Disembarkation went by class and then cabin numbers. He listened for his number, and then he and the men who had shared his cabin filed along. So close, yet America seemed an eternity away.

He could see ahead that two official-looking men in uniform were asking questions and reviewing papers as each of the passengers came before them. As he waited his turn, he became increasingly filled with fear. He tried, however, to appear confident and assured. His stomach was in knots, and though it was cold, he could feel sweat gathering on his back. This morning he had put on the only clean shirt he had. He had saved it especially for the disembarkation. His inquiries had led him to believe that even though he was not traveling in steerage and automatically subject to Ellis Island, nevertheless, he needed to look strong, healthy and sane. The agent in Nicastro had warned, "They will move you to the Ellis Island line in a heartbeat, if you look lame, disoriented, have oozy eyes, or show any impairment whatsoever." There, he would likely undergo a thorough medical examination and they would surely find out about his faulty eyesight and weak heart. He was sure if he had to undergo an examination he would be turned back.

He watched intently and noticed that a family with a babe in arms was sent to the other line. The little girl looked to have red eyes that were weepy. He held his breath and prayed as his turn came up. Surely, after all he had been through, God would not allow him to be turned back. When asked, he answered the questions as forcefully as he could to the agent, who spoke both Italian and English. The Italian was a bit difficult to understand, nothing like the mountain people's version of Calabrese to which he was accustomed. His voice faltering a little bit at the start, he stated his name. Yes, he had someone waiting for him in South Norwalk, Connecticut, a cousin, he answered. Yes. He had money in his pocket. Though the official showed no reaction to his answers, Michele concluded that he must have answered satisfactorily and looked okay, because he was not ushered to the tenders that took people to the dreaded Ellis Island, but pointed toward the gangway to disembark.

He finally breathed a sigh of relief. His emotions all came at once. He felt tears welling up. He did not undergo the "examination." It had cost him dearly. Almost all his savings and the money from the sale of his father's house, and after the expensive ticket cost, he was left with only a few dollars in his pocket to start a new life in America.

In what seemed an instant, he found himself dumped into the great New York City.

The strength he had mustered to get himself through the disembarkation process left him. It was replaced with a choking sense of doom. He was not sure if he was dead or alive. Perhaps he had dreamed the whole thing and he was now dead and in hell. He tried to get his bearings. The thing that struck him about America was the noise and confusion. The brief time he spent in Naples as a stop after leaving Vibo Valente also had seemed such, but this place was full of even stranger people, and vehicles pulled by many horses. There were horse droppings everywhere. The stench of that and other unknown smells brought the nausea back.

Surely, this wasn't America. People hurried on their way to somewhere. Others looked at him strangely. Everything was confusing. He felt himself falling. At the last moment, he spied a stone wall. He sank into it with a thud. All his resolve suddenly left him. As he slumped over, he said to himself, "I am here, America. Now what?"

The *padroni* were well known at New York's port. The *padrone*, or boss, was supposed to function as an employment agent, travel agent and sponsor. In reality, these *padroni* were free to swindle the ignorant immigrant, and they often did. Originally, the *padrone* would go to Italy and recruit unemployed peasants, paying for their passage and providing jobs in the US. The *padrone* often overcharged for these services and did not provide suitable living quarters.

Most *padroni* took a fee from the employers while also charging the immigrants for finding jobs for them. They mostly overcharged for transportation to job sites and levied exorbitant interest rates on loans.

Michele had been warned. He had specifically avoided signing on with a *padrone* though some had approached him in Calabria and then again at the port of Naples. Even if one didn't sign on before arrival, once in America, the peasant immigrant was easy prey for the unscrupulous *padrone*. Michele knew that to get a job you needed an intermediary, but he also knew he needed to be very careful. He knew these men were a necessary evil, especially since he and his fellow immigrants did not know the language. Despite the horror stories he had heard about these men, he also had heard there were some *padroni* who were honest and truly trying to help their own countrymen. These men, he learned, were those who were satisfied with the employer's fee payment, and perhaps you only needed to provide a small gift of gratitude once you settled in a job. Regardless of the shortcomings, this *padrone* system brought some short-term relief to the bewildered immigrants.

Now, Michele was barely able to remember his name or where he was from. The bewildering cacophony swirled around him. Coupled with his destroyed stomach and equilibrium from the voyage, his dehydration and disorientation, he found himself speechless when several men approached him asking him questions.

One of them spoke what sounded like a Neapolitan dialect. Another sounded Sicilian and one spoke Abruzzese, he thought. How could he discern whom he should trust? So, when they asked him questions, he did not respond.

Instead, in his weakened condition, he watched as he saw many people just leave from the Battery in Lower Manhattan toward what they had told him was a thirty-block walk uptown to Mulberry Street. What he had heard discussed on the ship that first night was that a large group would be walking with their belongings in tow to a place known as *piccolo Italia* or little Italy. The distance itself would have been nothing for him had he not been so weak. He had certainly walked up the mountain longer distances than they described. But now, he felt so unsteady that it seemed as far as walking back to Calabria. Through his confusion and dread, he recalled all the overheard conversations and admonitions and he decided that he wanted no part of New York's *piccolo Italia*.

He didn't know if it was the right decision or not, but he felt to succeed he needed to be in America, not in some smaller version of where he left. Unbeknownst to Michele, the slums of London that Charles Dickens wrote about in novels like *Oliver Twist* held about 175,000 people per square mile; the Lower East Side of New York City at the beginning of the 20th century held almost 300,000 people per square mile. One tenement might house 1,200 or more immigrants, perhaps ten to a room, if they were all male workers, or all of one family. Without knowing any of these statistics, the reputation of the squalid living conditions in "little Italy" had crossed the ocean and reached Michele loud and clear; even his hard life in Platania seemed better than that.

Like most southern Italians, Michele was self-sufficient. Most Italians chose not to seek help from institutions. In New York City in 1909, there were more than 2,000 mutual aid societies, but typically, most Italian immigrants shied away from them. Michele had grown up with an understanding that you could not trust the government or its so-called aid. Like his *paisani* friends and relatives, Michele distrusted most organizations of any kind. Most importantly, he, like most Calabrese, preferred work over charity, no matter how menial the job.

As he sat slumped against the stone wall, he felt a blackness envelop him and he thought it would be easy to let himself just slip away to another world. If you want me, God, I'm ready, he thought. He leaned against the wall and closed his eyes. His ears buzzed and he was nearly gone when a man who clearly looked the part of the *padroni* he had been told about shook him and offered him a cup of water. As he sipped, the man came into focus. He spoke an Italian that Michele only partly understood. He wanted to pull out the address for his cousin to ask for directions on how to go there, but he didn't have the strength. What Michele did understand was that the man said he had work for him, a place to sleep and something to eat.

Despite all his resolve to stay away from certain elements, he slowly accepted the man's outstretched hand to help him stand up, saying in Calabrese, "I need to go to Bridgeport." The *padrone* said he would put him and the three other young men that were with him on a train. Michele had understood that he needed to get on a train to find his cousin. The man asked about what money he had on him. Having strapped the money and address to his body in a type of sash, he was reluctant to expose it so he said nothing. The man took it that he was penniless, and Michele thought he understood the man saying that he could pay when he got to his destination.

In his weakened condition, the walk with the man and the others seemed interminable, but in reality was only about ten minutes. Sifting through the noise and bustling streets, they found themselves at a junction of tracks and a long line of box-type cars with open sides. The *padrone* jumped in one and then extended his hand to pull up one of the other men, then that young man pulled and another, who had not yet boarded, pushed Michele up into the car. Michele flopped to the floor and didn't move for hours. He was aware that at some point many more men had joined them in the boxcar.

As the world went in and out of focus, Michele noticed that another man associated with the *padrone* doled out some water from a tin and something to eat such as he had never seen before. It appeared to be a sausage wrapped in soft spongy bread. Michele nibbled at the corners and then clutched it tightly as he fell back into his drugged-like stupor. He had no idea how much time had passed; suddenly he was aware that the train car was moving and felt a wave of the all too familiar seasickness flood over him. Still he clutched the uneaten portion of the sausage, his instincts from Platania where food was scarce kicking in. The nausea passed, and he fell asleep.

Hours later, they arrived at a station where someone shouted "Philadelphia." Could it be that he was back in *Filodelfia*, the Calabrian mountain town by that name? How could that be? Then he broke from his reverie and turned to the source of a voice yelling that they needed to get off. He and the forty or so other men who had occupied the car, without seats or benches of any kind, poured out in the early evening twilight and walked off the tracks into the street. On the sidewalk, the *padrone* stood looking official with a stack of papers clipped to a board and a pencil with barely a point in his hand. He asked each of the men their names, when and where they were born, the birthplace of their parents, and if they could read or write. After each responded, he was asked to sign his name on a sheet of paper.

When it was Michele's turn to sign the paper the man had completed, he was reluctant. The *padrone* gave him a hard look and in a cold dialect that Michele barely understood, said, "If you don't sign you cannot work; if you don't work, you don't eat." Grasping the unstated meaning, Michele put his X where he was told, knowing full well that the paper had more to it than what he had provided in answer to the questions. Though the *padrone* didn't mention it, Michele would eventually learn the document said that he was three years older than what he had told the man and it promised that he would reimburse the *padrone* for the transportation, food, accommodations and other assistance that the man was providing in his first earnings.

As all the men finished giving their information and signing, a large horse-drawn wagon pulled up, and Michele and several other men were told to pile in. Michele asked the *padrone's* assistant who had passed out the water and sausage, if they were going to *Bridgeporto*. The reply, "*Certo, andiamo a Norristown, e vicino Bridgeporto*"—certainly, it's close to it—lulled Michele into thinking it wouldn't be long before he saw familiar faces.

One of the men in the wagon said to another, "*Andiamo alle minieri.*" Michele knew what that meant. He just didn't know how he got to this point, or why he was going to work in the mines. He had heard so many terrible things about the work in the coal mines. The accidents, explosions and the terrible air you had to breathe. But somehow, it seemed he was headed there now.

After a bumpy hour or so, Michele and the others filed into what looked like a campsite. Tents and makeshift shacks with dirty-faced children outside and the smell of cooking wafting in the air. A man dressed in a coverall came to meet them saying, "*Benevenuti, povere diavole.*" Welcome, you poor devils.

All directed to different areas, Michele was assigned to one of the shanties along with eight other men, some who had been with him on the trip out here and some who had arrived from somewhere else. He flopped himself onto the cot they pointed to. When he woke, despite the cold, he was soaked in sweat and full of terror. He looked around and, in the dark, he realized it had been just a horrible dream. However, as he took stock of his surroundings, he realized he had awoken into a dream just as terrible. Where was he?

"Where is this?" Michele asked one of the others.

A young man obviously from Naples responded, "*L'inferno!*"

———————

He lay awake a long time and watched the darkness give way to dawn. As others arose, he did also and asked where he could relieve himself. A man pointed to an outbuilding. Unlike Platania, everything here was made of wood. As he came out, the same man pointed to a shanty, saying *mangia*. He knew that there would be food there.

Two women, one most likely the mother and the other her daughter, were ladling out a hot chocolate coffee-type of drink. They chatted back and forth between them in a Sicilian dialect. The daughter, dark-skinned and with curly hair, caught his eye. He looked away. He took the hot drink and moved along to the mother, who wore her hair in a multi-braided bun at the nape of her dress. She ladled out something out and said, "*Polenta 'mericana.*"

Looking straight at her, he responded, "*Grazi,*" noticing her blue eyes. Just like my mother's, he thought. The woman smiled at him, and he noticed that despite a missing front tooth, she was pleasant looking, though like her daughter, very dark-skinned.

He looked around at the rough-hewn tables and benches and saw immediately there was a hierarchy of who sat and who stood. He decided to stand near the egress. Worried that he would not keep the food down, he ate cautiously and was ready to run outside if he felt sick again. In a quarter of a teaspoon full at a time, he ate the porridge, which compared with *polenta* was tasteless, and drank the beverage, which replenished him immensely. When he finished he felt a little better. Then someone yelled his name and motioned for him to follow.

In another one-room structure, a man not much older than Michele, sporting a barely-there moustache and wearing a white, buttoned shirt that looked like it had been slept in, appeared to be in charge. He called a few men forward, surname first. He spoke to each from behind a table where he sat with papers stacked in three piles. When Michele's name was called, he stepped forward and stood uneasily as the young man stared at him, clucking his tongue as if he had done something wrong.

Not saying anything for a very long pause, Michele inquired, "Is there something wrong?"

Finally, the mustached man spoke in a tone that seemed to exude empathy. "You are too young to work in the mines, though you look old enough, but they are cracking down now. Unions, making all kinds of trouble, so we will send you to work for the steel mill instead. I have a few I can transfer over there. We have to find you a place to live there, so you'll probably be here a day or two. We're gonna look out for you kid."

Again, Michele inquired about Bridgeport, but this time he had his address in hand. The man, who didn't look too much older than

Michele, looked at him as if he was crazy. "You do know you are in the wrong state, don't you?" Michele's heart sank. "This address is in Bridgeport, Connecticut. This is the state of Pennsylvania and we have a town called Bridgeport nearby, but you won't find your people there. The Bridgeport you want is closer to where you disembarked in New York."

Then the man lowered his voice as if he was taking Michele into his confidence and in his Neapolitan dialect, he said, "You would be better off not to mention or show this address to the padrone. If you do, you might get hurt. You need to work where the *padrone* sends you for a while, pay off your debt to him, then down the road, you can go and find your family if that's what you want."

Michele didn't say another word. He knew now, once the *padrone* put him to work, he would have to repay what the man had invested in him. Where the *padrone* was sending him would mostly likely pay the man a finder's fee,

Michele swallowed hard and asked, "How far is this steel mill I'm going to work at, when will I go and who will take me?" he said.

"Well, the *padrone* knows a lot of people, so he feels certain he can get you there in a few days. Here we sort of process people. Find out what they know how to do and we send workers where they are needed."

CHAPTER THIRTEEN

Cleveland, Ohio—1910

Michele had spent nearly a year at the Lukens Steel Company in Coatesville, before moving on to the coalmine area in South Pittston, Pennsylvania. His first job was cleaning latrines at the steel mill; there he had also, swept and moved debris out from the various work areas. It was dangerous crawling under equipment and disgusting to clean the toilets, but he had not been old enough then to work anywhere else, so he had been grateful for that work. As soon as he turned fourteen, he willingly moved on as soon as the Padrone could arrange other work because where he was paid next to nothing once he was done paying his expenses. The Padrone had said the mines are where you will make your money.

As he thought about that time, Mike recalled that his eagerness turned sour quickly. At the mining camp each morning before dawn, he left to walk down the dark streets leading to the mines. Outside, he would meet other young boys all headed to the collier, a machine that sorted the coal. There were many young boys doing the same job he did. He remembered eating some hard bread and coffee, and taking the tin pail prepared by the woman who ran the shanty where he lived with a dozen or so others. Dressed in a cap and coat over his threadbare clothes, he approached, with fear, the tall, gloomy structure where the coal was broken and sorted.

He hated the job first the first moment he arrived. Inside the breaker was a large, noisy room. It had high walls and a flight of narrow steps that climbed past the blackened wooden beams and grimy windows. Long iron chutes ran from the top to the floor.

He, along with many others, sat on pine boards placed astride the chutes. What Mike had learned was that not everything that came out of the mines was coal. It was, rather, a mixture of coal, rock, slate and junk all referred to as clum. His job and all of the other breaker boys was to pick out the clum as the coal flowed down through the chutes.

As each full coal car emerged from the mine, it was pulled to the top of the breaker by a long steel cable. There, a man threw a lever, the car tipped and the coal rushed out into a shaking machine, which pushed the coal toward the chutes.

As the coal streamed down the chutes toward him and his fellow breaker boys, it spewed black clouds of coal dust, steam and smoke, which settled over them like a blanket and turned their faces and clothing black. He remembered they all wore handkerchiefs across their mouths to keep from inhaling it. He used his feet to stop the flow of coal, as he had been taught. He picked out the clum from the chutes, and then lifted his feet so the coal could continue to the next boy. All around him was the monstrous, deafening machinery that crushed and separated tons of coal into various sizes.

When things were running flat out, he worked until six or six-thirty at night. His back ached from sitting in a hunched position all day. They could not wear gloves because the bosses said they could not feel the difference between the coal and the clum. That first week, his fingers had swelled from the sulfur on the coal and his hands had been shredded by the sharp edges of the coal.

The town, just outside of Pittston, where they lived in was even smaller than Platania, but unlike Platania, it had a river essential to the mine's functioning. At work throughout the day, he was always on the alert because many of the young men were often hurt; some were maimed or killed. He didn't want that to happen to him.

At the mining camp, each night after work, it took a good half-hour to wash the soot from his face and hands, but even after a thorough scrubbing, it clung tenaciously in the creases of his neck, ears and nostrils. He was sure the soot would slowly kill him. He had heard people talk about the black lung back home and now he heard subdued discussions about it here as well.

When one of the *capi* complimented him, saying "You do the work of three men; keep it up and you will soon be old enough to go deep into the mine; they only want good workers for that. That's where you earn the real money," the words had scared, Michele, even more than when he had encountered the threatening *Mafiosi*.

He thought back to that day after the first week at the breaker, earning seventy cents a day. As he was leaving the area where he had collected his money, a group of thuggish-looking chaps approached him and said, "You need to give us half your money so we can protect you; there are lots of bad people here who will get you hurt and hurt you badly."

Michele had been elated when he was paid. The boss had gone through an explanation of the deductions. He riddled through a list of items, transportation reimbursement, tools, food and lodging. In the end, it was a paltry amount for what he had done, but there would be a little left over after expenses. It had been horrible work. Nevertheless, he had some money for his labor and there wasn't anyone who was going to take it away from him.

He stood as tall as he could and, looking at what appeared to be the leader of the lazy spongers, said vehemently, "Get away from me. I will give you nothing. I know you people, and you won't get anything from me."

Expecting to be beaten up, Michele was surprised by the shocked look on their faces. Apparently, most people didn't stand up for themselves and most, like sheep, forked over the demanded protection money. Michele had been through too much to give up his wages without a fight. To his puzzlement, they walked off and never bothered him again.

His first job as a janitor cleaning latrines and other areas at the steel mill, where he had barely earned enough to buy food, and then later separating coal at the breakers—he knew there had to be more and better opportunities for him somewhere in this vast land. Close to a year after his arrival, he came to the conclusion that he wasn't getting the best of America yet. He just wasn't sure where that best was. That night of the compliment by the *capo* at the mines, he said to himself, "I didn't leave all that I know and sunny Platania for this."

Now, his days were long, but Michele didn't mind. He felt strong. With a steady diet that included chicken or meat at least once a week, he found himself more than able to keep up with older and bigger men. He noticed he was growing. His work pants, originally too large, now actually fit. The work here was backbreaking, but unlike Platania, he did not have to walk several kilometers in the dark before starting his workday. This road-building project in Cleveland had been a Godsend.

He reflected on how he had come to Ohio, recalling that fateful evening in the pub in Pittston. While he had no interest in the alcohol, he went to the pub on a regular basis to get the news and learn of the happenings in the area. It also offered some camaraderie away from the watchful eyes of the *capi*, or bosses. These *capi* were lazy men who seemed to exist on siphoning off others.

Ever on the alert for information that could be of use, he was gaining a clear picture that the breakers worked sporadically, and only real coal miners made any money. He was much too young and even if he wasn't, he recognized that coal mines were dead-ends. In his heart, he was sure he did not want to live and die underground. He had stood up to the bullies, the *Mafiosi*, at the mines, and they had left him alone since that first week. Nevertheless, he knew the mines were not his final stop.

Then the agent for the road-building project in Cleveland, Ohio had appeared to recruit men at an area near the pub in Pittston. These transactions had to be kept quiet, Michele knew. You couldn't let the *capi* know until you were actually leaving. There were too many stories, whether true or not, that those who tried to leave met with bad accidents.

As he talked with the agent, his eagerness to go actually caused the agent some worry. The agent knew that the mine *capi* did not want others poaching on their workforce. The agent wondered if the strong-looking young man was a plant for the people at the mines. But after questioning him for about ten minutes, the agent realized that the young man had no family or obligations, he did not appear involved with the *Mafiosi* and he looked like a good worker. So the agent felt confident he was not in danger of retaliation.

Then he asked what Michele thought was an odd question. "Do you plan to go back to Italy?" Michele's answer was, "No. I have no one there to see."

"Good. Then we can use you. You look strong and sturdy, and I don't want you, like so many do, working a few months then running back to the old country. We have a lot of work. I could keep you busy for a couple of years," the agent added.

Michele had jumped at the chance to get away from the depressive environment of the mines. He was intrigued by the odd-sounding name of this place called Cleveland, Ohio.

The other men who worked on the road-building project were mostly Germans, but there were some Italians. They were nice enough to him and he didn't feel threatened.

With the agent paying the fare, Michele had made the trip from Pittston to Scranton, then on to Cleveland. He had traveled with three others destined for the same job, based on the agent's coordination of their reporting for work. One of the men in the threesome had a wife and two children that he left in the watchful care of his brother and his family. He relayed to Michele that it was his intention to go first to determine if this was a better place than the coalmines. He also needed to be assured that the work actually materialized and that it paid the promised wages. They had all heard stories of false leads for jobs, where men left the mines only to return to beg for a job again, poorer than when they had departed from Italy.

By this time, Michele understood a good bit of the language. He had gone to some of the English classes offered nearby. But without knowledge of reading or writing in Italian, most of the writing instruction didn't make sense to him. However, he had a good ear, and he picked up the speaking part without difficulty. He learned to write his name and recognize letters. He wasn't afraid to say it wrong. He found that most people responded well when he tried to speak "Americano." Often they would laugh and gently coax him to say it differently. He chuckled with them and he'd try again. He enjoyed the challenge. He wanted desperately to become American.

That first winter in Cleveland had been the coldest he had ever experienced. The winds coming off Lake Erie were cutting. He had been cold in Platania, but in hindsight, he had never worked from early morning until evening in the subfreezing temperatures and bitter winds.

Now, close to two years into the life in Cleveland, Michele started to feel beckoned by the thin, piece of wrinkled paper with the address of some of his family living in America. Starting out as fragile as a butterfly's wing, the shred was now in danger of disappearing into dust. He had placed the gossamer slip between two pieces ripped from the rough wrappings that had contained the equipment he received his first week in America. He was adamant that at some point he would go there to this place called Connecticut. Not only was he longing to see and feel some contact with family, but also he knew his relatives lived somewhere close to his father's grave in a place called Bridgeport.

That night he went to sleep dreaming about what he would do when he got to the cemetery. In his dream, he placed a wreath of flowers on the grave and said prayers for his father's soul. He saw himself talking with him and telling him how glad he was to find him.

He had steady work and he felt he was getting ahead. He needed to work here a bit longer so he could buy himself a train ticket and still have some money remaining in his pocket, once he decided to go to find his cousin using the address he had.

Before coming to Cleveland, his wages had almost equaled his living costs. Yet there were others in the camps who at the end of the week owed money to the company. He had been careful, never wasting money on smoking, drinking or women. When he did have an extra few cents, he would find someone who could write and he would pay the going rate to have them fashion a letter, sending his greetings to his sister, Marianna.

He recalled the gratitude and pride he felt when he had put a whole American dollar in the first letter to her, saying, "*Questo e per le scarpe.*"This is for the shoes. By now, it had become a transatlantic joke between them because, after the first letter, she had begged him to stop.

"The shoes were a gift," she insisted in a letter obviously written by someone other than herself. He kept sending the money whenever he could. He wanted her to know he would never forget.

Unlike in Pennsylvania, Michele now lived in a rooming house with several men much older than he was. The German woman who ran the establishment at 2124 Woodland Avenue cooked meals that, though bland, served to fill him up well. Once a week she washed the few belongings that he and his housemates had, and she returned them neatly folded. Every Saturday night, she allowed the men a tub full of hot water for a bath in the one bathroom they all shared.

As he reveled in the water that had been heated on the wood-burning kitchen stove, he was pleased that he was only the second one to use the bath water this evening. It was not as cloudy as it had been many other Saturdays, and he relished in the luxury of a bath at all. His thoughts drifted to how much he had hated the mining camps. He felt he had lived out his purgatory there. Here, the sheets and his nose, neck and ears all felt cleaner, even if the work was in some ways much harder. The warmth of the water flooded his mind with visions of Platania where the water from the outdoor public fountain fed by the mountain springs was frigid in the winter months. There, full body bathing was postponed to late spring, summer and early fall. Then, the cool, rejuvenating cleansing and the warming sun made him feel reborn each time.

In rural Platania, everything happened outside. The peasants washed up at the public fountain, and communal bathing happened in the stream. Daily, they carried water to their outdoor kitchens with *vozza* or jug on their heads, or with buckets. This water was used only for cooking and simple hand- and dish-cleansing. Despite the limited facilities, the crystal spring water coupled with the incredibly warming sun, made everything seem splendid.

At least once a year, Mike, along many others from the region, had made a pilgrimage to Terme di Carone, to seek out the beneficial, therapeutic effects of the two-thousand-year-old thermal, sulfur spring waters that were fairly fixed at 39 degrees Celsius. Located at the foot of the Reventino Mountains, only a few kilometers from the Gulf of Sant'Eufemia, in a valley surrounded by mountains, inside an ancient forest of oaks, chestnuts and pines, the springs were famous and infused with strong beliefs as healing and rejuvenating, despite the rotten egg smell of the sulfur dioxide gas.

He often didn't understand his own fastidiousness. He wondered where he had gotten this curse to be washing and cleaning himself so frequently. Perhaps his father had been like that. His mother had kept the house clean, but was not as fastidious with her personal care.

He could stand all manner of slop and dirt when he was working, but he detested being dirty when he sat to eat. It didn't matter if it was a simple piece of stale bread and the dandelion coffee they made, or a holiday *soppressata* with fresh cheese. No matter what the fare, he felt his hands needed to be immaculate and his face clean. He had washed his mouth out with water and combed his hair every morning since he could remember.

The work at the road construction was dangerous, he knew. His brother-in-law had died at a similar site in another state. It was that disaster that had precipitated his father's heart attack and death. He knew he was vulnerable to such a fate as well.

After his Saturday bath, instead of going to bed, he walked the three miles to the train station. There, he asked the night agent at the desk what it cost to buy a ticket for Connecticut. As he made his return walk toward the rooming house, he mentally calculated how long it would be before he could go.

Once he climbed the stairs to the room with multiple cots, he undressed down to his underwear and slipped under the single cover. He made the sign of the cross and said his silent prayers as he did every night since he could remember. He asked God for forgiveness for any wrong he might have inadvertently committed, as well as his continual stubbornness. He thanked God for the job here, and for his strength to do the work. He added thanks for the food and for the woman who cooked and let him live where he was. He asked God to protect his mother, his sisters, his aunts, uncle and cousins. In closing, he begged God to help him find his way to his PaPa's grave.

Then he said to himself, "Just a few more months." As he drifted off to sleep, he was mentally already there.

CHAPTER FOURTEEN

He watched each town along the train route. He looked out the window the entire trip, never speaking to anyone. He noticed the subtle changes in scenery going from city to farm country to city again. Some towns he noticed were as filthy as Pittston and Scranton had been with the black soot of coal dust draped on them. Others were lush green, planted with some sort of crop. He wondered what they grew there. America was indeed a huge place, he reflected.

When he heard the conductor say, "New York, Grand Central," he knew it was where he would need to change trains, according to the admonishments of the agent at the ticket counter in Columbus. Suddenly it was dark. He hadn't expected the train to pull in underground. Once stopped, he found himself amid a cacophony of people, sounds and smells. He suddenly realized that this was the same New York City where just a few short years ago he had disembarked from the ship that brought him across the ocean. He would never forget that wonderful, yet horrible day. But now, he was not sick. He felt strong and excited. He was on a mission. No time to lollygag. He followed the crowds up some concrete stairs into what appeared to be a very large waiting room. Across the cavernous hall, he spied a row of metal-barred windows that he assumed was where he would find the ticket agents.

From somewhere in the station, he heard strains of the words and music of Enrico Caruso's song, "*Addio.*" He had heard the song for the first time about a month ago at the rooming house where he lived most recently.. The woman owner and housekeeper had something called a gramophone. He asked plenty of questions regarding the song with the words and title that meant goodbye. It had a beautiful melody, yet it evoked some nostalgia he had promised himself he would not feel. It made him think of his mother, sisters and cousins. He realized he missed them.

Since his arrival in America, he had never ceased to be amazed at the number of people who identified themselves as "Italian." He had always considered himself a *Calabrese* from *Platania*, or *Petrania*. Many of his fellow workers were *Abruzzese, Siciliani*, and *Napolitani*. But the *i'mericani* always said, "Oh, you're Italian."

From the first time he heard of Enrico Caruso, he was instantly smitten. He reveled in this man's magnificent voice and beautifully poetic songs that seemed to garner the adoration of people around the word and of many right here in New York. Caruso had been nothing but a poor Napolitano just a short while ago and now he was world-renowned.

This feat amazed Michele, and it marked when he first became aware that that all things were possible in America. Look at him. He was riding a train on his own. There was no unscrupulous agent buying a ticket for him at usury rates. No trickery about a great job and wonderful living conditions that resulted in exactly the opposite. He was doing this himself through the sweat of his own labor and his own volition.

As he took his place at the end of a long queue in front of the ticket window, he became mesmerized with all the sights and sounds enveloping him and went off into a reverie. So much so that he failed to notice how long he had waited. Suddenly, he snapped into the present and realized that the line hadn't moved. A man a few spots ahead of him said loudly, "It's closed." He understood. It meant *ciusso*. Not a good thing. He glanced at another window and it had an even longer line. He didn't know whether he should move to another window as others were doing, or stay where he was.

He decided he would continue to wait where he was and he was careful to watch if anyone moved ahead. Finally, he inched forward as each person seemed to be quicker than the initial person who apparently had such a difficult problem the ticket agent had to close temporarily. Then, after what seemed an interminable wait, he reached the window and somehow made himself understood by the agent by showing him the address on his now very worn piece of paper. It was the same piece of paper that the agent in Cleveland, Ohio had read and tried to explain to him that he could only sell him a ticket as far as New York City and that he would have to change trains and buy another to get to his final destination.

Now, this agent said that Michele had just missed the train leaving for South Norwalk. He would have to wait for the next train that left in an hour, at eight-twenty-six p.m., Michele would arrive at his destination close to ten o'clock.

He listened attentively to try to understand what the man was saying. "You'll have to take the train going to New Haven, but get off well before that in South Norwalk."

When Michele said, *"Scusa me; whata you say?"* a woman several places back in line, repeated the man's statement to him in a Neapolitan dialect: *"Pigio u treno chi è scritto New Haven e scendete ala fermata di Sud Norvocca."*

Michele thanked her and asked the agent, "Ow many stoppa to

geta off?" The man said to listen for five stops. His stop would be the one right after the town called Darien. The woman from the line assuming the role of translator said, "*Cinque fermata.*"

Mike mentally memorized the word Darien and repeated to himself "*cinque fermata.*" He paid the twenty-five cents the agent asked for and, taking his change from a one-dollar bill, tucked it and his ticket into his jacket's front inside pocket. As he turned to go, he profusely thanked the woman who had helped him. Then he moved off into the great hall.

He was awestruck by the station. An enormous clock in the center of the hall revealed that he had enough time to get something to eat. Carrying his cloth bag in one hand and his cap in the other, he walked toward the origin of the aromas making his stomach growl.

Stalls with foods from every nationality beckoned him. He passed them and stepped outside onto the New York City streets. He wanted to see if anything had changed since his arrival in late 1909. But he had not been to this part of New York on his brief visit the day of his arrival into the country.

Now, he exited the terminal on 42nd Street. Looking around, he thought the people seemed more well-heeled than he remembered from that first day. There were dozens of food and merchant vendors and shops with clothing displayed in the windows. Not grasping the vast difference in location from where he had disembarked at the port, he came to the conclusion that New York had prospered remarkably in the past two and a half years.

He took stock almost talking to himself. "Money in my pocket. Two pairs of underwear, three shirts and pants in my bag, a wool cap, and a sturdy pair of work shoes on my feet."

They weren't the best work shoes, he thought. They were more of a boot and not too different than the shoes he had come to America wearing. But his sister's precious gift, which had started out too large, had just two months ago been cast away. He had worn them to death. Not only the soles were worn through, but his feet were cramped in the toes. One of the nails on his left foot had become embedded and then infected. The kind woman at the rooming house had taught him how to clean it, bathe and wrap it each morning and night. She had told him he needed to see a doctor. He told himself if it didn't get better he would part with the money he was saving for his departure, but not now. As it began to heal, he put off getting it medical attention and saved his money.

He had cut a hole in his sister's shoes to relieve the pressure on his toe, but in the second week of his toe-relief effort, the foreman had noticed and said he could not work with his toe exposed. With that, he decided he would have to use some of the precious money he had been saving and make the footwear purchase.

Although he had been reluctant to part with the money, he now felt quite proud of his first purchase of his very own shoes. They weren't the best shoes by any means, but as he parted with the precious two dollars that they cost, he vowed that someday he would buy himself the best men's shoes available.

As he walked a little further, he heard a peanut vendor who sang an Italian ditty, and he bought a small paper sack of hot roasted peanuts. Walking to the corner of Vanderbilt Avenue, he found a hot dog stand and bought one of his American discoveries. He had learned to love the salty sausage-looking meat with a yellow, spicy cream called mustard. The hot dog had become one of his favorites. Something unknown in Italy and avoided by other Italians, it was both delicious and affordable.

Lost in his thoughts, he suddenly realized it had grown dark. He scurried to find the clock in the center of the great hall and saw that the small hand was on the eight, and the large hand at the one. He knew he needed to find the track and the train quickly. He didn't want to miss the train. The ticket agent had said the tracks were a flight down the stairs. He reviewed what he needed to do in his head. He needed to get on the train going toward New Haven, Connecticut, and listen for the stop that was South Norwalk; it would come right after the stop called Darien he repeated to himself.

Asking several people where the New Haven train was, he found the correct one just moments before the conductor yelled out, "Last call; all aboard." As he sprinted aboard, they closed the doors behind him, nearly catching his bag.

As the train lurched forward, he looked for a seat and walked through several cars before spotting one. He sat next to a man dressed in a business suit reading a newspaper. When he finished the man asked him if he wanted to look at the paper. Michele said thank you and glanced at the pages as if he could read. The front page had a large picture of what seemed to be a man playing baseball. He had learned about the sport in Ohio and had seen lots of young men and boys playing on Sunday afternoons in Ohio. He had once or twice picked up a stick and tried to swat one of the balls that others in his rooming house were playing. He smacked it away a few times.

As he flipped through the newspaper, he was fascinated by the arrangement of the letters, columns and pictures. He so wished he could read. He wondered what it would take to learn to do so. He promised himself that he would find a way someday to learn to read and write. He was doing well now writing his name. He had practiced and practiced at the school they had at the steel mill and later at the breaker.

He returned the paper to the man, politely saying, "Thank you very much." Then, he sat quietly with his bag on his knees imagining the joy of seeing his cousin Petronella when he surprised her with his arrival. Would his aunts Giovanna and Maria and other cousins be there? he wondered. He looked out the train car windows but could not make out very much as it was dark. Suddenly, he heard the conductor announce, "Stamford station." After the majority of people disembarked, including the man sitting next to him, he had more room. He noticed the man had left the paper behind and for some reason he wasn't sure of, Michele picked it up and tucked it under his arm.

Then, it seemed in no time at all, he heard Darien. Two people got off the train, and it moved on. Within minutes, he heard "South Norwalk!" This was it. He stood up by the doors as the train rolled to a stop. He was so eager to see some family. As the doors opened, he stepped into a deserted platform. No one else got off with him that he could see. He searched for someone at the windows of the small station, but everything was shut tight. So different from New York City with the multitudes of people, noise and excitement, this place seemed eerie.

He was at a loss as to what to do. He had the piece of paper with the address, but no one to ask or to show it to.

He thought he would find somewhere nearby to stay, but nothing appeared open. He saw lights in the distance, but where would he go without knowing? There was absolutely not a soul in sight.

Instead of walking on as he was about to do, he spied a long wooden bench on the platform and sat. He wasn't sleepy nor tired, but he recognized it would be a long time till morning when someone surely would open the window for ticket sales. He was glad he had eaten something. If he was in the wrong place, then he needed to buy a ticket to go elsewhere. Instead, he sat and began thinking back over the past two and a half years.

Thoughts tumbled through his mind... Would he stay here, or would he move on? He didn't know yet where he would call home in this vast country of America. He needed to see more of it to be sure before he decided. After a long while of musing, he stretched out on the bench, tucking his bag under his head and spreading the newspapers like a blanket over his chest and shoulders. He was a bit disheartened that he wasn't able to find his family here; he was also aware that he was homeless again. For a moment, he worried about robbers; then he said his prayers to God for protection and for forgiveness, and drifted into a fitful sleep.

CHAPTER FIFTEEN

South Norwalk, Connecticut—1912

He awoke to a cheerful sun and trembling cold. The fall air was damp. He felt chilled to the bone. As he opened his eyes and sat up, he saw there were signs of life around him. Two black men in coveralls pushed a big, flat green wooden cart with oversized wheels with red spokes. They moved toward what appeared to be a baggage room and began loading trunks and crates from it onto the cart. He watched as the men pulled the cart now laden with all sorts of freight and baggage to the edge of the platform.

Noticing that the station door now stood ajar, Michele quickly sprang up and went in search of a lavatory. Inside, he hooked his bag on the back of the door and stepped to the urinal to relieve himself. Bending over a small basin, he washed his hands and face with a medicinal smelling soap and icy water. Then, he cupped his hand and used it to get a little water into his mouth to swish around. Spitting it out, he cupped a little more to drink. With his right hand, he flattened his disarranged hair and straightened his shirt collar, then grabbed his bag and strode into the main part of the small station.

Throwing his shoulders back and standing as tall as he could, he walked up to the ticket window. Looking the man straight in the eyes, he said, "Gooda morning."

Without greeting, the man asked, "Ticket to Grand Central?"

Instead of replying to his question, Michele handed the agent the small piece of paper with his intended address and asked, "You know-a where? Maybe I getta taxi?"

The man studied the thin worn-out scrap, then looked up at young him wondering if he was joking. As he stared, the agent came to the realization that the lad must have arrived last night and not known where to go. It looked as if the kid had slept outdoors.

Taking pity on him, the agent pointed toward the left and said, "Burbank Street is right out back. Since you are already on the eastbound side of the station, just go down those steps," he said as he pointed. "Then, you walk just a short way down this street and it's right there. If you get to Wood Street, you've gone too far. Number 22 should be the corner house."

While he missed the meaning of some of the agent's words, he understood the phrase "short way" and gathered from the man's pointing that it was nearby. Shocked to think he could have walked there last night had he known, he regained his composure and sloughed it off saying, "Tanku," and rushed in the direction the man had pointed.

At the bottom of the station steps, he suddenly didn't remember if the man said to turn right or left. He was thinking he had pointed to the right, but as he was walking away from the station area, he spotted a black man and thought it couldn't hurt to check. "Gooda morning," he said. The black face looked at first wary and then broke into a large smile.

Michele asked, "You knows where Burbank Streeta iza?" The

man responded pleasantly and recognizing the accent pointed him to the general direction making sure that he knew to turn left onto the first street he came to. "That house is right on the corner."

Thanking the man, Mike started to walk away. But the man wasn't through with him. He spoke with a smile while giving a warning, "Watch out for Mr. Fred; he's tough."

He knew the word "tough" but didn't understand what the man said. His heart raced a bit as he approached the house with the number 22 posted near the door. He stood there perusing the three-story wooden structure and thought it impressive. He had been told that his cousin's husband had done well in America. The house sat behind a chain-link fence. The gate was locked. As he was trying to figure out how he could get past the vicious dog barking by the front door, a woman whom he recognized immediately came out. Looking right at him, she asked a bit harshly, "Whata you want?"

Michele asked, "Petronella, non me conosci?"

She had not recognized him. When she had departed for America, he was just a little boy. This person was a grown man. Nevertheless, with his question of "don't you recognize me?" a light went off in her head. The voice could belong to only one person. She put a key into the padlock and threw open the gate. Then she hugged and squeezed him until he couldn't breathe.

When he was able to pull away, he noticed she had a scar down the left side of her neck all the way to her collarbone. She was only a few years older than he was, yet she looked thin and worn. He inquired if she was all right and she shushed him, saying, "It's nothing. Have you eaten." He noticed the tears at the corners of her eyes.

Climbing the stairs, she began crying and laughing at the same time. As soon as they arrived on the third floor, she urged him to sit. "I'll fix you coffee. I have some good bread that I baked yesterday, and some cheese so sharp it will make your mouth pucker," she said breathlessly in her native dialect peppered with some American words. A million questions and comments flew from her lips in rapid succession. "Where have you been all this time? My sister Angelina wrote more than two years ago saying you was coming. I had given up hope."

He enjoyed the strong coffee. The bread and cheese had filled his otherwise empty stomach. The warmth of her smile and the embracing environment of her kitchen made him feel at home. He noticed the kitchen floor was immaculate. There were lace curtains at the windows streaming with sunshine. They had barely finished their coffee and his quick story on what he had been up to since arriving in America when she literally jumped up as if bitten by something.

"I have work to do," she said. "We have turned the first two floors of the house into a rooming house. I cook and clean for a dozen men who are boarders." She looked at him and something dawned on her. "*Miche, stati ca; c'e lavoro qui. Domenico ti aiuta a travore qualche cosa subito. chio uno letto vacante.*"

Hearing that there was work nearby and that she had an empty bed in her boarding house helped dissipate Michele's feeling of homelessness of the last couple of days.

He asked how far Bridgeport was from South Norwalk. She told him it wasn't far. She said, "You know our aunt, Zia Giuanna, lives near us here with her husband Zio Michelangelo Gallo. They have a little boy Cristofero. I think he's close to four years old. Maybe you know that Zio Pasquale Nicolazzo called our Zia Maria here with the three children after he earned some money. So sad though, she died last year only three years after coming to America. She's buried at the cemetery in Norwalk, named after her, Santa Maria.

"Zio Pasquale is such a nice man. The oldest girl, Innocenza, looks after the two younger ones, Michelangelo and the baby, Pasqualina. They all live just a few streets away. We will go visit them tomorrow. Today is washing day."

Michele asked how much she charged for the room and what he could expect to make in wages in the area and then did a quick calculation. Mentally he felt favorable to the idea, but thought he would wait to give an answer. He also was keen to meet his cousin-in-in law. "I will think about it," he said.

The night arrival at the train station and sleeping outside on the bench had made the area seem bleak and desolate. Now, in this spectacular morning sunshine, the place reminded him a little bit of Platania. It wasn't as pretty as Platania with its majestic trees and incredible mountain vistas, but all the houses he had passed walking from the station had little gardens in the front yards. On the downside of the growing season, they still appeared bountiful. He longed for some dirt where he could grow once again his favorite vegetables.

Wanting to make himself useful, he followed Petronella to help her take care of the men and the rooms. They spent the entire day chatting and working. She shared all she had heard from the letters she'd received from her sister and twin brothers. She updated him on the happenings in Platania and *ala Chianta*. He was saddened to hear of some deaths and elated that new babies had come into his distant family.

"Have you heard anything about my sister Marianna?" he asked in a tentative voice, fearing what she might tell him.

But his cousin had good news. "She and Francesco had a little girl less than three months ago. She went to visit my sister Angelina to ask if they had heard from you. My sister said in her letter that the little girl was adorable. They named her Marianna, just like her."

Petronella kept remarking on how handsome Michele was and whether he had a sweetheart. He told her no sweetheart. He had been focused on working and saving. "No time for girls," he said. She gave him a look and laugh that said she didn't believe him.

They washed clothes, scrubbing them on a washboard and then hanging them on a rope line outside with wooden pins. The linens that she had stripped from the beds were soaking in a smelly solution. They would be washed last, she said. They cleaned the toilets and re-made the beds with extra sheets she had. She washed the floors on her hands and knees. It was obvious that she kept everything spotless and that nothing less than perfect was good enough. Michele struggled to keep up with her.

It was well past the noon hour and she hadn't even talked of lunch. But after they finished the last bed, they sat for a few minutes to have a tomato and cucumber salad. After the salad, she made some fresh coffee. The delightful aroma made him feel as if he had been at Petronella's forever.

"It will be a while to supper time, but I will need to start cooking soon," she said. Coquettishly, she added, "When the wolves arrive they will be starved."

As they sat with their steaming coffee, Michele told her he had decided to stay. She jumped and kissed him many times as if he had just arrived.

"Wonderful! Get your bag and I'll show where to put it and which one will be your bed. Also, I have to collect the money for the room and board up front. My husband always insists on it. I know you are my family, but I can't break the rules, or Domenico will be very angry," she added softly.

Michele dug into the inside pocket of his jacket and parted somewhat reluctantly with his eleven dollars. He said, "I was only paying eight dollars a week in Ohio." Nevertheless, she said, "Domenico won't let me charge lower rates even for my cousin." As they cleaned vegetables and scrubbed potatoes the time flew. The day was nearly gone. Petronella alerted Michele that her husband would be arriving soon. Michele was just reflecting on what a wonderful day it had been when Fortunato arrived.

As he was introduced to his cousin-in- law, Michele noted that he was *Miletese*, Calabrese, but from the area of Vibo Valente, a little further south than Platania. A dark, short, brutish-looking man, his tone was extremely unfriendly. He expressed not the least of pleasantries, instead getting immediately to business. "I'm glad you have arrived, Michele, because we have an empty bed in our rooming house here."

Michele pondered his words and manner. He had never expressed any joy that his wife now had more family nearby. Fortunato was called Fred by the locals. They had even changed his last name from Prestia to Presty. He pulled out a chair and sat at the kitchen table, and immediately his wife starting placing food and wine in front of him. He tore into the food without even inviting Michele to sit with him, let alone join him in the meal. The man did not even look up at his wife. Michele had noticed that he hadn't greeted her when he first came, instead he started barking orders at her—get me this and fetch me that.

Petronella seemed cowered by him. She tended to him like a servant instead of a wife. Michele wondered again about the long scar on her neck. She had not offered him any explanation. Fred's manner toward him was clear. Michele didn't need any instruction.

Without a word, he went down the three flights of stairs to the first floor to introduce himself to the other boarders and to eat the evening meal with his roommates.

CHAPTER SIXTEEN

South Norwalk—1912-1916

"What are you doing, here?" joked Zio Michelangelo Gallo. Michele's Zia Giuanna's husband was a kind and generous man, unlike his wife, who was a tough cookie with a stern look that almost never softened. Michele and Petronella had walked to the Gallo home after she finished her most pressing chores quickly with his help. It seemed that all the family from his mother's side that he had in America lived within a few minutes of each other.

His mother's sister Giovanna, called Giuanna by the family, had finally joined her husband in America after a five-year separation. Zio Pasquale Nicolazzo also had come ahead to earn money, and his mother's other sister, Maria, had come to join her husband bringing her three children in June of 1905, well before Michele had even left Calabria. It was only his Zio Luigi and his children whom he had left behind.

He had been sad to learn from Petronella that Zia Maria had passed away in 1911. Of the three sisters, Zia Maria had been the most gentle, his mother and Zia Giuanna, more matter-of-fact, toughened by a difficult life. Not that Maria's life had been much easier, but her husband had sent good money while he was in America. And her husband's family had helped her with the children when they were in Platania alone.

Now, they all lived at number four Laura Street, which was just a few minutes from Petronella's place. Michele hugged them all, including Zio Pasquale, who still wore a black armband from the loss of his wife. Michele imagined how sad his own mother must have been to lose her younger sister. Now, with her sister Giuanna and her family in America, Rosa only had her brother Luigi and his family remaining in Italy; all the other siblings were now deceased or had emigrated.

It seemed that the Gallo and Nicolazzo families had settled among a neighborhood of people from *Ungeria*, or Hungary as they said in America. In fact, there was a church, St. Ladislaus that was solely for the Hungarian Catholics, just walking distance from where the Nicolazzo and Gallo families lived as tenants.

"We are among the few Italians in the neighborhood," Zio Michelangelo told Michele.

"I've lived on almost all the streets right around here, before Burbank Street," chimed in Petronella. "We lived just off Laura, then Bouton, Podmore and Cliff Streets prior to Burbank."

"In fact," joked Zio Michelangelo, "it won't be long before these streets as well as Ely Avenue will be taken over by the Italians." Petronella's laughter at the joke made her eyes crinkled up and they turned into slits with the azure blue barely a sliver.

Michele basked in the scene around him. He loved seeing Petronella, the uncles, aunt and cousins. Until that moment, he hadn't realized how good it would feel to be back among family. He had intended to just visit and move on, but now he began thinking a bit about staying.

Zia Giuanna made coffee and in her raspy barking voice asked him to sit and share all that he had experienced since leaving Calabria.

"I went to Pennsylvania, first I worked for the steel mill and later at the coal breaker. The coalmines were terrible. After I left Pennsylvania, I went to Cleveland, Ohio, to work on a road building project. It was cold there. I came here," Michele said, sharing a sparse list of facts, omitting all of the details, giving no clues about his heartache and loneliness. He didn't feel it was anything he needed to share.

Zio Pasquale said, "Michele, there's a family of Hungarians here with the name Ritzo! I think they write the name different from Italians, nice people, mind their own business. They work hard. He paused, then shifted his conversation to the topic of his wife's untimely death.

"We waited so long to be together. Now that we were in America, she's gone," his voice choked up as he expressed how cheated he felt and his children, as well.

"She was only thirty-three years old, and the baby was just a couple of years old. I'm trying to move to Bridgeport; I think we can do better there," Zio Pasquale said with a sigh.

Michele's ears perked up. "Bridgeport," he said. "I want to go there. Can we go tomorrow?"

Zio Pasquale said, "It's too far to walk. It's more than forty miles. We can get there with the train, but it's a big city and when you get there, everything is very spread out. I may have work there and if that job comes through I will eventually move the whole family, bring my son and daughters there. Then you can see Bridgeport."

Michele remembered the two children, his Nicolazzo cousins Innocenza and Michelangelo, from Italy. Though they had left for America with their mother, when Michele was nine, he remembered all of them well. Innocenza was then eleven years old; the boy, also called Michele, was six. The little girl Pasqualina, newly minted as Lilly, had been born in America just a year after his aunt Maria reunited with her husband, as he had come two years ahead of them to make a life for them first. Now eighteen years old, Innocenza, whom everyone called Jennie, announced that she was getting married in the spring. His cousin Michele, called Mickey, now approaching thirteen, was a small, wiry youngster. Good-looking and cocksure of himself, he boasted, "I can take you to Bridgeport, cousin."

Michele spent the day among his relatives, talking about jobs and where he might go to seek work. Zio Michelangelo offered to take him around to find a job. The consensus was that he shouldn't have any trouble getting work. They all saw him as strong and the bosses would snap him up right away, they joked.

The following three days he spent the mornings helping Petronella with her chores and then going out with his uncle to call on various companies seeking a job.

On the third day, Michele had become a bit discouraged. The Harris & Gan Company on Water Street had said they just hired two men and didn't need anyone right now, but to check back with them next month. The Ferris Coal Company on Washington Street said they needed help starting in two weeks.

As if he read his thoughts, his uncle said, "Don't worry Michele, there's going to be someone needing you. We just need to call on a few more companies. I feel certain of it. Did you see how that man at Ferris Coal insisted we come back in two weeks? He saw how strong you are, but the timing just wasn't right for them now."

As if on cue, the next place they went to was a coal, brick, lime and cement supplier located in the same general area as the earlier stops. The man at Bishop and Lynnes took one look at Michele and said, "Can you start today?"

All paid about the same wages for laborer work. Michele liked this company not only because he could start right away, but because they had a second location in the next town called Norwalk. Michele liked having options.

The work was hard, but nothing compared with what he had experienced before. He shoveled lime, coal and stacked and loaded bricks as they filled orders or made room for inventory that was delivered almost daily. The foreman and his work mates quickly changed Michele's name to Mike. He was happy to have a steady job and glad to be near some relatives. Mike, as he now thought of himself, also made friends with some of the workers and found that the whole atmosphere was more convivial then where he had been before. He went out for a beer with a couple of the men at the end of the workweek and smoked a cigar.

However, by his third week at Petronella's boarding house, he got more of the taste of the evil man his cousin had married. Fred had continued to be unpleasant after that first evening and had not warmed up at all. Petronella went with Mike to visit the relatives at Laura, Podmore and Cliff streets, but her husband never joined them. On Friday evening of the third week Mike was there, he and the other boarders had stretched out on their cots after dinner and were just talking. They heard the footsteps bounding down the stairs. Fred walked into the room and announced, "Something smells bad in here." Then, without a moment's hesitation he said, "Mike, it's your feet! I don't want anybody here with bad-smelling feet."

Mike was horrified. His feet most certainly did not smell. In fact, he was the only one whose feet did not smell. He wanted to say, it's your own feet you smell. Though he was offended, he didn't say a word in response. After making his grand pronouncement, Fred turned and went back upstairs.

Mike brooded all night. By morning, he decided that this was

Fred's way of saying, "Get going." It was clear to him that Fred had been upset that he had helped Petronella with her chores. On several occasions, Fred had commented that Mike liked to do woman's work. Mike observed that his cousin seemed not to notice that her husband was a tyrant. He recalled how he had not stood still when his mother had been slapped by his stepfather and he knew he would not be able to restrain himself if he saw Fred strike his cousin Petronella, which a few times he seemed ready to do.

Tomorrow, I will look for a room somewhere else, he thought to himself. Though he was enjoying his cousin, her pleasant manner and delightful personality, he knew he did not want to spend any more time than needed in the presence of her tyrannical husband.

On Saturday, after he helped Petronella, he walked to the Central Hotel at the corner of Monroe and Chestnut Streets and negotiated a room with board for twelve dollars a week, they had wanted fourteen. Though a bit more expensive, the place was newly renovated, clean and comfortable. The owner told him the Italian social club where men played cards on Sunday afternoon was right nearby. As a bonus, the room gave Mike more privacy than the boardinghouse his cousin ran. The hotel owner, Mr. Disesa, seemed to be a decent fellow. He ran a bar and a band and he was full of good stories.

When with bag in hand, he told Petronella he was leaving, she was upset. He comforted her by saying, "You'll always be my cousin and you'll have my respect. I won't forget what you did for me, taking me in. Blood is blood."

"You're going right now?" she asked. Then, she kissed his hands and got teary, but in her heart, she realized it was for the better. Her husband had been especially nasty during this time that Mike had been here. She recognized that Fred didn't want anyone related to her in the house to see his comings and goings. She knew he slept with the prostitutes that frequented the bar that he ran. In fact, the scar she had on her neck was from a knife wound he had inflicted upon her early in their marriage when she had complained that she had seen him go into a back room of the bar with one of them. It had turned ugly in a flash. The words just came out of her mouth and he had seethed, "Don't you ever question my authority or anything I do. I will kill you if you dare to say a single word about what I do."

At the time, she did yet know his capacity for violence. Foolishly, she tried to explain, but she never got to finish. He picked up a knife and slashed her neck, warning her that his words were not empty threats. The neck healed with an ugly scar and she had learned to keep her mouth shut. Within six months, she had contracted a venereal disease from her husband's continual promiscuity. The infection wreaked havoc, and she had to undergo a hysterectomy. As a result, she would never bear children, something she wanted more than anything. What could she do? She felt trapped. A woman without a man was as good as dead. Such was the lot of women, she resigned herself. She prayed for her husband's black soul and for herself. She prayed for a child that might come to her by some miracle.

Mike had come at her lowest point. He had been great company and a joy. But his presence wasn't worth her upsetting Fred. He was her husband and she needed to obey him. As sad as she was, she determined it was good Mike was leaving. She shuddered as she thought about what might happen if her cousin intervened when Fred was in one of his moods. She could tell that Mike was not like many of the black folks around the neighborhood that Fred intimidated easily with his threats. She didn't want her husband and cousin to tangle. It could be disastrous.

CHAPTER SEVENTEEN

South Norwalk, CT—1914

As Mike walked up the hill, he went past the Hungarian Catholic church to 8 Cliff Street, which intersected Bouton Street, to visit Zia Giuanna and Zio Michelangelo. Their little boy, Chris, was growing up. This Sunday dinner he would also find his Zio Pasquale and his Nicolazzo cousins who had moved to Bouton Street. It was all within just a stone's throw, but the families had moved into a real apartment instead of a one–room, shared-bathroom situation. At the dinner, the family topic was about the upcoming wedding. Mike was excited. Jennie, Zio Pasquale's daughter, was getting married to Nick Fiumare. This would be Mike's first American-Italian wedding. Zia Giuanna was acting as mother of the bride so Jennie would have all the information she needed to help her through the womanly needs of preparing for marriage. Zio Pasquale was ecstatic. He liked his son-in-law-to-be and was thrilled that despite the lack of a mother, his son and daughters seemed to be faring well. Though, he did worry a lot about the boy who seemed more than a bit wild. He was learning to work hard like his father, but it seemed to Zio

Pasquale as he confided to Mike, that for his son Mickey it was all about wheeling and dealing. He didn't like his son's friends. He urged Mike to take him under his wing, even though he was only two years older than Mickey.

For his part, Mike didn't have the heart to tell his uncle that he was right not to trust the people his son called "his pals." They were not of the good life. Mike felt certain that nothing good could come of his cousin Mickey's association with this crowd. But he felt he had to try because it was a request from Zio Pasquale. After they finished the wonderful meal their Zia Giuanna had prepared, Mike invited Mickey to come with him to play cards at the Italian social club.

After a friendly hour of conviviality, Mike broached the subject of Mickey's dubious friends. No sooner were the words out of his mouth than Mickey retorted with a conviction Mike had not seen before in this cousin of his, "Mike, I know everything I need to know about my friends."

Using the pejorative terms for Italians, he went on to say, "The *Guineas* think if they work hard and save their pennies, they are getting somewhere. I'm not going to be like my father who works every day like a slave. For what? So he can pay rent to someone else so there's only four of us sharing a place to sleep instead of eight? That's not for me. I remember how many times my mother, sisters and I went to bed hungry in Petrania. It's not enough to fill my belly, I'm going to be somebody!" Mike tried to interject, but his cousin wasn't yet finished. He practically spat out, "People are gonna respect me!"

The conversation ended abruptly with young Mickey storming down the stairs and out of the club house. Mike remained seated for a few moments trying to digest his cousin's passionate outburst. Then he decided he should go after him. When he got to the outside porch, he watched as Mickey took off with some of his wise-guy buddies. Then, he turned to look back and seeing Mike, yelled over his shoulder, "Cousin, don't tell my PaPa that I didn't stay with you all afternoon."

PART TWO

Acqua passata non macina mulinu
~ old Platanese Proverb

Water that's past, won't turn the millstone

CHAPTER ONE

Mike, as he now thought of himself, had been in awe of all the companies and businesses that seemed to be prospering in Norwalk. Almost every corner had businesses, factories, and supply companies. The population was similar to that of the area of Nicastro, Sambiase and Santa Eufemia in Italy, and though a mere fraction of the size of the population of New York City, Norwalk was nevertheless a melting pot of diversity. In the short few years, he was living there, he had come to love Norwalk. He worked with people from every nationality, religion and race. He found everyone interesting.

His biggest disappointment was the discovery that he didn't find common ground with a lot of the people who called themselves "Italian." Some were involved in what he called "the bad life." Working at illegal pursuits, running numbers, women and liquor, Mike steered clear of those types. Instead, he developed some close friendships with men of Irish heritage, their last names Magner and Leonard. Good men. He found them honest and loyal. He sought their advice on many matters. They both told him, "Mike, the future is Norwalk." Mike took their prognostications seriously.

Just a few years back, the two towns of Norwalk and South Norwalk had consolidated into one city called Norwalk, with designations of East Norwalk, South Norwalk, Norwalk and Rowayton. Within those distinct designations there were areas people referenced by the former use of those areas such as Cranbury, Winnipauk and Silvermine. Working and living in South Norwalk, he started to give serious thought to moving to Norwalk.

Zia Giuanna and Petronella were still in the same general area where they had always lived, but early in 1916, to his disappointment, Zio Pasquale moved his family to Strafford just outside of the big city of Bridgeport. He loved the man and was very fond of his daughters, Jennie and Lilly. Mike felt that his uncle was under the mistaken impression that if he took his son, Mickey, away from his circle of questionable friends, he would help him start fresh.

Mike worked hard and saved his money. He told the truth. He never spoke ill of anyone and without trying, he found that people responded in kind to him. He often turned over in his mind the words his cousin Mickey had spewed. The boy was right, your friends are important and if you want to be respected you have to do what it takes to earn that respect. Where they differed was the method to achieve that goal.

———— ❦ ————

It was a cold Sunday morning. Mike had boarded the train to Bridgeport from the South Norwalk train station, and the landscape from the windows of the moving train car was just showing the promise of spring. Today, he was making another attempt to find his father's grave. The last time he had tried to find it, he had been ill prepared. It had been within the first two weeks of his arrival at his cousin Petronella's place.

Once in Bridgeport, he had made several inquiries about the cemetery. He learned there were three cemeteries that could have been where they had taken his father. He also learned the devastating news that the church had had a fire in 1906. The fire had consumed all of the cemetery records for all the Catholic cemeteries in the area to that time. He had been crestfallen. There was no documentation he could ask them to check. Could traces of his father have dissipated so completely?

He insisted someone show him where the cemeteries were located. On that trip, he had gone to one cemetery there called St. James in Bridgeport. He had walked the cemetery and looked at almost every headstone and footstone with his uncle, who could read them. They returned to South Norwalk that night without speaking. His dreams of so many years, that he would lay a wreath on his father's grave, were shattered. He just couldn't believe there was no recourse to finding his father's grave. He had to think of something. He was unwilling to give up his quest. He had placed the wreath he brought with him that day on the largest marker he saw, bowed his head and said a prayer not only for his father, but for all those buried here whose families might not know where they were.

During these past four years, Mike had learned a lot in bits and pieces, each giving him new hope. He learned that St. James had stopped taking new burials well before his dad died in 1900, so that's why he wasn't there.

He discovered there were two other Catholic cemeteries in that area, both with records lost in that same fire, but he thought he could visit with family members who could read, walk each of those with them and he would find a marker with his father's name on it. The blanket of snow during the months following his arrival in

South Norwalk made checking other cemeteries impossible. Then, work demands, coupled with the distance and his transportation limitations had prevented him from going back right away. When he finally got there, the overgrown weeds and grasses made it impossible to see what was there.

It was almost two years before he was able to explore the second lead, St. Michael's Cemetery in Stratford. Still an active cemetery, it had taken burials before the time his father had died and since then. He had been full of hope on that occasion as well, only to come up with nothing.

Then, he learned of the St. Augustine Cemetery. This was the most likely one for his father to have been buried in, he was told by someone at the Bridgeport diocese office, because it was closest to where most of the immigrant workers lived. The area was full of boardinghouses. Located on the east side of Bridgeport, at the northeast corner of Helen and Arctic streets, it was the first Roman Catholic cemetery in Fairfield County. Consistent with the ethnic makeup of greater Bridgeport in the mid- to late 1800s, most of the burials were of Irish heritage, although there also were many Polish, Czech, Italian, Russian, Hispanic, and other ethnicities represented. No one knew exactly how many individuals were buried there. Estimates of 1,000 to 2,000 were thrown at Mike during his inquiries. Unfortunately, because of its location it had been the target of vandals numerous times.

Today, he was meeting his Zio Pasquale and together they would walk St. Augustine Cemetery. They had chosen early spring because the snows had stopped and not too much brush and undergrowth would have grown yet.

He was full of hope, but it was tempered with a healthy dose of realism.

CHAPTER TWO

Working as a laborer on the tracks for the Connecticut Railway Company, Mike had found an apartment at 19 River Street in Norwalk, just off Wall Street, to bring his new bride, Maria Raffaela Russo, whom he called Raffaela. He had rented the place in the fall of 1917, right after they decided they would get married. Despite the preparations, it wasn't until the couple had gotten their marriage license just before Christmas that the impending marriage seemed real to Mike.

The three rooms were dark and tight, but the apartment afforded Mike and Raffaela some marital privacy despite the fact that Salvatore, Raffaela's brother had come to live with them.

As she went about sewing, cleaning and preparing meals, Raffaela was flooded with an overwhelming sense of gratitude that God had sent her this gift. She had thought she would never marry. Now, she often reddened with embarrassment at the open adoration by this young man, Mike, almost nine years her junior. He had come into her life so unexpectedly. After her mother had died, she tended the three males in her life in Mileto, a small town in Calabria, just twenty-five miles southwest of where Mike hailed from. Founded by the Greeks, her town, also in Calabria, had suffered tremendously from earthquakes in 1905 and 1906. Although the big earthquake that devastated Reggio and Messina at the end of 1908 was less damaging to their region, her father and older brother emigrated to America shortly thereafter with the promise to send for her and her younger brother as soon as they could.

Though just a young girl herself, she had cooked, cleaned, mended and maintained a home first for all four of them, then after her father and older brother, Giovanni, emigrated, just for herself and Salvatore. To Salvatore, six years younger than her, Raffaela became the mother. Her father and older brother had always been sweet and kind to her. Considerate of her, they had worked to become self-sufficient.

Antonio Russo knew the time would come when his daughter needed to marry. He had told her often that she was a beautiful girl. He had been adamant with his sister, Concetta, keep a watchful eye on his growing girl while he was gone. After a few years, Raffaela and Salvatore joined their father and older brother in America.

Raffaela felt herself change after coming to America. She had blossomed into a full-bodied woman. Her father and older brother wanted her to be happy. They often encouraged her to come to some of the gatherings that happened regularly where most of their *Miletesi paisani* lived in South Norwalk. On the other hand, the young Salvatore, who was sourly and demanding as a youngster, only grew more so with time. As a teenager, he followed in his father and brother's footsteps—first as an apprentice and later as a full-fledged cobbler. He eventually split from his older brother's business and opened his own shop.

Raffaela worried about him incessantly. After their father's death in 1913, Salvatore seemed to have developed an exaggerated possessiveness of her. Then, their brother Giovanni, now known as John, proposed to Antonietta Zambarelli. Instead of being elated for his brother, Salvatore declared, "Everyone is leaving me!" He proceeded to beg his sister never to leave him. By the time he was seventeen, he had developed a reputation as a rogue—taking up smoking, drinking and gambling—and he had developed quite a reputation with the young women, with fathers wary if he noticed their daughters. Raffaela was distressed that he seemed devoid of commitment.

John, on the other hand felt his sister needed a life of her own. At twenty-eight, she was considered an old maid. In their social circles, most Italian women were considered hopeless if they reached twenty without at least an engagement. It wasn't as if there hadn't been suitors, but the ever-devoted Raffaela had turned them down when the offers came because her "baby" brother needed her. It seemed after she turned twenty-two, suddenly there were no longer any marriage-makers sending the 'mbasciata. The 'mbasciata was the message delivered by a go-between communicating an interest in a match. No one seemed to cast an eye in her direction any longer. Those men who had been interested when she was younger were long married with children, not that any of them had intrigued her. It seemed that almost overnight, despite her thick, wavy hair, tiny waist and ample bosom, she seemed to fade into that category of the unseen.

Her outings were limited to church, the market and home. However, once John had married, his wife, Antonietta, became an avid matchmaker on her behalf. But Raffaela seemed disinterested. Her sister-in-law urged her to come to the numerous gatherings her family held. Including other families from Mileto, all of these social occasions were populated by *Miletesi*. It was rare among the immigrants who identified themselves by their town or province that outsiders would be included. However, it did happen now and then.

It was late April, and the Connecticut sun finally began to warm a little from a long arduous winter and the tulips were responding and casting pretty splotches of red, yellow and purples on an otherwise dead canvas. Giovanni Russo took the occasion of the start of preparations for the feast of the Holy Mother, slated for May 8, as an opportunity to invite a non-*paisano* to a game of *bocce* at the St. Anne Club on Ely Avenue. The gathering after the sport would involve food, but also work and planning for the upcoming popular festival in honor of the Holy Mother, daughter of their patron St. Anne.

John's sister Raffaela hadn't wanted to go to the gathering, but Antonietta had said they needed help with the food as well as with writing the petitions to the Holy Mother Mary. Appealing to her beautiful penmanship, Antonietta told Raffaela, "*Abbiamo bisogno dello tuo bello scritto per fare le letter alla Madonna.*" Raffaela's need to be needed won out, along with her sister-in-law's indication that only she had the script to craft the petition letters to be pinned on the statue of Madonna for the yearly ritual. The statue would be paraded around the square and all the intersessions pinned to it would be heard by the Holy Mother.

The intersessions started coming in to the club around the beginning of March, so they were already piling up. The locals organized this event annually in the traditions of their town in Italy. Most of the immigrants in the area could not read nor write. Yet, Raffaela had gone to the third grade back in Mileto and she had not only learned her lessons well but the teacher had complimented her on how well she had mastered them, enough to teach others, and better than those who had attended school far longer. Her teacher had also felt that Raffaela's penmanship, her "hand," as she called it, was exquisite. A gift from God that should be shared for good purposes, she had often told the girl.

Contrary to her homebody nature, Raffaela accepted the plea to attend the social gathering at the St. Anne Club on that semi-warm day in late April. With a dish of eggplant *parmigiana* to contribute to the planned buffet and her fountain pen, which she treasured like a piece of gold, she went reluctantly.

There she sat with some of the women dictating their own petitions and what they had been told by others, Raffaela translating them onto the small scraps of paper torn from a much larger sheet by hand. Each that she wrote would be pinned to a wide ribbon hung on the Madonna's statue.

After the *bocce* rounds wrapped up, all the men washed their hands at an outside faucet strategically positioned to water the immense vegetable garden that was tended by the club members and shared by all. Cleaned up, they filed past the table laid out for a feast. One by one, they filled their dishes and took a seat at the makeshift table and long wooden benches fashioned from planks and stacked cement blocks.

Mike Rizzo had spotted her seated with pen in hand from the *bocce* court. He was intrigued by the scene before him. He didn't know many men in his group who could write, let alone a woman.

He noticed she was lovely. He had been very respectful and asked someone about her. When he was told she was the *zitella* Russo, he was stunned. He was nearly twenty and she looked about his age. How could she be an old maid?

He was gripped with something he couldn't describe—a mixture of awe at her intelligence and beauty, and permeating sadness that she was being referred to in such a pejorative manner. At the same time, he felt oddly elated that she wasn't married.

Motored by some unknown force, he walked over toward the women to talk with them. On his approach, he heard her voice as she said to another woman, "I'll go in and check on putting out more *parmigiana*." The sound of her voice was like a thunderbolt strike. He was smitten. Though she never reappeared from inside, he sat there hopeful that he would get to talk with her.

Though disappointed, after the planning and his promise to help the day of the feast, hope sprang eternal as the men invited him to come back the following week for another round of bocce, food and festival planning.

She wasn't there on his subsequent visit, though he enjoyed the camaraderie and the food. On his third outing among the Milatese, he went to speak to Giovanni, Raffaela's brother. He expressed his worry about his sister, because he had not seen Raffaela again after his first visit, and he hoped she was not ill. Her brother explained that she didn't normally come to these gatherings, but the women had tapped into her good nature about the petition letters. Michele tried not to betray his intentions lest he be rebuffed. However, John, recognized the signs, and because he loved his sister so much and because he had grown fond of the young *Platanese*, he asked Mike to come to dinner at their home the following Sunday.

Raffaela thought back at what a strained affair that meal had been. She had recognized that her prospects for marriage were nil. She had tended her brother's needs and selfish demands, and she had become a *zitella*, an old maid. Now, here she was, married.

The wedding had been a lovely affair in St. Mary's Church on West Avenue, January 7, 1918. Her brother John had walked Raffaela down the aisle amid the lace and ruffles of a dress she had made herself. As an experienced seamstress, she had taken great care with the most important dress she had ever sewn. Her husband, Mike, looked so handsome.

He had insisted they have a wedding portrait taken. Definitely, an extravagance they couldn't afford, but Mike had been adamant. It was so important to him. The photographer told them they could pay a little at a time for the portrait and when they finished paying for it, they could have it. Now after fourteen months of marriage, the colorized full-length portrait decorated the wall of their tiny place. She basked in the thought of it all as she gazed it frequently throughout the day these past two months since they had made their last payment.

———

During this first year of marriage, her brother Salvatore had become almost unbearable. He expressed his feelings to his sister in a frequent and vehement voice. "You have been fooled by this boy-man. He isn't particularly smart or handsome," he had said just this morning. "You have made a terrible mistake." It wasn't the first time he had said it. She expected it wouldn't be the last. Salvatore raged often that Mike was taking her heart, time and life.

Sadly, she recognized that the concept of men and women and marriage had escaped her little brother. He didn't remember their parents' marriage. It seemed to her that he had little to focus on but his own plight. Though he objected mightily to the marriage, somewhere in his brain he had the mistaken notion that even though she married, she would remain his surrogate mother, totally devoted to him.

Raffaela reminisced over this first year of marriage. For her and Mike it had been a year of wonder and discovery. They learned how much they had in common. They now knew what it was to adore someone more than yourself. At first, she had felt embarrassed that Mike was much younger. Yet he had proved to be a serious and committed husband. There seemed to be none of the failings that she heard about so often from other woman. He seemed to be totally oblivious to other women except as people. She was the apple of his eye and his eye remained focused on her.

Secretly, she was thrilled. She had been warned by the neighbor woman who had helped her prepare for marriage about men in general and younger men in particular. Her brother John seemed so much like her father, a one-woman man, but her younger brother had declared his love and then left several girls along the way. And he was still doing that. The trail of upset girls and fathers was getting longer every month.

She had been pleased that Mike had agreed to have Salvatore come live with them. She had told Mike she couldn't marry unless he did. However, the two didn't get along particularly well. Often, she felt torn. It was true that Salvatore treated her as his doormat, as Mike had said to him whenever they exchanged harsh words. Mike took great offense at Salvatore's demanding ways and inconsiderate behavior toward her.

She was in a bad spot. She loved Mike so much, and yet she felt guilty and obligated toward her brother. There were times Salvatore said such awful things when Mike was out that she thought to herself, "Perhaps I should not have gotten married." Then, after nine months of marriage, she had become pregnant for the second time. The first time was only two months after the wedding, but she had lost the pregnancy almost immediately. The midwife had comforted her and upset her all in one sentence. She'd told her not to worry, it was common to lose the first pregnancy. Unfortunately, the woman had added that that many times "older" women never could carry a baby full term, crushing her hopes.

As summer approached, the baby was growing inside her, kicking, turning and very much alive. Due in just a few more months, Raffaela was busy sewing and knitting the baby's layette. Today, she was taking comfort in making the gown that her son or daughter would be baptized in. Using the fabric from the train on her wedding dress, her joy danced around her like pixie dust. She momentarily reflected that it seemed that the more her belly grew larger, the more her brother grew sour. Just as quickly, she smiled to herself thinking, as my belly has grown, it seems Mike beams from morning until he falls asleep at night.

"Rosa, that's what we will name her," Raffaela declared. when their infant arrived. Even before Mike could say anything about it, his wife had determined that tradition would prevail. Their first child, a beautiful girl with a head full of dark hair, cried lustily. He had not given any thought to a girl's name. He was sure it would be a boy and he would name him Antonio. Though he had never succeeded in finding his father's grave site, he had eventually settled for knowing the general area where he was buried and he had placed a wreath on the entrance in memory of his father just before he and Raffaela married. Deciding he would honor his father by naming his child after him brought him comfort.

But it wasn't to be, at least not yet. Mike had ambivalent feelings about his mother. But his feelings for this lovely creation, his daughter, were crystal clear. He was flooded with an overwhelming sensation of love and protectiveness for both the mother and child, born at home. Mike didn't want to leave them for even for a minute. His brother-in-law had been the one to register the baby at the town hall.

Now close to a year old, Rosa began to make her first steps, when she became Rosina or Rosie to her parents. She was their joy. Not long after Rosie's birth, Raffaela had become pregnant again. The new baby would be born two months after Rosie's July birthday in September.

·—————⟨∽⟩—————·

Mike's cup was full. He and Raffaela were very happy together. Their second child, also a girl, had been born September 9, 1920. They named her Angelina after Mike's oldest sister, who had gone to Argentina, again with Raffaela dictating the naming traditions of their heritage. The child quickly became Lena to everyone. Different from her sister in personality and temperament, she too was a beautiful baby with gorgeous hair, a ready smile and a dimple in her cheek.

The family had now officially outgrown the apartment on River Street. "We need to move," he said to Raffaela. "We have a little money saved. I don't know if it's enough yet to buy a place, but I need to start looking to find a place to rent. If something good comes along we can afford to buy, that would be best." With her ever-present needle in hand, she nodded an affirmative at her husband. Stroking his wife's cheek, and patting his daughters on the head, Mike left to meet with a friend.

They needed more room and they needed a place of their own. He didn't know if he could afford both.

He spent the day talking to people he knew in the shops, inquiring about property for sale and potential apartments. He had learned early on that if he could find something word of mouth, often it was more affordable, or negotiable, than properties reported in a newspaper or listed with agents. Everything he looked at was way out of his reach. He had some savings now, but they were meager when he factored in the need to pay the loan, eat and provide for a family of four on his labor wages. He knew he would have saved enough money in a couple of years, but they needed the space now.

Calling it a day, he decided to go to talk with his friend Jim Magner at the funeral home before heading back to River Street. Jim said, "You know, Mike, you are doing the right thing looking for a property to purchase. I hear there was a house for sale on Henry Street. It backs up to the Center School property. It was a big house that could easily be turned into a multi-family dwelling, they said."

When he went to look, it was indeed big. He calculated that if he could somehow come up with the down payment, he could rent out part of it and cover his mortgage and have a place for his wife and children. He liked the street and it had an ample yard for him to grow his vegetables. In their apartment, the owner had allowed him to plant some vegetables along the back in a strip, but the rest of the yard was for the owner's use. There was no dirt in the front as it sat right on the street.

He was excited. He took his brother-in-law and his wife and children to see the place. They all remarked about how much work it needed to make it livable, but Mike was no stranger to work. Raffaela became excited about the prospects. Her brother John had just bought a home on Cross Street, which was nearby.

There was only one problem. When Mike went to the bank for a mortgage note, he didn't have enough of a down payment.

He talked with Raffaela's brother, who said with compassion in his eyes, "Look, I would do anything for you and my sister, but I just bought this place for my family. I don't have the money, but you know who does, my brother Salvatore. He may be a rogue, but he's making money and he has been living with you and my sister and paying no rent nor spending any money on food. I think he would loan it to Raffaela, if she asked him."

A dilemma for sure for Mike. He didn't want to be beholden to his ne'er-do-well brother-in-law. The only disagreement Raffaela and

Mike had ever had between them was about her brother. But Mike eventually decided he had to swallow hard and do this for Raffaela and his daughters.

He approached his brother-in-law the very next evening when he wandered in smelling of liquor about eleven-thirty. At first, Salvatore responded in an falsely sweet tone, "Of course, you want my money. First, you take my sister, now you say that the money is for her and the children. Sure. Sure. I can loan you the money." Mike was a little frightened by the docile attitude tinged with sarcasm.

Then Salvatore starting banging doors and slamming things down. The children started crying being awakened from a deep sleep. Raffaela flew out of the bedroom with her nightgown on and spoke softly and firmly to her brother. "You say you love me. Yet anything that makes me happy, you try to destroy. These children are all you may have some day, when you are old and I am gone. They are the love of my life. As much as I love you, I love them more. My husband is working every day to do the very best he can for all of us," she said.

"You live under his roof, you ungrateful oaf. When will you wake up? You are biting the hand that's feeding you. We need the money. We will pay you back. If you don't loan it to us, pack your bags now and get out." She turned and went back into the bedroom, shutting the door in his face.

Shocked at his sister's quiet but chastising tone, he knocked at the door and begged her forgiveness. Her words had cut him as if stabbed by a knife. She did not respond.

Humbled, he turned to Mike and said, "How much you need? When you buy the house, I will give it to you right at the bank. I will not live with you when you move. It's time I go out on my own."

CHAPTER THREE

"*Fa freddo,*" she said softly as Mike arrived from his night watchman's job at eight-thirty a.m. "*Siamo quasi finiti i legni.*" It's cold and the wood is almost exhausted. They huddled close in the small apartment in January of 1924. Two of their three daughters were playing on the kitchen floor because it was the warmest place in the house.

They had already had a simple breakfast of latte and biscuits. It was Wednesday and they would have meat on Saturday, when he went to the butcher and bought some ground chuck. Raffaela had some food waiting for him as he came in, but before he ate, he had to clean up. He washed his face in the enamel basin in water that she had heated on the wood-burning stove, in anticipation of his arrival.

That wood stove had kept them snug the past four years since they bought the house. With no central heating, the house was nothing more than a large wooden box with a flat roof. Mike had worked hard, several jobs at a time, to buy the place. Costing nearly $2,300, when the opportunity came before they had enough to put the down payment on it, Salvatore had lived up to his words and loaned them the $400 they needed to make up the difference. They had been shocked at the bank when he had requested that his loan be treated as an official lien on the property in case they didn't pay him bank. More than a little offended, they swallowed hard, and said nothing in front of the bank officials. They had offered ahead of time to write up an official note of loan and payment, separate from the bank loan. But Salvatore kept saying, no need. I'll meet you at the bank and give you the money then. They walked out of the bank owning two mortgages.

Despite owing money to her little brother, and paying every six months on the note from the seller, they had done fairly well. They had paid Salvatore back and he removed the lien he had on the house. Moreover, Mike had done an enormous amount of work to make it livable and to turn it into a multi-family dwelling. He was able to collect rent that helped provide some additional income with which to pay the two mortgages.

They had rented out the first floor to a family with children who were from New York. In the second upstairs apartment, backing up to theirs, lived a childless couple from Calabria. The Rizzos' second-floor apartment was the larger of the two.

Though more spacious and more pleasant than the dark rented apartment on River Street, the apartment that had seemed quite large when they moved in, now barely contained them and their three, soon-to-be-four children. Despite the house's lack of esthetic beauty and its never-ending need of repair, Mike often basked in the good feeling of ownership. He openly hoped there would come a day when he could take the entire upstairs for his family.

The three little girls were growing beautifully. The third one, Concetta, had been born two years after Lena. They all had gorgeous smiles. Now, Raffaela was pregnant with their fourth child. He loved his little girls, but he hoped this one would be a boy. He wanted so much to have a namesake for his father Antonio.

All the inquiries had gotten him nowhere; he had never been able to locate his father's grave. With all the records destroyed in that fire of 1906, no matter what he had done, he hadn't been able to locate it. He had held great hope for that last of the three possible cemeteries. He tried to walk the entire area at the abandoned St. Augustine Cemetery along with his Zio Pasquale. The ground had been overgrown and the stone markers knocked over; it was impossible to discern anything. According to the caretaker back at the church where they had gone to see if there was any other recourse, they learned that some of the graves had been marked with wooden crosses. For the most part, those that survived the fire had been ravaged by the snow- and ice-laden winters. That day, he had been able to see the area where some crosses still stood and he had stared at them a long time. He felt at a loss to assume that any one of them marked where his father was buried. At first, he was so heartbroken. It was as if his father had just died. As time went by, he slowly began to feel better because, better than flowers, he had decided he would honor his father by naming his first-born son after him.

The cold weather that had started in early November of 1923 didn't let up until April of 1924. Now it was May and they had had almost a month of beautiful weather; he knew it wouldn't be long before the unbearable heat would descend upon them. That morning as she was fixing coffee, Raffaela doubled over in pain, and Mike realized she was in labor, though she was not due for a couple of weeks yet. He ran down the stairs two at a time, and knocked on the house next door, imploring Mrs.Tavella to contact the midwife, who appeared about thirty minutes later.

He wanted to hold Raffaela's hand through her pain and through delivery, but once the midwife arrived, she scolded and banished him from the bedroom, saying this was women's work. Instead, he focused on taking care of the three girls, bringing them outside as a way of helping. His thoughts wandered. He had been at work when Concetta was born and he was so happy to be there with Raffaela at this birth.

From the street and through the open windows, he could hear Raffaela's screams. Suddenly, all went quiet. He held his breath. Then someone shouted from the window, *"Figlia numero quarto."* Daughter number four.

He bounded up the stairs, elated to see Raffaela, tired and drained as she was. The first thing she said was, *"Me dispiace che non è maschio,"* expressing her regret that she hadn't delivered him a son.

He said to her in a choked voice, "It's okay, we'll name her Antonietta after my father Antonio. He will be smiling in heaven."

CHAPTER FOUR

Godfrey Street ran perpendicular to Main Avenue. Its positioning was excellent to the bus line and a reasonable walk into the north part of city's business and retail area. Most importantly to Mike, it was at the opposite side of town from what was pretty much known as the center of the Italian population, South Norwalk. The road had originally been known as Henry Street, and the city had to change the name after the consolidation of Norwalk and South Norwalk revealed that there were two streets with the same name.

When he had purchased the house, it had backed up to land owned by the town where the Center Elementary School stood; the school the girls would attend. However, the majority of the property was an empty, hilly wooded area that extended all the way to the parallel street recently renamed School Street. Now, directly behind his house, the town was constructing a new school on the empty portion of the parcel. The new building would house the middle-grade students. He was pleased that his children would not have to walk far in the nasty winters until high school. The area was covered in trees, and the clearing before construction was now under way.

It was a comfortable morning at 72 degrees nearing the end of July in 1924, when Mike noticed that the workers behind his house were taking the felled trees and cutting them up with a large chain-run buzz saw. The next day, he had gone to talk to the workers. Thinking ahead to the cold winter sure to descend on them later in the year, he asked if, at night after they quit work, he could use their equipment to cut up a few of the trees himself to use in his wood-burning stove for heat.

The head worker told him, "Yeah, after we're done if you want to come on over, we don't have a problem with that. You just can't be here in the daytime when we're doing our work. You'd be doing us a favor because we need to get rid of everything before the construction can start."

A few evenings later after he had worked a long day at his own job, at about six-thirty, he went over to the school construction site, the area clearly visible from their apartment window. It had been a smart idea to try and take advantage of a wasteful product and plan ahead for the coming winter, he thought.

"You are tired; go tomorrow," said Raffaela as he headed over to the clearing site.

"I'm fine. I'm just gone be a few hours, then I'll come and eat my dinner," he told her.

As he headed away from their house, she went to the window to watch him. From the window, she said, "Be careful," as was her custom.

The headline in the local paper the next day read, "Arm horribly mangled by buzz saw, is amputated at Norwalk Hospital."

As he was using the chain saw, he had bent over to move one of the cut logs away. He lost his footing. As he slipped, his shirt sleeve was caught by the chain. Raffaela, watching him from the window, saw him go down. She ran yelling to the people next door. Mr. Bredice, a local man with a brand-new car, put Mike in his vehicle and drove him to Norwalk Hospital. However, the car didn't have enough power to make it up the steep hill to the top of Stevens Street where the hospital was located. From there, he was manually carried up to the hospital. By the time he was attended by a physician, he had lost a tremendous amount of blood and was barely alive.

The doctors realized that the arm was horribly mangled and to save his life, they would need to amputate it. The cut came just above his elbow. For several days afterward, he was delirious and unaware of his surroundings. He slowly came around, and opened his eyes to see the worried face of his lovely wife and her brother John. He had no recollection of the events that put him in the hospital. He saw their concerned and tired faces and only slowly became aware that he was forever left-handed.

He made a protracted recovery, but eventually was released to go home. He watched with guilt as his beloved Raffaela, with three small children and a baby in tow, waited on him hand and foot because of his incapacitation. He became despondent. What had he done? How could something so stupid happen? He had been worried about making sure they had wood for warmth, and now he didn't know how he would be able to work to feed his family. He tortured himself pondering how he had become a burden to Raffaela, just as he had perceived her brother, Salvatore, to be.

He continuously asked himself, how could he put this saintly woman through this? They had four children. Now, she had a fifth, a one-armed husband. He cried as he sat and watched his family. Then Raffaela hugged him and cried, too. Before long, the oldest girl, Rosie, came over and hugged and cried with them. He spent the next couple of months wallowing in self-pity.

Friends and family came to visit expressing how sorry they felt for him. Their pity, though well intentioned, was depressing in itself. His self-flagellation about what he had done was relentless. Three months after the accident his friend Jim Magner came by and gave him the talk he needed.

Unlike all his prior visitors, when Jim came. his demeanor and words were stern and clearly non-sympathetic. The moment he got into the bedroom where Mike had holed himself up, his normal friendly, compassionate manner was nowhere to be seen. "Get off your ass, Mike," he bellowed. "You are a strong man, you're young and a hard worker. There is no reason for you to stay inside nursing your wounds. Get out there. Take care of your family and stop feeling sorry and blaming yourself about what happened. That won't put any food on the table!"

It was a hard blow. Stunned, Mike sat not saying a word. After about three minutes of ranting, his buddy paused and said, "I don't care if you ever talk with me again, but I just had to tell you."

To Jim's surprise, Mike said after a long silence, "Thank you. You are a good friend." Mike spent the rest of the evening no differently, than he had the past three months. But the next morning, he told Raffaela to leave him alone when she asked if he was ready to have her help him get dressed. Instead, he told her to take care of the children; he was going to rest a bit longer. With the door closed, he got up and attempted to put on his clothes for the first time without help. He struggled and was frustrated but kept at it. Right-handed all his life, his left hand was relatively useless. Then he'd scold it. "You bugger!" He'd chastise its clumsiness. But he didn't give up. Raffaela was surprised to see him come out of the bedroom some-what dressed.

"Why didn't you call me so I could help you?" she asked.

"I need to do this myself. You work so hard with the children, you don't need me to be another one of your babies," he said, nearly sobbing.

Within a week, he became proficient at washing himself and getting his clothes on.

He quickly moved to attempt to help his wife with the household chores as he had in the past. By the end of October, he had mastered hanging the washed clothes on the line with his one hand. He even managed to tie his shoes. He held his infant daughter and played with the girls.

Each night he would make his sign of the cross with his left hand. He prayed morning and night, imploring the Almighty, "Dear God, help me do what I can and make the most of what you give me."

CHAPTER FIVE

What an angelic child, he thought as he looked at his daughter Concetta sleeping. At the other end of the crib was the baby, Antonietta. Barely two years old, she had a smile that could seduce the hardest curmudgeon. He walked over to the other small bed where the two oldest girls slept, Rosie and Lena, both lovely youngsters. If asked he couldn't not have said which was the prettiest. Rosie, at seven and half years old, seemed the most adult though not quite fourteen months older than Lena; she was a huge help to her mother with the younger children.

It had been an exceptionally cold winter and they were still in the depths of it. He had been gone all day doing some laborer work at the nursery in the farm area north of Norwalk, called Westport. There he and two other men had covered plants, wrapped small shrubbery and stoked the heaters to ensure the indoors was protected against the cold. The days were short and the cold seemed to whip through the windows. He wished he had as much material at home as they did at the nursery to keep the elements at bay.

His left hand touched each of the girl's heads one at a time. Then he sat down to eat his very late dinner that Raffaela had kept warm for him. She had seemed quiet and tired these last few days. He didn't know what was wrong, if anything, because when he asked, she said she was fine. He wondered if she was pregnant. He had asked, but she said she didn't think so. They surely had been blessed with children. All healthy, beautiful and seemingly very quick and smart. He ate slowly as they talked quietly not to wake the children. He didn't turn on the radio as he usually did, deciding that the morning would be soon enough to hear of the happenings around town and the world and listen to music.

It had been almost three years since his stubbornness had cost him his right arm. Once on his feet, he had made great strides in getting work. At first most of the bosses looked at him as damaged goods and worried that if they brought him on, they'd have to pay someone who would sit out most of the labor assigned. Instead, his reputation as a hard worker, adept at handling any task, quickly made the rounds. Most days at the labor line-up, he was chosen in the first round for the day-laborer work.

He had found some more steady employment at the nursery. He and his two co-workers handled everything from digging up seedlings and potting them to repairing and reinforcing the structure to keep the cold out. In the spring, they would take down the glass and wood and expose many of the plants to the sunshine and warmth. Now, in the middle of February, that seemed a long way away.

Gardening, landscaping, tending the land and the plants were in his blood. He had learned how to coax out vegetables from a stubborn soil in Platania. Every year since he had bought the house, his backyard was lush in vegetables. After he lost his arm, he found he could still wield a shovel and plant the fresh vegetables his family needed. The business of landscaping and tending plants was a good place for him to work.

Raffaela had cut out a dress for Rosie while waiting for him to come home. Her seamstress talents ensured the children always looked well-dressed despite their meager circumstances. She was always on the lookout for price-reduced fabric at the dry-goods store. Then, when she found something, she'd have it on hand for when she had a few moments. She'd fashion a pattern, cut and sew each little dress, going through the lineup of daughters one at a time. Now, she was back at the oldest, the other three having gotten a new dress over the past six months.

Admiring the small cut-out form of the dress, she said, "Rosie will love this little blue fabric."

"Let's get some sleep," Mike said to her. "You look very tired; you work too hard."

They readied for bed and he waited for her to join him as she went in to take one last look at the girls. The full moon flooded the room with light through the windows. When she came to bed, he kissed her forehead and both of them closed their eyes and cuddled close to keep warm. She suddenly complained of a terrible headache, and turned her head up to him. In the moonlight, he saw her contorted face. In an instant, he recognized something was terribly wrong.

Within moments, she made a convulsive sound. He screamed, "Raffaela, Raffaela, talk to me," but no other sound came. He pulled on the lamp chain and reached out for his pants intending to run next door for help in getting her to the hospital. But before he could even get to them, she rolled her eyes. He grabbed her tightly and began screaming like an animal being slaughtered. The screams woke the tenants from the apartment below. They roused and banged on the door. The commotion awoke little Rosie, who promptly began to cry. But when he shouted to her to open the door, despite her tears, she let the couple in. They found him with his wife in his arms, screaming, "Don't leave me. Don't leave me."

"She looks so pretty, like she's sleeping," Lena whispered to Rosie. The girls sat politely as friends and neighbors viewed the open casket with the lovely mother of four. The girls couldn't understand why their mama would not talk to them. The neighbors had told them she had gone to heaven to be with God.

The casket sat in the church among the numerous flower arrangements brought by friends and relatives. Connie leaned over to her father and asked with an innocence only a four-year-old could express, "Why did she have to go?"

A vise gripped his heart, he could barely breathe. He tried to say something comforting to his daughter only to have his voice choke and the faucet of tears he had been working so hard to control opened up full blast.

The death certificate said she had died of a cerebral hemorrhage—an aneurysm that had been like a ticking time bomb in her brain for many years before now, the doctor had said.

Mike sat in a daze throughout the visitation and funeral mass. He was inconsolable. He had had angry words with Salvatore, who accused him of killing his sister. Salvatore's words had cut to his heart. Perhaps it was his fault. She was a bit older than most women when she started bearing children.

A week after the funeral he was no better. He had slipped into an abysmal depression. His friend Jim stopped by the house to check on him and was appalled at how Mike looked, he barely acknowledged his presence. Filled with compassion Jim, spoke gently to his friend, hoping to get Mike to register the world around him. "Mike, you've got to get yourself out of this, you've got these four children. Only you can help them." Mike heard him as if through a dense fog. He struggled to focus on them, his sense of loss so vast that he'd sunk into a deep well with nothing to grip on to pull himself up. After Jim left, Antonietta who had been pretty much in the care of a neighbor for the first few days after the funeral crawled on his lap and hugged him. Looking at her dirty face, he felt ashamed. How long had it been since he had noticed his children. Slowly, he recognized his girls were the incarnation of his beautiful wife.

His thoughts ran together and overwhelmed him. He sat for a long while sorting things out in his head; all the while, the children who had seemed to be afraid to approach him came close and hung on him. He knew he had to work. How would he take care of them, he wondered. In a daze, he got up and washed their faces and helped them change into clean clothes. Then, as if struggling through molasses, he began to work out arrangements where the two youngest girls would be cared for by a woman who lived nearby who could come to the apartment to watch them, at least for a short while. The two older ones were in school during the day and he'd worked it out so his brother-in-law's wife could watch them after school.

Two days of that routine of going to work and coming back to find the youngsters dirty and hungry was enough to demonstrate that this plan wasn't going to work. With his one hand, he tried to clean them up and make them some food as best he could. Then, on the third day, the woman left early, leaving the children alone. When he arrived, they were screaming in terror. He pulled them onto his lap and cried with them. Calming himself, he thought there had to be a way he could get them through the next few years, by then Rosie would be old enough to help with her younger sisters.

The next day he didn't go to work, figuring he would need to make other arrangements for his daughters. However, someone had already reported to children's services that there were four little girls in peril. The knock on the door sounded like another death knell.

"Mr. Rizzo, it has been brought to our attention that there are four children here who are being neglected." He was stunned. He loved his girls. He had never even swatted them on the bottom when they tipped the rice all over the floor. He worried about them constantly and he did all he could; they are not neglected he thought. However, he was immediately aware of how it must of looked to the caseworker. The house was not clean. The girls weren't properly dressed. Their faces were not spotless. He felt a stab of total despair and then immediately brushed it away. I have to be strong for my daughters, he thought.

He listened respectfully as the woman said. "Unless you bring in a nanny, or get married, we will have to bring the girls to the Children's Home on Westport Avenue. There, they will be treated well, given proper meals, appropriately bathed and dressed, and sent to school. I must be honest with you, bringing them to the home makes them eligible for adoption. You will be declared an unfit parent and they will become wards of the state. They are lovely girls; someone will adopt the two younger ones quickly."

He could not speak. Finally he managed to eke out in a voice that was barely audible, "Will they be kept together?"

"I'm sorry, there are no guarantees, mostly likely not. I can't think of anyone in a position to adopt all four," she said as if she was talking about taking out the trash.

He didn't say anything for a long time. He was silent for so long that the social worker grew impatient and prompted, "Have you been listening to me, Mr. Rizzo?"

He struggled to keep the tears out of his eyes and his voice under control. "I will come to talk with you on Monday. I will be here with them over the next three days, and I know I can get my sister-in-law to help me with them for a few days."

"All the paperwork can be done then, Mr. Rizzo," she said as a parting shot. He shut the door, sat in a chair and cried. The pain was unbearable. He'd lost Raffaela, now he would lose her daughters.

The girls, who had gone into hiding when the woman was there, came out, hugged and kissed him. Rosie had understood everything. "Why do they want to take us away, PaPa?"

He wallowed in his misery that entire afternoon and evening. The next morning, he bundled them up and walked with all of them to his brother-in-law's house on Cross Street. Hearing what had transpired, John empathized with the predicament. Then, Antonietta said, "Mike, there is a widow we know who would make a good mother to the girls and a good wife to you. She has two children of her own."

"I can't," he said. "I can't take that chance."

"What chance?" Antonietta asked, mystified that he would not jump at the idea.

"What if someone mistreats them? How can I do that to them? They are innocent children. They should not be punished for their mother's death. It's my fault," he screamed. "I will make this right. I don't know how yet, but I will make it right."

"Antonietta," John said softly, "please make some lunch for my nieces," as he beckoned Mike out to the front porch. The sun was bright, but the temperature was twenty-six degrees. Once out of earshot of his wife and the girls, John said, "Mike, what are you gonna do? You can't stay like this. They are too small yet."

"I know there are women out there who take in children as boarders. I just don't know how to find them," Mike sobbed. "You know so many people through the shoe shop, surely someone you know must have a lead on a name. I beg you to help me find someone."

Before returning inside, John said, "I will do what I can."

After they had stayed a while and had a good meal, Mike took his little band home. Once there, he heated water and bathed them, put on their nightclothes and put them two each to a bed. Rosie slept with Antonietta and Connie slept with Lena. He hugged them a long time. It was cold and they giggled as he snuggled them.

Once they were tucked in and no sounds came from the bedroom, he heard a knock on the front door. The family who lived downstairs had been away for the day and they wanted to invite him into their kitchen for a cup of coffee. He listened at the bedroom and didn't hear any sounds from the girls, so he went down.

In their own way, the tenants who had been very friendly with him and Raffaela were trying to help him. As they served coffee, they too encouraged him to give up the two youngest girls for adoption. They spoke of how much they wanted children and hadn't been able to have them. Though they never came out and said it, it was clear they wanted to adopt one of his. He listened and expressed his appreciation for their efforts, but he was not consoled. He finished his cup of coffee, thanked them and went back upstairs. He looked in on the girls and then turned on the radio very low to get some music. Raffaela had loved the radio when he bought it second-hand a little over a year ago. It had been a wonderful addition, though expensive even used. Mike had been fascinated by the wireless radio technology that spurred the radio craze starting in 1920. He bought the small table top with two dials because he felt it would brighten Raffaela's long days when he was working. Together, they had enjoyed the novelty of it, most especially the music programs. He had come to depend on it for the news reports as his information source.

As he sat there in the quiet with the soft radio, he heard the chugging train and the music and words to a popular song, *"I see a* new horizon , My life has only begun, Beyond the blue horizon, Lies a rising sun." Suddenly he said aloud with no one to hear him, "I will never give them up for adoption! I don't want anyone to split them up and the only way I know no one will mistreat them is for me to raise them.

"Dear God," he cried, "help my girls, even if I'm a wretched, worthless sinner. Please help me find a way."

On Sunday morning, the woman from downstairs knocked on the door. "Do you need any help getting the girls ready for the day?" she asked brightly. She had heard Mike's cries from downstairs the night before. She felt a deep empathy for those beautiful children. She too prayed for them and for him. She secretly hoped that he would offer one to them for adoption.

He opened the door and accepted her gracious offer with a nod. After the girls were all dressed and fed, she announced she and her husband were headed to noon mass at St. Mary's Cathedral. "Mike, you and Raffaela always went to mass, now is not the time to stop. You and the girls need God's grace and peace," she said. He agreed. She helped them all put their coats on and off they went.

He carried Antonietta in his arm and told the others to hold each other's hands and Rosie to hang on to his jacket pocket as they walked to the church where he and his wife had married. The organ music was like a salve to his soul. He had first felt angry with God that he had taken Raffaela. Then, he had self-flagellated in his belief that he had killed her. Eventually he moved directly into the abyss of despair. Now, two months after she was gone, he was in a quiet resignation filled with sadness and easy tears. I have to get hold of myself, he scolded himself inside his head. He did not want to upset the girls more than they already were.

Leaving mass, he ran into Mr. Bredice. The man had saved his life when he drove him to the hospital after the chain saw accident. At the time, Mr. Bredice's car was brand new and the man hadn't even hesitated a moment, he just drove him to the hospital, bleeding and all. Mike thought the world of him.

Mr. Bredice was as polite as ever. He chatted with the girls first, then looked up at Mike and said, "How are you faring, Mr. Rizzo?" It must be so hard with the girls so young, and you with your one arm." The empathy in his face made Mike confide in him. Though uncharacteristic of Mike to do so. He felt this man who had driven him in his new car when he had nearly lost his life, was kind and knowledgeable and could be trusted. As he shared his desire to keep his daughters, Mr. Bredice nodded as if in agreement.

"Surely there is someone who could take care of them just until the baby is a little older and Rosie is old enough to help me look after them and tend them when I'm at work," Mike said.

All of a sudden, Mr. Bredice had a brainstorm. "Mrs. Racanelli," he said. "Frank Racanelli's widow who lives on Aiken and Ward Street, backing up to Ohio Avenue, I know she takes in children. The word is that she's competent. My sister is a schoolteacher and has a little boy in her class who lives there. She says he comes to school neat, clean and seems to be well fed. Maybe you could go talk with her."

Mike was filled with hope. "Thank you so much. God bless you. You are a good man," he said with a catch in his voice. Instead of walking home they went directly to Mrs. Racanelli's house. Knocking on the door, he looked around at the grounds. The house was a big one, with a large porch in the front and spacious property surrounding it.

"Yes?" said a very round woman as she came to the door.

"I've come to talk with you about boarding my children with you," Mike said.

"Are these the children?" she asked sweetly. "They are lovely. Come on in, my dears."

There was a swing in the backyard and a sandbox in one corner. Inside there was a room with a large table and some books and a few playthings. The girls were impressed with the surroundings, but awaited their father's signal before venturing to try anything.

"I run a very clean boarding house," she said, "The girls will be fed, bathed, sleep, and go to school from here. I already have three other children I have taken in. They have to behave for me and do as I tell them. But because I have a daughter of my own who is somewhat sickly, I don't have enough room to sleep four more; I can take only three of them."

"How much you charge?" Mike asked, sure it would be more than he could pay.

"It will cost you $3.00 a week, cause the little one will be a little extra."

He did a quick calculation. She would take the youngest three. He could leave Rosie with John and Antonietta. Antonietta was expecting, but did not yet have children. Rosie was already a great little helper. Antonietta would appreciate having her.

If I can do this for a little until I get on my feet, the state can't take them away, Mike thought.

"You can come visit them each day if you like," the woman said. "On weekends, you can even take them home for a day or so, but I still charge the same."

They stood there in a very long silence. Mrs. Racanelli broke the ice saying, "If you decide you want me to take over their care, bring them back tonight with all their clothes."

"No, not tonight," he said quickly, "We will start next week."

Then, he took his family home and together they spent the rest of the afternoon and evening playing games and listening to music on the radio. He made them some dinner and made sure they cleaned up before they went to bed. Then he sat with them as they said their prayers, and he tucked them in.

After they had fallen asleep, he made his way into bed, too. It had been an exhausting three days. Before he fell asleep, he made the sign of the cross and said, "Thank you, God to send me Mrs. Racanelli. I promise to take good care of my girls."

CHAPTER SIX

"I've got to re-tar the roof or imma gonna have some leaks soon," Mike said to his neighbor, Dominic Mangone, as he took a respite from having turned over the dirt in preparation for planting his garden early next month. He would spread some lime on it and then let it sit for a couple of weeks. It was a spectacular Saturday morning in April, just two weeks after Easter.

Mike watched as his girls played with Dominic's stepdaughter, Josephine, on the street. Whenever they were outside, the girls were like honey, they attracted a swarm of bees. There were as many as a dozen kids out there most of the time with them. Playing tag, hide and seek, hopscotch, they seemed to have an endless abundance of energy.

He looked on and felt a glow of goodness wash over him as he relived the miracle of having them all together under one roof again. He had felt that way almost every day since they had come home. Rosie had been the comfort. She had pretty much been home with him all along except for the first few months after their mother died when she had stayed with Rosa's brother and his wife Antonietta. As the oldest, Rosie was a great help to him. Wonderfully behaved, industrious, always pleasant and cheerful, she had kept him sane.

The three younger girls had remained at Mrs. Racanelli's until this past November, when he took them back suddenly. He had planned to bring Lena, Connie and Antonietta back when Antonietta turned five, on May 28 of this year. They had been at the foster home for fourteen months. During that time, Mrs. Racanelli was able to keep them safe and clean while he worked.

By his own calculations, he needed to wait until the littlest one turned five before bringing them home. It would mean Rosie would be nearly ten.

That first Christmas after their mother died had been difficult. He avoided his empty house by trying to find ways to earn money so he could provide for the girls and going to visit them every chance he had.

Mrs. Racanelli's foster care was not cheap. He was trying to keep up the house payments and work had been sporadic for him, after Raffaela died. He rued the day he had been so foolish when cutting the wood and turned into the one-armed man trying time and again to get people to realize he could do the work they wanted. He had cried aloud one night when despite his efforts he found he did not have enough money to buy the children even a small doll for Christmas. He still couldn't afford a stone for their mother's grave.

Their mother had been so talented. Her hands wove magic with bits of fabric and her tiny, neat stitches. She had sewed the girls' lovely dresses, homemade dolls and always seemed to bake some little delight for them.

The City's Children's Fund, however, had saved the day. They had stopped over to Mrs. Racanelli' s and delivered little toys all wrapped in bright paper. He thought highly of Mrs. Racanelli. However, his second oldest, Lena, often said she was mean because she was strict with them about everything—but Mike realized the woman was not without a kind heart. He was most grateful to her. If not for her, the girls would have had to be split up and he wouldn't even know where they were and they wouldn't know each other.

He was particularly grateful that Mrs. Racanelli had never broken her promise to not lay a hand on them. "If they izza bad, you talk to me," he had emphasized. "You no hitta my girls." She had been true to her word. She had never struck them, in an era when he knew corporal punishment was frequently meted out.

Every Sunday when he went to visit, he would bring a little bit of hard candy and take them for a walk. Without their being aware of what he was doing, he would get the full report about everything from the past week.

"She's so mean," Lena had said with her little hands on her hips.

"How's she mean?" he had questioned.

"Well, she's always saying, you come right back from school, and don't do this; do that. You all stay together when you walk to school. Don't dawdle. Come right home. Only walk on the sidewalk. Oooo, she's so bossy." Lena had mimicked Mrs. R's voice and her stance. He remembered now how Lena had gotten upset because he had smiled when she had demonstrated not only her voice but Mrs. Racanelli's mannerisms as well. Lena accused him of not believing her. He had reassured his second oldest daughter that he surely believed her. But he reminded all of them that it was Mrs. Racanelli' s job to be sure they behaved, went to school and that they were safe.

"Did she spank you when you took too long to come home from

school?" he slyly added.

"No. She doesn't have to spank us," was Lena's quick retort. "Her looks can kill you."

The girls were too young to understand, but Mike knew that Mrs. Racanelli, a widow herself, was doing all she could to keep things going by raising foster children to keep up the payments and taxes on the property that her husband had purchased before he died. Without a husband, she had raised a son and daughter by keeping children for the state and others for several years. Now that her son and daughter were grown up, you'd think she would have had it a bit easier. Instead, in recent years, the woman's daughter had been quite ill. Certainly all the medical costs must have been a drain. The daughter, a very pretty young woman, was working at a good job when she was stricken with a painful, chronic condition. Mrs. Racanelli hadn't shared with Mike what the illness was, but often she indicated her daughter was in bed, or in the hospital. It was just about six months ago that tragic events sent Mrs. Racanelli into her own sickbed and brought his girls home earlier than he planned.

It was about midday, Wednesday morning, November 7, 1928, that the twenty-six-year old Grace Racanelli, who had been despondent for some time with the thought that she would never recover from the painful illness she was suffering from, committed suicide by plunging to her death in Healy's pond near Aiken Street.

The pond was only a short walk from the Racanelli home on Ward Street where Grace lived with her mother, brother, and the motley crew of foster children her mother had cared for over the years. Grace was seen by two teenage boys who were trapping at some distance from the shore when she appeared to jump in. They heard a splash and then moaning, and she disappeared. They ran to a house nearby to get help and they knocked on the door of a police officer who had been at home having his lunch. His heroic efforts to jump into the ice water to get the girl out were all for naught. She could not be resuscitated.

Mike knew from conversations with her mother that the lovely, dark-haired, vivacious girl had undergone a recent operation in at Yale New Haven Hospital. Nevertheless, this course of action to take your own life was beyond his comprehension. When police arrived to tell her what had happened, Mrs. Racanelli had become so distraught she fainted and fell flat on her face in her dining room. She was barely functional during the visitation and funeral, her face and nose all smashed up, swollen and purple. She had trouble keeping her balance. Mike remembered how awful it all was. He couldn't bear to see the pain in her face.

The news had spread quickly and Mike went right away and swooped up his girls who were being watched by some of the neighbors until he arrived. That first night back home, he held them so tightly, they squealed. They knew what had happened to Grace because the police had come to the house and Mrs. Racanelli was taken to the hospital.

But for every black cloud some sunshine pierces through. They had had Christmas here on Godfrey Street this year. Right in the room where Connie and Antonietta had been born and where their mother had died. The Children's Christmas Fund had again brought presents, but this time, Mike, too had had a little money to buy them each a small token gift as well. He also had shamed his brother-in-law Sal into buying his little nieces some new things. Then, just after the New Year, he had taken them all to the photographer's studio where they had their family photo taken. It had been important to Mike that they record events in their lives, because he had never ceased to wish he had had even a photograph of his own father to see what the man's face and eyes looked like.

During the photo sitting, Antonietta wanted to sit on his knee as she often did at home. So he let her climb up. She felt extra special because of her special status as the baby. Connie, daughter number three, was very proud of her Mary Jane shoes: she felt they were more stylish than her sisters' tie-ups. The two older girls huddled around knowing he loved them all. He told them that they were all beautiful no matter what they wore, but they loved the new dresses and he was happy that they were happy.

The last time he had had a photo taken was when Raffaela was alive. At that time, only two of the girls had been born and she was expecting Connie. He loved reliving the short nine years he had had with his lovely wife.

Dominic Mangone broke him out of his reverie saying, "Looks like the heat's gonna start early. I'm gone plant some beans." Each year the two men planted vegetable gardens. Dominic with his two hands planted a much larger piece of land than Mike. In fact, the man owned an extra building lot that he had no intention of building on, he used it entirely for his garden and chicken coops.

Even after he lost his arm, Mike had never stopped planting his entire back yard with beans, tomatoes, cucumbers, eggplants and whatever else caught his eye. During the summer when the vegetables started to mature, Dominic made his usual assessment of the two gardens. "Mike, you have one hand less than me and land about half the size, but you always reap twice as many vegetables. What you puttin' in the ground?"

The standing joke, Mike would reply, "I got better sun than you."

Today Dominic took a different tack. In his very slow, soft voice he said, "Mike, while you fixing your roof, I'm gonna putta my beans in so they get a head start over yours."

Acknowledging the joke with a chuckle, Mike turned to the serious project ahead of him. "With this flat roof, it's important to put fresh tar on it every two years; otherwise it will leak. We had a lot of snow this past winter and it just sits on the roof. I gotta be sure it's secure," he said.

"I'm gonna tar the roof tomorrow morning. Is your wife gonna be home in the morning? I just want to be sure the girls don't climb the ladder when I'm up there. I know Rosie understands, but sometimes the younger ones could forget. If your wife could keep an eye while they play outside, I 'ppreciate it."

Turning his body like a short, stocky robot, the small, sweet man saluted an affirmative about the kids, then walked to his garden shed to get a hoe.

The next morning was a little chilly. After they had gone to nine o'clock mass, they all went inside to change. Making sure, they would remain in the house playing, Mike lifted and placed the heavy wooden ladder against the house. Then, he hoisted the rope that extended the upper half of the ladder till it hooked into the eave of the roof. Mike climbed with his one hand, carrying what he needed to do his roofing job under his stump on the first two trips up. Before making his third ascent with the buckets hooked to a belt so he could climb with his hand, he went inside to check on the girls. Connie announced that they were going over to play with Josephine.

"You all go next door and stay away from the ladder," he warned. "Watch Antonietta cause she's still little."

He watched them race next door and Mrs. Mangone greet them. Then, he climbed with the heavy belt strapped to the buckets and slung crossways over his neck and other shoulder. Once up, he got busy laying the tarpaper before spreading the sticky, black goo to one half of the roof. It would be too much to do the whole roof in one day. He would do half today and half next weekend. Moreover, he still had to make lunch for the kids.

From above he saw the girls playing next door and he went about his work. He was deeply absorbed for a good hour when he heard a small voice say, "PaPa, what are you doing up here? Are you playing a game?" Shocked, he saw Antonietta on the top rung of the ladder looking across the roof at him.

Though alarmed, he moved slowly and talked calmly and quietly. "Oh, baby, you don't want to be up here. It's all black and dirty. Why did you climb up the ladder? You remember I told you not to?"

"Oh, PaPa, I forgot because I wanted to see you."

Grace Racanelli' s lifeless body sudden came before him.

He got to the ladder and assessed the situation.

"Okay, baby, I'm gonna talk with you and you climb back down very carefully."

Then from below, Connie, Lena and Rosie yelled. "Antonietta, we've been looking all over for you. What are you doing up on the ladder?"

Suddenly, Antonietta looked down. "PaPa," she screamed, "I can't go down; I'll fall. I'm sorry, PaPa. I'm scared." She began to cry.

Not sure, about what to do, he thought quickly. "Dear God, help me," he said aloud. "Okay, come on up the final step, I'm a-holding you."

With her on the roof and off the rung of the ladder, he then positioned himself on the step she had just come off of. Then leaning up against the ladder heavily so as not to lose his balance, he urged Antonietta to hug him. "You close your eyes now and hold me tight around the neck." Then, with his one arm wrapped around her little body, but his fingers holding on to the rungs, he backed down the twenty feet to the backyard. His other daughters were holding their breath, watching with scared faces.

When they got to the bottom, they all gave a cheer. Connie said, "I don't know how you did that PaPa!"

Mike, though, suddenly felt sick. What if something had happened to her," he thought? He didn't even know how he had pulled that off with only one arm. He hadn't been sure if he could hang on to her and the ladder when he started down.

Regaining his composure, he took the little girl by the hand and her sisters followed them inside, where he made some lunch. Rosie and Lena put dishes on the table and Connie helped him with the food. Then, with all sitting at the table, he said softly. "When I tell you something, it's very important you listen. You could get very hurt if you don't listen. You can fall from ladders. Terrible things could happen."

They could tell from his voice and his look that this was important. Antonietta hung her head. They all nodded, and said, "Yes, PaPa." The silence hung and Mike knew they got the message.

Then they jumped up as if on cue and they were a well-practiced dance troupe. Quickly they cleaned and put away their plates, gave him a quick hug and kiss, and scurried back outside again.

Mike sat there with his head in his hand. He lingered over his yet untouched food. Then he said out loud, "Thank you, God. Please don't take any one of my girls. I need them all."

CHAPTER SEVEN

Mike fought hard to tamp down his rage as he fled the rectory on West Avenue at almost a run toward Wall Street. He swallowed hard. He immediately began thinking about what to do about his problem. Fleeting thoughts came and went. When the wisp of a solution emerged, it was crowded out by his anger at the priest whom he was forced to address as Monsignor.

As he made his way down toward Wall Street, a whipping frigid wind cut at his face and bare head. The thin jacket he wore was suitable for early October, but it was no match for the December Connecticut arctic-like temperatures.

He realized slowly that he was more angry with himself than the Irish priest. He should have known better. Nevertheless, his friend Jim, the local undertaker, had lulled him into thinking this was a viable option. Mike had tremendous respect and affection for his friend, so he had acted on his guidance.

Nevertheless, this wintry Friday morning, Mike had told Monsignor Finn in no uncertain terms that he would never set foot in his church again. He now was feeling the tugs of regret at his outburst, though delivered in a quiet voice. Mike and his family had found St. Mary's, the second oldest parish in the Bridgeport diocese, a comforting place. The parish dated back to 1848, though the original wooden church had been burned down by members of an anti-Catholic, anti-immigrant group. Since moving to Norwalk from South Norwalk in 1916, Mike had enjoyed the big organ and the beautiful stained glass windows of the Irish-immigrant-built, Gothic-revival-style cathedral. When he and Raffaela had planned to marry, it had been Mike's choice to leave South Norwalk, where the Italians were fully ensconced, to move to an area of town and a church that he knew was definitely Irish domain. Despite the horror stories he'd heard, he found several Irishmen who had been sincere and kind to him, so he accepted Jim's recommendation as being valid for Italians as well as the Irish. Each of the four girls had been baptized at St. Mary's, even though most of the baptisms on any given month were Irish babies. And, it certainly was a beautiful church.

He struggled now to remember what brought him to humble himself as he had this morning. Yet, he knew full well that swallowing his pride was not too great a sacrifice for his children. It wasn't their fault that their mother had died. They had no part in the disaster that had taken his arm. The depression that made finding work impossible was the world's doing, not theirs. Yet, these innocent little girls were facing a winter without shoes. He had put cardboard in each of the four pairs twice. Now, there was barely anything left to hold the cardboard in place, the soles almost completely gone. Antonietta's shoes were too small and yet he continued to shove her feet into them. Her sisters were close to outgrowing theirs. He had hoped for more for his children than he had had and he would be damned if they would ever go barefoot. He never let them even in summer though they complained mightily at his insistence that they keep their shoes on.

He had heard snippets of conversations that referenced the church's generosity from several of the men as he waited in line after line to see about possible jobs. Then he had confided in his friend Jim that he had no idea what he was going to do about getting the girls the replacement shoes that they so badly needed.

"Mike, you need to go down to the parish house and talk with Monsignor Finn. He has a pot of money he gives to the poor for things like shoes for their kids."

Mike had pondered the information for several weeks, hoping some other solution would materialize. Then, when the thermometer took a nosedive, he mustered the courage to go ask the church for money to buy his kids shoes. He knew the Irish stuck together. The discrimination of the Irish against Italians was legendary.

Against his better judgment, he rationalized that the Irish priest would take compassion on the children whom he saw in the front pews at mass every Sunday. Rosie and Lena, the two oldest, had already made their first Holy Communion and the two younger ones were in preparation and would receive the blessed sacrament this next May. The third child, Connie, had commented that Monsignor had asked her name a few Sundays ago. When she answered, "Concetta," he had said it was a beautiful name. Connie had remarked on how nice he was. To top it off in Mike's mind, the church was in the process of a major renovation, during a depression no less; he felt sure they could spare a few dollars to help him.

Mike had knocked at the front door and when the housekeeper who opened the door asked what he wanted, he had simply said, "I need to talk with the Monsignor." He was not even offered a seat while he waited, then after nearly thirty minutes standing, she returned to say that Monsignor Finn would see him now. The frail-looking clergyman asked him to sit in a wooden chair available for visitors. He wore a simple black cassock with a big cross hanging from his neck. He had a ring on one finger with a large red stone set high. The man's hands looked soft and delicate. The office had two walls with shelves filled with books. Mike thought how wonderful it would be to able to read what was inside. The pastor sat behind an impressive desk made from solid wood. A crucifix hung on the wall facing Mike, reminding him that this wasn't the office of an important businessman, but rather the office of a man of God.

The Monsignor had seemed impatient as Mike tried to relay his predicament. He started out by saying that he had heard Monsignor was a generous man who took care of those in need, avoiding the word poor. The priest could clearly see the man had only one arm, but Mike did not reference it. He wasn't asking for anyone to feel sorry for him. He wanted something for his children. Something very important. He was providing food for them in every way he knew how and a safe roof over their heads, but the shoes were eluding him. It was a terrible time.

Mike never got very far in his planned statement. Instead, the priest cut him off, saying in a heavy Irish brogue, "You got it wrong. I have no money to help you for shoes, food or anything else."

Mike had at first sat stunned at the heartless manner in which the clergyman had delivered the words. Then, he stood up. In a choked voice he said, "You help those you want to help. God is watching and he knows your sins."

The Monsignor had responded by saying, "You better leave now," perhaps afraid that his visitor might strike him.

As he turned to go, Mike quietly said, "You'll never see me set foot in your church again."

Now, embarrassed, angry and humbled, he still had to figure out a way to get four pairs of shoes for his girls. He began to have misgivings about not allowing Antonietta and Concetta to be adopted. However, he brushed the thought aside quickly. He couldn't bear thinking that he might not see them. What if someone mistreated them? That they might be separated from their sisters and himself was a crushing thought.

But he could not buy them shoes. What kind of a father was he?

During his fifteen-minute walk home, he figured out a plan. It too would involve asking for something, but it wouldn't be charity. He didn't want charity. He had simply made a mistake in coming to the church.

The following Sunday he walked the girls to church, but he didn't go in with them. He had said his prayers that morning and that night before going to sleep as he always did, but he had told God he couldn't go in and honor that sinful man who was posing as a man of God. Then, he asked for God's forgiveness.

CHAPTER EIGHT

Springtime 1933

"Chocolate pop a nickel," hawked Mike right after he blew the squawk horn. It certainly got people's attention. He had parked himself near the baseball field on New Canaan Ave. It been a little more than two years that he had been performing the five-nights-a-week, Saturday-and-Sunday-afternoon ritual of selling ice cream pops, gum, candy, and cigarettes at all the sports events at the fields in the Broad River section of town.

He had asked John, his brother-in-law the cobbler, to fashion a leather shoulder strap that attached to the right handle of the pushcart loaded with his wares; he would sling it over his right shoulder when he needed to push the cart along. The wooden peddler's cart had two large front wheels with wire spokes and two sturdy wooden peg legs in the back. Inquiring at the bus depot, he had secured a coin machine like those worn by the bus drivers, and he strapped it to his waist.

Each afternoon during the warmer months, he would push his cart laden with the sundry items down Godfrey Street, over to the

Crystal Ice House on Crescent. Then he would walk up Commerce Street, over to Wall Street to get to Knight Street, where he purchased the ice cream from a company called Fro-joy, a division of the Sealtest company. He could cover the one-mile distance quickly, but the real work was wheeling the heavily laden cart to his choice location on New Canaan Avenue. The walk was nearly one and a half miles and took him a good forty minutes. Once he arrived, he would unhook the strap from his right shoulder and use his left to do all his work. With that one sturdy left hand, he served mothers, fathers and kids the tasty chocolate-covered ice cream pops on a stick, kept firm by the ice he picked up each afternoon at Crystal Ice.

Unfortunately, the games often went to well after nine. By the time he walked home, pushing the cart up the hill, he would find the girls had gone to bed as he had instructed.

On the nights he didn't sell all of his creamy treats, he would wake them up. "Hurry, you gotta eat the ice cream before it melts," he'd implore.

Bleary-eyed, they would comply. They never ceased to enjoy it even though it was delivered a good hour after they had been asleep. They sat up and ate, sometimes more than one apiece. With chocolate smudges and happy faces they quickly went back to sleep.

During the winter months, he parked himself outside of factories in the area. In fact, that was how he had started. Cigarettes, gum and such were the favored items. On those days, he brought home enough to cover his expenses and some for groceries and to save a little something toward the girls' needs—like shoes.

In the better weather, his ice cream sales helped clear enough to help toward paying some of the utility bills and to put toward the mortgage payments. The mortgage was his largest burden.

He remembered that embarrassing day with Monsignor Finn. He had begged God to help him and suddenly the idea for the pushcart hit him like a thunderbolt. "Why didn't I think of this before?" he said to himself.

Since putting together the pieces, getting the required food peddler's license, and paying back the cost of the cart made for him by the carriage house people, he was doing okay. As a peddler at night, he had the ability to get work during the day on most days during the spring and summer. This spring things seemed to be picking up. Each morning he'd go to the corner of Main and Wall streets and wait with a dozen or so other men for the callouts. He often would get an assignment working as a laborer on a variety of projects around town. He had worked on numerous projects already, such as widening the sidewalks and digging ditches for the sewers and storm drains. He heard there was more to come and he felt that good times were ahead. There was talk of some new schools and a post office to be built, but not for a couple of years yet.

After a long period of nothing, the work assignments were coming almost weekly now. If he worked at least two days, he could manage. The work day ended at four-thirty p.m. On those days, he hustled to get all the supplies he needed for his cart and work at least one ball game. In the spring and fall, it was dark earlier and if he worked, he skipped the ice cream offering because he couldn't get the ice and the confection and get to the field in time to do any business. He would focus on the sundries. On the weekends, he could work several games on Saturday and Sunday; those were his most lucrative days.

Everyone seemed to look for him and he had become a well-known figure at those events. He was grateful for the cheer he seemed to bring others and the small profits were like a treasure to assuage his great need in providing for his daughters.

After his upsetting encounter with the Monsignor, he had swallowed his pride and had gone to see his brother-in-law Sal. He had shamed the girls' Uncle Sal into buying them their communion dresses and loaning him the money for the shoes. That winter after two months of selling the small items from his cart as the factories let out at lunch time and for the evening, he had earned enough to repay him for the girls shoes.

Rosie had always been a bit frail and sickly and he worried about her health. He made sure to buy fresh fruit during the winter months, and his garden in the backyard that had always been a source of enjoyment for him now was a lifeline providing manna from heaven with fresh vegetables for them. He worked it as much as he could, and the girls helped, but it was difficult to do more with the need to go to look for a job every day. Despite the summer garden, there were things he could not plant. Like bananas. He bought his girls fresh bananas whenever he could after the woman who was the principal of the high school had told him that growing girls needed the vitamins found in them. The girls loved them, and they soon discovered that not everyone had them. Bananas were an extravagance. It wasn't often that the girls had something others did not.

"We have fresh bananas," became their favorite line to say aloud for their friends and acquaintances to overhear at school.

He kept the girls' hair very short. He was concerned they would get the dreaded lice and be quarantined. With the other three watching and making signs showing that it was extremely short, the one seated under the scissors often cried or sat petrified. He reminded them, "*Sta sodo*"—stay still. He didn't want them to be unhappy, but he had to keep them all looking neat. Most of all he had to prevent them from getting the terrible bugs and being quarantined. That would be a horrible ordeal and one sure to have the authorities look in on him to ensure he was not being negligent. He lived with the ever-present fear that they might take them away. Lice would be a signal for the schools to send a social worker.

With his one hand and well-sharpened scissors, he managed to trim their hair straight and he washed their hair every day in the kitchen sink.

It had been an adjustment after losing his right arm, but he had learned to do pretty much everything, including tying his shoes, that he had done before as a right-handed person with two limbs. He felt bad because the girls were home alone quite a lot. He had admonished them never to leave the house at night and never to open the door for anyone

CHAPTER NINE

November 1934

"PaPa, we're freezing," they said simultaneously. He looked at their bare hands and they were pink, so he said, "Just a li'la bit longer."

They huddled as he lifted the cap on the lamp to expose the wick and his two oldest daughters cupped their hands around so Mike could light it. Then he carefully placed the cap on and set it down. When they had helped him light four, he dragged the sawhorse across the road to block off half the street, then carried the wooden ladder and propped it against the first post. Hurrying back to where the girls were, he took the two lanterns into his one hand over to the post. Placing one lantern on the ground, he climbed up the ladder holding the one lamp in his hand while holding onto the ladder at the same time.

That one hung, he scurried back down the ladder, carried it across the street, set it against the post and repeated the task of going up the ladder with the lantern in hand. Returning to the girls, he repeated the process several more times while they waited.

Mike had been at this lamplighter job for several months now and it was going pretty well doing it alone. But on the windy nights, he would wait until the two little ones had fallen asleep and take Rosie and Lena with him. Then, they would lock the door, alerting Mrs. Perri in the apartment downstairs that they were going to be out for a few hours and to keep an eye and ear out for them. He wanted to be sure she knew they were up there alone in case of a fire. He was so grateful to Catherina Perri. She and her husband were childless and she always was very kind to the girls. All four of the girls were sound sleepers and once asleep never woke up until morning.

On those windy evenings, Rosie and Lena helped protect the flame from the wind for him, because with the one hand, he could not light it and shield it from the wind at the same time. Evenings like tonight were typical. After the girls had helped him keep the flame from going out, he would turn the wick up carefully and proceed to hang the lanterns. His section of responsibility was Main Avenue from the end of their street at the corner of Godfrey all the way up to the Winnipauk section, just beyond Broad Street. When they did the lamp at the corner of Main and Broad, he would gently remind them, "Your mother is buried right back there in St. Mary's Cemetery," pointing down the road. But in the twilight, it was impossible to see. They never went to the cemetery at night, but always went on Sunday mornings after church.

Being a main thoroughfare, Main Avenue needed the gas lamps. Most other streets didn't have lights. Mike knew that the entire state of Connecticut was converting to electricity. In Norwalk, electricity mostly was used to run the trolley lines now, but the electrification of the area was occurring at a rapid pace and this job would be gone soon, too.

The November wind was whipping high; without gloves, Rosie

and Lena were feeling it. Mike quietly urged them on. He watched carefully that their little hands still had color.

"Keep your hands in your pockets tilla I com'a back," he instructed as he hung the recently lit ones. They waited for him to return. Then together they did another four. Stamping their feet and jumping up and down, Lena and Rosie joked as they watched their PaPa in the distance.

"What do you think, Ro? Have we had enough? Let's tell PaPa we can't stand the cold any longer. He'll feel bad and let us go home," Lena said mischievously.

"No. We have to help him. He can't do it alone; it's too windy. Yes, it's cold, but not that cold. Besides, we just have a little more to go and we'll be done," came Rosie's quick retort, in a scolding tone.

Not to be outdone, Lena ribbed her older sister, saying, "You always think you're the mother."

"Somebody has to help PaPa with our little sisters," answered Rosie hotly. "What is PaPa going to buy food with if he doesn't work? The trouble with you, Lena, is you don't think about anything. You just like to play."

Overhearing part of the conversation as he was walking back, Mike felt himself crumble. They were just little girls. Why did he need their help? He had accepted the job because he needed it and he assured the boss that he could do it. Yet he had failed to figure out how he could do this job on the windy nights without the girls' help.

He was determined to keep them together; he hoped they would understand when they were a little older. He just had to get them through this difficult period. Work was extremely scarce. The bank, where he had had his $400 in savings, closed. He had lost his entire savings in the bank run in 1930. It had been a devastating blow. He had needed that cushion to pay his mortgage in case he couldn't work and to take care of his girls. After that bank run, work opportunities shriveled and he found himself behind in his mortgage payments. Often, his tenants didn't have the money to pay him either. He understood. Lots of them were struggling, too.

During the worst of the past few years, Mr. Chase, from whom he had purchased the house and who held his note, had been extremely patient.

Mike remembered his embarrassment when he had come to the house saying, "Mike, you didn't send my payment."

Humbly, he said, "I no gotta it. I'll getta next month." He was grateful for the mortgage holder's kindness when he said, "I know it's tough times." He agreed to wait for yet another month for the bi-annual payment.

The past several years had been a test, he felt sure of it. Despite the personal and economic challenges, he truly believed that things would be better in time. He missed Raffaela. Yet he found that hole in his heart and life was being filled by the girls. They were his sanity and his all-consuming concern. He worried about leaving Concetta and Antonietta in the house asleep; during the nights when the wind was calm, he would leave Rosie to watch them all. He felt she was mature enough to get help if something were to go wrong. On those nights, it took him longer to finish, but he did the job alone whenever he could. When Rosie was there to watch Lena, Concetta and Antonietta, or the little ones were left behind, under the watchful eye of Mrs. Perri, he never shook the gnawing feelings. What if one of them became sick while he was gone. What if there was a fire? And what would the woman from Child Services say if she knew? He shook off the terrifying thought. He would die if they took his children or if something happened to them.

Hurrying as much as he could, he checked the color of their hands; he still saw pink. He checked frequently and as soon as it looked like their hands were pale, he would tell them to scurry on home.

This job had been a godsend. He scrounged whatever he could do. Often there were periods when he could find nothing. It was so ironic. He had saved enough and the girls had grown up enough that he get them all home again, and the market crash dealt yet another blow that set him back.

Now as they were getting close to finishing, he noticed that Rosie had gotten quiet after the first few. He didn't know what she was thinking, but he guessed.

As they repeated the process several times along the last stretch of Main Street, he remembered how she had seen him head in hand crying in the kitchen when her mother was alive after his accident. He had been pitiful. Rosie was old enough to remember the aftermath of his accident and amputation. He remembered her worried face when he watched her at lunchtime in the schoolyard after their mother died. She came over to him each time. He would pat her on the head, her eyes responding to his love.

As he turned to walk toward them, they were faced away from him and he overheard Rosie saying to her sister.

"Lena, I'm not going to complain to PaPa about the cold any more. After all, he doesn't complain. He could easily have sent all of us to the children's home," she said, sounding like an older woman with years of experience. "You know he never said so to us, but I heard the grownups talking when they came to visit after our mother died."

Lena remained quiet.

As they made their way home that night, Rosie said, to no one in particular, but loud enough so her PaPa and sister could hear. "PaPa, the old lamplighter, and we're his little band of princesses!"

CHAPTER TEN

Christmas was almost upon them. It had been a bleak year, even worse than the past one for work. He was barely making it at all. He had started a small grocery store in the spring to try to earn money, figuring everyone needed to buy food. Right along Main Avenue, the location was perfect. In an empty storefront on the corner of Main and School Street, he'd worked out a deal with his brother-in-law, who owned the building. Appealing to Sal's love for his dead sister's children, he had asked if he could have the space for free because it had been empty a long time. Mike didn't see any prospects coming for it anytime soon. However, when Sal insisted on ten percent of his earnings, Mike said okay; he didn't want charity.

He also worked a deal with a supply house for the food stuffs. The girls helped him stock shelves and bag groceries. Everybody who came in loved the girls and things went well pretty much throughout the Summer. In early September, the girls went back to school and though it was just a hop across from the schoolyard, they had school work to do in the afternoons. They were great helpers on Saturday. Everything closed on Sundays.

Overtime, more and more people came who wanted to buy on credit. Mike felt sorry for them. Money was scarce. They appealed to him with their hungry children in line, and he was a softy.

By the time November rolled around, he was in trouble. The extended credit didn't come in, and he needed to pay his supplier. He realized those who did pay could not earn him enough to cover those who couldn't. He operated another month and said, "Sorry, no credit." He remained open one more month until he sold everything he had. Paid his debts and shut it down.

This past week, when the woman from Children and Family Services had come to do a home visit, she whispered to him that she would put all the girls' names into the Children's Christmas Fund. They would all get something for Christmas.

He was pleased and tried not to have his pride injured because he didn't like charity, and he hated it that he couldn't afford any extras for his children. He could only manage to feed them, dress them, house them and love them. By paying Mrs. DiStasio who lived across the street to sew the girls' dresses, they always looked lovely. He'd learned from Raffaela how to look for the fabric sales and the DiStasio woman was talented. She took the fabric he brought and fashioned it into dresses with pretty pinafore fronts.

He thought back to the year that Rosie had learned in school that you needed to hang stockings so Santa would come. Not knowing any better, she had strung four of his large stocks on a line tacked from one end of a corner of the kitchen to the other. Poor child hadn't realized that the kerosene stove would burn them in short order.

"You gonna burn the house down," he scolded. "What are you thinking, Rosie? You know better."

"But PaPa, they told us at school if we hang our stockings Santa Claus will come. Santa can't come to bring us something without them," she sobbed.

Mike had pulled the stockings down, all the while thinking if he hadn't come home early he would not have been able to avoid the fire that surely would have resulted.

Fire hazard removed, he went to seek Rosie and found her lying on her bed. He hugged her and told her, "You gotta keep vigilant about fire. The kerosene stove could have burned those stockings and the smoke could have killed you all.

"You're gonna have some presents. Santa Claus doesn't need the stockings. You are very special girls; he's a-gonna find you."

Now, with the girls asleep and the radio playing music with the volume dial set at the lowest level, found himself weeping as he sat alone by the window looking out at the snow-covered street.

He learned from a neighbor that for the past week, the girls had sat by window playing with a candle, watching other kids in the snow out on the street below. He had told them that when he wasn't home they were to remain inside. Obeying his rules, they sat playing with a lighted candle in the window—despite the fact that he told them fire was dangerous. He feared a fire more than anything. He had watched a house off of Main Avenue burn to ashes because of a knocked-over candle not too long ago.

They might accidentally burn the house down. He had been upset to learn of the nightly activity fearing they might get hurt. Nevertheless, he smiled inside as he recognized they had indeed followed his instructions and were just doing something to entertain themselves.

They were such good girls he didn't have the heart to scold Rosie again, nor her sisters.

Each night in the summer months when he had come home

from his push cart sales foray, he had put all the coins out on the single dresser they all shared. While they were asleep, he counted it carefully. He had told them only once, when he first started this business, that they were never to touch his money. He found in counting it each morning that they had never taken even a penny. He was pleased and proud they had mastered the importance of obeying him.

They were growing up honest, loving and charming. They often made him laugh by repeating his miss-pronounced words. They seemed to get the most pleasure from his articulation of the breakfast cereal corn flakes, which they claimed always came out, "corn flags" and when he tried to tell them the teachers were very strict about the rules for good reason, they claimed it sounded like, "strickle"; instead of taking him seriously, they laughed.

Sometimes on Sunday afternoons before he would head out to ply the crowd at the ball games with his cart in the summer, they would ask him for money to go to the movies. It was an extravagance, and his first answer was usually, *"Lasciami stare."* The girls had gotten used to his Calabrian dialect phrase for "leave me alone." They would keep pestering him until he eventually gave in. Then, as he put out the four nickels on the kitchen table, they would grab the coins and run out, yelling, "Thank you, PaPa!" while he reminded them in a forceful voice, "Watch out for the train and always stay together!"

They were growing up so fast. Soon they would be young ladies. He felt a pang of guilt as he thought of the void in their lives. He wondered who would talk with them about the womanly things when it was time for them to marry, the kind of things a mother says to her daughter when the time comes. Mrs. Perri, who lived downstairs in the house and who had no children of her own, had always loved his girls. She had taught them to make bread and about other important household things. He knew she and Mrs. DiStasio across the street had talked with Rosie about becoming a maiden, when Rosie had turned 12. The adults were counting on Rosie to pass the information to her sisters.

He was ever reminding them never to go anywhere or with anyone alone and that all four of them needed to stay together wherever they went. He implored the neighbors to keep an eye out for them. The girls were extremely popular; they had made friends with several of the other children on the street. However, not until recently had he allow them to go out with anyone but their sisters. The two girls who lived next door were their ages—the Salvato girl, Rose, and her cousin, Josephine; there were several others from two enormous families on the streets. The Tavella and Calzone girls living next door and across the street, all made for a happy group playing outside in the summer time. Mike enjoyed hearing all of the lilting voices and the chatter and giggles. It made his heart feel good to see them all happy.

It suddenly occurred to him that he needed to start thinking about when it came time for them to marry. They were beautiful, thoughtful and engaging and, no doubt, they would find husbands worthy of them. Will I have the means to give them a proper wedding? he wondered. As worry swelled within him, he thought, There's time enough to make it happen. There are more important matters ahead of that now. I will think about it another day.

CHAPTER ELEVEN

It was Sunday morning, one of those bleak fall days with gray-white clouds and the sun nowhere to be found. The stump that was his right arm throbbed continuously. He knew it would rain at some point.

He worried about Rosie. She was such a tiny creature. At sixteen, she carried the weight of the world. His oldest child was now a woman. She had stayed with him after her mother died; she was eight years old when she had to assume the role of mother for the other three, all so little. Antonietta had only been two and a half years old when Raffaela's life had been snuffed out that fateful night by the cerebral hemorrhage. A tiny blood rupture, the doctor had said. Now, eight years gone, he still missed her tremendously. He could almost taste the saltiness of her skin. She had been a tiny woman, just like her daughters, and full breasted. She was a quiet and serene woman. Almost nine years his senior, she had been almost childlike in her love and devotion to him. Rosie, his oldest, was a lot like her mother, not very social and outgoing, but tenderhearted, organized and smart.

He had found Rosie a job in a garment factory in South Norwalk. He felt terrible that she had to leave school, but at sixteen she could read and write better than many with much more education. She had to help him, though. It was critical for their well-being and for her own future. He had to find some way to amass some savings so he could someday provide for them to marry.

Rosie had told him the work was hard. In some ways she was so hearty and in others so frail. He was scared that she might fall ill or something might happen to her. There were so many frightening stories of what went on in those factories. Each night he pried gently for information on what had transpired during the day. Today, she had confessed that they had made her uncomfortable. They had asked her to model a full slip. The woman had told Rosie, "A man will come in and look at you to see how the sample fits, because you have a model's sized body." The woman had promised that the man would not touch her or the garment in any way. And, Rosie had said, it had been just as the woman had said, the man had not touched her or the full length slip. Moreover, the woman had remained present throughout the time he was checking to see how the slip fit.

Regardless of the purpose or intentions, it was obvious this had made Rosie quite uncomfortable. Mike was furious. She was supposed to be boxing clothing, not modeling. He struggled with his thoughts. She was so pretty and with her tiny, perfectly formed, full-figured body, she would be called upon other times to model. He could not put his daughter in harm's way. He pondered the situation. Was it really harm? Had the company owners' actions been a glimpse of bolder things to come? He didn't want his daughter to be uncomfortable and he certainly did not want her to become a model. He feared the implications of such a profession. Yet, he knew they had not paid nor offered her any more money than the agreed-on laborer's wage, so perhaps this was a one-time thing.

"Dear God, what must I do?" he gasped. "I have gotten them this far. They are all four very good girls." They always remained in the house until he came home. They went everywhere together, as he instructed, chaperoning each other. He had been truly blessed. So many girls their ages were headstrong and gave their parents grief beyond belief. Yet, he, a single parent, had four angels as children. Early on, he struggled just to keep them, then to feed them. Now that they were sixteen, fifteen, thirteen and eleven, he had even more to worry about. They were all now maidens, and could get pregnant. How could he talk to them about such things?

Just a few years back, the neighborhood women had told Rosie the essentials and Rosie had passed the information to each of the others as their time came. Lena had been the first to get her period. She had cried aloud, screaming, "I'm bleeding to death."

He had kept quiet. He didn't know how he was supposed to respond. Rosie thought she was keeping all this from him, but he knew everything, though he never let on. He knew they needed their privacy, despite the tiny living quarters.

They each had one half of drawer in the chest that all four shared. There would be more for them once they all went to work. Then they would each have the ability to buy some clothes, attract a nice young man. For his part, Mike focused on keeping them safe, feeding them and providing them with a constant in their lives—unconditional parental love. He made sure to instill the values that he knew—honesty, industriousness, being polite and, above all, for them to do well in school. What he wouldn't have given to have gone to school. Someday, when they were grown, he would go and ask the teacher on West Avenue to teach him to write and read.

He dozed with his head on his hand and when it dropped, he awoke startled. He thought he had felt Raffaela's hand on his head.

She had told him he was doing good for their children. He felt a single tear slide down his cheek. He got up and walked down the flight of stairs outside to wait for the girls to come back from mass. When they arrived with the red on their cheeks like poster paint and their smiles and hair all aglow, despite the dismal day, he made his decision.

That night he told Rosie, "You no go to that job anymore. Tomorrow, I find you a new job."

Secretly Rosie was pleased, but she didn't reveal her elation, except to say, "Yes, PaPa." She had been afraid to tell him; but knew she should. Now, she recognized that no matter what, she couldn't keep anything from PaPa. She was PaPa's favorite. Though he had never said so, she had always known that. PaPa had held her hand when she was sick. He had patted her head when she was playing in the schoolyard, when the others had been boarded at Mrs. Racanelli's after MaMa died and she was staying with Uncle John and Zia Antonietta. He would call her over and ask how they were treating her. He looked so skinny and so sad, then. She wanted to tell him how awful it was to be apart from him and her sisters, but she didn't then. She knew he would keep his promise.

"I gonna take you home soon," he had assured her after she had stayed only briefly with her aunt and uncle. "Now, you have to stay here, because you and your sisters are little. I have to work; and there's no one to take care of you."

True to his word, Rosie came home first to be with him again. Then, after about a year, the others had come home. In the interim, he had gone almost every night to check on them. While it was only about a mile and a half away, without a car and with his very late hours from painting houses and other odd jobs, he often came home well after ten p.m. On Sundays, he always took her to visit her sisters.

Yes, PaPa had kept his promise. She could count on him. In the morning, they went to look for a new place for Rosie to work. Riding the bus, they hardly spoke. But she smiled at him and he smiled back. He was so proud of her.

CHAPTER TWELVE

Early Spring 1936

The shop was nearly empty as Mike walked to the counter. He spotted the owner of the Brandman paint store on Main Street and waited until he caught the man's eye. Mike had purposely gone late in the day when he knew the shop would be slow. Brandman was a good man who had seen Mike on many occasions around town digging and shoveling ditches or lighting lamps. Most often, Brandman had seen the one-armed man walking with at least a couple of his daughters in tow going into downtown Norwalk. Brandman also knew Mike because the man had run a small grocery store for about a year in the neighborhood, though it was now closed. He had stopped in there a few times to pick up something for his wife. He remembered the shop was poorly stocked, but it did have the essentials, definitely put together by someone without any capital to get it going.

Mike caught Brandman's eye and removed his hat and asked pleasantly, "How you?"

The storeowner eyed him with reserve. He knew the man was a

hard worker and always polite, but he wondered what Mike would want in a painting supply store. He hoped it wasn't a request for charity. He knew the man had been through some difficult times, but the Brandmans had been approached by so many people who thought because theirs was a thriving business, the Brandman family could give away everything.

"Can't complain," he responded a little petulantly.

"I been'a working lots of different jobs around town with the WPA," said Mike, matter-of-factly. "At one of the schools, I was the cleanup man to the guys painting the building inside. They mak'a good money and they work only eight hours a day.

"I think I can do this painting pretty good. I try it on some of the walls not yet done after the painters go home. My hand is very steady. I 'ma strong, but I don't know how to mix colors. I was hoping you could learn me something about it," he said in a humble tone.

Caught off guard by the question, Brandman felt guilty for his earlier thought.

"Mike, you would do well at painting on someone's crew, but if you do this on your own, you have to deal with ladders, brushes, paint cans and the lids. There's a lot of things involved that with all respect you might have trouble with," he said in a compassionate tone. The Brandman family business had been there on Main Street since 1907 and the family had a second location in South Norwalk. All the sons worked in the business, which seemed to stay busy five days a week with painting contractors. On Saturday, the patrons were mostly housewives and their husbands who were coerced into doing a small project.

"You mean because of me having one arm. I can handle the ladders and everything, but I don't know how to mix the colors. I know lotsa people who need someone to paint for cheap. I don't charge a lot. I can get work."

Brandman thought for a few minutes. "Well, the colors are the least of what you need to worry about. I can help you with that. You take this card with the paint samples and when your customer picks the color they want, you bring it to me and we will mix it up to make just like the picture here.

"You need to find out if they want high gloss or flat finish. The high gloss works really well for kitchens and bathrooms. People seem to like the flat finish for bed and living rooms. Outside paint is different from inside paint," Brandman said.

"The outside paint is made to resist the weather. It also costs more. The colors available also are different. With outside work, sometimes you have to scrape and get off the old paint that's peeling. You often have to sand it smooth, then cover that sanded finish with a primer. The primer will even everything out and then you apply the paint. Most often with the old houses, you will need two coats. You can price the job also based on the number of coats a customer wants. If they want two coats outside, and use the good paints I sell, they will not need painting again for a very long time.

"Here. These brochures here are for outside paint," he said, handing Mike two cards with color squares ranging from two shades of white to dark blues.

"You'll need paint remover for spills and splatters. I'm sure if you watched the crews at the schools you saw how they put down a drop cloth and cover the floors. It will be harder in a home because people have sofas and refrigerators you can't move. So covering and taping everything is probably the biggest part of the job. When painting a house on the outside, you have to be very careful you don't lean your ladder on critical things like electric wires and windows.

"We can sell you everything you need right here. But you'll have to pay cash. If we do enough business together then I can extend credit for a month and I'll give you the paint contractor's discount," he said.

"With all the supplies you will have to buy, such as ladders, brushes, coveralls, drop clothes and the paint, you will probably have to get your money up front from your customer. Otherwise, it's a pretty big cash outlay."

Mike had listened intently and then asked, "Is the paint always here, or do I have to order ahead of time?"

"Except for very unusual requests, you can get everything the day before you start painting. Please keep in mind that we are extremely busy until noon time, so I'd say come in after that and we'll set you up. You'll need a truck or a car to carry all the supplies. We deliver only to very large contractors. However, when you buy your ladders and equipment the first time, we can deliver it all for a small charge."

"I 'preciate it a lot," said Mike. Thanking the man profusely, he left the shop.

Once outside, he put his hat on and walked from the store to Godfrey Street but instead of going up the hill to his own house he stopped at the Bernards' home and went to talk to them about painting their house. He had noticed it looked bad from the outside. He had no idea how much to charge, so he asked them what they wanted to pay him. He imparted the newly gained knowledge as if he had done this work forever.

The Bernards knew Mike to be a resourceful man and never questioned whether or not he knew what he was doing. They agreed on fifty dollars for Mike plus the actual cost of the paint. The project would start next Saturday, and Mike could stop by Thursday and pick up the cash to buy the paint. After he showed them the color sheets, Mr. Bernard decided he liked the slate grey. Mrs. Bernard liked the green.

Mike said, "You look at it for a coupla days. Then, you tell me which color when I come to get the money to buy the paint."

As Mike walked up the hill to his own house he thought, "Now I just have to figure out how far one bucket of paint goes. I don't wanta buy too much and have it left over."

It never occurred to him that he couldn't do the job.

CHAPTER THIRTEEN

Disappointed was a mild word. He didn't want to force his daughters to do anything, but he had hoped that all of them would graduate from high school. They were all smart. The teachers had told him they had great penmanship. "Always respectful and they do their work," the principal had told him.

Now, Connie was telling him she was leaving school at the end of the eleventh grade. With just one more year to graduation, he could not believe it. She sounded like her mind was pretty well made up. In September, she would have been going to the new high school building, which was nearly finished.

It had been awful for him to take Rosie out before she finished, but they had needed the money so badly. He had been extremely careful that she not be put in uncomfortable situations. She was a quiet and shy girl, more like her mother than the others in her demeanor. The money she had earned had saved them. Now all of them had decent clothes. He had been working more steadily and they had bought a little car for Rosie to drive. She had been a great savior in taking him to talk with people about painting jobs, going to get the final payments when the work was finished, and taking him to buy groceries and supplies.

He was confident that Connie would work it out. She reminded him of himself. She had the same eyes and same attitude, he thought.

When he had come home from a painting job one night in June on what was the last day of school, she had shared her news with him.

"I quit," she stated nonchalantly. "PaPa, the teacher made me so mad; Mrs. Bushnell, my economics teacher, last month said I could help her clean up after school 'cause I don't have to catch the bus like a lot of other kids. I said no because it would have been dark by the time I walked from West Avenue to home. Now, she gave me a zero as my grade! I did all the assigned work in class and I did well. How can she do that?!"

Before Mike could say a word, she rushed on to say, "Rosie is working and I know I can find a job, too. The people at Amherst Knitwear, across from Patchen Brothers butcher shop, are looking for help and said they would hire me. I start next week!"

He couldn't fault her. She had found a job; she had a plan and she was smart. He recalled how she had recited the entire Gettysburg Address that President Lincoln had given during the Civil War. She had a keen nose for news and history, as he did. They often listened to the news together and discussed the topics of the day. The only difference was that his daughter could read and write beautifully. He couldn't hold a candle to her reasoning. She was a good girl and she'd do well with that bright mind and beautiful smile.

He remembered the day she went off to work for her first day. It was a beautiful June day. Connie was excited about her independence. She was a working girl now. That evening, she shared that she had reported to work early and the owner was very impressed. She was assigned to work with the cutters who gave her fabric all jumbled in bins. Her job was to sort them by colors and bundle them together.

Now as summer was winding up and a few leaves already falling, Connie confronted her father as he walked up the drive. He knew she wanted to get something off her chest, so he pulled up a chair outside and sat near the barrels he had filled with water to swell in preparation for the winemaking that would take place as soon as the grapes arrived from California. He pulled one over for her, but she didn't want to sit.

"PaPa, yesterday I was thinking about my carefree time of summers past. I wished I were outside. I know I was daydreaming because all of a sudden I couldn't remember what the instructions were about the fabric in the bins. Some days I have to do different things with them. Anyway, so I did what I thought I was supposed to, just like the last few days. But when I got to work this morning, I was in trouble.

"The boss lady yelled at me saying I had mixed up all the colors up. She said she had spied on me from the back and saw me looking out the windows," Connie ran on, "I said just one thing to her, 'I guess you don't want me here anymore.' So I walked home with my face looking up to soak in the sun. I didn't like the people at Amherst anyway. " Mike looked at her and understood. But he was worried about how she had left it with the employer.

Recognizing the look on her father's face, she immediately added, "PaPa, don't worry I was respectful. I said thank you. And I'll find another job."

"I know," was all he said.

Within a month, Connie was working at Frederick-Speier Footwear on Muller Street in Winnipauk off Broad Street. "PaPa, I love it. The minute I walked in, it felt like home. Not only is Mrs. Spires a wonderful person but some of my friends work there, and there's a cute boy named Babe Rasmussen who sits opposite me in the workroom. I operate the cement machine. Babe has graduated already."

Mike sat back and enjoyed the descending day and listening to his daughter. He had spent many years worried about all four of them. As he gazed out at the sky turning a kaleidoscope of red, orange and yellow, he realized that they looked in one way or another like their mother, but they were a lot like him.

CHAPTER FOURTEEN

Rowayton, Connecticut–Summer 1939

The atmosphere was charged with excitement as the sounds wafting from the big structure at Roton Point served as giant magnets pulling them in. The four girls had just stepped off the trolley, an investment of forty cents for the four of them. This monthly extravagance was thrilling. They burst onto the bustling scene like gulls to a dead fish on the beach. They had arrived at the prettiest park on Long Island Sound. While less than six miles across town to the Rowayton section, it was a big deal if you didn't drive a car. Fortunately, the trolley ran every twenty minutes.

"Remember what PaPa said," Rosie cautioned. "We have to stick together, at least two of us."

Connie chimed in, "Ann, you stick with me, cause I want to ride the Skylark roller coaster and Rosie's a chicken." Making a face at their younger sister, Rosie and Lena strode off arm in arm headed for the arcade.

During the summer months, Roton Point was especially crowded as steamers from New York City spilled escapees of the city summer heat to enjoy the beach, amusements and music.

It was a Friday night in late August. They knew to stay away on Saturday because the park would host the Miss Connecticut pageant. Last year at pageant night, it had been reported that 12,000 people came in from New York. The pageant winner would go on to the Miss America contest in Atlantic City, New Jersey. The pageant ticket cost out of their reach, the sisters consoled each other with comments about not wanting to outshine the contestants. They had been told by the boys who lived on their street that all four of them were far prettier than any of the girls in the beauty contest. Lena had joked that if pinching pennies, tending house or the garden could serve as a talent, then any one of them could easily be a winner, as none of the four had had any ballet, voice or baton lessons to display during the talent portion of the competition.

Two weeks before, the girls had come on a Saturday night and walked around, played games, and listened as the sounds of Duke Ellington skipped on the water to their ears. Somewhat of a second-hand concert, they enjoyed it enormously nevertheless. Tickets to see and dance to the big band leaders in person cost a ransom. However, passengers on the steamers running from New York City across the Long Island Sound dumped enormous crowds with plenty of cash each weekend the bands played. They came to hear Tommy Dorsey, the Duke and so many others who played regularly in the pavilion during the summer months.

Though Antonietta was the youngest of the four, she was the bravest. She would lure the others to the airplane swing ride and the coaster. Lena and Rosie were partial to the bumper cars and the Scooter. They all reveled in the two-story slide when exiting the fun house. They never missed playing in the penny arcade; sometimes they were even lucky. Enormous prizes were given like a bag of groceries, or even a hundred dollars.

The day had been warm, but now with the cool breezes by the sea, the girls forgot the heat and enjoyed the music while they hoped some cute boys they had met earlier would make an appearance like they promised.

Lena was especially dolled up. She had met a fellow named Frank a few weeks before. He had casually dropped words to suggest that he and his friends were coming to Roton Point on Friday night. Now, Lena was tingling with anticipation.

The Rizzo girls were not alone in their love of the place. Arguably it was the favorite place of young people far and wide; Roton Point was a cool place to be. Whether or not a band was playing, on any weekend you could count on fun things to do and lots happening. There was a pier into Long Island Sound on the east side for excursion boats, but it was also fun just to walk down it to enjoy the moon and stars.

Now as the pairs of sisters reunited at the concession stand, after an hour of perusing and playing the amusements, someone yelled out to them, "Hey, Rizzo sisters!"

They turned and there was not only the tall and handsome Frank Casavecchi, but with him were at least four other cuties.

The young people spent the remainder of the evening laughing, dancing to the distant music and gentle teasing. It was clear that Lena's magnetic smile was having a hypnotic effect on the somewhat stoic Frank. Of the four, she was the most into fashion and concerned about her appearance and it wasn't lost on Frank, who seemed to appreciate her efforts.

At ten-thirty p.m., Rosie reminded all that they needed to catch the trolley. Frank said mournfully, "Guess there's too many of us for me to give you all a ride." He pecked Lena on the cheek and said, "Hope to see you again soon." Without saying a word, her respective smile said all he wanted to hear.

CHAPTER FIFTEEN

April 1940

"Papa, did you go get yourself fitted for the tuxedo?" asked
Lena in a taut voice.

"I went last week."

"Well, don't forget you have to go pick up the suit on Thursday.
The rehearsal at the church is on Friday night at six. You have to
be there."

Mike scrutinized his second daughter with an eagle's eye. She
had been terse and bossy for the past couple of weeks, but he
understood her apprehension. She and Frank were getting married
on Saturday. After all the preparations, the big day was less than a
week away. Still, he wanted his fun-loving, smiling Lena back. He
thought for sure her prenuptial jitters would disappear by the time
of the ceremony. At least he hoped they would.

Mike had been giving a lot of thought to his daughter's choice
for a partner in life.

Lena had met Frank Casavecchi in 1939 when she and Rosie
worked in the factory located on the third floor of the Centennial

building on West Avenue. Frank had gone to the dentist located in the building where they worked, now the Regent Theater. As the sisters, with their friend and neighbor, Rosie Salvato, waited for the bus, Frank had driven by in his brand-new '39 gray Chevy and asked them if they wanted a ride. Since they were all three together, the girls said yes.

During the ride to Godfrey Street, they asked him a million questions. Though blue-eyed, blond, tall and fair, he was Italian, they discovered, and they thought he was cute. As he dropped them off, he asked Lena for a date. She had said, "Only if one of my sisters comes along." He was charmed and quickly agreed. So he brought his friend Buddy with him and she had brought her sister Connie. Together the four had gone out for a drive to watch the planes fly up at the West Rocks airfield. "We had lot of fun," announced Connie upon their return.

The relationship took off quickly after the girls met him and his friends at Roton Point; from then on, Frank took Lena, and at least one or more of her sisters, out in his new car to dances, the movies and the amusement park.

Frank was an apprentice carpenter and was a hard worker. Mike liked that. To his daughters, Mike seemed outwardly calm about Lena's impending marriage to the young man.

He had met with Mr. and Mrs. Casavecchi when the couple had become engaged. The Casavecchi family, who had emigrated to America from northern Italy, was educated. The father, who had a comic personality, was also a wise businessman. Because he had bought real estate, they were very comfortable despite having five daughters. They had originally lived in Ridgefield and even after building the expansive home on Gregory Boulevard, they kept the their original home.

When he had met with the parents, Mike did what he was

supposed to do. He offered to pay for half the wedding. Italian people were big on that. He was also supposed to buy the dress, pay for the cake and the band. He and his daughters had been saving for this day. The girls had all learned to put away their money for the time they would marry, ever since each of them started working. The past few years, earning money with painting and his tenants actually being able to pay the rent had put Mike in a much more comfortable financial position. He still worked as hard as ever, but he never spent any money frivolously. He didn't drink or gamble. His only vices were making homemade wine and playing cards at the San Rocco Society once in a while. There the ante was pennies and big pots were quarters.

He was trying to imagine what life would be like with one of the four missing. Lena had been gone a lot over the past six months. She had been spending an enormous amount of time with Frank's family. She had become close to Frank's sisters and only Rosie had been chosen to be in her wedding from her own sisters. Rosie would be maid of honor, as the oldest, and the younger sisters, who also adored Lena, had understood. Still, it stung him that all of his daughters were not asked to be in the wedding party. Nevertheless, he kept his mouth shut. He watched the sisters' exchanges and saw it was all playing out just fine.

However, it hadn't escaped his daughters' notice that none of Frank's family ever came to their house. It seemed as if neither Frank or his sisters felt that this end of town was good enough for them. They considered themselves in a different class, was the opinion of his daughters.

Mike didn't quite understand that assessment. He waited patiently for the invitation to their home to meet them and since it never came, he invited himself there to meet the parents. When he returned from the due diligence trip, about six months ago, he was pressed by his three other daughters curious about their future brother-in-law's family.

His observations were that the father enjoyed his drink, but comical and pleasant. The man had joked that he would chew garlic when he was driving so if he was stopped by the cops they couldn't smell the liquor. Mike thought the father a bit old-fashioned Italian, but he was very nice. Frank's mother was a quiet, big, handsome woman with her hair braided at the nape of her neck. He admonished his daughters for their assessment because he had found Frank's parents pleasant, down-to-earth people. He chalked up Frank's sisters not coming to the Rizzo home as having been indulged too much. Maybe the Casavecchi daughters didn't want to be associated with anything they felt was "guinea." With their father owning multiple houses and land in another town, perhaps the Casavecchi daughters felt they were a type of landed entry.

But, according to his own daughters, who often spoke about how they missed their sister now that she spent all her time at her future in-laws home, Lena's sisters-in-law-to-be all put on airs, and that's why only Rosie was going to be in the wedding and Frank's sisters were the bridesmaids and not them.

Mike wasn't worried about any of it. He was sure he knew how Frank felt about his daughter. It was clear he adored her. His biggest worry was how to accompany his daughter down the aisle without crying.

The Saturday morning of the wedding was exciting as the girls all helped Lena get dressed. She looked absolutely dazzling. That morning, she was acting like herself again. Suddenly, she blurted out with tears in her eyes, "I'm going to miss you all so much." To prevent a crying fest, her sisters joked saying, "Oh, you'll have all the nice clothes you've always wanted; you're marrying into money. You won't miss us!" Though she laughed with them, Mike could see that she would indeed miss them all and they would miss her. The love that swirled around them tugged at his heart.

Mike had hired a car to pick them all up at the house and take them to the church. Assembled in the church's narthex, the grandeur of the organ music, coupled with the lovely, white lilies adorning the altar, he choked up seeing Rosie, attired in her maid of honor finery poised to process down the aisle ahead of them. As he moved forward with Lena on his arm, he gazed at the scene before them with friends and family filling each side of the aisle pews, and realized how blessed he was. As he walked his daughter to the altar, he prayed to God and all the saints that Frank would treat his daughter well and that she would be happy. At the altar as he lifted Lena's veil and kissed her cheek, tears sprung into his eyes. Recognizing the significance of this day, he composed himself and turned to sit in his appointed pew next to his two younger daughters. It was the beginning of a new phase in the life of his family; the natural order of God's plan unfolding. Lena embarking on her path as a wife, the others would soon follow he knew. He felt enormously grateful for everything. And, somehow, he gotten through this gut-wrenching ordeal of letting of his child go, without embarrassing himself or his daughter.

———— ⋰⋰⟨⨳⟩⋱⋱ ————

Rosie had been dating Steve for a while. Unlike Frank, who was the only son among many sisters, Steve Mola was one of eight boys; he had only one sister. As they prepared for the marriage set for November 20, 1941, Mike was finding dealing with his eldest daughter's fiancé's family quite pleasant. He had known Mr. Mola for several years. He was a barber with a shop in Norwalk where Mike went on occasion to get his hair cut. From Salerno, the Molas were warm and friendly people. Steve's uncles were also barbers and some of Steve's older brothers could wield the scissors, too.

The plans were that when Rosie and Steve married they would live in the house on Godfrey Street.

After her marriage to Frank, Lena had gone to live on Gregory Boulevard with her in-laws so the couple could start saving for a house of their own.

When Rosie had taken Mike for his tuxedo fitting for the wedding, she shared what her sister had told them all when they were last together, "Frank is wonderful, but I'm not too happy living here. I can't tell you how many times I've wanted to keep come back with all of you," Lena had said. Mike had felt hurt to hear it, but recognized that as close as the sisters had been, it was to be expected that living with her new husband's family would be an adjustment. "No worry; Lena's gonna be alright," he assured Rosie.

The Molas had been happy to have him pay his half of the wedding and he was most pleased that all of his daughters would be in the wedding party. Lena would be matron of honor, reciprocating for Rosie standing up for her. Connie and Ann, as the girls all called Antonietta now, would be in the wedding as well. He was looking forward to seeing all four of his lovely girls at the altar dressed in finery and at the big celebration party that would happen after the ceremony at St. Vincent's Hall on Ely Avenue. There were several hundred Italians invited to the big event. The Molas knew a lot of people.

Rosie had found a seamstress who made custom dresses. The woman had sewed a beautiful wedding dress for someone else; unfortunately, the marriage had been called off. She offered the dress to Rosie for the price of the alterations to make it fit her. Mike assumed the woman must have already been paid by those who had abandoned it. The dress was a work of art. Now, the wedding day here, Rosie looked exquisite.

"Time to walk my number one daughter down the aisle," he said to her.

As he stood with Rosie beside him in the back of the cathedral behind the wedding party waiting for their turn to process down the aisle, he thought about how this tiny person, his odlest daughter had been a pillar of strength. She had stayed with him when he was alone; she had played mom to her younger sisters. He felt bad that she was the only one whom he had not been able to encourage to stay in school. At that time, he needed her financial support to help provide for the younger girls. She had borne the brunt the loss of their mother, the recession and so much more. When she was seventeen he had bought a car so she could drive him to get paint jobs. Her feet not reaching the pedals, they had propped them with cans. She had driven him faithfully and waited even on chilly nights, while he was inside talking with people to get paid. He hoped she would be wildly happy with Steve; she truly deserved it.

He lifted the veil and kissed his lovely daughter. He saw her mother in her face and though he was prepared to avoid tears, once he saw hers, he was unable to control his own. He turned to take his seat in the front right pew where he sat alone watching the tableau on the altar with his all four of his gorgeous and generous daughters in finery that he could never have imagined when he was a boy growing up in Platania. He made the sign of the cross with his left hand, and gave thanks to God.

PART THREE

Ama a chine t'ama e rispundi a chine te chiama.
~ Old Platanese Proverb

Love those who love you and answer those who beckon you.

CHAPTER ONE

Barbara Drive, Norwalk—July 1946

"**V**iani con me. Che fai ca. E tempo che ti diverti nu pocu. Fami compagnia. Io vio a trovarmi una mugliara," said Antonio Chieffalo in his most familiar dialect—a mixture of Sambrasino and Nicastrese. As he asked Mike to go with him, back to Italy his statement that he was going back to find himself a wife was as candid as could be. He implored Mike to keep him company on the trip, cajoling him by saying, "What you doing here? Your daughters are grown and don't need you anymore. It's time for you to have some fun; divert yourself." Mike had responded that he did not need a wife, and that he had not left anything in Italy that he needed to go back for.

After they parted, Mike listened to the radio news. It was a bitter cold February. After all of the heartbreaking news of the past several years, now in 1946, there seemed to be some good news at last. The Marshall Plan was in play and some rebuilding of Europe was under way. It had been a long, cold and painful war. Since 1939, he had anguished over the unfolding events in Europe, especially in Italy.

He had been devastated that Mussolini's Italy had been at war against the Allies. He had many cousins and distant family there. He could only imagine how terrible the bombing, the blackouts and the hunger had been.

He was proud of his daughters' husbands, who had fought for freedom in Europe and the Pacific. He had feared for them. His daughter Ann's husband, Harold "Babe" Rasmussen, had given his life on a beach in France in December 1944. The news of Babe's death had been a belly-stabbing blow. Two officials had come in person to City National Bank in South Norwalk where Ann worked. Babe's unit was part of the 143rd Infantry, 34th Division, at what the news was referring to as the Battle of the Bulge. His body had not been returned home; instead he would be interred at the newly established US Military Cemetery in Epinal, France, not far from the battle site and where more than five thousand American service men and women were buried from the area battles.

They all had flocked to the Rasmussen home in Rowayton when it happened. Rosie and Lena's husbands had come home, as had Connie's beau—of the sisters and their friends, only Ann was a wartime widow.

"Thank God, she and Babe did not have any children," Mike thought. She was an intelligent and beautiful woman. He was just now starting to see signs that she was moving back toward the vivacious woman he remembered. She had been a wonderful student at school. Then, after high school graduation, she had worked at Frederick-Speier Footwear along with some of her sisters, then at the telephone company and eventually at the bank. He had often thought there was not anything she could not do.

He proudly told everyone who'd listen, "Ann could drive a Mack truck if she wanted to." She was gutsy and a trouper through whatever he had asked her to do when she was young. Now, in the quiet moments, he saw and felt her heartache.

He hurt with double compassion for the Rasmussen family and for all those who had sacrificed their sons for freedom. Throughout the war, Mike had followed every detail on the radio, and at the local meetings downtown he would pick up more information as the men discussed what they had read in the daily paper. At the movie theater, he went sometimes just to see the newsreel and hear the world reports.

At the weekly San Rocco Society meetings, he would remain for the social hour, playing cards. There, he gleaned more news about various stages of the war. During those candid moments, he would hear the personal accounts of the simmering hatred leveled against his fellow Italians in America and even in Norwalk. In Italy, its people suffered as Benito Mussolini joined forces with the devil; the Italians bearing the worst of the outfall from that unholy alliance that opposed the Allied powers.

Mike was an American. He cried as many nights as he had prayed for his cousins and remnant family in Italy. At the same time, he wholeheartedly supported with all he could the American cause, even buying war bonds.

Though he wished he could help Ann, he didn't feel especially useful to her now. Because they had all been so very close to each other and to him, he had been puzzled that Ann had married Babe on what seemed to him a whim when she had gone with Babe's mother and sister to see him off just before he shipped out to France. She had kept the marriage a secret not just from him, but from her sisters as well.

Everyone knew and loved Babe. Though he was not Catholic and of Danish heritage, Ann knew that neither her father nor her sisters would ever allow such things to color their opinion of the winsome young man. Mike knew her sisters were disappointed not to be there, but he still didn't understand why she hadn't entrusted them with the secret. Connie and Rosie had expressed their puzzlement to him, asking, "Why?" Of the three, only Lena didn't seem to have a problem with it. For her part Lena understood fully that Ann wanted to make Babe happy, that's why she agreed to his request. Babe wanted to leave, knowing Ann was waiting for him on his return. It was something Lena would have done, faced with the same situation. When the news of Babe's death came and the secret marriage was revealed, Ann confided in Mike that she had felt guilty about not having a proper wedding. It hadn't felt like a real wedding. "PaPa you and my sisters weren't there; it had happened so unexpectedly."

Despite all their disappointment of learning of the marriage only once she was widowed, they put aside their personal slight without hesitation to comfort her. They all rallied around Ann and none held it against her. For his part, he understood she was better comforted by her sisters than by him. What he wanted to tell her, but couldn't, was that he too knew firsthand what it meant to lose your spouse. Though she and Babe had no children and never lived together, they had been sweethearts for several years.

Ann had been not been quite three years old when her mother had died suddenly. The loss and pain he had felt had been a deep wound that had taken at least ten years to mend. Even then, it had healed with a huge scar. He still missed his wife. He took great solace that she lived on in her beautiful daughters. He was doubly fortunate in that even when they married, they all remained close to each other and to him. He was grateful to God that his other three daughters got their men back alive and intact. So many young men had returned without legs, arms, or without their sanity. He certainly knew bodily mutilation first hand. He also knew that amputation of the spirit was far worse.

Sadness had given way to joy, as Mike Marotto, Connie's

sometimes beau returned from the Pacific in December 1945, a hero with a purple heart. A handsome, fun-loving young man, who was a great dancer, he had easily won Connie's heart and they waited just six months from his return to take their vows.

The Marotto family was from Campobasso in eastern Italy on the Adriatic coast. Nice people, Mike had met them and liked the father and the mother very much. The Marottos had three sons and daughter. He was happy with the match. Not that he had necessarily expected or desired his daughters to marry into their heritage. He was not opposed to any religion or ethnic group. His standard was the same for Italian and non-Italian; he wanted his daughters to marry men that came from honest, hardworking families. He was elated that his daughters had the values he had instilled and they sought mates with those same values. He was especially pleased when he accompanied his daughter to be married, that it was from this house on Barbara Drive.

He was proud of his second homeownership. The house represented for him an "arrival" of sorts. The multi-family dwelling on Godfrey Street had served them well and he would never sell it. However, it was an old house in continual need of repair. He had built this new home for them, a little too late. "Too bad, only Connie and Antonietta ever got to live here," he thought. Though Lena and Rosie lived with their in-laws while their husbands went off to serve in the war, they were frequent visitors on weekends, so the house was often full of the laughter and joking he so loved.

No more than twelve hundred square feet, it was not a large place nor did it have anything special about it, but it was a brand new house and every element in it he had made sure was quality material. He had kept the apartment on Godfrey Street empty in case any of the girls wanted to live there with their husbands to start out. Indeed that was the plan, but with the husbands going off to war, they needed to be nearer their mothers-in-law.

So, when his good friend, Antonio Chieffalo, cajoled him about joining him on a trip back to their homeland, Mike, who had never had any desire to go back, considered it. Indeed, he never shared with his daughters anything about the harsh life he had lived there. Unlike other Italians, he never pined away for sunny Italy. He lived in the present as much as he could make himself do so.

***

Like Mike, Chieffalo had known his share of tragedy and loneliness. A widower, Chieffalo had raised three handsome, intelligent sons alone. The night before the family was to emigrate to America, his oldest son was struck and killed by a bus at the bridge from Sambiase to Nicastro. Now that the remaining two were grown, he found himself lonely. Chieffalo and Mike had some shared relatives through some of his cousins' marriages, but they themselves were not related. But as he was a tenant in Mike's house, the two had developed a kindred spirit based on the heartbreak and the shared familiarity of the region where they were raised.

"There's nothing there for me," Mike had responded to the often repeated urging to go to Italy. Though he had often thought about seeing his Marianna one more time, only now for the first time, had he entertained the idea before casting it aside immediately. While he felt this might be a good opportunity to see his sister, Marianna, whom he had not seen in thirty-five years, he was reluctant to relive the pain, hunger and rejection he knew in Platania as a boy. Before this, he had the very real excuses that his daughters needed him and that he didn't have the money. Now, he had to be honest with himself; those reasons were no longer valid. He was at a different point in his life. He was comfortable. He owned two houses. The world was finally at peace. His daughters were grown and doing well. Except for Ann, they all were happily married. However, Ann had a good job and seemed happy surrounded by her sisters and many her friends. And, though she had never yet left his home, she had severed the paternal strings when she had married Babe without him.

As he looked around, he recognized that while the house on Barbara Drive was a joyful and lovely place, he did not think any of his daughters felt it was really home. For them and perhaps for himself, Godfrey Street would always be home.

He mulled over his desire to see Marianna once more and the compelling "pull" to visit all his cousins on his mother's side, and especially his cousin Angelina Folino, now married to Antonio Bonaddio. It had been she who had directed him to visit Norwalk all those years ago to see her sister Petronella, shaping his destiny before he ever left Calabria. Norwalk had been his destiny. He was button-popping proud of his adopted New England town with its straight-laced mores and industrious people. He enjoyed visiting Pennsylvania, Ohio, New York, Boston and other places, but in his heart, he felt there was nowhere as good as Norwalk.

All the same, the more he thought about it, the more the idea grew on him. He didn't want to spend his time yearning for his daughters' attention. They had their own lives. He knew they all loved him as much as he loved them, but things had moved to another plane.

On Sunday afternoon at the card game, he told his friend of his decision to accompany him on a trip back to Italy. Later that evening, he told his daughters he was going. They had all been so close. Rosie cried, Ann looked stricken, and he got a bit emotional himself. Yet, in a flash, the girls all put aside their own feelings and told him how much they wanted him to enjoy his trip. They assured him they would all be fine. His daughters were unselfish to the core. As they talked among themselves, they took pleasure in knowing he would finally do something for himself.

CHAPTER TWO

Platania, Italy—1946

The ocean voyage back to Italy was much more comfortable than the initial trip he had taken more than thirty years before. He was older and wiser; he knew English; he wasn't sick. And, unlike his first Atlantic crossing, he didn't feel afraid or embarrassed at any time during the voyage. With his friend, Antonio, Mike enjoyed the days on board ship, talking with different people, playing some cards and watching movies. In his quiet times, Mike thought a lot about his childhood in Platania. In his mind, he expected it to be much improved during his absence.

The pleasant transatlantic crossing was the end of his romantic notions about what he would find. As they disembarked in Naples and looked for transportation to the train station, the two men were jolted into reality. Once aboard the train to Calabria, the Mike never spoke. Throughout the six-hour, non-stop viewing of the burned-out landscape going south, Mike was aghast at the prominent scars of the struggles of the final years of the war, the German occupation and the Allied bombing to root out the Nazis. He was shocked by the devastation and ravages splayed out before him. Here it was 1946, and southern Italy was just barely in the beginning of a recuperative stage.

As bad as his childhood had been in Platania, he was appalled by what he found when he arrived at his hometown. Somehow, even though he had followed the war closely on the newsreels, the radio and discussions, nothing had prepared him for the devastation he was seeing up close and personal.

"*Michu, nomeno ti conscio,*" Marianna said when they met; she had barely recognized him. He couldn't tell her how aged she looked. He could see all that had transpired on his sister's face, the result of living in fear for more than five years. Tears of joy flowed in seeing her again, and he cried too for the pain of everything he saw around him. It was worse than what he remembered.

Marianna introduced him to her two children. While he had known poverty and hunger growing up, he remembered the homeland as beautiful, sunny—almost majestic in its rawness. In its place, he found a gouged, desolate, scorched landscape. Poverty and hunger ran rampant. The few men left around were either old or maimed. All the able-bodied young men had been sacrificed by Mussolini for his own vision. Those remaining had been chewed up in the aftermath of the resistance and Germany's anger at Italy's about-turn. Even the children bore the scars of bombs. Everyone had a shell-shocked appearance, made more prominent by the long years with barely enough to eat.

He walked around Platania and visited briefly where he was born and where he stayed in those years after his mother re-married. He could not conjure up the tiniest shred of a fond memory. There was no laughter to relive. His heartstrings were tugged only by the loving compassion of his sister Marianna. He had never forgotten her generosity and tender care. He was so happy to embrace her again. She was effusive in her gratitude for the gifts he had brought as well as those he had sent over the years. Now these cheeses, clothes, soaps, and fabric, though seemingly simple items were treasures to her. He had gotten help with his purchases from his friend Antonio's sister-in-law, Francesca, who had been making many trips back and forth to Italy for years. She understood their needs.

He implored Marianna to go with him to the valley to visit Petronella's sister, his cousin Angelina Folino. While trekking down the mountain, he thought to himself that he would visit his cousins for a day or two. Then he would change his ticket to return to America as quickly as possible. He couldn't stay here too long. It was too painful.

As he and Marianna walked down to the Canetto area of Nicastro-Sambiase at the base of the mountain and then across the river, he spotted her. His cousin Angelina, the woman with eyes the color of a cloudless sky, was exactly his age. Yet she seemed aged, bent, and she wore a depressingly plain dress in the universal symbol of mourning—black. Her sister Petronella had told Mike all that had transpired not only in Angelina's life but also what the region had suffered.

Angelina, daughter of his uncle Luigi, had married Antonio Bonaddio; together they had ten children. Their first-born, Vincenzo, had been killed by a German mine during the horrors of the war. The irony of the tragedy was that it had occurred not at the front lines where he had served and been injured twice, but close to home while recuperating from an injury.

Italy's participation in the war had been a complex mix of disparate ideologies and politics. Coupled with antiquated weaponry, the lack of good leadership and a clear unwillingness of the Italian soldier's desire to achieve Mussolini's goals, the Italian people paid dearly for allowing the dictator to fill their vacuum in leadership.

Mussolini's Fascist regime had ambitions to restore Italy to the glory that was once the Roman Empire. Southern Italians, who had endured numerous invaders over the centuries, had little interest in these pursuits. However, they did desire the other promises that were tagged to these grandiose illusions. They wanted jobs, education, food, security and the trains to run on time.

After nearly four years of a war they did not ideologically support and were not equipped to fight, Italians wanted to move away from the unhealthy alliance that they felt had sold out their land to Hitler. By summer of 1943, Benito Mussolini had been arrested by order of the King, provoking a civil war. The northern half of Italy was occupied by Germans, while the south was governed by the King and liberal forces, which fought for the Allied cause in the Co-belligerent Army, which provided over 20,000 men for the Allies. Coupled with these were the partisans of the Italian Resistance who fielded up to 80,000 men on the Allied side.

Angelina's son Vincenzo had been wounded as a result of Mussolini's ill-conceived campaign and defeat in North Africa in May of 1943, but he was among the lucky ones to come out of it alive. Though seriously injured by shrapnel to his leg, he had felt at the time it was a blessing in disguise, Petronella had told Michele.

The Bonaddio and Folino families had rejoiced when Vincenzo was allowed to come home after a several months in a military field hospital. During the brief visit with his wife and children before his scheduled return to the front he had shared his disgust with the Axis Powers plans for world domination. He felt the war was close to being finished and he wanted desperately not to have to go back. He wanted to help rebuild the country for his family and neighbors. He hated the hunger he saw around him. He was sick with the thought he would once again have to leave his wife and children.

It was the fall of 1943. Italy officially had changed its allegiance to the Allies. The Italians had been carrying on secret negotiations with the Allies and on September 8, 1943, the Allies released the announcement. Instead of an end to the bombing and conflict for the southern Italians, they were faced with occupation and civil war. There were rumors of Italian troops captured by the Germans and given a choice to keep fighting with the Germans; supposedly about 94,000 Italians accepted and the remaining 710,000 were deported as slave labor to Germany . No one seemed to know what was true and what was rumor.

Vincenzo's wife, Giovanna, had given birth to a son—their fifth child—two months before his short medical leave. Reveling in his children, Vincenzo had confided in his wife the tenor of a soldier who had no stomach for Mussolini's vision and even less for the Fuhrer's. Italians had fought bravely and fearlessly, he hold told his wife, but the Southerners didn't feel this was a fight they wanted to be a part of.

He was dealt his fatal blow when he led a small group of locals, mobilized with a cart pulled by oxen, to the next town to secure a load of rice rations for their community from the distribution center across the Amato River. The Germans had blown up the bridge over the Amato, as well as all other bridges on the retreat route, as they were chased by the Allies out of the area. However, the Germans had left some souvenirs behind in the river in case there was an attempt to cross through the waters. When the cart and ox entered the river, they tripped a German land mine and the explosion killed them all.

Though Angelina was still in mourning for her firstborn son, gone less than three years, she believed it was God's will. As she laid eyes on her long-lost cousin Michele, her eyes twinkled. She screamed, and squeezed him as hard as she could. She couldn't believe that nearly four decades had passed since the day she had bade him a good voyage.

"When you left we were kids, as freshly made as mozzarella. Now, your body is broken; you have only one arm. And I have a break in my heart that cannot mend," she said.

The Canetto spilled over with children and extended family—more than one hundred in all. They ranged in ages from a few months to late eighties. The few men in the prime of life had the hollowed faces of witnessing too many comrades dying in their arms; many were missing limbs. Countless older women wore pictures hanging from their necks of sons still prisoners in camps in Africa.

With almost a magical telepathy, the family compound slowly filled with extended family as Mike's grandmother's siblings made their way into the courtyard littered with scrawny chickens, barrels and other agricultural paraphernalia. The return to planting had begun a little more than a year ago. Each person came with some small amount of food, wrapped in a dish towel or in a tiny basket to greet their long-lost cousin from America. They never mentioned that the gift they brought was most probably something they had been saving for the Easter holiday months away.

As Mike was offered a seat outside on a not-too-sturdy bench, his cousin's husband, Antonio, brought out some wine. This was unusual, as he had been told that Antonio had not ventured out of the house since his son was killed. At first, the talk was subdued. Fresh tears were shed as Mike expressed his condolences at the loss of their son.

Mike noticed the marks of war on each face. There were children of every age with gaunt looks of hunger and scars. Several men had missing limbs, a hand, or a leg—all ravages of bombing air raids, mines and stray shrapnel. Though his cousin Angelina wore a long, unadorned black dress, she still looked as beautiful as ever. However, he hadn't known she'd had so many children. It seemed unfair to Mike that her sister in America had none, and she had given birth to ten. Now, her oldest was gone.

"He left four beautiful children," Angelina said, smiling and sobbing at the same time and waving her hand across as if to show Mike her grandchildren.

Among the many children gathered there that day, Mike had noticed a handsome boy of about twelve or thirteen, somewhat short for his age with a wary and concerned look. Mike thought the boy was asking telepathically, "Is this one-armed man here to cause trouble?" From the moment Mike had been ushered to the courtyard and everyone gathered around him, the boy had appeared to Mike to be quietly gathering up his younger siblings like chickens being protected against the wolf approaching.

"This is the oldest of Vincenzo and Giovanna's children, Antonio," Angelina said as she beckoned her grandson to approach.

The boy had been a bit shy, but warmed up quickly when his paternal grandmother said, "*Questo e mio favorito cugino della'merica.*" She had given her stamp of approval to this one-armed stranger, and that made it okay with him. The boy looked at Mike and gave him a hug as instructed, but said not a word.

After nearly an hour of visiting, talking and determining where Mike would sleep during his visit—hotel accommodation were out of the question—it was worked out that he would sleep at his cousin Michele Folino's home. With the two houses only a few steps from one another, Mike was in a position to enjoy the company of not only Michele but his twin brother, Antonio, and of course, their sister and his favorite cousin, Angelina. The three siblings had nearly thirty children among them.

Mike said, "Let's send someone into town to buy some food for all of us." With a sign of relief, his cousins volunteered to go. Cousin Michele had spent the past hour worried about how they could possibly feed one more. His wife had said, "Don't worry; God will provide." But he had not been able to shake the feeling that having brought out their *supressata* to the gathering, they would find they had nothing to create even a meager Easter feast. His wife had been right; God, or his American cousin was going to provide.

Well aware of the hunger that surrounded him, Mike felt an expansiveness that made him want to give every hard-earned cent to this loving group of people. His people, he could see, had suffered tremendously during the war. The fields, the house, all were in disrepair.

With an affable personality and a willingness to help his mother and grandmother, young Antonio seemed to be forever jumping up to scurry up the stairs of the former fortress now serving as the home for three families.

The boy's mother, however, had yet to make an appearance. Mike asked about her well-being. Without having seen her, he felt a tremendous empathy for the woman. He, too, had lost his spouse abruptly and been left with four children during a terrible time when there was little to provide for them. Yet, as bad as that was, what he saw here made his plight for food and clothing seem paltry. All of these children and adults were gaunt and in rags.

As Angelina proceeded to share the story of her ill-fated son and his devoted wife, Mike took in the surroundings as if he had never been there before. Her house was a former fortress of the Brigands with two-foot-thick walls. Their adjacent farmland showed signs of having been fertile and productive in better times. In addition to her own children, she told Mike that her daughter-in-law, Vincenzo's widow, Giovanna, also lived there with the four children. Mike had at first thought they just lived nearby.

Angelina said, "I am in mourning, but my poor daughter-in-law could be described as a member of the living dead."

She went on to explain that Giovanna Cuiuli and Vincenzo

Bonaddio had been childhood sweethearts, their marriage cemented by a passionate, all-consuming love. She had given him five children; the second child, a daughter, had died of measles at age two in her arms as she ran to the city to find a doctor, while Vincenzo had been in the army. The youngest boy had been but four months old when the mine exploded. They had tried to console her with the fact that Vincenzo lived to see the child they had named Giuseppe.

"Giovanna was so grateful when Vincenzo came home from the front," Angelina relayed. "The leg injury did not appear too serious. She was just happy to have him near here. All the time he had been away, she had fretted, worried and prayed. Just like me.

"When he came home he told us he was tired of the fighting, the killing all around him. He believed that Italy should have allied itself with America. He didn't understand how Italy could have been so stupid.

"He was worried about Giovanna, the children, and his family. I could tell that my dear son's body would mend, but his soul was very much in need of care and comfort. Giovanna felt she had shared him with the Republic for far too many years. It was very difficult for her, Mike," she went on in a soliloquy like fashion.

"After they were married, Vincenzo had to report for his mandatory military service. After fourteen months, he was discharged, only to hear the rumblings of war start almost immediately upon his return. He was conscripted and being such a tall, strong man, he was sent immediately to the front lines. Oh, how Giovanna cried. She lived for any news of him. They had these very beautiful babies,

"The recent leg wound was the second time he had taken some shrapnel. We all saw how, despite his war weariness, he comforted Giovanna. He loved her so much. He was overcome with emotion when she relayed little Giuseppe's birth in July during the air raid.

"The three-month-old was beautiful but very thin when Vincenzo arrived home. My son was angry because he hadn't been here when his son was born. He hated it that he could not relieve their hunger. We all talked about how, now that America was in the war and Italy had surrendered to the Allies, perhaps it would all end soon. Instead," she sobbed, "as his recuperation was winding up and his leg healed, he was killed."

CHAPTER THREE

Giovanna's Story

Giovanna would never forget that fateful day in December when the mine exploded. Her oldest child, Antonio, was just a little over ten years old and that morning, she had sent him with his father to help. At some point, Vincenzo had decided to leave the boy in the field to work, telling him he would return for him that night on his way back.

While the whole town had grown somewhat accustomed to the sounds of war, Giovanna had gone with Angelina, her daughter, to get bread. Then, suddenly her heart stopped, ripped open at the sound of the explosion, even though it was obviously many miles away, she knew something very bad had happened. She hurried home without the bread and waited anxiously the remainder of the day. Although Vincenzo and Antonio were not expected to come back until very late, she somehow knew they would not return. Without the benefit of phones, radio or television, when friends came late that night to tell her, she already had the news from some telepathic communication that only love can transmit.

She languished a long time after he died. She was debilitated more than most. The pain and heartache she had lived through more than once. She had lost him so many times. He had gone off to the military service shortly after they were married, because every man in Italy serves. After all the prayers and worry, he came home, only to have war break out. Then she prayed and worried about him being killed in Africa, in Ethiopia. When he was wounded and he came home again, she was grateful that God had spared him. Now, to have him die so close to home and it seemed the war was ending—the irony; the pain, was too much for her. Her son Antonio was her rock. She had leaned on him as the man of the family while his father was away. Just a little over ten years old, he was like a grown man in his compassion and work ability.

Then, despite the horror of what had occurred, Vincenzo still showed her his love. Antonio was alive!

Antonio had waited patiently for his father to come. He waited a very long time in the field, but his father had never returned. But he was an obedient boy. He did not leave the appointed spot. He knew his father was coming for him. Late in the night, someone found him and brought him home.

His mother gave thanks for her son's life being spared. After that night, her voice disappeared at Vincenzo's loss. She could not care for her children. Her milk dried up. Little Giuseppe was passed to wet nurses to keep him from dying of starvation. Her sisters-in-law, almost children themselves, cared for the kids. Her husband's next oldest brother stepped up and helped in every way he could. He even wanted to marry her.

Now, a few years had passed and she was beginning to pay attention to her children again. She was facing another crisis, because they had no money and no pension. Although a veteran of war, Vincenzo had been on leave at the time of the fatal explosion.

Because he had not returned to report for duty, and the paperwork in Italy was a bureaucratic nightmare, the Italian government considered him AWOL. It took some time for them to sort out the facts that he did not come back because he was killed by the very war and the mines that he had met on the front. So her children languished without a pension for some time. When her mother-in-law's cousin Mike came to visit, they were near starvation. Even for those who had some money, there was nothing to buy in the stores. Giovanna had gone to her father and asked for money. He was very angry because she had married Vincenzo when he had not wanted her to do. She felt as if everyone was against her, and there she was with four children that she didn't know how to feed.

Several men had come around checking to see if she would have them. And, although some had some means, she couldn't bear to think of them touching her. Her vivid memories of Vincenzo destroyed any chance of desire or feelings of womanliness.

So she lived with her mother-in-law and her father-in-law, who was a tyrant and, since the death of his son, a raging alcoholic. Her own mother would sneak food or money and give it to her behind her father's back. Her father, she knew loved her, but was adamant that she should not have married Vincenzo and her current plight was of her own doing.

Her ever-faithful son Antonio urged her on most days to get up and get dressed. He tended the younger children as best he could and he worked the fields like a grown man, trying to coax a little something out of the burned-out land that they might grow to sell.

And there she was when Mike arrived to visit his cousin Angelina, her mother-in-law.

And so, toward the end of 1946, Mike made some indications about his intentions to Angelina about her daughter-in-law and her children. Giovanna would hear nothing of it; she was both angry and embarrassed by the attention. She had been a very attractive and charming woman. Many had vied for her before she married Vincenzo. And, after she was widowed, she had had other suitors; others in her family had intervened to reason with her. A woman alone with all these children could only come to no good, they told her. She had held out. She was starving, but she would not marry. She and Vincenzo had promised each other they would never marry if something happened to either one of them.

And she didn't want to marry Mike. She was concerned that another man would mistreat her children. She did not want them to be adopted or step-fathered by anyone. Her mother-in-law urged, "Oh, you'll take my grandchildren to America; they'll be saved. We are all starving here. Mike is my cousin; he will take good care of them, and treat them like his own. He raised four daughters alone and he will be good to my son's children, too."

Mike had come to Italy in American clothes; he told them that he owned two houses. He bragged of what America was and what America held for immigrants. He told them how he had arrived hungry and with nothing and had taken advantage of all the opportunities. He shared what was in his heart and told them it was the best country in the whole world. He assured Giovanna that they would never have to worry about where their next meal came from. With that plea, he began to convince her. Yet, in her heart of hearts, she felt that to remarry was a grave sin. After all, she had promised Vincenzo.

While she had no desire for another man, her children were starving. There was no hope in sight. Often she had asked, why had he left her? Why had he gone? Vincenzo had always been able to figure out everything. He had been optimistic. Playful. Even in the darkest times, he could make her smile. What was she to do but be strong and make the best choices she could for their four children? Neither his parents nor hers could help them. The war was over, but for her and the children it had just begun.

She examined her thoughts. She concluded that Michelangelo Rizzo, called Mike by everyone, was a handsome man. She could sense he was a good man—after all he was a first cousin once removed to her precious Vincenzo. Hadn't he raised four fine daughters alone? Like her, he had a place in his heart for someone he had loved before. A love lost. He had only one arm, an amputee. The war had created a large stock of amputees in her world circle. It didn't strike her as odd or uncomfortable. Yet he was certainly not the man that her late husband was. Her dead husband had been six feet tall, incredibly handsome. Strong. Muscular. He picked her up as if she was nothing. He adored her, showering her with affection. They had pet names for each other, and codes between them that they delivered with their eyes. Her children looked like him, most especially the boys. Antonio, now fourteen, and the others just a little younger displayed the passion for life that was their father's.

Still, at her in-laws' urging and against her own father's wishes again, she agreed to marry Mike. Her own father did not want her to marry because she would leave them and go to America. He told her that it would break his heart and her mother's heart if she did so. The first time she had disobeyed them for love, the second time she disobeyed them for necessity. And again, she broke their hearts and in turn was filled with remorse about what she was doing to them. Giovanna and Mike married February 9,1947, at the Church of the Madonna of Mount Carmel in Sambiase, Calabria, and she became Mrs. Michael Rizzo.

Marriage brings advantages. However, it didn't end Giovanna's troubles. She had just swapped one type of woe for another. To be sure, her children now had food, and she had a reliable source of income and someone to provide for them. She regained the respectability that at one time in southern Italy was only afforded to a married woman.

Then the unexpected challenges of coming to America began to weigh in. Mike and Jennie, as he liked to call her, started a new life together in the same home in the *Chianta* where she had lived with her first husband. Jennie lived with the ghosts of her late husband and her two-year-old deceased angel. Mike was excited and thrilled to have such a lovely, young wife. After so many decades of being alone, he was experiencing an almost drunken joyousness. There also was his secret hope of someday having a son. Her children, most especially the eldest, were beautiful, respectful and affectionate, something sorely missing in his life. His daughters, he felt, though they loved him, no longer needed him.

Nonetheless, he was eager to return to America. American money bought them food, but there were none of the meager comforts he had grown accustomed to stateside. What he hadn't anticipated was a U.S. government that, while embracing his naturalization and stalwart citizenship, had great difficulty accepting his new family, members of a foreign power that was very recently an enemy state. Suddenly, it appeared nearly impossible for his wife to bring her children into America.

The government bureaucracy didn't recognize Jennie's children as Mike's children. He was not their father. Jennie and Mike had decided that adoption was out of the question. She felt strongly the children were the offspring of Vincenzo Bonaddio. Nor did Mike think it was right to change their name. Until his dying day, he always displayed a reverence for the man who had been Giovanna's first husband. Whenever he talked about him, his voice choked up. He felt an obligation to help this man's children, who were also related to him, without changing their name, which he felt would be disrespectful.

Those were the circumstances causing Mike to leave his new bride, pregnant with child, and return to the USA to work out the details of getting his stepchildren into the country, in August 1947, only six months after his marriage. Upon arrival in Connecticut, he visited his congressional representative and made contacts in Washington, things he was unable to do from Italy.

CHAPTER FOUR

"It's a girl," Rosie's husband, Steve, said with tears in his eyes. They were all gathered in the Norwalk hospital lobby because husbands were considered persona non grata anywhere near their wives during a delivery at the hospital. Steve was flying high and Mike couldn't help but think about when Rosie herself was born at home on River Street. He remembered that he was thrown out of the house by the midwife. At least he had been able to remain nearby. He heard not only his wife's screams, but the baby's first cry, from the back porch where he had worried and waited for those nearly eight hours.

His son-in-law Steve was a good man, Mike thought to himself. But as a family of eight brothers he probably was none too happy with a daughter. Yet he seemed moved and excited.

Looking at the baby through a glass panel, both men were moved to tears as the tiny bundle with a mop of dark hair squinted and made a face at them.

He gave his daughter and her husband a few minutes alone before he walked into the room.

"PaPa, she's beautiful!" his eldest daughter said, beaming at him. "Just like you were," he said with a catch in his voice.

"Don't worry that she's so small, she'll grow up strong," Mike said confidently.

"We are going to name her Shirley," Rosie declared.

"What kinda name is that?"

"It's America, PaPa." We don't want our daughter to have some guinea name," she chuckled lovingly at her father and added, "Grandpa!"

As Mike walked the couple of miles from Stevens Street to Godfrey, he had a smile on his face as he realized he had just become a grandfather for the second time in less than a year. Lena's first child and his first grandchild, Barbara, had been born while he was in Italy. He had come back to find a beautiful toddler with dimples. He was indeed blessed, he felt. In Italy, his wife would soon be giving birth to their child. He would be a grandfather and a father all in the same month. He had been disappointed that Jennie had refused to come to America in her eighth month of pregnancy. But he did understand her fears. He was furious with the consulate for taking so long to expedite the papers for his new wife to join him. She would have been here with him now to meet his new grandchild. The past few years had been like a dream. He had gone back to his birth land reluctantly, yet it had changed his life. So long alone, he was totally in love with his much younger wife. He couldn't wait to have her wonderful kids all together with his four daughters and their children. It was the large family he had never had and always wanted.

He hoped his new baby would be a boy. Jennie had three boys and one girl; surely they would have a boy together. "God, forgive me for wanting a son," he prayed. "I know you sent me the very best daughters a man could ever have. Sweet souled, pretty, hardworking, polite, wonderful personalities and with a loving heart toward me. I am grateful. But I still want a son to make sure our name Rizzo continues. If it's wrong, I'm sorry." He made the sign of the cross as he walked past St. Mary's on West Avenue.

Rosie, Steve and Shirley were living upstairs from him on Godfrey Street. They are a nice little family, he thought to himself as he was finishing up his mid-day meal of fried potato chunks and a cubed steak just two weeks after Shirley had been born. He sat as he often did, thinking as he sipped his glass of homemade red wine. The wine had come out just so-so this year. But he wasn't going to throw it away. Since he had returned from Italy, leaving his new wife behind, the house had a hollow quality. At one time, he had worked so hard and long each day to raise his daughters, the house had always been abuzz with activity. Now at age fifty-two, a grandfather twice, he was married again with four stepchildren and a new baby on the way.

He had amassed a good bit of savings in the past eight years. He owned the house on Godfrey Street with the three apartments that he rented out. Of course, he was only charging a token amount to his daughter, as he had with Lena. He had just sold the house on Barbara Drive for a profit. He regretted the terrible neighbor who had caused him to have to do that. He had built that one-family house. It was a badge of success. It would have been a great place to take Jennie. It had a pretty yard and was just off Westport Avenue, a very desirable neighborhood.

Mike had several painting jobs lined up starting in March, but he hadn't been working much these past several months. No one wanted to paint a kitchen or a bedroom close to the holidays, and with the extreme cold, the paint fumes made people uncomfortable because you had to open windows. So between the Thanksgiving and Christmas holidays and through the deep freeze of January and

February, he hadn't worked. When he first returned from Italy, he had not sought out any work, he had been too busy trying to wade through all the complications of getting his wife and her children to America. Everything was still not in order about her children.

He remembered the conversation with his cousin Mickey Nicolazzo, the son of Zio Pasquale and Zia Maria, who had changed his name to Nicholas. Mickey had said, "Mike, we'll go talk with the Congressman and he'll help us get it sorted out." Though he was reluctant to do so, Mike had sought help from his cousin, who had straightened out his life after his stint in jail. All those years ago, Mike had tried to steer the young man in a better direction, but he had gotten into big trouble before turning himself around. Learning his lesson, now he had indeed many people who respected him. Mike had always kept in touch and often visited every family member he had in America, including his mother's sister Giuanna, who still lived in South Norwalk with her one son, and his cousin Petronella, and the Nicholas cousins, Mickey, Jennie and Lilly.

He thought about the disappointment he often had felt that neither his aunt or his cousins had ever been generous with his daughters when they were growing up without a mother. However, he didn't hold it against them. He always went to pay his respects on holidays, but there was no comradery among them.

Suddenly, he had a fleeting thought that perhaps he had taken on more than he could financially afford. He wasn't getting any younger. Could he raise all these kids? he wondered. He pondered what the future would look like, as he sat staring out the kitchen window into a snow filled back yard he thought, "Jennie's oldest son, Tony, will be able to go to work soon and help if we need it." He brushed away the thought as soon as it came. No, he couldn't bring those kids here and expect them to go to work. He wanted them to learn and do well like his daughters.

Then he saw a man walking up the driveway. He knocked at the door and Mike rose from his chair to greet him. "Western Union telegram for you, Mr. Rizzo," he said, giving the name an American pronunciation. Mike fished for a coin in his pocket to tip the young man. Then he said thank you and held the paper in his hands a long time.

Finally, he stepped out and knocked on the door to the apartment above him where his eldest daughter lived. Rosie came down the stairs to answer the door, with little Shirley in her arms.

He bent over and kissed the baby and said, "I gotta telegram, you read it for me."

Rosie opened the envelope and said softly, "PaPa, you have another baby girl."

CHAPTER FIVE

New York—May 1948

The ordeal was nearly over. Newly married, he'd spent nearly ten months alone. Mike had never imagined the difficulty he would encounter trying to bring Jennie and her children to America. He was a citizen of the United States of America. He had a document to prove it. When he passed his naturalization tests and was sworn in on May 7, 1936, he could not have been prouder. Yet, after he married Jennie, he was astounded by the barriers that seemed to crop up at every turn. He'd felt from the beginning that U.S. citizenship should trump any of the arcane laws on the books. However, it was not to be. The worst part was that he'd found it was impossible to bring Jennie and her children at the same time.

The Immigration Act of 1924 was still in force. It had established a quota system according to national origin that severely limited the number of immigrants and refugees able to enter the U.S. That law had been the principal reason that the waves of immigration from Italy had stopped.

He had spent months going to talk to everyone who would listen.

He'd made inquiries and gone by bus to meet with Congressman John Davis Lodge, in Westport. The man had been extremely polite and appeared to have sympathy for Mike's plight, but spent a lot of time explaining why he could not do anything to expedite the process. The children would have to follow their mother. He felt confident that a law in the works would pass in Congress sometime soon that would provide a window of opportunity for the children to come into the country as displaced persons. He couldn't promise when, but things were looking optimistic, he said.

After Jennie came, the congressman indicated he would help pave the path to bring them in as displaced persons. Before that happened, they would not fit the criteria.

Several weeks after his meeting with Congressman Lodge, Mike was shocked to learn that Lodge's grandfather had been instrumental in passing the law that kept immigrants from certain countries out. He almost understood the bias against Italy based on Mussolini's alliance with Hitler. What he couldn't fathom was a law that deliberately discriminated and kept families apart.

Complicating things further was the government's assessment of his assets, indicating they were not enough to serve as a legitimate bond for the care of his four stepchildren. The government didn't want anyone coming into the USA who might end up on public assistance. Mike had no interest in relaying that he had maintained his home during the Depression, and he taken care of his four motherless daughters himself. He had no interest in having his stepchildren go on any public assistance. His stubborn self wanted to walk out, yet he'd learned a thing or two over the years and kept his ire in check, deciding some things were better left unsaid.

Instead, he appealed to his cousin Mickey Nicholas, who had married again and had amassed a goodly set of land assets; Mickey, who seemed to hobnob with political types, agreed to provide the bond for the children. One thing, they learned from the congressman's aide was that they needed to get Jennie's oldest boy here first, before he turned sixteen years old. Apparently, the Italian government, their manpower depleted by the war, was making a serious effort to hang on to some of its young men by preventing those approaching sixteen to leave, though conscription was at age nineteen.

Then, when Jennie's papers had finally come through for her to emigrate, her brother had responded to the telegram that she was too late in the pregnancy to travel.

Now on this lovely day in May, he awaited his wife and a daughter he had not yet seen. He was full of anticipation. He bragged to his daughters about how lovely Jennie was and that he was sure they'd love her. The girls were excited that they were going to get three brothers; they'd never had a brother.

He had bought Jennie and the baby first-class passage. He wanted her and the baby to travel comfortably. He knew how horrible the trip across the Atlantic could be; he wanted the experience to be lovely one for Jennie, she had been through so much. It was bad enough, that she'd been upset because of leaving her other children behind.

Built in 1926, the Vulcania had had a long history; reconditioned in 1946, it now carried 240 first-class and 860 tourist-class passengers. Its run between New York, Naples and Genoa was its current service. Mike, along with his new son-in-law Lester—Ann's husband—his oldest daughter Rosie and her husband Steve, all waited with anticipation near the first-class disembarkation area, because those passengers came out before the tourist class. Mike had positioned himself so Jennie would see him quickly. With his daughter Rosie holding flowers, and her handsome husband Steve beside her, and his tall, handsome son-in-law Lester standing beside him, they looked like a greeting party for royalty.

People started pouring out. No Jennie. After the first wave passed, Mike began to get nervous. It had now been more than an hour since the process of disembarkation started and there was no sign of his wife and baby daughter. He didn't want to leave the spot they had lest Jennie come out and feel frightened that no one was there as she didn't know anyone else; so he asked Lester if he could make his way against the crowd to talk with one of the stewards. Lester disappeared for a while, making Mike exceedingly anxious. He tried to abate the scenarios in his head that they had been taken ill. He knew people who died at sea were buried at sea. He knew she had been aboard because her brother Francesco had telegraphed once when all of the issues with Raffaela's passport came up and then once again when he had seen the ship pull away from the port in Naples.

Finally after nearly three hours, after all the passengers had disembarked, they found a frightened and bedraggled Jennie with a babe in arms, the last person to come off the ship. The bursar had told Lester that the passenger he sought had not been in first class, but rather in tourist class in a cabin with portal, below the waterline. She had been very seasick, but the baby had been even more so, and they had transferred the child to the infirmary.

"Why weren't you in first class?" Mike asked with tears in his eyes. She began to cry. She was so glad to see him. Worried about meeting Mike's daughters, she relaxed in Rosie's embrace; exuding warmth and affection, Rosie spoke to her in dialect. And her husband Steve did as well. And though Lester didn't speak Italian, she saw immediately that he took charge and was extremely considerate of her needs. Speaking no Italian, he made her understand that they would get her luggage and then get her something to eat and help her with the child. The entourage had come in two cars and once the bags were loaded in Lester's car, Mike, Jennie, Rosie and Steve followed him to the designed location.

Once at the restaurant, she was again bewildered by all she saw. It was like the first night on the ship all over again. Rosie helped her relax. Jokingly she kept saying, "*Mangia. Mangia.*" Jennie understood that her eldest stepdaughter, only seven years her junior, would be her friend.

After they had eaten and the baby was fed, Mike finally got Jennie to share what had happened. She explained that when she boarded in Naples she was in such an emotional state, that she wasn't thinking straight. She was shown to a lovely cabin with a balcony. Everyone around her was very well dressed and spoke impeccable Italian. She felt that she didn't belong in first class; she was ill at ease and there was no one to talk with. She couldn't speak the way they spoke. She was miserable. All she could think about was the pain and anguish of the night her brothers lifted her on the train leaving Nicastro. She had collapsed; the pain of leaving her children behind was overwhelming.

Then, with the ordeal they had encountered at the American Embassy in Naples, she felt she'd never make it to America. Waiting in Naples for the medical exam for her and the baby, she had met some people from a town in Cosenza; they had emigrated to American decades ago, but had gone back to Calabria to visit family. They spoke the dialect that they had left with decades before and they were now returning to America from that trip. The older woman had been very kind, holding the baby for her while she had gone into the examining room. The husband and a teenage daughter had been so helpful.

Once they boarded and her bags were situated in her cabin, Jennie had gone to the upper deck, along with everyone else, to watch Naples recede as they sailed away. There, with tears in her eyes for all she was leaving behind, she ran into the same family. Seeing her tears and comforting her, the older woman asked Jennie if she was all right. Jennie poured out, not only the story of the four children left behind, but also how uncomfortable she felt, even after being in the first-class cabin for only two hours. Full of compassion, the woman had said, "Why don't you come and be with us?"

Jennie shared how foolish she had felt; after all she knew how much it must have cost Mike to send her first-class passage. So, when she went back to her own first-class deck for dinner, she was mortified. The table had more china, silver and crystal glasses than she had seen even in the big store in Nicastro where people from the city bought their wedding table settings. Never having owned anything but basic utensils herself, she didn't know what to do with all the silverware and glasses. She watched others, but it was so stressful, that when they started bringing out food, she ate nothing.

Continuing her story, she told her new family that after that first evening's painful dinner on board ship, she asked one of the women who cleaned the cabin if there was a way to find a family who was in tourist class. The maid, a woman from Abruzzo, took pity on her and pointed her to the bursar. There, the maid asked for Jennie if they would help her find this family. The bursar had been kind and said, "Absolutely, madam. Only those in tourist class cannot come up here, but you are welcome to visit there as much as you like."

When she finally made her way to her newly made friends, she broke down. The woman's husband went to talk with someone who put Jennie in an unoccupied cabin near them. It was the only remaining cabin. At first Jennie had felt so much better being with people who talked and dressed similarly and they were so very kind. But, then, when they were way out at sea, both she and the baby were sick continually. She feared for the baby's life and consequently was worse off herself. "I kept praying and worrying that my little girl was going to die," she sobbed in the restaurant. "They had the baby in the infirmary for most of the trip."

Looking at his wife and daughter and the condition they were in, Mike was trying hard to damp down his anger. How could she have been so foolish to allow herself to be put in tourist class, let alone get herself moved there voluntarily!

Lester said, "Don't worry, Pop, we'll get you the reimbursement for the difference in the fare, which is tremendous, I know."

"Thank you," said Mike. He sheathed his ire, and said, "I'm not angry at you, Jennie, but I'm angry that you were so uncomfortable and then so sick. I wanna give you the best I can."

CHAPTER SIX

Norwalk—August 1955

Mike had always loved seafood. Clamming was something he could do with his one hand. Whenever he could get someone to drive him to Calf Pasture Beach on Long Island Sound, during the summer months, he went. Tonight was special. Tony had said they would go fishing for shiners and clams as soon as he got home from work. Sunday night he was off and he would wrap up the painting early to be ready.

When Tony arrived, he and his stepson Joey, along with the two youngest children Raffaelina and Mikey all piled into Tony's old Plymouth. Buckets, nets and bait all in the trunk, the three young ones in the back, he had a chance to ask Tony about work and how the apprenticeship was going. Ever the grateful and respectful young man, Tony shared how he was learning so much. When Mike asked him, "Are they working you hard?" With his iconic wry smile, he turned and said, "I'm so happy for the chance to learn a trade; you won't hear any complaints from me."

Periodically, Tony turned his attention to Joe, Raffaelina and

Mikey in the back seat; they all seemed to be having a hard time containing their excitement. "Sit still, we are almost there. If you aren't good, I'm going to have to spank all four of you."

Raffaelina, in her bewildered seven-year-old voice said, "But, Tony, there's only three of us!" Tony answered calmly, "Somebody's going to get it for two."

There were no sounds from the back seat for the remainder of the trip. Mike appreciated how Tony looked after the younger ones. Mike knew that spanking was not something Tony would ever do, but he appreciated that he kidded with them and made them know there might be consequences to misbehaving. He always basked in his oldest stepson's company.

Upon arrival, Joey jumped out quickly to help his older brother remove the nets, the buckets and other paraphernalia. At twelve years old, it was as if Joey was emulating his brother in being a man. Both of them deferred to Mike and made him feel special. Their mother had done a great job instilling in all of the children the importance of respecting their stepfather and all their elders in general. They were all very polite. It was something Mike prized.

Joe worked to set up the net. He, along with Mike, took one side of the pole, and Tony took the other. The tiny *nunnata*, ultra-baby smelts, were perfect this time of year. Jennie would make a delicious batter in which she dropped in the tiny silvery creatures, less than an inch long, and fry up the patties that were a delicacy. On their first drag, they got nearly half a bucket full. The two young children were busy playing at the water's edge and were fascinated with the catch as they dumped it into the bucket and cleaned the net of some of the stowaways like crabs that they picked out and threw back into the sound. For the second drag, Joe announced that he could handle the second pole alone and that PaPa should rest.

On that cue, Mike went out to dig clams. He used his hand and fingers to dig in the muddy bottom along the rocky breakwater. Leaving the two youngsters to "guard" the catch, making them feel important in the operation, he waded out. As he pulled out some clams, he'd put them in the pockets of his bathing trunks, then when he had four, he'd wade and dump them one at a time into his zinc bucket containing a little seawater in the bottom. He did that trip back and forth quite a few times.

Just as he was unloading his last haul, Tony and Joey had finished their second catch. He had dug more than two dozen clams while Tony and Joey had filled their bucket with the tiny smelts. Mikey and Raffaelina were all a glow with the process and the catch.

Everyone was tired and yet still excited. They loaded everything to head home where they all knew MaMa would be waiting with batter ready and a pot boiling to steam the clams and they would all eat dinner. "MaMa is gonna be happy about how much *nunnata* you caught. Are you going to eat the clams, PaPa?" Mike answered by telling them all to sit still and not make too much noise. The voices in the back eased into a gently ribbing and joking. In the front, Mike started talking to Tony about the fall's upcoming mayoral race. He liked sharing his political views with Tony.

Once home, Joey and Tony went to clean the net and the buckets after they deposited the clams and the tiny fish into their mother's care. Upon their arrival, Jennie quickly flew into production mode. She had a family to feed and everything else was ready, just waiting on the catch.

Standing over the sink inspecting the catch, Mike was thrilled that he had gotten not only some blue mussels, but also some of the cherrystone clams, which he especially loved. He knew Jennie did not like clams, though she loved the *nunnata* and that had her attention now. She had already steamed the clams slightly so they would open up. The rest of the job was his. Therefore, he began the meticulous, painstaking process, of cleaning out all of the bad stuff in the clam over the kitchen sink. He had developed a system that worked for him. Then he would squeeze a lemon in to the open clam, he would then suck it down. Delicious! He announced.

His young daughter was watching with big eyes. Then he cleaned another, squeezed the lemon and putting it to her lips, he said to her, "You sucka it up." Jennie admonished him, "Don't give that to her, she won't like it." Nevertheless, the child moved in and did as he said. Her face lit up; he knew she was feeling the texture blended with the taste of lemon and salty sand. She said, "PaPa, that was delicious; I want another one. I loved it. It's too bad you don't like them, MaMa!"

Mike was ecstatic; at last, he had one child who shared his love of clams.

CHAPTER SEVEN

Norwalk–Early October 1958

Mid-October in southwestern Connecticut can be warm and beautiful, Indian summer playing out the changing colors of the leaves in yellow, reds and orange. The temperatures had begun their decent in the evenings. The snap in the air this Saturday morning at 46 degrees served as a harbinger of the winter ahead. It was October 4 and the new school year was no longer new. The children had started back to the classrooms on the first Tuesday after Labor Day as they did each year. However, this year that was on September 2.

Mike was walking with his eight-and-half-year-old son, Mikey, Jr. down Main Avenue. As they turned right onto Wall Street, Mikey asked his father, "PaPa, where are we going? I was playing with my friends; they need me to play baseball. We have only a few weeks left, then it will be too cold to play again until next spring. I gotta get back early cause this afternoon we have to watch the World Series; the game starts at quarter to three. The Yanks are playing Milwaukee at Yankee Stadium."

"Be patient; you'll see," Mike answered. He did not want to tell Mikey just yet where they were headed. Mike was proud of his little boy, a handsome, joyful lad, the only male heir to his family's name; he wanted him to appreciate the importance of buying something of quality. He had noticed his son's shoes had the tongue flapping out for several days. Jennie was at home with her usual Saturday morning chores; though not at the factory today, she had no time to waste. "She works hard," he thought. She'd bought Mikey the shoes he was wearing at the Woolworth's in South Norwalk, on her way home from the factory where she worked as a sewing machine operator. They hadn't lasted long. Unfortunately, Jennie did not understand that because the item was cheaper, it didn't necessarily make it a good deal.

Mike had rounded up Mikey, who already was playing with his friends in the schoolyard behind the house, when he woke from his short rest period that he took each day when he returned from his night watchman job at eight o'clock each morning. On most weekdays, he had a painting job that he went to around midday, during the longer days; he could get in six hours once he got the job set up. Right now, he was between painting work. He had just finished a big house on West Avenue. The gingerbread detail on the house had been a persnickety feat, but he had earned more for that one. He had a much smaller job that would start next week. He would be taking Joey with him to get the ladders to that location in South Norwalk next Saturday.

Joey was a hard worker and he had proved to be a great help with most of the painting work Mike did during the summer. With Joey's help, he was taking on work that before he had his stepson's help he would have had to turn down. During the summers, Joey also kept an eye on Raffaelina and Mikey while Jennie was at work. All three children had chores their mother expected them to do and to do them diligently on a daily basis.

Joey was old enough that he came with him often to help with the paint jobs. At ten years old, Raffaelina, whom his daughters had renamed "Marie," was a great help with household chores and good in school. Whenever they could not find her, she was sitting on the front stoop engrossed in library books. In fact, all three walked to the public library on Belden Avenue at least twice a week during the summers. Mikey didn't have too many assigned jobs; mostly the youngest enjoyed playing baseball. He had been somewhat adopted by the Vasil family who had a son, Billy, just Mikey's age. Mike felt he had some lessons he wanted to impart to his son, but between working all the hours he could, and the kids being in school and playing with his friends it was difficult, but he took every chance he could. He was grateful; they were all good kids.

Tony, his oldest stepson, had married this past spring. It had been a lovely wedding. Mike's cousins from Bridgeport had all come and he and Jennie had basked in the gathering of so many friends and family. The bride was a gorgeous woman with raven hair, and he and Jennie enjoyed the company of her parents and their other children. Mike was extremely proud of Tony, who had completed his apprenticeship and was now a journeymen plumber. While working originally at the Character Novelty Toy factory, Tony displayed his valued work ethic, but Mike had wanted him to learn a trade. He knew he would do well at it and plumbers made good money. Mike had approached his son-in-law, Michael Marotto, to inquire about who to talk with to get Tony in. It was very difficult to have someone agree to take on an apprentice. The union-run training program included three nights a week at a school in Stamford for several years. That was in addition to a full five days a week he put in on the job as an apprentice. It was hard, but Tony was no stranger to hard work and he had something else, a fantastic attitude.

As they walked, Mike thought about his other two stepchildren, Frank and Angie. Jennie worried insistently about all her children, but most especially about these two. Angie had had a difficult time. Her marriage had been tumultuous and disastrous. Who would have known the man was an illegal and would be deported? She was now living in her own apartment upstairs from them on Godfrey Street. Mike had found her a job at O'Brien Press, where she worked in the composing room. She was beautiful, smart and hardworking, but she and her mother tangled frequently.

Frank was a senior at Notre Dame Catholic High School in Bridgeport. Living with Mike's cousin, Mickey and his wife, Doreen, since shortly after he came to America, Frankie seemed to thrive in the environment that his wealthy cousin provided. Like Tony, Frankie had a great attitude, he was easygoing and amiable. Despite the lovely home Frankie lived in, Mike was concerned about the lad's future. "Uncle Mike" as the kids all called his cousin Mickey, was pushing hard for Frankie to go to college. Frankie, although smart, did not want to go to college; he had confided this to his mother when he had come for an extended visit during the summer.

Mike's four older daughters were married and living their own lives with their children. Rosie and Steve would come to visit tonight as they did most weekends. Lena had come to visit during the day this week. He had spoken with Connie on the phone and he was glad to hear she and the three children were doing well. Ann had come to visit from Meriden two weeks ago with her husband, Lester, and their two girls. Linda, their oldest, was exactly the same age as his boy, Mikey.

During the fifteen-minute walk, Mikey had interrupted his thoughts a few times early on, but had remained quiet in the last ten minutes. Mike liked to think; it was something his little boy seemed to be getting used to about him. As they turned onto Wall

Street and past the bank, the boy got his hopes up. He thought they might be headed to the Fanny Farmer candy shop, not that anyone from his family ever went in there, but it was a great place to look in the window and the chocolate aromas wafted onto the sidewalk. Instead, Mike stopped in front of the Stuart Shoe Store right next to the woman's store, Polly Perry. Then, Mikey got excited, "Oh boy, are you going to buy me new shoes, PaPa?" The boy stood at the window and pointed, "I want those."

"*Sta sodo,*" Mike shushed his son and with one dialect phrase that he used often communicated for his son to be still and quiet. As they stepped into the small shop and sat in one of the seats, a young man he did not recognize greeted them. Mike inquired after the owner and the young man said his father was only working weekdays now; he was capable of handling the store on Saturdays for his dad.

Sitting at Mike's left, Mikey lifted the leg of his pants to display the nearly destroyed cheap shoes. Mike said, "You measure his foot and get a good, strong pair of shoes." Mikey, enthused, "I like the loafers in the window." Mike instructed the salesman, "You bring some sturdy ones to try on so his feet grow good."

The young man brought both the Buster Brown style shoes and the loafers. Mikey tried on both. The stylish ones cost five dollars and the Buster Brown tie shoes cost three-fifty.

Mike examined the loafer thoughtfully and said, "I don't think these are built too good; see these seams; they're gonna pull apart and gonna break quick like the ones you got on. They got no support for your feet."

Mikey looked at the combat-like style shoes, the ones his father favored. They had round toes with laces. Mikey squirmed and said, "But PaPa I really like the other ones."

"*Stati chitto,*" Mike answered, telling him to be quiet. The shopkeeper said, "You had better listen to Grandpa; he knows best."

"Whatta you mean?" Affronted that the whippersnapper of a shoe sales clerk thought he was his son's grandfather, he asserted, "This is my son!"

"Oh! I'm sorry."

Mike stood up. "We buy these."

He saw the disappointed look on his son's face, as they walked to the front to pay, but knew the shoes with the laces were the best choice. Beyond the disappointment of the style, Mike realized that his son had just become aware that his father was old. He hoped that someday he would understand about his choice of shoes and appreciate the importance of buying quality and sturdy footwear. He wanted to tell his son that he had not had any shoes, or a father, old or otherwise, that he could remember. His heart was bursting to share so much with the boy, but he kept quiet.

Their purchase in hand, they walked from there to the Army/Navy surplus store and the shopkeeper an older woman, greeted Mike warmly. They had known each other for years. Mike bought Mikey some sturdy pants and a couple of shirts. Then, as they walked back, they stopped in Sip and Sizzle on Main Avenue and he bought a Mikey a Coke. The boy guzzled it down, "That was so good, PaPa!"

Now as they were getting closer to home, Mikey was getting antsy. "PaPa, the World Series is gonna start soon."

"Not too long, we gonna be home," he said. And Mikey knew not to say anything else. Then, Mike made a familiar stop at the Brass Rail Tavern. Telling Mikey to sit at one of the tables off to the right side of the tavern where they served food in the evenings, Mike stood at the bar and ordered a beer. Knowing the routine, the bartender, drew a Pabst Blue Ribbon with a fine head and headed it to Mike. Then, he walked around from behind the bar over to the tables where the boy sat quietly. He turned on the TV so Mikey could watch the ball game and said, "Gotta root for those Yanks."

The smile on Mikey's face said it all.

Leaning on the bar, Mike turned to watch his boy glued to the World Series, a game he was totally disinterested in. Then, he turned to the bartender, who was now back behind the bar and was ready to fulfill his role as confessor to his regular clients. He said to Mike, "The boy's growing up. I remember when he was born; I kidded you about being around to see him grow up."

Smiling, Mike said, "I felt young then, now I'm not so sure." As Mike nursed his beer, he said, "Almost lost him when he was born because of a breathing problem. Then, again when he was five when he and my stepson Joey had been on the swing we rigged on the maple tree in our driveway. I never knew whether his hand slipped or the boys decided to jump, but Mikey hit his brow on the edge of a cement block. The blood was everywhere. Jennie was hysterical. While it took only had a few stitches to close the wound over his eye, I was scared he'd have some damage to the brain. Thank God, though it was swollen and ugly for about a coupla weeks it healed just fine."

"Mike, the boy seems sharp and smart. I guess no lasting harm from that. I can hardly see that small scar above his eye," the bartender reassured. Mike turned and observed the boy engrossed in the TV. They had had a nice afternoon together. Yes, he thought, he was grateful that there had been no apparent lasting injury from that fall.

What Mike didn't know, and Mikey couldn't express, the boy was blind in that eye.

CHAPTER EIGHT

"Hey, Mike! How are you?"

"Not too bad."

"How's your wife? What did the doctor say?"

They walked a little farther.

"Beautiful evening," he said, stating the obvious, as they walked past the men's shoe store.

"What's happening with the grapes, Mike? Any news from Cocchia? You making wine this year?" asked Mr. Mola, the barber. Mike moved closer to the man standing at his storefront to share what he knew.

"It's been dry; they shoulda start pickin' 'em next week; I hearda it'sa good grape season this year in California. The wine shoudda coma good. I ordered eighteen boxes of Elegantè Bouche and two boxes of zinpadella. I'ma gonna blendem and maka good glass of wine." Mike went on, "Last year I did that, too, but I mixa in too much zinpadella. This yeara, I cutta back the zinpadella; I putta the barrels outside. I fill 'em with water already. They're swelling.

Shoulda be about 'nother two weeks. How about you? What you doing this year; same grape mix you do before?"

The barber answered quickly, "No way. I am out of the winemaking this year. The price went up too much on the grapes and last year I lost all of mine. *Amuffa*. Once the mold sets in, you can't use those barrels. I have to get new ones and can't afford that this year."

"You make a tonna money here," joked Mike.

"Yeah, but my wife has plans for it. Business is okay, but it could be better," the barber sighed.

The conversation then turned to local news and politics. Mike noticed his youngest daughter was getting fidgety. With a smile he abruptly announced, "Gotta get to the Norwalk Savings Society before it closes. See you later."

Putting his hat back on, he took his daughter's hand and they walked on. A few steps more toward the bank, Mr. Kydes, the owner of Champion Shoe Repair, was outside his shop said, "Good evening, Mr. Rizzo. Are you busy?"

"Heading to the bank and then on to the A&P to getta a few things for my wife."

"You still working?"

"I got small kids, I'm gonna work till I die."

"Come see me next week. The shop needs painting and my wife wants the kitchen painted, too. Stop by and give me a price."

"You know I work cheap," Mike said jovially. "I'll comma Tuesday afternoon 'bout four o'clock. You be home?" Seeing a nod, he moved on.

Walking across the Norwalk River, he began to realize that these walks into town were tiring for his daughter, whom he had never been able to bring himself to call her Marie, as everyone else did. Now eleven years old, she was quiet but smart. She never gave him any trouble and she helped her mother at home immensely. Mostly on these weekly trips, she said nothing, though to be fair, he was pretty quiet himself. Walking into town always made him feel good. He got to see people who knew, liked and respected him. His child was a comfort and he felt proud of who he was within the community.

From when she was very little, Raffaelina had accompanied him on his Friday night jaunts into town. Often, he was delayed quite a bit. She seemed to wait patiently, always watching everything around her. She was more than a bit shy. He was trying to help her be more outgoing.

As they crossed the bridge, he slowed down. She always liked looking down at the water. Since the flood five years ago, the river was more exposed at the Main and Wall Street bridge. The devastating flood took several buildings with it and changed the appearance of the town forever.

As he thought of his adopted home town of Norwalk, he got a bit choked up. It was getting close to fifty years since he had arrived. Much had changed since then; it was so long ago. For one thing, the town had grown considerably from the twenty-five thousand or so residents to more than sixty thousand who lived there now.

Sitting on Long Island Sound, it was only forty-one miles from 42nd Street in New York City's center. The thirty daily trains each way, and the hour commute, had turned Norwalk into a bedroom community to the metropolis, despite its own commercial manufacturing and oyster fishing. New people moved from the city more and more to escape the crowds. They also came to Norwalk for the public schools, its lovely beaches and the rolling hills and appealing countryside. The town had an interesting history dating back to the 1640s. It had consolidated with South Norwalk shortly after he had arrived and it had grown and prospered since. He envisioned it changing even more over the next decade as city escapees could build or buy a much bigger house with a yard and live in quiet on the weekends, commuting into the big city Monday to Friday.

At sixty-three, he had an eleven-year-old daughter and a nine-year-old son. While it meant he would be working for a long time yet, he was proud of his son and of his youngest girl.

When father and daughter finally arrived at the bank, several men he knew were standing outside. As was typical on Friday evenings, the bank remained open until eight p.m. and the A&P at the end of the Wall Street on Belden Avenue remained open until nine.

"Mike, you gonna come to St. Rocco's Sunday afternoon? We're planning an extra good time with a tournament of *briscola* and some new card games. Haven't seen you for the past couple of weeks," said one fellow club member, whom he wasn't especially fond of.

"My wife's been sick. I'm gonna come this Sunday though."

"Who is that with you, your granddaughter?" the man asked.

"No. It's my youngest daughter. I brought her from the old country. I gotta boy a little younger." The response elicited a whistle from the fellow's sidekick, a small, wiry-looking man that Mike knew only as Pasquale, he sometimes played with them. "Mike, all these years I've been playing cards with you at the club, I never knew what a sly dog you were," Pasquale joked with a funny expression on his face.

Raffaelina was looking at the man closely. She suddenly looked down.

Mike was a little miffed at the way the man had spoken in front of his little girl, but let it go with the thought that some men are just rude. He excused himself and moved on into the bank.

All during his walk into downtown, only one other person had even acknowledged the child was there. She had mostly hidden behind him as people talked with him. Now, entering the stately building, Mike removed his hat. As he walked into the lobby he glanced to the right. He told his daughter in a gentle tone, "Pick your head up and say hello to people at the bank."

The office on the right was unoccupied except for a lone woman sitting behind a huge mahogany desk. Mike took a step to the entrance as she beckoned him in. The executive vice president rose and extended her hand. "Mr. Rizzo," she said brightly. "How lovely to see you." She shook his hand. "How have you been? I spotted you last month as you walked past, but unfortunately the people I had in my office didn't leave until well after you did. I've been gone to a conference for a few weeks."

"Things izza good though my wife's been sick. She is going to work on Monday though." With almost a reverent tone he asked, "How are you? It's busy in here tonight."

"Oh, it's been a very busy day. We can't complain though, lots of customers. That's a very good thing. Big thanks to you for much of this, Mr. Rizzo. Every one of the customers you have recommended has always paid their mortgage on time and many make weekly deposits into their accounts. We rely heavily on the immigrants' business. They represent the backbone of our bank. I don't know if I have ever thanked you, sir, for all the people you have brought in to us."

"Youse all been very good to me. I know you gonna treat'em good, with the best rates."

Then she turned her attention to the shy child who was hiding behind her father. "Please sit, Mr. Rizzo." She pointed to the two chairs. "And you, too, young lady."

Mortified that the important lady had spoken to her directly, she looked up. It was a kind and pleasant face. The woman was dressed in what the girl thought were "old lady" clothes. Nevertheless, she was tall and her hair was wrapped in a bun at the nape of her neck. She looked elegant in a classic sort of way.

Raffaela sat at the edge of the chair, hardly breathing. Suddenly, she found herself at the center of attention, something she dreaded.

"What grade are you in at school?" the bank executive asked.

"Fifth."

"Is that at Tracey?"

"Yes, m-mam."

"Do you like school?"

The response came quickly before she could think about it. "I love to go to school."

"I'll bet you are a good student."

To that statement, Mike replied, "The teachers say she is very good."

The woman stood, signaling her need to attend to other business, but instead of saying goodbye, she walked Mike and his daughter to a teller window that appeared vacant. Immediately a woman from a side desk came to the window. Mrs. Raymond said very pleasantly to her, "Mr. Rizzo here is one of our best customers. Please help him so he doesn't have to wait in these long lines."

"Thank you so much," Mike said quietly.

"You are most welcome. And you, young lady, keep up the good work at school. I'm gonna be watching out for you to take my job one day." With that, she turned and walked back to her office.

As they left the bank and headed past Woolworth, Genung and Tristam & Fuller department stores, Mike looked down at his little girl and decided she was old enough for him to share some of his hard-learned wisdom.

In a soft voice and sober tone he said, "When you are older, you go to the bank and you always talk with the head person. You say hello and ask them how they are. You work good. You save your money every week at the bank and you'll be good. You will get ahead. You gotta be polite and talk to people. Never talk fresh. Remember, when you talk to people you look 'em in the face. When you say you gonna do something, you do it. You only have your good name. Nothing else. Take good care of it."

Then he smiled at her. She looked at him and smiled back. And he knew she would be all right.

CHAPTER NINE

New York City–1960

It was 1960, a new decade. American business depended on people power and the United States Postal Service to expedite work orders and to communicate important information.

Only very trusted and dependable individuals were tapped for such critical tasks as carrying the official signed work orders for a print job, or ad space placement. These human couriers were a mainstay in business expediency.

Armed with a leather briefcase under the stub of what remained of his right arm, Mike shuffled off the crowded Lexington Avenue subway at Blecker Street one November morning. He knew what street number he had to look for and he knew his numbers. His eyes were heavy from his tour of watchman's duty from midnight to eight a.m. As he did every Monday and Thursday after the eight-hour evening shift, he had trudged the two-minute walk up the small hill from O'Brien Suburban Press, where he had worked since the 1950s on Main Avenue, directly perpendicular to Godfrey Street. The company employed about two hundred pressman and other people and printed publications for other media outlets as well as printed and sold their own products. Most of the $1.6 million worth of work products was generated out of business orders from other companies in New York City.

The Rizzos now lived in four rooms on the first floor, in the house Mike had bought with his first wife, Raffaela, in 1919. There were tenants occupying the two-room apartment also on the first floor and the other two, three-room apartments on the second floor. Altogether, four different families lived in the box-shaped house that was built long before indoor plumbing and heating was even a filament of an idea. Mike would clean up and then dress in his one good suit, buttoned shirt and a fashionable tie and head back down the hill to catch the eight a.m. bus for South Norwalk, where he would take the New Haven Line Commuter Train into New York City. Once there, he would most often go downstairs within Grand Central terminal, and take the Lexington Avenue subway downtown, then walk to whatever office he needed to go to among a handful of small and large publishing companies whose print jobs O'Brien Press depended upon. There were a few in the mid-town area that he called on to which he could walk the distance.

Once at one of these customers, Mike would buzz and be let into the building. Then, he would take an elevator up to the appropriate floor and usually be let out at a small office reception area. There he exchanged a sheaf of papers with the receptionist, who would ask him to wait. Sometimes, he had nothing to give them; he would only receive orders that he would bring back to his employer. In most cases, he would wait about an hour, then he would receive a small piece of paper that was a carbon copy with several numbers on it. The important thing he knew to look for was the signature at the bottom. Alternatively, he might get a large manila envelope sealed shut with checks inside. Armed with the paper or envelope, he would reverse his route. Tonight as the Lexington Avenue subway rumbled along, toward Grand Central Terminal for his ride home on the New Haven line, he dozed as he often did. When the subway came to its stop, there was usually no time to dally. He always raced to re-seat his felt hat firmly on his head with his huge left hand. Then he would rise, grabbing the briefcase that held the all-important work orders, and tuck the briefcase under his stub.

It was an important job for a night watchman to serve as the messenger into New York City. He had been chosen because he was known as reliable and honest. He was chosen because they didn't know he could not read or write. He appeared intelligent, knowledgeable and worldly. And, when they had asked if he knew how to get around New York City, he answered, "Of course." He had never lived in New York City. He had only arrived there in 1909 before being whisked to places he didn't know, and he had gone to New York to board the ship that took him back to Italy in 1946 and returned him in 1947. In between, he had been to New York just a handful of times. He'd gone with friends to the Bronx to buy Italian oils and cheeses and he had gone once or twice by train to the famed San Gennaro Festival held each year in September centered around Mulberry Street in Little Italy.

Once he had landed the additional responsibilities to his job that increased his weekly pay, he asked someone he knew to show him around and help him sort out the subway system. Mike looked the part of a businessman, because he had always felt it was important to buy a very good suit and a smart, high-quality hat, and a good pair of shoes. Nothing made a person take a man more seriously than good manners and being well groomed. His suit, purchased about once every five years, always came from Ed Mitchell's clothing in Westport, a respected fine men's clothier.

The commuter train ride into the city usually took about an hour.

But before the train, there was a bus ride from the stop at the foot of the hill of his street. Twice a week, he dropped a token into the coin collector's slot as he greeted the bus driver with a hearty and pleasant good morning. About thirty minutes later, he would stride confidently into the South Norwalk train station and line up at the ticket counter to purchase a ticket on the New Haven line train into Manhattan at Grand Central Terminal.

Often, the train into the city was crowded; he stood holding the pole with his hat gripped firmly between thumb and index finger and three fingers wrapped on the pole. The all-important briefcase was tucked under his right arm stub. Although he knew it would be easier to leave his hat on when on a bus or subway, he never did. He was illiterate, but intelligent. He was very clean of body, mouth, and mind. Neatly dressed in his one good suit, he was, after all, a gentleman.

"Good morning," he would say in his pebbly, slightly accented voice to no one in particular. He always removed his hat as soon as he got on.

When he got a seat, whether on the bus or the two types of trains, he invariably would start a conversation with whoever was seated next to him.

On this particular misty November morning, he greeted the black woman seated next to him on the bus from Winnipauk to the line's end at the South Norwalk train station. "How are you today? Looks like it's going to rain; we need it," he said. Like most days, he had barely enough time to buy a ticket and catch the 9:05 into Manhattan. At Grand Central Terminal, he became part of the throngs of commuters who pounded the pavement like troops marching on a battlefield, all moving to a harmonious crescendo. He took the stairs to the lower level and turned toward the subway tunnels. Another token in the turnstile gave way to entry into the subway. It had been an uneventful trip to the publishing company's offices, and they had been a little quicker than usual in their turnaround.

And now here he was. With orders in hand, he knew he had the important paper with a signature confirming the factory would have work for its employees for the coming week. He couldn't read the documents, but knew of their value. Today's treasure had been the carbon slip with the all-important signatures.

He trekked briskly to the subway station and he was a bit excited because it looked, if all went well, he'd be home by eight-fifteen or so instead of his usual nine or nine-thirty. He might even be able to catch an hour's nap before starting his watchman midnight shift.

He had beamed when the receptionist had commented on his new hat, barely a week old. He had bought a really good hat this time. It had cost quite a bit, but it was distinctive and very smart-looking. A dark gray, almost velvet-feeling felt fedora with a leather band and silk lining inside, it was the well-known Bostonian brand. There hadn't been any room on the train to hold it, so it had to be placed in the luggage rack above him.

Suddenly the subway car lurched. Had he overslept his stop? His reactions were slow and the door was beginning to close. He gathered himself in the nick of time and jumped through the doors as they were closing on him. He was safely off the subway and would easily make his train. As he watched the subway zoom swiftly to its next mission, he suddenly remembered his new hat safely stowed on the rack above his seat, now halfway to what might have been another world. He swallowed hard, clutched the briefcase with the valuable contents, and stood up very straight. He walked to the information both and gave the details of his lost property and they asked for his phone number in Norwalk, but the man behind the glass didn't want to give him any false hopes.

Mike wiped the pit of disappointment from his mind and moved quickly to catch his train back to Connecticut. With no hat to keep him from the cold November winds, he shivered as he walked from the train station in South Norwalk to the bus stop a few hundred yards off. As he stepped on board the bus, his good evening greeting to the bus driver hid his emotions. When the driver asked him how he was this evening, Mike simply and reverently said, "I forgot my new hat on the subway in New York." The driver seemed to understand the significance of this loss, and simply remained quiet out of respect.

Stepping off the bus at the foot of the hill, he trudged up Godfrey Street. When he came in, his daughter Raffaelina was in the kitchen setting the lone place for his dinner, because on Monday and Thursday nights the family always ate without him, keeping his food warm on the stove. Jennie was in the cellar tending to laundry. As his daughter started to lay out the food, he plodded into the bathroom to wash up. He went into the bedroom slowly to change from his suit to his midnight-watchman work attire, tan chinos and a tan pullover shirt with a soft collar and a red panel in front that formed a vee along the three-button placard. Then he sat down at table.

As he looked up, he said to his youngest daughter in a voice that might be used to convey the news of the death of a good friend. "I left my hat on the subway train in New York."

He bowed and gave a silent prayer of thanks for his food. Then he looked up again and began to eat in his slow, pensive fashion that was his trademark. His daughter stared, saying nothing. She seemed to understand. The entire kitchen seemed to be in mourning.

PART FOUR

Megghiu namicu ca centu ducati
~ old Platanese Proverb

Better to have a friend, than one hundred coins

CHAPTER ONE

"Mike, you didn't punch all the clocks last night. Did you fall asleep or go home?" asked the foreman in a kindly tone.

"No. I beena working here long time. I never leave my post. I musta forgot one. It won't happen again," he said, humiliated.

It had been a while now that he'd been feeling the nightly duties as a serious weight. His stump throbbed and his shoulders ached. The fingers on his left hand were gnarled and swollen. He was painting less and less, but when he took a small paint job, the night watchman work was more than he could handle. It was all getting more and more difficult. Walking through the factory, checking all the areas, punching the clocks used to be a snap. Now, it was a sentence. He didn't know how much longer he could keep it up.

He had hoped to work until about seventy. Raffaelina and Mikey were still children, the girl fourteen and the boy twelve. It would be awhile before he could feel he had enough money to get her married and the boy started in life. He could collect Social Security now, but he was trying to wait as long as he could because he had been told he'd get more money if he waited. But now going on sixty-seven, he didn't think he could delay any longer.

Jennie had stopped working since she slipped on the ice on her way to work last winter. The black ice was invisible on the front walk. She seemed never to recover from the concussion that left her without her sense of smell and off balance. It had had a traumatic effect on her. She seemed unable to function. He wasn't sure if she would ever be able to work again.

It had never been his intention that she go to work in those sweatshops anyway. But she had insisted that she needed the money. It had begun because she wanted to send money and packages to all her family in Italy. Then she found that his money didn't allow for the little extras she craved. For his part, this was the first time he was experiencing a menopausal woman. He had talked with the doctor about her anxiety and nervousness. The doctor had explained that patience during this time was critical. Sometimes he had it and often he didn't. Now, it was all affecting his ability to work.

He'd been respected at O'Brien Suburban Press. He had been working there for decades and had been their trusted messenger into New York for many years. To have this young foreman question his integrity was demeaning. But if he had failed to punch a clock, it was serious. He would have to be sure and get more sleep during the day.

This weekend there would be lots of company. Jennie liked to have people over. Not feeling well, she like to surround herself with distractions. When she was well, she just liked the fellowship. No matter how you sliced it, there was no time when the house was truly quiet so he could rest. He felt himself on edge and testy. He was short-tempered a lot. He didn't like himself when he was like that.

He clocked out at seven a.m., left the factory, crossed the street and trudged up the hill to his house. The children had gotten themselves off to school and Jennie was resting on the couch when he came in.

Before he could say a word, she lit into him. "The furnace broke, you gotta call someone to come and fix it."

"Leave me alone," he responded before he could think about it.

"That's all you ever say. Now, you gonna go to sleep and later you won't be able to find anyone. It's already gotten cold."

Grudgingly he fixed himself some breakfast and found that she was right; it was already getting cold in the house. At about nine a.m. he called the heating company and asked them to send someone to fix the burner.

Then, after getting washed up, he went to bed. About two hours later, he was awakened by a slamming of the cellar hatch door. The furnace repairman had arrived. He knew Jennie wouldn't deal with repairmen, so he dragged himself out of bed, pulled on his clothes and went out and into the cellar.

"Good morning, Mr. Rizzo."

"Morning, Bill. How you? What's it look like?"

"Well, I haven't had a chance to look at it too closely yet, but it looks like it won't fire up. You have plenty of oil."

Mike sat himself down on a little bench that he had made from the grape crates and watched as Bill Santaniello, brother of the probate judge, pulled apart the furnace.

He felt himself dozing when Bill said, "Sorry to say, Mr. Rizzo, you gonna need a new burner. This one is shot."

Mike sighed. "I figure it was gonna be time soon. That one is about ten years old. How much they costa now?" When Bill told him the price. Mike sat quietly. then, he asked, "Can you wait till next month to get paid?"

"I'm gonna need twenty-five percent of it now, so I can get the parts. My labor, I can wait up to sixty days for you, Mr. Rizzo, but please don't let anyone else know. I got little kids, too."

Mike sat there feeling bad. Tired, dejected and ashamed, he couldn't pay the man whom he knew worked very hard. Fifteen years ago, he thought all his money troubles were behind him. He owned two houses and had $2,000 in the bank. Now, a year past retirement age, he was working two jobs and he didn't have the money he needed for necessities. How did he get into this position?

He went back upstairs. Jennie asked how much and he said, "Never mind." He was depressed.

He went back to bed but sleep wouldn't come. He knew Jennie was unhappy, yet he couldn't seem to do anything about it. He was unhappy, but didn't know what to do about it. He tried to focus on his kids. He had two lovely kids with Jennie. And he loved his stepchildren. The oldest, Tony, was a godsend. He had two beautiful little children. Mike appreciated his stepson's sense of humor and his respectful manner. Tony's wife was also respectful to him.

His other stepchildren were also wonderful to him. Angie and her husband and children were always around. Joey often helped him with repairs to the house. Mike enjoyed playing cards with Joey and his other stepson, Frank. Grown and married, all of them stopped by often and invited him and Jennie to their homes frequently. He always enjoyed going to their homes for birthdays, holidays and other occasions. The stepchildren often came to pick them up and drove them back home.

His older daughters all had lives of their own and teen and pre-teen children. His oldest daughter, Rosie, and her husband came to visit frequently. Lena and Connie stopped in sometimes for lunch and Ann came a least once a month from Meriden. About once or twice a year, Jennie gathered them all for dinner, though it was a lot of work for her.

He counted them all up. He realized he had gone from no family to an extended family that was the envy of others. Every one of them good-looking and smart, he thought. They were all clean and respectful. So why was he depressed?

He needed to find a way to relieve his money pressures. If he did that, he felt certain he would feel better. He was getting old. If he died while his two youngest were still in school, who would care for them? He needed to be sure to leave a little money for them. He felt himself falling to sleep.

In his dream, he was on a search. But he couldn't seem to find what he was looking for. He knew he was getting close, then it was snatched away. He awoke in a cold sweat. He felt sick and he had a searing pain in his belly. He tried to get up, but couldn't. He yelled out for his wife.

She took one look at him and called the ambulance. Then, she quickly dialed from memory each of Mike's daughters. All except Lena were at work. Lena arrived to pick up Jennie and they headed to the hospital.

His daughter Raffaela Marie was the first to arrive home from school. She found it unusual that both MaMa and PaPa were gone. Mrs. Salvatore, the next-door neighbor, came within moments of her arrival and said, "They took your father to the hospital in an ambulance. I don't know what the matter was." As she pondered what to do, the phone rang. It was Lena.

"Marie, PaPa is having a heart attack!" she said.

Young Marie had waited for her brother to arrive and then asked that he go stay at his friend Billy's house. She locked the door and walked to the hospital. Once she arrived, she found her way to the ward Mike was in and learned that her father was resting comfortably. They would be running more tests. No, it wasn't a heart attack, they said. They believed he had a very large kidney stone. It would require major surgery.

Lena brought Jennie home, and Marie remained there in the

hospital. Once he was out of surgery, they made her go home, too.

At the house, Jennie was praying the rosary. The phone rang every few minutes with people inquiring about Mike's condition.

The next day after school got out, his daughter Marie again walked to the hospital. There she found Mike awake. He said Lena and her mother had just left. He was in a great deal of pain. She then did what he had always done for her during her hospital stays when she'd had her tonsils out and a cyst removed from her the base of her spine; she held his hand and sat quietly.

Eventually, she noticed sitting on the bedstead table next to Mike's hospital bed a clear jar with a beautiful orange-colored stone the size of a golf ball inside it. She stared at it and then she asked aloud, not expecting an answer, "I wonder how our bodies can make such a thing."

Mike wished he had the strength to answer her. He took a few sips of liquid from the cup she held up to his lips. His left arm was wrapped to a board and two intravenous needles were inserted in the veins of his hand making it useless.

"How are you feeling, PaPa? Are you going to be okay?" she asked him, her face a bundle of concern.

"Not too good now, but I'm gonna be okay now that they take that stone out," he said.

"How did it get in there?"

"My body just made it?"

"I'm gonna stay with you tonight."

"You go onna home. Do your school work. You come tomorrow again."

"Not yet, PaPa."

He dozed.

After a while, a woman in a gray uniform arrived with a food tray. Lifting all the lids of what seemed like an elaborate tray, Marie found some green Jell-O, a cup of clear broth, some hot water for tea.

"PaPa, you should try to eat some of this. It says on the paper a clear diet." She spooned up some of the Jell-O. He ate most of it. He sipped the broth and immediately grimaced. Too salty, he said. He didn't want the tea.

He laid back exhausted as if he had run a marathon. His daughter sat quietly holding his hand. He started to think back to the day before yesterday and recalled his sense of despair. He knew his hospital bill would add to his money woes. But as he watched this little waif of a daughter with the worried look on her face and her attentive behavior, he was flooded with a sense of peace. He heard voices and realized that his daughter Rosie and her husband Steve had arrived. Then, he thought he heard his stepson Tony's voice and others. They all sounded so distant. In the fog, he realized he didn't need money. He had treasures worth more than gold. He had children who loved him, people who cared. As he drifted off to sleep, he felt certain God would take care of the rest.

CHAPTER TWO

After nearly a fifty-year love affair with his radio news, Mike looked to Walter Cronkite on CBS for his daily update on the world. Mike had grown to trust Mr. Cronkite. He liked his demeanor and his respectful manner. Despite that move from radio to TV for his world update, ever the news junkie, Mike never failed at nine, noon and three to turn on the radio with his heavily clubbed index finger and the thumb of his only hand to catch the WNLK Norwalk news. He didn't want to miss any important happenings locally or regionally and he didn't mind hearing the world updates according to the local broadcaster, whose voice he had come to depend on years. There was always something of interest in those reports that certainly Mr. Cronkite would not cover.

Like much of the rest of the world, Mike watched and listened intently to that intense July 16, 1969 report, as the United States launched Apollo 11 via a Saturn V rocket from the Kennedy Space Center in Merritt Island, Florida. The U.S. space program had gone full throttle in 1961 when President John F. Kennedy challenged the nation to claim a leadership role in space; land a man on the moon and return him safely to earth before the end of the decade. By the end of the 1950s, the Soviet Union, America's Cold War rival, had surged ahead of the U.S. with some spectacular achievements in space that struck fear into the hearts of many Americans, Mike included. The Soviets had used these accomplishments as a testament to Communism.

Now America was within striking distance. Mike said little as all the world listened and watched the events that July unfolded like an epic movie. The Apollo spacecraft launched that July, unlike the previous Apollo missions, had a cabin for three astronauts, a lunar landing module and a return booster to get the astronauts back to earth.

For nearly four days, he had been ultra-quiet and wore a look of worry. Jennie, never liking silence, kept cajoling him to converse with her. As was customary for their daughter, Marie stopped by every afternoon before heading home to prepare dinner. Her baby was just two and a bit mischievous, so over the last several months she had stayed briefly, worrying that the toddler was too much for Mike, now seventy-three years old.

Jennie had phoned Marie after she had returned home the afternoon of July 20 and complained again about Mike's lack of responsiveness. He overheard the phone conversation. She was worried that he looked worried. Never one to complain, Jennie and her daughter discussed whether Mike might be sick and not telling them. But he seemed to have put that bladder stone surgery ordeal behind him and had been eating well for about three months and looking like his old self.

Mother and daughter had decided to keep an eye on him and if he wasn't better in the next day or so they would make an appointment with Dr. Andrews and take him to be checked out. The night of the 20th most of the world remained glued to the television broadcast. Marie had said she was staying up to watch as Neil Armstrong took one step on the moon and one giant step for mankind at four minutes to eleven p.m. EST. It was an enormous event. Along with nearly half a billion communal viewers, all recognized it as a defining moment in history. At twenty-one, Mike's daughter, a lot like himself, was prepared for a brave new world of adventure and otherworldly happenings. She was taking it in stride as something that would happen without anxiety or any thoughts that it might fail. Her comment was, "We are America." Naively, she thought there wasn't anything America couldn't do well.

The following morning, concerned about her father, Marie came over for lunch. Mike, ever the quiet one, sat with his daughter as they devoured her MaMa's gourmet meal of homemade chicken soup with broken pieces of linguini floating inside the bowl. The fresh garden basil made it aromatic as well as delicious. Together they also enjoyed a salad of Mike's vine-ripened tomatoes with his crispy cucumbers. Jennie had a way of tossing them together with light vinegar and oil dressing. They used the crusty Italian bread to sop up the juices left by the tomatoes in the dressing, and reveled in the otherworldly goodness of the flavors and Jennie's amazing culinary talents.

As they finished eating, Mike said to Marie, in almost a whisper, "I never thought I'd live to see it."

Suddenly, it all made perfect sense to his daughter. A man of few words, Mike knew she understood. For her part, Marie got it right away as she thought, "PaPa was nervous that something might happen to prevent the landing, a malfunction, or that the astronauts might be hurt or, even worse, killed."

He had been following the space program closely and he thought all the success to that point had been shining examples of America's greatness. His recent surgery alerted him to the fact that he might not be around when the big event, the biggest he had ever experienced, happened. She had never realized until that moment that he had been cautiously awaiting the milestone for a long time. His voice and demeanor told her he was not only awestruck but grateful that he had lived to experience it.

He had come to adore the brave astronauts. He reveled in every display of American ingenuity and success. He had embraced change throughout his life and never agreed with the naysayers who predicted that the Americans would fail or, worse yet, watch as the astronauts were gobbled by some alien being.

The achievement was monumental to him. He had come from being a barefoot hillbilly with an empty belly to experience the wonder of the telephone, see the horse and buggy acquiesce to the automobile, watch radio give way to television, and now to see man make his way from earth to the great unknown of space and the moon. He had seen many changes and he felt they were all ways of advancing Americans. While having great confidence in America, he had been worried lest something happen to the astronauts and shatter his dream of seeing it happen. He felt the achievement was a living testament to the lofty dreams of the late President Kennedy, whom he had adored.

They sat together for a bit longer. Then, he said to Jennie, "The soup was very good!"

CHAPTER THREE

It was right after Labor Day, when Mike and his twenty-year-old son, Mike, Jr.—Mikey to the family—left on a night flight from New York's John F. Kennedy airport via Alitalia Airlines to Rome. Boarding at nine-ten p.m., the flight was packed with nary a seat to spare. However, before the airlines reconfigured the planes in 1978 and put more seats in the same space to maximize profits, coach seats were a bit more spacious and not too uncomfortable.

During the flight across the Atlanta, Mikey thought his PaPa especially quiet. That he didn't say much wasn't unusual, but this time he seemed especially pensive. Once the flight took off, Mike told his son he was cold. Being a dutiful son, Mikey asked the stewardess if he could get a blanket for his father. The attendant wasn't particularly keen on tending to the coach cabin as she was normally assigned to first class. She grudgingly found a blanket and then tossed it in an off-handed manner into Mike's lap. Mikey was shocked at the rude behavior.

However, when his PaPa grabbed the tossed blanket, she became immediately aware the man had only one arm. Never one to allow rudeness to dictate his behavior, Mike graciously said, "Thank you very much." The stewardess looked instantly embarrassed by her actions and quickly apologized.

During the flight, both father and son slept a bit. Mikey, for his part, kept wondering what they would do once they arrived. He hoped PaPa knew where he was going because he certainly didn't. He worried that his Italian dialect was rudimentary at best. Would he be able to communicate once he arrived? He knew his PaPa hadn't been back to Italy in twenty-one years. As his father sat quietly, Mikey kept wondering what was going on in his head, because it was certainly unusual for PaPa not to engage the people near him into even a short conversation. Though a man of few words by nature, PaPa was always social and gracious, asking people where they were from and where they were going, commenting on the weather or asking about the happenings in the news. Yet during the course of the entire trip, he eschewed his usual pleasantries.

It struck Mikey that PaPa was somewhat apprehensive about the trip. Throughout the nine-hour flight, PaPa never complained about anything, which was a little surprising since he suffered from terrible arthritic pain, and one of the main lures for making the trip was to bask in the legendary cures of Caronte's sulfur springs. For a man who suffered gnarled fingers, stiff joints, knotted shoulders and lower back pain, he remained unusually calm and undemanding throughout the flight.

No one gave any thought to the fact that this was PaPa's first time on a plane though he was nearly seventy-four years old. As the morning sun streamed through the plane's small portals, Mikey could see Rome splayed out below them. He became excited. Once they deplaned in Rome and went through customs and Italian immigration, Mikey asked, "Do you know where you are going,

PaPa?" as he looked bewilderedly at the signs written in Italian.

PaPa's gravelly voice was commanding. "You no worry; we need to catch the *Rapido.*" Mikey noticed that once on terra firma, PaPa appeared in command and in the know. Mikey was immensely relieved.

What Mikey hadn't thought about was that PaPa had come by ship out of Vibo Valente, and into Naples on his initial voyage to cross the Atlantic. On his second trip he went from New York City to Naples and again returned by ship after nearly a year. But this was PaPa's first trip to Rome. To top it off, Mikey thought, my father has had absolutely no experience with planes and airports. And yet what Mikey also hadn't grasped was that PaPa had done what he always did when faced with the unknown—his homework.

He had inquired from people he respected about plane rides, the airports, and how to catch a train from the airport to Calabria, which train was best and much more. Mike senior had ferreted out everything he needed to know to ensure he and his son made it safely to his hometown. Just as he had mastered New York City for his messenger service job, he employed his manners and his internal antennae. He cast a knowing eye, then walked directly with his son in tow to an information counter, and asked about the train station. They went via shuttle from the Fiumicino to the rail terminus. Once in the massive *Roma Termini* station in the heart of the eternal city, he said, *"Due biglietti sul rapido per Nicastro, provencia di Catanzaro."* Handing the agent thousands of lire for the two tickets, he then asked, *"Che tracca?"*

The man at the window answered with what sounded to Mikey as proper Italian, *"Benario dodice,"* using the proper Italian word for track, but knowing very well that *tracca* was dialect for *benario* in most southern towns. What neither PaPa nor Mikey knew was that the ticket master was a southern, like hundreds who went north to work supporting a family somewhere in Calabria or Abruzzo. His polished language skills were the result of a family who had kept him in school though they could ill afford to do so, with the desire that their son could get a good post. These jobs were considered plums for the southerners, though considered beneath them by most Romans.

With tickets in hand and the track identified, and a two-hour wait ahead of them, they bought something to eat and drink at a little stand within the station so they would be fortified before boarding the train for the long trip south. Mikey tried to order by himself and successfully communicated the need for coffee and a sandwich, which he learned quickly was called a *panino*. He listened to the buzz of voices and found that while he understood a lot of what was being said around him, the Italians spoke very differently from the amalgamation of part English and part Italian hillbilly dialect of *Platanese, Nicastrese* and *Sambrasino* that he was accustomed to hearing in America. Somehow though, he and his PaPa made themselves understood.

The train ride was a tedious eight hours, but Mikey found it quite interesting. He enjoyed watching the various towns and countryside fly by. The orange tile rooftops and the stucco houses were fascinating to him. Everything seemed crowded. At one point after the train stopped in Naples, Mikey was mesmerized seeing the blue waters of the Mediterranean off on the right from the train's perch atop the steep cliffs. He was sure he had never seen a place more beautiful.

They got into Nicastro close to nine at night. MaMa's niece's husband, Giuseppe Mercuri, as if by magic, appeared to pick them up at the Nicastro train station. Mikey figured that PaPa or MaMa had undoubtedly arranged it beforehand. They planned to stay at Giuseppe and Peppina's house for the duration of their stay.

Peppina's other two sisters—Maria and Franca—were as excited as little children to learn what *Zia Giovanna*, Jennie to her husband, had sent them from America. Knowing her penchant for generous giving, they waited with anticipation for their *Zio's* arrival because he would surely bring gifts from America. Sure enough, Zia Giovanna did not disappoint. She had sent thoughtful presents for all.

To Mikey, it seemed everyone was treating his PaPa like an elder statesman. "It's just like in Norwalk where everyone knows my father." Mike and Mikey went to visit all of PaPa's cousins, having dinner with a different family every night. The Folinos, Zio Michele Bonaddio, Zia Caterina Bonaddio and so many others. A distant relative, Frank Torcasio, was there from America at the same time. And both Mikey and Mike were grateful for someone who spoke English. Father and son went with Frank to San Eufemia where his family lived, and he drove them both to PaPa's home town of Platania in the mountains above Nicastro.

Talking with his sister, Marie, months later, Mikey expressed his awe at their father's celebrity. "PaPa arranged for the two of us to spend a lot of time with his old and dearest friend, *Compare* Antonio Chieffalo," he told his sister. She reminded Mikey that it was *Compare* Antonio who had been responsible for PaPa returning to Italy, the trip when he'd met their mother. *Compare* Antonio had served as best man at their wedding, hence the "*compare*" title of respect bestowed to people involved in sacramental occasions such as best men or maid of honor, baptisms and confirmation. "If not for him," thought Mikey, "I would never have been born." *Compare* Antonio's son Franco and his grandson became constant companions to Mike and Mikey. And, since they all spoke English, Mikey was especially happy.

Mikey was struck by the fact that everything in Italy was made of marble, in the bathrooms, the foyers and hallways. In his experience back home in America, marble was rare in ordinary homes, and was always equated with wealth.

The pair also went to visit Jennie's older sister, Angela Cuiuli Talarico. Living in the rural countryside on her husband's family farm, she was surprised and pleased to see them. Mikey was struck by his aunt's beauty. Though an old woman, she was tall, fair-haired and blue-eyed. In a letter to his sister back in Connecticut, Mikey remarked, "Our aunt's features are distinctly similar to our mother's despite the difference in height and coloring." Zia Angela Cuiuli seemed pleased that this American-born nephew had come to find her. "She gave me a beautiful, happy smile. Later I learned that she rarely smiled. I know I was special to her."

Mike and Mikey received wonderful receptions wherever they went. Distant relatives and friends of friends rolled out the red carpet, prepared food and shared their wine. It never occurred to young Mikey that for many of these relatives the food they shared was all they had.

They traveled from Sambiase and Nicastro up the mountain to Platania. They made several trips there during their stay in Calabria. Zio Michele Bonaddio drove them there the first time and Cousin Giuseppe, another. Their last trip they made was with their friend Frank.

Mike shared with his son that he had walked up and down that mountain more times than he could count. "I was young and strong then."

"On the first day visiting there, PaPa didn't say too much," Mikey wrote in the letters back home. "The Rizzo house was down past the church of St. Michael the Archangel. To get there, then, we needed to go off the road, we walked down another quarter mile to the left. We got close enough; PaPa said his house had been around the bend and down a very steep incline. There were only a couple of stucco houses closer to the road, but not much of anything else in the area. Where the Rizzos had lived was still extremely remote. We couldn't get any closer. The three-wheeled truck we came in wouldn't be able to keep its balance there, and for PaPa it was too steep a climb with his bad arthritis. We got really close, but stopped short of going to PaPa's actual house."

Now at seventy-four, Mike wanted to show his son where he lived. Mike reminisced to his son that in the last couple of years before he left, he had had a cow and chickens. "We walked down to Nicastro to sell the eggs, we justa keep eggs for ourselves on a holiday." Though things had changed dramatically since he was a boy, the rough terrain and the distance from any type of road along with his arthritic condition made them stop before they could get close to exactly where his family's house had once stood, or even to see if there existed any remnants of the rustic abode.

Mike felt proud that his only son was interested in his past. Mikey was struck by the distance from *Petrania* to the valley of Nicastro; with all the switchbacks and hairpin turns, it had taken an hour in the car to get from the valley to *Petrania*. When finally at the town, Mikey asked his father, "You walked this entire way when you were a kid? How did you do it?"

Mike replied, *"A fame ti fa fare qualunque cosa che è necessario fare."* Hunger makes you do whatever you need to do.

The next time father and son went back to Platania, they went up there on the feast day of St. Michael, September 29. It was the biggest day of the year in the small mountain town. St. Michael the Archangel was the patron saint of the town. It was quite a festival

Mikey learned that each year the parish of St. Michael the

Archangel of Platania honors their patron and protector with faith and pride. There is a procession through the streets of the town carrying the statue of San Michele Arcangelo with followers demonstrating reverence with songs and prayers. After the procession, torches are lighted in the spirit of peace and hope for the children of the area. Then, the parish priest celebrates mass. The feast day is preceded by three days of preparation with the recitation of the rosary and the celebration of Holy Mass with homilies that offer the faithful a chance to meet Jesus through listening and meditating on His Word. The prayers of the faithful are addressed to the patron saint so he may turn his eyes to the suffering and hardship of the people.

The events of the day were so familiar to his father that Mikey wondered if his father's faith had been honed here at this annual demonstration of love, reverence and hope. The day ended with a spectacular fireworks display.

The next day, Mikey wanted to return to Platania because he had spotted a cute girl that he hoped to talk with, plus he had such a great day there with his Dad. But Mike responded, "No, you go." And, even though Mikey tried to cajole him to come, Mike didn't want to go back to Platania again, even though they remained in the valley for another three weeks. He had had his fill of Petrania. Despite the pleasant day and his pleasure at being able to show his son where he was from, the bad memories still haunted him.

He shared with Mikey that he had worked all the time when he was a boy. He had tended the cow, and then he went somewhere else a good distance to tend the chickens, tend some potatoes and gather the *fraschetti*, the firewood. It had been a hard life and he was glad to have spent the lovely day of the feast of his patron saint with his son in his hometown, and now he was done with it.

His life, his best memories were in America. He enjoyed his relatives and friends and greatly appreciated their hospitality and loving attention, but this was no longer his place. He belonged on Godfrey Street in Norwalk, Connecticut, in the United States of America with his wife Jennie, he told Mikey. While his son went the next day back to *Petrania* searching for the cute girl, Mike went to visit some of his cousins. The previous week, the pair had been at the same cousins' home when the Folinos were making the wine. It was that time of the year for the harvest of the grapes here. He looked forward to making his own wine when he returned home. The harvest in California would have started already.

Mikey returned saying he had another great day, but failed to see the girl he had traded eye contact with.

The entire trip allowed his son Mikey also to spend a lot of time with cousins on mother's side from her first marriage. With Mimo, Michele and Benedetto Arzenti, Mikey played a lot of *briscola* and drank the homemade wine. The storytelling often went on well into the night.

While his son went out with the male cousins who had immediately befriended him, , Mike went frequently to the sulfur baths at Caronte to help ease the terrible arthritic pain.

Three days after the feast in Platania, Mike and Mikey went to visit Mike's Folino cousins again and stayed the entire day. There, Mikey was given some slick rubber boots and all the young men stomped the grapes. There was a big hole in the floor with big oak boards around the perimeter. Once that chore was done, they feasted on cheese and fruit and drank the old wine. The both reveled in the sweet sickly fragrance of the ripened grapes and the musty smells that followed.

Mikey told his father how much he enjoyed Zia Carolina's sons, especially Mimo. Fun-loving and pleasant, they had never been to the USA and desperately wanted to visit. Together, the young men went to restaurants and gatherings of younger people. "I didn't think I'd like it here, but I'm having a lot of fun, PaPa," he confided to his father.

Early in October, Mikey, Frank Torcasio and Mimo Arzenti went to another town in the province, called Cosenza. There they ate *fice d'india*, or cactus pears. Then, they traveled on to Tropea, to the Church Santa Maria dell Isola; it felt like there were a million steps to the top. The long ago builders had carefully arranged the ascent in blocks of thirty or so. Mike sat it out in the square, but the young men climbed to the sanctuary, going to each landing, then another and another. People were coming and going up and down. Mikey remarked to his companions, "It seems as if Italians have no trouble with stairs; me on the other hand, I can barely do this."

Mike was happy Mikey was enjoying himself. For his part, he was seeing beautiful parts of Italy that he had never experienced as a child. Cars made such a difference, he thought.

After a Clint Eastwood movie in Italian one evening back in Nicastro, they all went to get pizza, after the movie and then going to the *passeggio* on the *corso*, a fascinating custom Mikey thought. It seemed every evening the entire town came out; they walked along arm and arm, stopping for espresso or gelato, visiting with friends, chatting, all wearing their best clothes. For the young men it was a great opportunity to see the eligible young women; for the young women, it was an opportunity under the watchful eye of mothers, sisters, fathers and brothers to artfully pretend to ignore them.

The next day, Frank took Mikey to one of the many beautiful beaches in the area, for an entire day, on his prior visits; they had visited the churches and sites. Now, splayed out on the white sand enjoying the deep blue water, Mikey's eyes nearly popped out; there right in front of him were many women bathing topless. Mikey had always thought that Southern Italian women were straight-laced and modest, based on the Arab invaders in previous centuries. Now, he observed all their buxomness in full display before his eyes. As a young man, he was shocked, delighted and excited.

Telling his father that evening of the day's events, Mikey also remarked how different the temperature was from where Mike had come from and where his mother grew up, where they were staying at the Nicastro-Sambiase town line. It was semi-arid in the valley, but in the mountains, you needed an undershirt as well as a sweater and jacket.

Father and son spent a lot of time *a la* Chianta, playing *briscola.* They played a version called "boss," to control the distribution of the beer or wine. Then it happened. Someone came to talk to Mike about a daughter; they wanted to do some matchmaking with Mikey. Mike talked to his son about it, but was clear that he did not want him to do anything he did not want to do. "I no force you," he said.

After an enormously pleasant two-month stay, Mike said to Mikey, "We're leaving day after tomorrow. It's time to go back," he said matter-of-factly. Mikey was taken by surprise. He did not know what prompted his father's decision. Mike never explained to his son. Everyone had rolled out the red carpet and it was obvious to Mikey that his father was extremely well respected. He was having a great time; why leave now?

However, things were moving quickly, so before they left, Mikey's cousin Peppina and her husband Giuseppe, with whom they had stayed these two months, wanted Mikey to help pick olives off his mother's land. Jennie had left the land in trust to her niece Peppina, since it was not likely she would be coming back; and her niece's family needed it. At six o'clock in the morning, Mikey and his cousin went to pick olives. Bending for several hours picking olives off the ground, Mikey learned the meaning of farming without tools. Then, after lunch, Peppina's husband, Giuseppe, who had kindly picked them up two months before, transported them to a different train station for their return. From the Sant'Eufemia station, the two men took the *rapido* to Rome.

Once in Rome, Mike and his son, got something to eat and talked a bit. Mikey said, "I had a great time here, PaPa, but like you, I'm ready to get home."

With a nostalgic look on his face, Mike said, "I never wanted to come back here again, but I'm glad I got to show you where I was from."

CHAPTER FOUR

Norwalk—July 1974

"You've got arthritis, Mike. The constant pain you're feeling is due to the trauma your body suffered all those years ago when you lost your right arm, to wear and tear on your joints from the work you've done, and a bit of heredity," Doctor Andrews said.

"Warm compresses, showers or baths can help ease it as well." Joe Andrews had been Mike's doctor since he started his practice in 1970. Most of the Italians went to Dr. Falzone, a somber Italian man. Mike preferred a younger man's approach. He figured this doctor just learned about all the new medicines and how to treat old-time diseases.

"What can I take, Doctor, to make this pain better; it's bad?"

"You can safely take Anacin. It is an anti-inflammatory and it will dull the inflammation and the pain; it will not cure the arthritis. Nothing can. Keep moving as long as you can, although it hurts. It is important."

Mike thanked him, left the office after visiting with the receptionist, and descended to the first floor via the stairs instead of the elevator. Though the pain was excruciating he had noticed that when he moved his joints it actually helped. He stepped out onto East Avenue and began his walk back to Godfrey Street. Every joint in his body hurt. He knew his painting work had put a lot of stress on his joints. Some days he had painted for hours on stepladders and in odd positions, his left arm taking the brunt of the load. Now he could hardly move the arm. His hand had become gnarled, clubbed, swollen.

There had been a long period in his life when he had been grateful to live past the age his father had. Now that his kids were grown and he did not need to work anymore, he was nearly crippled with pain.

He always felt better in the warm weather. Lately, he had dwelled on the possibility of moving to Florida. In fact, he had mentioned it to Jennie just yesterday. Her response was vehement. She wanted no part of it. She had gone on and on about how she would not leave the children and grandchildren. "Who do I have in Florida?" she asked without expecting an answer.

"We'll just go for the winter months," he replied. She went silent after that. Unusual for her, that meant she would not even give it any consideration.

It was a damp, gray day. The sun looked as if it was trying to escape the grasp of its gossamer shroud, making short, faint appearances. He longed for warmth and sunshine. As he approached Norwalk's small retail business area, it seemed he was seeing for the first time the aging process of the community and it was not for the better. He realized that he too had aged and not too well. At one time, he could not take two steps without being stopped by shopkeepers, friends and foes asking after his family. They were all gone now.

He made the trek up the small Godfrey Street hill that today seemed a mountain. Arriving home, he was delighted to find Cliff, the mail carrier, sitting at the kitchen table. For several years now, Cliff had been coming for lunch at around three-forty-five in the afternoon.

"Hello, Mr. Rizzo!"

"Good to see you, Cliff. I'm glad you're here today."

"Sorry, I had to handle a different route for a bit, but I told the boss I need this route back because my friend Mr. Rizzo will miss me."

Jennie chimed in, "You no change route; you come here and eat with us."

"Mrs. Rizzo, I ain't ever tasted good cooking like yours. And, Mr. Rizzo, your wine is outstanding! I enjoy the political and social discussions, too. I feel like you've adopted me and I'm a grown man with kids myself."

"You could be my son, too," said Mike, very much meaning it.

"I'm just gonna wash up and I come and eat with you."

He headed to the bathroom, his right shoulder joint and his arm stub throbbing. He thought about when Cliff had first started delivering the mail to their house. It had been sporadic when he would see the large, handsome black man, laden with his mailbag. He had always greeted Mike with a beaming smile. Mike recalled that he had asked Cliff to tell him what was in the packet of the mail bundle he had delivered to him. It was then Cliff realized that the man, with whom he had exchanged occasional comments on the news of the day, could not read.

"Telephone bill. Electric and water bills. This looks like a letter from attorney Santaniello's office. These other two things, I'm sure are junk mail," he had said.

Mike recalled that he had asked Cliff to open the letter with the return address from his attorney, and read it to him please. As nice as Cliff had been in all their exchanges, his request led to a disappointing answer. "Sorry, sir. If I open your mail, I could go to

jail. I got a wife and kids. You wouldn't want that to happen to me."
Gasping, Mike immediately apologized for asking him.

The next day, when Cliff delivered the mail, Mike was eating a
late lunch. He beckoned Cliff inside through the screen door.

"Come an' eat with me, Cliff."

The mail carrier's smile turned into shock. He appeared not to
know what to do. He had not yet had lunch, and he had taken a
liking to this old man who was full of surprises, but the invitation
presented a difficult dilemma for the civil servant.

"Thank you, sir. I can't eat, but I'll just sit a minute or two and
keep you company if that's all right. My bag sure is heavy today;
we have a lot of flyers on Wednesdays."

Despite his having said he couldn't eat, Jennie had immediately
placed a dish of spaghetti in front of him with a thin-looking tomato
sauce. "You eat. It's just plain pasta. I have a veal cutlet for you after
you finish that," she had urged.

"Mrs. Rizzo, what are these green exotic-looking leaves? They
smell really good."

"*Basilico.* You say basil in 'merican. I putta olive oil, garlic and
fresh tomatoes to make the sauce, and I putta the fresh basil. It's
what makes it good and tasty."

Despite his protests and concerns, Cliff was lured by the fresh,
fragrant dish. He ate it.

"You like it?" Jennie asked him.

With his mouth full and look of delight on his face, Cliff nodded
in the affirmative.

Then, Mike offered Cliff a glass of wine.

"Oh. I'd love to try it, sir. But I'm still on the job until three-thirty."

Mike had the solution to that. "You eat now; then come back
at three-thirty after your shift and have a glass of wine with me. I
make it myself. It's good."

Cliff had done just that for several months, coming in the late afternoon for an after-work glass of homemade red wine. Then Jennie had suggested that Cliff come to eat after his shift so he could enjoy the wine with his food. So now, for several years, at least once or twice a week, Mike would wait and eat around three-forty-five so he could share it with Cliff. Sometimes Cliff came for lunch several days in a row and sometimes they didn't see him for a week or two.

Mike respected the man. He admired his integrity about his job. There was no temptation to do what he wasn't supposed to. Mike admired that quality. Over the years, they had exchanged life stories as well as present-day news commentary. Mike loved Cliff's company. Over time, he had learned a lot from Cliff. He was a pleasant, hardworking, dedicated family man. He had served his country. But also Mike had come to understand that the plight of the black man was different, yet similar to, what he had lived through as an illiterate immigrant sixty years ago.

In recent months, they had discussed their disappointment with the Democrats. They commiserated that their party had forgotten about the working man. The two men were nearly two generations apart, different races and religions, yet they had so much in common.

Today, Cliff's uplifting presence was a godsend. Not only would it help Mike to focus away from his pain, but also because it was pleasant for Jennie, too. She loved to talk and to serve food. She was a very charming woman, and when engaged in conversation it helped her take her mind off her many physical ailments. He would see glimpses of the younger Jennie he had fallen in love with. She was still there behind all her suffering.

Often, when Cliff was there, after they finished eating, she would get on the phone to check on the well-being of the children and grandchildren, leaving Mike and Cliff to discuss the world in quiet. Jennie hated discussions about politics. Cliff, on the other hand, loved to talk the topics of the day. With a ready laugh, he also seemed to enjoy Mike's jokes and stories. The two men discussed the world, their pasts and their families, and shared their thoughts, hopes and fears.

It seemed that lately, Jennie nagged him about everything. She nagged about his napping. She nagged when he was doing a chore for her. He thought it ironic. She expressed her love for him through her cooking. She never failed to prepare him a fine meal, laying everything in front of him. When they had eaten as a family with the kids at home and now when they visited with their own children, or when company was at the table, she always served him first. She respected him in a way that made him feel important.

He prized these seemingly small, but supremely meaningful acts on her part. Jennie was a generous woman who loved everyone. About ten years ago, she had suffered a concussion after a bad fall one morning on the black ice. As a result, she had lost her sense of smell and had trouble with her balance; she was often dizzy and uncertain. She had been energetic and lively, and then became fearful and tentative. Suffering from agoraphobia, she would often have panic attacks. Her heart would race and she'd break out in a cold sweat.

Mike well understood that her past life's challenges and her present health ailments had changed her. She now tended to carp. It was not her fault, he knew. She didn't like being a complainer, she had said to him often. She was perhaps a bit disillusioned with him as well. He'd aged. He had gotten a bit fat. He, too, was a bundle of aches and pains. Yet, despite her own ailments, each night she would arrange the heating pad for him in the bed, then after rubbing Ben Gay on his back and shoulders for him, she would go to sleep on the sofa because the pungent smell would make her cough and her eyes watery. She was always kind and compassionate, helping him in the evenings. Tenderness flowed between them during those times in the dimness of their bedroom in which she rarely slept any more. She barely slept at all, in fact. She'd stretch out on the sofa propped up on her arm. If he moaned, she'd come right in to check on him. He often accused her of sleeping with one eye open.

However, in the daytime, everything changed. When the sun was up, it seemed no matter what he did, she was unhappy with it. Her mind worked nonstop. She worried about everyone and everything. Yet, all her meals were prepared with painstaking care and served up with love. He could feel it. Sometimes, she would make him laugh with her salty mouth. He loved her. But he was aware of his inability to express it appropriately either.

Stepping back into the kitchen, Mike said, "Jennie, you give Cliff some of that good eggplant parmigiana you maka and I'll get the wine." Then, to Cliff, he said, "I wanna you tell me about your trip to Florida. I'm thinking of going there someday."

CHAPTER FIVE

"**J**ennie, come hold the ladder for me," Mike said from the garden as Jennie stood at the kitchen window washing some lettuce. From his short time in the garden, he had observed that the kitchen window trim paint was peeling.

"I gonna scrapa this off and then I paint it tomorrow."

"With your arthritis, you shouldn't be doing this. Mikey can do it when he comes over on the weekend," she responded.

But he insisted and she came out and held the ladder steady. He scraped most of the peeling paint and then Jennie announced that she had to get lunch going. She headed inside. And Mike put the scraper away and the ladder and came in.

Jennie never missed anything. She often remarked that not even a fly could pass by without her noticing its color or its size. As she stepped to the screened door, she observed a car she didn't recognize parked in front of the DiStasios' home directly across the street from her house.

The man and woman inside looked as if they were talking and

relaxing in the car. Then, when they saw her, they got out and walked directly to her.

The man was distinctively dressed with a casual, colorful shirt and tan slacks. He had expensive-looking tan leather shoes and she noticed he had no socks on. The woman was dressed in almost a matching skirt outfit. The man said, "Hello. I'm Haskell O'Brien. I used to live in this house when I was a little boy. I remember a wonderful man who owned the house, Mr. Rizzo, and his four lovely daughters. I was just telling my wife about my fond memories of the time we lived here."

Jennie said, "I'm Jennie Rizzo; you must mean my husband, Mike."

With that, the man dropped his jaw. "You mean he is still alive? I guess when I was little I thought he was old. I just assumed he would have passed away."

"Miche!" Jennie yelled. "Somebody here who knows you."

Mike had been intent on his chores and hadn't heard the conversation, but as he walked around from the back of the house, he saw the visitors.

Haskell looked shocked. Then regaining his composure, he immediately strode toward Mike and hugged him, "Mr. Rizzo! I can't believe it! It's me, Haskell O'Brien!" The way he carried on, it was as if he had seen God. Mike was more moderate in his response.

"Haskell, you are not only grown, but you an old man now," he joked. Immediately, Jennie invited them in. Mike excused himself, "I justa go clean up anna I comma sit down. You sit. Jennie will get you something to drink."

With that, he stepped into the bathroom. And Jennie began peppering the visitor with questions. "When did you live here? What do you do? Where do you live now? How many children do you have?" In a few short minutes, she had ferreted out all of the pertinent details.

Haskell, who was the son of a musician, had also made somewhat of a name for himself in the music world. The former bandleader and drummer had been living in California for many years. When Mike stepped out of the bathroom, Haskell began his gushing again. "I just can't believe it!"

Then, he shared a captivating story. Haskell's son, was Cubby O'Brien, a Mouseketeer on the Mickey Mouse Club, Disney's first TV foray. He spoke of Hollywood and TV; he talked about Las Vegas and the many places he had been. He explained that this trip was to reconnect with his roots. He wanted to show his wife where he came from.

"Mr. Rizzo, I have been a lot of places and met a lot of famous people, but you know, I have never forgotten Godfrey Street and most especially you. You know, we didn't have anything." With a catch in his voice, the man continued, "My dad barely eked out a living or paid the rent, but you always gave us vegetables from your garden, you checked on us and treated us with respect, and your daughters were my friends."

Jennie broke in and said, "You stay for lunch." She immediately went to work to enlarge the meal she was preparing. While Mike and Haskell talked, she dialed all Mike's daughters, and their children as well. Everyone was working. She was frustrated. She wanted so much to have Haskell see Connie, Rosie and Lena, the friends of this visitor's youth. Antonietta lived too far in Meriden to get there in time, so she didn't phone her. Finally, she located their youngest child, Mikey. He came right over.

Mikey walked into the kitchen in less than ten minutes from his mom's call. He watched as the visitor effusively spoke with his father. Mikey thought to himself, "You'd think he had seen God, and it's just PaPa." What was with this guy? However, the unexpected visit was fortuitous. Mikey wanted to know all about Walt Disney, and what it was like to be part of the Hollywood scene. He politely directed several questions to Haskell. While Haskell politely answered young Mikey's questions, it was obvious he did so only out of respect and affection for Mikey's father. He quickly returned his attention to talking with Mike.

Mikey was struck by the esteem the visitor held for his father. What had PaPa done that had made this man remember him so reverently all these decades?

Mike pulled out the wine. Jennie starting serving food, and all the while, Haskell O'Brien kept telling Mikey how proud he was that he'd grown up in this house and how great it had been to live on Godfrey Street. Looking Mikey right in the eyes he said, "Your father was very good to our family."

CHAPTER SIX

Godfrey Street, Norwalk—October 23, 1976

"You getta me a sock in the top drawer, Gianni," he said to his grandson. They had just finished talking about politics and the strides in aerospace, the seven-year-old was like an adult in his interest, knowledge and attention. He had been enthralled when his grandson described to him in vivid detail the Viking Lander on Mars and what the scientific outcomes would be from the mission.

His daughter, Raffaelina, had been helping Jennie with canning the tomatoes, a huge job. He had been playing *scuppa* with the boys to keep them occupied; they seemed to enjoy learning the Italian card game and were actually very good at it.

Mike's stub throbbed relentlessly from the chill in the late October air. Over the past several years, he had taken to wearing a woolen sock over the stub in the cooler months; it seemed to help the pain.

When he returned, the boy unpinned Mike's hanging right sleeve, and rolled it up to his shoulder, then he slid the sock under the short sleeve of his undershirt and over the arm's short stub. Rolling the sleeve back down and pinning it in place, Mike was pleased with all the help and attention he frequently got from the twenty-two grandchildren that he and Jennie had between them. All seemed intelligent and did well in school. None seemed at all bothered by his amputation; he didn't mind their sometimes curiosity about it.

"Does it hurt, Grandpa?" asked Gianni's five-year-old brother, George. A lively, blue-eyed blond with a charming smile, he and his sibling were as different as night and day.

"Not too bad," he answered.

"Okay if we go outside?" asked Gianni.

"You go, but you no go in the street," he admonished as they glided out the door.

Mike sat thinking about the cold winter ahead as he watched his grandsons play. He wanted so much to take a trip to Florida. He had asked just about everyone he knew who had ever been there to tell him about it; over time he had become convinced that his arthritic pain would ease there during the winter months.

As his wife and daughter emerged from their labors in the cellar, he asked his daughter a question. "You think you take a trip with me to Florida?" Before he even finished, she said, "Sure, PaPa! I can get some time off from work in January if you want to go then. I'll see about airfare. Gotta go now." With a hug and kiss to him and her mother, she went out the door calling her children to pile into her little white car sitting in the driveway.

Jennie looked at him with a worried look, but said nothing; she just proceeded to start the dinner preparations.

He turned on the radio and immediately a song called, *"Don't Go Breaking My Heart"* started playing. While he didn't like some of the crazy songs of the younger generation, he did like a lot of it, as long as it wasn't playing too loudly. The lyrics and tempo were good, he thought. He went to put the cards away and then cleaned off the table to help Jennie in his small way.

They sat down to an early dinner, as was their custom on Saturdays, when Jennie decided to break her silence. "I can't fly, you know that, and I know if you go to Florida, you will want to spend every winter there. I don't want you to leave me alone."

CHAPTER SEVEN

"When you die, I want to bury you at St. John's cemetery," Jenny said, as matter-of-factly as if talking about the weather. Without even looking up, he said in an even voice, "That cemetery is built on a swamp; it's all water. No good."

"It's much better than right next to the railroad tracks where you have those plots at St. Mary's. There's trash everywhere along the tracks. I want you buried right next to me. I don't want to go there with your first wife," she said with emphasis, in case he was not paying attention.

A loud ring emanating from the black rotary phone on the wall interrupted her tirade. Jenny moved effortlessly from the kitchen counter where she was putting together the final elements of her husband's lunch into the tiny alcove that separated the kitchen from the living room.

"'Allo, she announced loudly in her Italo-American accent. "Marie," she said in recognition of her daughter's voice. During the short probing discussion with her daughter, she managed to ferret out all the information she was seeking. She had left a message earlier at Marie's office to elicit a stop by before she went home from work. Secure that her daughter had eaten, that the boys were well and that Marie would definitely stop by to write a check for them for the electric bill, she moved on to other matters.

During the phone call, she had stretched taut the phone's cord so she could finish the luncheon salad. The conversation, though mostly in her native Calabria dialect, was also well peppered with broken English.

Admonishing her daughter to "no work too hard and to leave work on time," she hung up. Turning to her husband of thirty years, she sliced in again as if the interruption had not occurred.

"It's not wet. It's *spazioso* and sunny, and I don't care whatta you want. If you die first, I'm burying you there," she stated almost petulantly. "Besides, my name is Giovanna and I want to be buried in my namesake cemetery—St. John Cemetery." She continued with her well thought out arguments. "St. Mary's Cemetery is old. Kids are always vandalizing it. If I die first, promise me that I'll go to St. John's."

She paused. Her tirade ceased while she strained the pasta. He found his moment and said, "We have a very good place at St. Mary's. It's dry and on a little hill with shade over it. That's my place and there's room for you, too, right next to me. The stone is already in place," he said calmly.

"Why do I have to be buried near your first wife? I'm your wife now; you shouldn't want to go there," she stated like a well trained attorney trying a civil case as she dressed the pasta with sauce. He ignored her and sat looking out the screen door, reveling in the aromas that were emanating for her culinary handiwork.

She placed the bowl of pasta and her other creations on the table family style.

"Eat your lunch before it gets cold," she ordered.

"Oh, be quiet about the cemetery," he said firmly as he turned his attention to the magnificent bowl of *buccatini* just off the stove swimming in a light fresh tomato sauce addled with an aromatic abundance of basil from their garden. In another serving dish were two fragrant, cubed steaks fully dressed in fresh parsley, garlic and herbs from his garden. In an oblong platter were lovely green beans. She had picked the beans from their garden just that morning, wearing a long-sleeved old shirt to avoid the itchy leaves of the pole bean plants. The tender lettuce leaf and cucumber salad was drizzled with oil olive and garnished with fresh radishes with the tails on them. He helped himself as she did also. They ate contentedly.

The conversation had neither worried him or upset him. She had brought up the topic before in a conversation. He wasn't worried. He knew his daughter would respect his wishes and that Jennie would come around. He also knew that were she to die first, he would honor her request as well.

PART FIVE

Vo' sapiri qual è lu megghiu jiocu? Fa beni e parra pocu
~ Old Platanese Proverb

Want to know what is the best game? Do well and speak little.

CHAPTER ONE

A Daughter's Perspective

Norwalk—Summer 1977

"Y̲ou comin' down?" he asked. I knew from the glitch in his voice that it was important.

It was August. The early morning phone call had been from my mother. The topic, her usual. How were the kids? Had my husband gone to work? What did I have planned for the day? What was I going to make for dinner, she wanted to know, even though we hadn't yet had breakfast.

The kids were out for the summer. I, Raffaela Marie, was working for the *New York Times* Magazine Group, at their Connecticut offices of *Golf Digest, Tennis* and *Hockey* magazines. This was a change from when I worked at the Board of Education in the Education Office. Then, work had been literally in my parents' back yard and holidays coincided with the school system's.

Now, I planned vacation days around my children and parents' needs. Today, I had taken off to get my two sons' annual physical examinations and immunizations handled.

My career was no longer compatible with summers off to be with my children and my parents. When after a few minutes, MaMa said in Calabrese, *"Aspettta, PaPa ti vo parare."* I wondered what was on his mind. It was most unusual that my father would want to talk on the phone. To him the phone was not for idle chit-chat. It was for emergencies. A non-emergency call was made only for a very distinct purpose to convey valuable information. PaPa's conversations on the telephone were always brief and to the point.

My mother had decidedly different ideas. She used the telephone to remain connected with her children, grandchildren and the world. It was her social media outlet. She had never driven a car. Suffering from agoraphobia, she didn't get out much even when we invited her to go out with us. Yet, through the convenience of the telephone, she kept up with all the activities and happenings of her children, stepdaughters, grandchildren, friends, *paisani* and other distant relatives. She cared about people and it mattered to her what was happening in their lives. Perhaps because of the tragedies she had suffered in her earlier life, she wanted to be sure that all her children, no matter how old, were safe and well, and she needed constant reassurance because life had taught her that tragedy could strike in an instant.

MaMa was on the phone more than a secretary in a busy office. The long spiral cord on the black wall phone allowed her to make coffee, cook and reach the sink while talking. To dial the rotary phone she had to stand in the tiny nook that separated the kitchen from the living room, but once connected she talked for a long while, doing all sorts of things and never missing her deadlines for meal preparation.

Since there were no cellphones or message answering machines, when her ringing went unanswered, MaMa would redial as many times as necessary until someone came home to answer. She called all of the children at least once, more often twice a day. Her second call was usually to check if everyone was home from work and to ensure the children were well and fed. More often than not, her calls were to her daughters-in-law, asking them to stop by the house before going home from work. She would remark often that she recalled vividly the burden of putting in eight hours working at the factory and returning starting the meal for her family. To help alleviate their workload when they arrived home, she would often prepare extra pasta sauce, eggplant parmesan, meatballs, or some fresh garden string beans fixed with olive oil and mixed with garlicky potatoes, or whatever was the vegetable in season. All fragrantly enticing, no one ever refused her care packages. If the truth were known, it may be that it was just a ploy to see her adult offspring and make sure they were fed properly, but the work and thoughtfulness she put into the preparations were her essence. Generous to a fault, there was nothing she wouldn't do for her family.

In some families, the words "I love you" are generously and casually expressed. In our family, that was not the case. Neither MaMa nor PaPa casually spoke those words to us children. MaMa said them to me about a dozen times in my life. And the two occasions my father said them to me are etched in my heart.

Nevertheless, I remember all the "I love yous," said without words.

During summers, my mother called me at least six times a day. I concluded that my mother truly believed that if she didn't remind all of her children about what we were supposed to do for our family, that we would let our kids go hungry, or leave them alone to play with matches.

That's why I figured if PaPa asked me to be sure and come by, even though I did so on most days after work, that it was probably something important. Without asking PaPa why he wanted me to see this afternoon, I assured him that I'd come after taking the children to the doctor for their annual physicals.

"I'll be there around two," I said.

The morning went quickly. I prepared breakfast for my two very active sons and got them dressed. Made beds, cleaned breakfast dishes, took a shower and pulled on some shorts and a sleeveless blouse. Then I ran a load of laundry, picked up toys, and made peanut butter and jelly sandwiches on whole wheat bread, packed them up and announced, "Since it's special for Mom to be home during a weekday, we'll take our sandwiches and eat them over at the Westport Nature Center. They have someone talking about animal habitats today. And you'll get to see the new snake they have."

"Yeah!" they said in unison.

About five miles away on Woodside Lane in Westport, the fledgling nature center was a favorite with my kids because they were both interested in science and nature, but more importantly, it was all about touching and experiencing. They reveled in that type of activity.

"Now, we'll listen to the talk, pet if they allow it, but no trails today. You have to remain clean because we are going to Dr. Weinberger's office after that."

"What, no trails?" moaned George.

"You heard me then."

After a scintillating visit where we learned that snakes are not slimy, and we were all allowed to touch the head of a snake that the keeper held still, we jumped on the expressway to the pediatrician's office.

Their back-to-back physical appointments were set for one-thirty and two-fifteen p.m. The office was packed when we arrived.

The wait longer than usual, the boys busied themselves with blocks in the play area. Eventually we were called in. After the boys had been measured, weighed, poked, prodded and questioned, I met with Dr. Weinberger to get the exam results and to cover my list of questions and concerns. George's asthma and allergies seemed to be under control. I thought he seemed thin, but the doctor said he was in the appropriate weight range. Gianni's hearing had been worrying me, but that too proved to be normal. He asked about their behavior at home and what was going on and then assured me they were both healthy. With charts and papers in hand, I paid at the exit desk and then went down two flights of stairs back to our little white Datsun.

By the time we arrived at MaMa and PaPa's house, it was nearly four o'clock. PaPa smiled like a sunbeam when we arrived. He always delighted in the hugs and kisses from his grandchildren and me. MaMa quickly swooped up the kids and asked them if they were hungry. Always ready to eat and the early lunch already dissipated, they devoured two meatballs apiece and then quickly ran outside to play.

PaPa observed in silence, amid the flurry of food and little boy excitement that filled the small but warm kitchen. Once the kids found other interests, I sat on the opposite end of the chrome-legged, enamel-top table waiting for what I thought would be a request to write something for him, a check or a letter, perhaps.

Instead, PaPa got up and went without speaking to the kitchen cupboard closest to the window. In his big hand, he brought out something wrapped in a clean, freshly ironed white handkerchief. He set the bundle on the table in front of me and gently pulled back each corner with his one hand as if he was unveiling a very delicate gift. In the center of the white cotton handkerchief were three perfectly shaped and freshly picked figs. They were the Italian white variety, a tender green the size of an egg.

"You eatem," he said.

I marveled at their perfection. I loved figs. There was almost no commercial fig production at that time. I had spent much of my childhood hearing about all of the fig trees *ala Chianta* back in Italy. Growing up, my brother Joey and my sister Angie always spoke about the abundance of figs they had there. They talked about how much they loved them and of all the sizes, the purple ones that resembled eggplants and the dainty "white" ones, really a tender green. When people came from the old country to visit PaPa and MaMa, they always delivered some dried figs laid out in cruciform, called *croci,* that a cousin or other relative had sent. The *croci di fichi* always had a walnut half planted in the center of the cross. I loved those dried figs as well. But the fresh fruit was something I truly prized.

PaPa's fig tree in the backyard in our home in Connecticut was an anomaly. The tree had been a passion of PaPa's. Fig trees don't flourish in cold environs and long winters. Initially, PaPa's tree had been nothing more than rootstock, about six inches long. Then, PaPa planted it in the corner of the garden with the most sun and where, once it grew, it would not shade the vegetables. When it grew taller, the small tree had to be buried or completely covered in carpets and other weather-resistant materials to survive the frigid Connecticut winters. With his one arm, once the tree grew to more than five feet tall, he could no longer bend it to bury it. He needed help. A son or son-in-law or a neighbor would be enlisted to help as each year the fig tree underwent its hibernation.

Only every other year did the tree bear an abundant amount of fruit. On the off year, it could be coaxed to produce just a few figs. And it took diligence to fend off the birds. One might think the small handful of fruit was hardly worth it. But PaPa never complained about the work, or how little fruit it bore. It was a labor of love and a connection to perhaps his few good memories of childhood. I don't know. But he knew how much I loved figs.

He put the three oval-shaped figs in front of me urging me to eat them while he watched. I took a bite. It was an exquisite sensation. The lusciously sweet, reddish brown flesh, combined with the smooth skin and crunchy seeds, sent me straight into a fit of ecstasy. I looked up to see my PaPa looking at me. I saw a love so pure it brought tears to my eyes. His face was so serene.

I was so lost in the moment that I nearly forgot to offer him one. Thankfully, my senses come to me and I insisted he take the third one. He did so with reluctance, but then he bit in. I sat back and watched him eat it. I smiled as I recognized he loved them as much as I did. Our love went full circle. No words were necessary.

CHAPTER TWO

Godfrey Street, Norwalk–January 1978

The cancer had spread throughout his abdominal area. He was weak, too weak to stand even with help. He could no long turn himself in bed, both from the cancer and from the lack of substance. Despite his physical weakness, his mind remained alert, his memory perfect and he spoke slowly but firmly as he had for several months now.

My brothers, Tony, Frank, Joey and Mikey, had dropped in regularly as had my sisters Rosie, Angelina and Connie. They all lived within a three-mile radius. Antonietta, who lived the farthest, in Meriden, had made several trips recently with her husband, Lester. On her most recent visit, PaPa's deteriorated state had upset her tremendously. Recognizing she might not see him alive again, she left in tears with her husband gently guiding her to their car.

My brother, Mike Jr., the baby of the family and my father's only son, felt more and more that he needed to be near PaPa as much as possible. He knew, as we all did, that it was only a matter of time before God called him.

Despite the tremendous suffering, PaPa displayed an incredible desire to live.

The evening of February 13, 1978, PaPa had not been able to down more than a quarter-teaspoon of baby food. The Ensure product that my brother Mikey tried to make him drink resulted in just an ever-so-tiny sip. Then, close to the time when we would go through the ritual of readying PaPa for the night, Mikey received a series of imploring phone calls from his wife to come home. It was snowing heavily and she did not want to be alone if the power went out; she sobbed into the phone. Mikey felt torn. He knew PaPa was bad. Yet his wife's calls wouldn't let up. With each call, he recognized that she was more unhappy and frightened. At around eleven-twenty p.m. he said, "I'm going to go home; my wife is scared with all this snow."

As he was leaving, he implored, "Call me right away if anything changes." I wanted to say to him, "Don't leave, Michael." However, I kept my silence. I didn't want to make it tougher for him than it was already.

"Be careful on the roads," implored MaMa. As I heard the door close and moments later his car start, I remember thinking, you shouldn't be going.

I sat quietly by PaPa's hospital bed, ensconced in the middle of the bedroom. He seemed to be resting comfortably. I didn't want to disturb him to change him.

At the kitchen table, my husband's brother, who was living with us at the time, sat with my mother as she lamented the condition of her husband and worried aloud about her son driving in the bad weather.

Then, as PaPa stirred, I called my brother-in-law and MaMa to come help me get PaPa ready for sleeping.

I washed his face gently with a soft washcloth heated with warm water. Then with Nick's help, we turned him on his side to change out the wet pads beneath him and to help him move his chest fluids. My mother left the room with the wet pads and my brother-in-law went with her. With a glycerin stick, I swabbed the inside of his mouth, around his teeth and across his parched tongue. I said, "PaPa, now you'll rest well tonight, you are nice and clean just like you like."

Suddenly, he grabbed my hand and almost lifted his entire upper body from the bed. There was a look of fear in his eyes as he said, "I die."

I called out for my mother, and she and my brother-in-law gathered at the foot of the bed. PaPa still held my hand tightly and I squeezed back just as ferociously. He repeated his words, and from somewhere I do not know, calm came over me and I said, "PaPa, do not be afraid. I love you. Do not be afraid."

My mother began wailing, but he was undistracted. She immediately called Mikey and said, "Come right away, your father is dying."

PaPa seemed oblivious to what my mother was saying and doing. His eyes remained fixed on me. Then his eyes calmed. I was suddenly aware of a gurgling in his chest. He grasped my hand even tighter than I thought possible and I found myself a broken record saying, "PaPa, don't be afraid." He continued to look straight at me. Then his eyes went from me to somewhere above and beyond me.

A few moments later, he spoke no more. His eyes remained fixed on the spot above and beyond me as if he had seen a great light. He looked calm and radiant.

My brother-in-law then said, "That's it. There is nothing more."

At that moment I hated him for speaking those words; at the same time I was grateful for his presence because he took my mother, who was inconsolable and brought her to the kitchen. It had all happened so quickly that I realized my father had actually now passed to the world of life everlasting. I refused to leave the room because I felt his spirit was still in the room. I sat in the chair and continued to hold his hand. I became ultra-calm. I felt I was becoming him. How would I handle this?

MaMa called Dr. Andrews. Then, Mikey arrived. He was so distraught. I will never forget the pain in his voice and eyes. "I missed him. I knew he was bad. The snow is so terrible; I couldn't drive too fast," he said, covering his face. I couldn't bear to watch him. My brother's pain was palpable.

"PaPa's spirit, his soul, is still here. Reach out to him," I said. Then, I left PaPa with his son.

Eventually, Dr. Andrews arrived. He had cared for PaPa for so long and he had grown to love the man. He asked me, "Did you notice the time?" I remember looking at the clock on the dresser and it had said 12:02 a.m.

He asked us whom we wanted to do the arrangements. Without question, I said, "Magner." PaPa's old friend's son would be doing the honors.

Dr. Andrews seemed intent on knowing all the details. "Exactly what did he say as he passed away?" he asked gently. I recounted the events. He listened and seemed to be making notes in his head. All of it became extremely vivid, as if a neon light had begun to shine. The room. The house I grew up. The hospital bed PaPa had lain in these last several months.

Then, I walked over to the door and I gazed through the large glass pane. Outside I saw the beautiful white fluffy blanket that covered the road and hooded the streetlights. The reflection upon the snow made it glisten like a million tiny diamonds.

It was peaceful. It was calm and lovely, like PaPa was now. I prayed that his soul went straight to heaven. That all the suffering he had done throughout his life was enough.

"Please, dear God, no purgatory for PaPa," I begged. Tranquility overcame me spurred by an inner knowledge that I didn't understand, but it told me all was well with PaPa.

I called my husband. We continued to wait for the undertakers. When they arrived with a stretcher, they asked us to leave the room. In short order, they came out with what looked like a black vinyl zippered bag, strapped to the stretcher.

It struck me then. He was truly gone from this earth. Quiet tears welled, then flooded and dropped. Through the door, I watched as they loaded his body into the car. Then, after they took PaPa away, we packed up things my mother would need, and my brother-in-law and I headed for my house with her. Mikey went home to his wife. From the house to the car, from the car all the way to my home, MaMa was still wailing, keening really. Once at my home, she didn't want the empty bed in my kids' room, but rather stretched out on the living room sofa.

When I got into bed, the water gate broke and a torrent of tears poured forth like a monsoon down my face, soaking my nightclothes.

Why? I thought. I was prepared. I knew he was fatally ill. I didn't want him to suffer any longer. The conversation in my head raged at a high pitch.

Had I been kidding myself that I understood that?

The pain was indescribable. A physical pain that started from my stomach progressed through my liver, kidneys, and heart and then it seared into my brain. It cut a hole into my entire being as if someone had dug a tunnel through my middle and driven a truck through it. My arms and legs felt limp. I remember thinking, I didn't know anything could hurt so much.

CHAPTER THREE

A solemn-looking man came out to greet us. "We are the Rizzo family," I said. "We have an appointment."

"Yes. Thank you for choosing Magner. We collected your father's body about twelve hours ago. We will be glad to handle all the arrangements for you."

With that, he pulled out a multi-page form and proceeded with his questions.

"Is there an insurance policy?"

"No," we said in unison.

"Oh," was his stunned reply.

"I assure you our father set aside sufficient funds for a dignified funeral," I said quietly. With that verbal assurance, he laid out all the decisions we needed to make. Calling hours, church, cars and caskets. Once satisfied that he had all the information he needed, he asked that we follow him downstairs.

I recall that the puzzled look I must have worn was mirrored on the faces of my brother Mikey and my sister Rosie. At the bottom, the funeral director pulled out an enormous key ring from where I do not know; then he unlocked the door and opened it just a crack.

He slid his hand in to hit a light switch. Then, he swung open the door and invited us in.

What I saw startled me. It looked exactly like a new car showroom, brightly illuminated in some areas, and soft spotlights focused in other areas. There were coffins of every type and model. Wooden caskets, bronze models and metal ones. The collection was showcased on angles, on risers or upright. Some were open, to show the satin and velveteen linings. There were metal pinks and charcoals, and light and dark mahogany wooden ones. The funeral director commented on each model that he deemed appropriate for a man. Most had the prices right on the model. One even said, "Price reduced."

Among us, we reached consensus quickly. We knew what our father might have liked. We zeroed in on a smart, quality and sturdy choice. Once we settled on the casket selection, he asked us to think about the lining and draping, again making suggestions about what he thought would look best. He indicated pricing for each item as everything was an a la carte cost. Lastly, he announced that the coffin should be encased in a cement liner to protect it from moisture. Moreover, he had a small model of the types and styles and the difference in pricing.

"Upstairs we will finalize all the arrangements," he announced. We ascended to the upper floors and Rosie and I went to the restroom before going back into his office. When we got back, he was gone. We sat awaiting his return. I felt tired and mentally exhausted.

Returning, the funeral director offered us coffee, which we gratefully accepted. As we sipped our hot beverage, he went through each of the charges shown on an intricately detailed invoice. As executor, I signed the papers showing the total cost, a scary sum.

Then he added, "You will need to bring a full set of clothing, as you have chosen to have an open half casket." As an afterthought, he added, "But you don't need shoes since they won't show."

My brother Mike and I looked at each other and said in unison, "PaPa needs to be buried with his shoes."

CHAPTER FOUR

The outpouring of love and the hundreds of people who filed through Magner's funeral home was mind-boggling. The flowers were profuse, beautiful and suffocating. We all remained attentive to my mother, who was inconsolable. I recognized we all had our own pain as I watched the faces of my sisters and brothers. Many of the visitors were people I did not know, but they had known PaPa throughout the years. Some came though they hadn't had contact with him in a long while; however, they came because as they said, "I wanted to pay my respects," and then would proceed to tell us what PaPa had meant to them.

Many were friends and coworkers who hadn't known that the one-armed man in town was our father. Among the ten of us, we all were outgoing people with friendships extending throughout the community and beyond. Many who came to call shared words of praise with each of us for the man who looked so stately and handsome in the mahogany box.

At some point during the three-hour visitation period, my son pulled at my hand as I was being hugged by a procession of people that seemed to never end. He said, "Ma, look, Mr. Cliff is here." There, at the coffin, kneeled the kind mail carrier. His large hulk and handsome, dark face crying uncontrollably while he spoke to the soul who was gone.

After a few minutes, he rose and came over to hug my mother, seeming never to let go. Then, he spoke only very briefly to me and said, "He loved me." Then, he left.

CHAPTER FIVE

The last prayers said, the funeral director wanted us to load up into the limousine that would take us to St. Mary's Church and later to the cemetery. We had learned that the ground was so laden with ice that the procession could not make it into PaPa's burial site on Broad Street. Instead, after mass, we would all go to St. John's Cemetery for a graveside service to be held indoors at an outbuilding. St. Mary's cemetery being very old and historic had no such accommodation. "We will then transport the coffin later and bury him where he belongs," assured Mr. Magner.

My brothers, sisters and mother proceeded to our final goodbyes before they closed the coffin for transporting.

My thoughts were a jumble. I thought back to my growing-up years. My mother and my father. I remembered so vividly when I pressed him for the forty-four-thousandth time, to tell me why after all those years of being alone he had married my mother, a widow with four children. His answer was short, but spoke volumes. I could still see his face and hear the catch in his voice as he said, "I saw those children without a father and my heart went out to them. They had no father, nothing to eat, no one to guide them." Then he added, "And your mother was very beautiful."

Now, walking up to the bier, I was once more taken aback by the enormous collection of flower arrangements. The fragrance was overpowering. I walked to the bier holding PaPa's coffin, and stood for a few minutes before kneeling to say prayers for his soul.

He looked good.

His suit looked smart. His unlined face, despite its eighty-one years, handsome as always. His one hand lay on his chest as it often did when he rested. I thought about its significance in this man's life and our lives.

That one hand, it was large, strong, and it had prominent veins that stood out like blue dunes on a brown desert. Solid and dependable, that lone hand had never made apologies for its lack of a right-side mate. In the later years, it became thick, gnarled and clubbed by arthritis. However, even in this afflicted state, it never wavered. This one hand had raised two families—three by some people's count. It wore its disappointments no more prominently than its triumphs. I was in awe of all that it had accomplished.

It had ignited the flame in the gas lanterns of the town and had bagged many groceries. It had dug ditches on railroad beds, and swung a pick ax building roads. It had mixed the oils and tints in drums full of paints. It had hoisted its owner up heavy, wooden extension ladders and wielded the brush that restored brightness and color to countless three-story, Victorian-style homes. It had set clocks at sequenced intervals during the wee hours in factories, and counted change to the numerous customers who clamored for ice cream, candy and cigarettes from his pushcart at the local ballgames.

That lone hand had carried a briefcase, ferrying important documents into New York City for a printing company, and annually planted a huge vegetable garden that grew tomatoes, peppers, eggplant, basil, parsley, squash, green beans, and even a fig tree. On occasion, it had held a cigar to its owner's lips. It had hauled crates full of grapes, and turned them into delicious wine every year until his last.

That hand had played a sharp game of *briscola*. It often had been used to cross himself as he prayed every night before he went to sleep. It had held my hand through sickness and hospital stays and as I came out of surgery.

This same hand had gently bathed his four motherless daughters. It had neatly cut his first four daughters' hair in a Buster Brown look that kept them lice-free. It patted us on the head, and stroked our faces when we cried. This hand's owner had stood vigil with dying friends and had mourned with their families. It had helped its owner work for a living, yet it never lived just for today. It carefully and systematically put small amounts of money into a passbook savings account each week at the Norwalk Savings Society Bank on River Street.

This hand had shaken warmly and strongly with politicians, judges, bank officials and company leaders as proudly as it had with the last coming Italian *paisano* who needed guidance and help finding a job. It had lovingly caressed the only two women he had ever loved. It had learned to pen a name although the owner was illiterate, and it had faithfully pulled the lever in the voting booth in every election since he had become a naturalized U.S. citizen in May 1936.

It had bought lacy lingerie, for his second, much-younger wife. And, for some twenty-five years, it sported an elegant gold ring with a flat, jade stone centered with a small diamond, on the third finger.

Despite all of its talents, there were many things this hand had never done. It had never driven a car. It had never taken or paid a bribe. It never intentionally hurt or cheated anyone. It never destroyed anything and it never went to war.

What had kept it going? Its spark flinted by a passion for living, its engine fueled by respect, love, and compassion, it served *Michelangelo, Michele, Miche* or Mike Rizzo, or Ritzo, or Ritzzo, as well, if not better, than any pair of hands, or any hand you and I have shaken any day of the week.

I thought to myself, no, PaPa was not famous or accomplished in the modern sense. He did not write books or invent the internet. He was not a politician and he never had a 401(k), or even a life insurance policy for that matter. He was not particularly athletic; he was neither tall nor short at five feet nine inches. He was not outstandingly handsome, nor would anyone ever describe him as homely. He was distinguished-looking and very clean of person. He admired quality and good taste in contrast to flash and gaudiness.

He was an enormously complicated, yet a simple man, never following the convention, but creating his own. He had numerous acquaintances, inquired about everything, yet kept his lone counsel. He was the living embodiment of incongruity—caring and tough, compassionate and cold, smart and stubborn, humble and proud, doggedly determined and yet reverently afraid.

No wonder he had such a profound effect on me. How could you ever say "I can't" to a one-armed man?

AFTERWORD

Fernandina Beach, Florida—September 1999

It was one of those spectacular September days with just a hint of nip in the air portending the coming fall, yet the cloudless sky and blazing sun intimated that summer was still kicking.

The long awaited re-opening of the Catholic school, St. Michael's Academy, had made the start of this new school year extra-special in the small town of Fernandina Beach on Amelia Island, Florida. The restoration of the one-hundred-seventeen-year-old structure had begun two years ago. In August, it had opened with classes from pre-K to fourth grade.

Once again, the landmark three-storied school with the mansard roof and the cupola graced the historic block looking exactly as it did in the photographs dating back to the early 1900s. The sixty or so children, looking learning-ready in their uniforms and excited to be with old and new friends, appeared oblivious to all that had transpired over the past one hundred twenty-five years or so to bring them the education they were about to receive. It was an education created by selflessness, humility, and love, committed and fashioned in a Christ-centered environment striving to challenge them to grow academically, physically and spiritually.

Those who know me best are privy to my lifelong quest of seeking understanding about where goodness comes from. In psychology classes this nature vs. nurture question is often debated and unanswered. Education tells us role models and a father figure are important in a child's development. All know that family and staying connected means everything to me.

Perhaps someday, I thought, these children would learn of goodness as demonstrated by the historic sacrifices of the Sisters of St. Joseph from Le Puy, France, who had left their home, language and culture to come in response to the request of their bishop to teach the newly freed slave children in the 1860s. They came willingly, hearing the call of the Holy Spirit to their mission, to serve those in need. Their primary focus was education, but the quote *"that all may be one,"* from John 17:21, was their mantra.

They came and established free schools for blacks, for whites, for boys, for girls; they took in orphans; they set up a boarding school for girls from families who could pay. They taught French, English, and the three "R's," as well as art, music and piano. They worked selflessly under conditions almost on the level of the stable of Christ's birth. They looked upon everyone as children of God, rich and poor, no matter what race or ethnic background.

My thoughts wandered. I had moved to Florida in January 1990, a result of a corporate relocation. I had quickly become immersed in community organizations as well as the historic St. Michael's faith community. "PaPa, you always wanted to come to Florida. Here I am, living the Florida for you," I whispered. "Guess what, PaPa, back in Connecticut, you have three handsome grandsons with your last name, courtesy of Mikey and his lovely wife, whom you never met."

I gazed up at the stained-glass window with the beautiful colors depicting St. Joseph, and I wondered about this spiritual, faithful, selfless man who cared for Mary and Jesus; once again, a life demonstrating goodness. And, again my thoughts return to those women who call themselves the Sisters of St. Joseph, teaching, guiding, loving, protecting and emptying themselves for the glory of God.

No grand monuments mark the heroic nuns who nursed the town during the mysterious fever that only ten years later became known as the Yellow Fever Epidemic of 1877, and again in 1888. When the fever struck, the Sisters had been on retreat in St. Augustine. Filled with the Holy Spirit to move quickly to the side of those who desperately needed them back home in Fernandina, they went knowing full well they might be going to their own deaths; they did not hesitate to race to the aid of others. As the island was cut off by quarantine, they nursed the sick, bathed fever-wracked bodies, fed the hungry and abandoned, sewed lifeless bodies into shrouds and even buried the dead with quick prayers of faith and consolation.

Again, my wandering thoughts returned to family, particularly my father. I thought of the unselfish love he, a man of few words, had lavished upon me, after raising his first four daughters without a mother. He had worked against all odds to keep those girls together, always treating them with kindness and care, and they had grown into loving and wonderful women.

"I'm proud to have them as my four sisters. My younger brother, my half-siblings, we all learned so many important lessons through your quiet example, PaPa," I whispered. "I continue to marvel how you took on MaMa's four children. Not your own, but you provided for them as well. I thought of your loving relationship among all of us—whole, half, step, all irrelevant labels," I breathed.

Could I be as courageous as the Sisters of St. Joseph, or as PaPa, if called by the Holy Spirit to live such a selfless love? I wondered.

I moved to the wall where a small plaque indicated that the stained-glass window depicting St. Joseph had been restored in the memory of Michael and Jennie Rizzo. It had been a small sacrifice to pay for that window restoration, but I had felt compelled to do it. PaPa, a humble father, honest citizen, loyal friend, a faithful believer; he was a man of goodness.

For many decades, I have searched to understand where goodness comes from. Is it taught? Is it learned by example? Without any of that, where, PaPa, did you get your goodness?

In that moment, in that chapel, the wellspring of goodness came to me.

Clear as a school bell, I heard it. "Goodness comes from God. We are all heirs should we choose it." I recognized then that it doesn't have to come from epic events or great acts of heroism. It is, rather, built from all the little things that demonstrate love for our fellow human beings in the glory of God Almighty.

As I left the chapel, I murmured softly to no one in particular, "Thank you, Sisters of St. Joseph for your selfless examples of courage, love and humility, all adding up to the greatest sacrifice, that of your life for your fellow man. Thank you, St. Joseph, for taking Mary and Jesus into your care, love and protection. And I'm eternally grateful to PaPa and MaMa, for teaching me that where you come from, and what you materially have or have not, have nothing to do with your character, your integrity, the love and compassion in your heart and most of all your goodness."

ACKNOWLEDGMENTS

Though I sat alone for many, many months at my computer to compose the words, this book could never have become a reality without the generous gifts of time, talent, encouragement and love of numerous people.

I appreciate the dedicated curators and volunteers at historical societies and museums everywhere, especially, Paul Keroack, at the Norwalk (CT) History Room; Richard Stanislaus, Pennsylvania, Anthracite Heritage Museum, Scranton, PA; Bode Morin at the Eckley Miners' Village in Weatherly, PA; Elizabeth Van Tuyl at the Bridgeport History Center; Teen Peterson at the Amelia Island Museum of History and Paolo Nicolazzo, Pro Loco Platania-Italy.

To my extended family and friends in Italy who showed me all the places and helped me get the records; to my cousins in Australia who remembered their birth land and the events.

To my dear friends and champions who fanned my frequently stalled flame of writing over the years, Shiela Fountain, Suzy and Patrick Sabadie, Martin and the late Marsha Arnold. To Roseanna White for her talented cover and design. To Emily Carmain and Cheryl Duttweiler, who made this book better in every way.

A million thanks to my late mother, Giovanna, who painted pictures with words and provided me the insight into her soul, the ethos of Calabria and to share what my father found too painful; and, to my late father, who told me the important stuff, each word as precious as a gold nugget. To my wonderful sisters and brothers living and in heaven, Rose Mola, Connie Marotto, Lena Casavecchi, Ann Redican, and Angie Ciliberto, and my brothers Tony, Frankie and Joe Bonaddio and Michael Ritzzo. Over the years in addition to looking out for me, they all shared numerous stories of the old days in Norwalk and La Chianta and times they shared with PaPa and MaMa. For sharing their remembrances, thank you to my children, George and Holly, and all my many nieces and nephews.

A heartfelt special thank you to my dear friend and mentor, Don Shaw, who met with me weekly, believed in me, made me read my manuscript aloud for the first time and helped me stay the course to the end.

Saving the most important for last, to my best friend, my love, my husband, Mark. Thank you for your exceptional patience, understanding, love, support, encouragement, technical skills, delicious dinners and adopting the Calabrian olive tree for me. You have shared freely and unconditionally and for all these things and much more, you have my eternal gratitude and love.

With much gratitude and thanks to you all, and may love be your deepest emotion.

- RMR

ABOUT THE AUTHOR

Raffaela Marie Rizzo is a former senior executive with numerous business and marketing communications awards. She earned an MBA from Jacksonville University and a BA degree in media studies from Sacred Heart University in Fairfield, CT, where she graduated magna cum laude. She has been a life-long volunteer in community and faith-based organizations to help bring comfort and solace to those in need. Her passions are people, family stories, community, genealogy, history and travel. Born in Italy, raised in Connecticut, she and her husband now make Amelia Island, Florida, home. To learn more, visit www.rmrizzo.com.

From humble beginnings in the
Mercuri-Tedesci area of
Platania, Italy.

Circa 1913—Michelangelo Rizzo arrives in Norwalk, CT after a circuitous route from Calabria in time to share in his first family milestone in the new world, his cousin Innocenza Nicolazzo's wedding. Mike, second from left, sitting; to his left, his cousin Mickey Nicolazzo; on his right, cousin Pasqualina; standing behind her, Mike's Zia Giuanna, his mother's sister.

*Michelangelo Rizzo married Maria Raffaela Rus-
so at St. Mary's RC Church in Norwalk, CT Jan.
7, 1918. It took a year to pay for the portrait and
have it released to them by the photographer.*

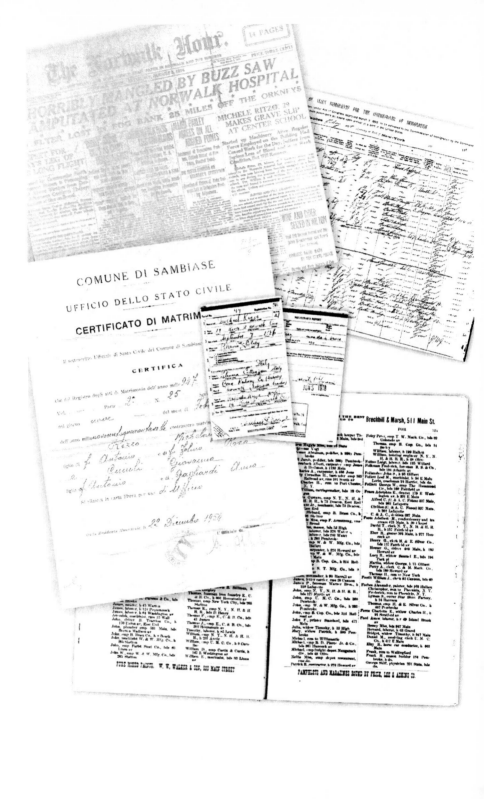

*January 1929 - Mike gets his four daughters home
and takes them to memorialize the re-united family.*

Mike at work at O'Brien Press, circa 1957

Circa 1964 - Mike and his second wife Giovanna "Jennie"

April 1958 - Mike, with his wife Jennie, at the wedding of her son Antonio Bonaddio to Maria Parisi; also in the photo are Jennie's other children, Angie, Frank, and Joey, as well as their children together, Marie and Mikey Jr., and Mike's Nicolazzo cousins.